Praise for *Stealing Mr. Right*

"A sexy, fun, cat-and-mouse chase that hooked me from page one!"

—**Jennifer Probst**, *New York Times* & *USA Today* bestselling author of *The Marriage Bargain*

"The minute I finished reading...I started it over. That's how good this book is! I laughed, I cried, and I fell totally in love with Grant Emerson and Penelope Blue, one of the most fascinating book couples I've ever read."

—**Sandra Owens**, author of the bestselling K2 Special Services series

"Tamara Morgan has masterminded the perfect heist of the heart."

—**Katie Lane**, *USA Today* bestselling author

"A rollicking romp that packs a surprising emotional punch."

—**Jenny Holiday**, author of *The Engagement Game*

"This sexy cat-and-mouse game between an FBI agent and a jewel thief had me furiously flipping the pages until the very end."

—**A.J. Pine**, author of *The One That Got Away*

Praise for Tamara Morgan

"The opening of Morgan's Montgomery Mansion series highlights her sensational sense of humor and development of colorful characters, pitch-perfect relationships, and daring plot twists."

—*RT Book Reviews* 4.5 Stars
TOP PICK for *If I Stay*

"Utterly unconventional and wonderfully smart, demolishing readers' expectations with zany, deeply sympathetic characters and a charmingly irreverent style."

—*RT Book Reviews* 4.5 Stars
TOP PICK for *The Derby Girl*

"Morgan possesses a rare talent for conceiving the most unlikely and surprising couples."

—*RT Book Reviews* 4.5 Stars, Contemporary Love and Laughter Nominee for *Because I Can*

"Totally unanticipated and genuinely fulfilling."

—*RT Book Reviews* for *When I Fall*

"An uplifting, irreverent, and emotionally satisfying novel."

—*RT Book Reviews* 4.5 Stars
for *The Party Girl*

"Morgan is at her snappy, outrageous best in this quick-witted, clever tale of con artists and lonely hearts. Her characters are beautifully quirky and utterly endearing."

—*RT Book Reviews* 4.5 Stars
for *Confidence Tricks*

SAVING
MR. PERFECT

TAMARA MORGAN

sourcebooks
casablanca

Published by Sourcebooks Casablanca, an imprint of Sourcebooks, Inc.
P.O. Box 4410, Naperville, Illinois 60567-4410
(630) 961-3900
Fax: (630) 961-2168
www.sourcebooks.com

Printed and bound in Canada.
MBP 10 9 8 7 6 5 4 3 2 1

THE HEIST

1

Infiltrating the FBI is a lot more difficult than you might think.

The seventh-floor waiting room in the New York field office is one I'm intimately familiar with. There are no windows to penetrate from the outside and no air vents big enough to squeeze through, which means it's impossible to access this floor unless security clears you first. The fifty-something woman at the desk *seems* nice, what with the glasses perched on the end of her nose and the fresh flower pinned to her chiffon blouse, but she'd shiv you sooner than let you through the door.

I know this because in addition to the gun she carries, Cheryl also has a letter opener that doubles as a throwing knife strapped to her upper thigh.

And I know *that* because I'm the one who gave it to her.

"Hey, Penelope," Cheryl says with a smile that welcomes me and warns me not to make any sudden movements at the same time. "It's lovely to have you visit us today."

Loosely translated, this means: *I know you're a thief, and I'm packing. What do you want?*

"I'm so happy to be here," I reply. My own smile stretches wide and full of meaning. "How are the kids? And Dan?"

In other words: *I'm not scared of you. Also, I know where you live.*

"They're good, they're good. Dan got that promotion he was after, so that's been pretty nice for us. We finally bought that gun safe we've been eyeing."

Meaning: *We keep extra weapons at home. Don't even think about it.*

"Safety is so important," I agree.

"Do you want me to let Grant know you're here, hon?"

"If you don't mind. He's not expecting me."

"Oh, how lovely," she says. You'd think, from the way she beams at me, that she means it this time. She doesn't. "Is it a surprise lunch date?"

It's a surprise *something*, that's for sure. But all I do is offer her a bland look and say, "In a manner of speaking."

"I'll buzz him."

And with that, I'm in as far as I'm going to get on my own. Only once in my life have I made it past Cheryl's desk, and that was in handcuffs. It's not an experience I'm keen on repeating.

To pass the time until my husband's arrival, I settle into one of the austere metal chairs set against an even more austere white wall and struggle to suppress my air of expectation. A buzz of adrenaline is common before a big job, and since it's been more than six months since

I've so much as *looked* at a lock the wrong way, my expectations and my buzz are flying.

The fact that things are progressing exactly as planned only helps my high. I haven't always loved the FBI—what with their spying on my every move and the arrest of my father earlier this year—but I can always count on their love of protocol.

To Cheryl's credit, she doesn't make excuses as the minutes tick by and there's no sign of my husband. To *my* credit, I don't let my anxiety at his delay show. There's a small window of opportunity for this particular job, and I need him to appear before Riker—my best friend and coconspirator—gets things started down below. In about five more minutes, I'm going to have to do something drastic (like fake a seizure) to get Grant out here.

Fortunately, my acting skills aren't put to the test. A shadow appears in the doorway before I hear the impressively faint sound of footsteps, and I know it must be Grant. No one moves as silently—or is as deadly—as my husband.

"You're here!" I cry. All six feet two inches of him fill the room—and my heart. Even considering what I'm about to do, I'm honestly happy to see him. He didn't come home last night until the wee hours of the morning, and he left for work while I was in the shower—a schedule that's been on repeat for much longer than I like. The occasional late night is par for the course when you're married to an FBI agent, but tacit avoidance has become our default mode as of late.

In any other marriage, such a thing might indicate waning sexual interest or a general lack of communication. In *our* marriage, it means one of us thinks the other has started stealing again.

I'll let you guess who.

Grant accepts my proffered hug warily, one eye on the door, the other on his watch. I'm tempted to tell him it's exactly 2:13 in the afternoon, give or take thirty seconds, but that might give too much away. I only pay such close attention to the passing of time when I'm up to no good—a fact he knows from personal experience. I want to throw him off guard, not set him on high alert.

"My sweet darling, how I've missed you!" I say instead, dialing my beaming smile up to twelve. "I've been waiting for the chance to wrap my arms around you all day."

He doesn't miss a beat. "Okay, who are you and what have you done with my wife?"

"That's unfair." I feign outrage with a flick of my ponytail, the more-blond-than-red hair pulled back in the lifelong style I can't seem to shake. As my role in the breaking and entering circuit used to involve squeezing into tight spaces, I grew accustomed to minimizing the amount of space I took up—hair included. Nothing is more disastrous than squeezing yourself inside an air conditioning duct only to have your hair sucked into the blades. "Can't I be happy to see you?"

"You could be, but you're not."

I fake a pout. "How can you tell?"

"For starters? Not only have you never called me *my sweet* anything before, but your skin is flushed, and your pupils are dilated. What are you up to, Penelope Blue?"

I bite back a laugh. His air of distrust is offset by the familiar playful rhyme, a singsong form of address he's used since the day we first met. It's always been one of my favorite sounds—that combination of suspicion and adoration in Grant's voice. I like to think it's how he shows his love.

"I'm not up to anything." At least, I'm not up to anything *yet*. The action isn't set to start until 2:20, which means I've got about five more minutes to keep his attention focused by being suspiciously charming and wifely. "Maybe I'm flushed because I'm happy to see you. Did you ever think about that?"

"Once. Maybe twice. Then I learned better."

His eyes narrow as he continues assessing me from top to bottom. I attempt to keep my breathing mostly even and my posture just a little too relaxed—I want him to be suspicious, but I don't want him to *catch on* that I want him to be suspicious. It's harder than it seems under his special brand of scrutiny. Grant is very good at his job.

He's so good at it, in fact, that his face doesn't register even a flicker of surprise when he reaches my feet and catches a glimpse of my footwear. Normally, I'm all about functional flats and comfort soles, but this is a special occasion. Today, I've paired my black skinny jeans with bright-red peep-toe heels that threaten to topple me with every step.

The shoes were a gift from Grant—a gift *and* a reminder, and a large part of the reason I'm here today. It's a thing with him, a tradition of sorts, to give double-edged presents. The habit goes all the way back to our early courtship, where each date could end with an arrest as easily as a kiss. Instead of confronting me with his suspicions like a normal man, Grant likes to toy with me to see if I'll break.

I'm on to you, Penelope Blue, he all but said with a few shiny pieces of patent leather. *The Peep-Toe Prowler better not strike again.*

Which is totally unfair, by the way. Even if I was the burglar currently working her way through a string of Upper East Side homes—which, for the record, I'm *not*—I wouldn't wear heels while I did it. I prefer to make my getaways quick and painless, thank you very much.

"Well? Am I a threat to national security?" I ask when it appears he's finished his assessment. I even give my foot a sassy kick for good measure, but I elicit no response and almost lose my shoe in the process. "Do you want to place me in one of the interrogation rooms until you get the all clear? I'm partial to the one Simon uses. Such fond memories I have of being held there against my will."

Grant sighs, his exasperation causing a crease to form down the middle of his forehead. I resist the urge to smooth it away. Don't get me wrong—my husband is and always has been devastatingly handsome, and no amount of annoyance can change that. His hair is the blondish-brown you typically find on frat boys and surfer dudes, and he has these huge brown eyes that exude sleepy innocence and puppy-dog friendliness. It's the perfect look for lulling unsuspecting cat burglars into falling in love and spilling their secrets.

"This better not be one of your tricks, Penelope."

"It's not!" I lie.

"You said you were having lunch with your grand-mother today."

"She had to cancel," I lie again. "I never see you any-more, that's all." I run my finger up the line of his suit jacket. It's loose and crumpled, which says a lot about his current state of mind. He usually wears his suits like they're made of neoprene. "You've been spending all your free time at work lately, and even when you come home, it's like you're not there. I miss you."

"Stop batting your eyes at me. I'm not falling for it."

"I'm blinking. You want me to stop blinking?"

"I want you to tell me why you're really here."

"My profound love for you isn't good enough? Thanks a lot."

His lips twitch in amusement, though I wouldn't go so far as to call it a smile. When Grant really smiles, he does it with his whole face. His eyes crinkle at the edges in a way that sets my heart skittering and makes me wonder what I did to deserve such a gorgeous, strapping beast of a man in my life.

"I mean it." He places his hands heavily on my shoulders. "I'm in the middle of something at the moment. There's been a new development in the case I'm working."

Aha. Now we're getting closer to something interesting. By *new development*, I can only assume he's talking about the ruby bracelet that went missing from one of New York's elite inner circles last night. This makes half a dozen pieces in all, each one worth more than the last. They're saying this one clocks in at over a million bucks.

I almost feel sorry for Grant having to head up this investigation. With such high-profile victims as the CEO of a chain of hospitals and an energy tycoon known to contribute in presidential campaigns, he must feel the pressure to find the culprit before any more rich people are outraged.

But the thief—again, *not me*—is a good one. According to the newspapers, there have only been two clues worth note. The first is a bath mat bearing the imprint of a woman's size seven shoe. The other is a maid who claims to have seen a pair of peep-toes poking out from under a curtain in the same room where a diamond watch later went missing. It's not much to go on, but I assume Grant has dozens of theories and facts he's not sharing with the world.

Theories and facts that appear to be pointing to yours truly.

"What kind of development?" I ask.

"Nice try. I know I've been distracted lately, but I'm not *that* distracted." He squeezes my shoulders again, and there's a finality to it that lingers long after the pressure is gone. "I'm sorry, love. I appreciate you coming all this way to see me, but I need to get back. I'll have Cheryl show you out."

"I wish you wouldn't." And not only because I need to keep him distracted for a few minutes longer. The truth is, I don't like feeling shut out of his life—of *our* life.

But all he does is sigh in frustration. "Why don't you go home and enjoy the rest of your day? Aren't you supposed to be finishing that novel for your book club?"

"I tried, but it was about zombies. It gave me nightmares."

"What about your plans to overhaul the garden?"

"Too many bugs." I give a delicate shudder. "They also give me nightmares."

"There's always that volunteer gig at the rare books room you were talking about..."

I let him trail off, refusing to pick up the bait. Of all

the book clubs and garden plans and volunteer opportunities Grant keeps dangling in front of me, that one is by far the most appealing. I've always loved the New York Library, and that room, in particular, has personal meaning for me. But the larger issue isn't about how I spend my leisure time—it's about how he doesn't trust me to find a productive way to fill it. To him, the succession of long, empty days I've faced since renouncing my life of crime is nothing more than an opportunity to get in trouble.

It's sweet that he's so concerned for my well-being and all, but it's almost enough to make me want to give the real Peep-Toe Prowler a run for her money.

"You're such a man sometimes," I say with a *tsk* of real annoyance. "You just have a thing for the sexy librarian look."

He tilts his head, playing along. Our voices are low to prevent Cheryl from overhearing, but there's no mistaking his interest. "Hmm. Maybe I do, now that you mention it. A pair of glasses here, a tight skirt there…"

Oh, he's good. A tight skirt and its immediate removal does have its appeal. I can feel myself faltering already. "I am *not* volunteering at a library just so you can get off on your weird, repressed fantasies," I say.

My insult, neatly aimed, goes wide. He laughs. "Nice try, but there's nothing repressed about the things I'd like to do to you."

"Don't look at me like that," I say, though not very convincingly. I happen to adore that particular dark-eyed stare of his. "I'll have you know I'm more than a pair of legs."

"True. But you have to admit they're very nice legs."

Sure. *Now* he looks, his gaze intense as it moves from my toes along every curve of my calves and thighs. Dammit. That's not what the shoes are there for. I put them on this morning to take the lead in the cat-and-mouse game of our marriage, not to get sidetracked by seduction.

"Stop it," I warn, "or you're not getting anywhere near these legs again."

His smile only curves wider. "Oh, really? Is that a threat…or would you rather call it a dare?"

"Let's call it a promise."

"Excellent. A promise." His voice comes out in a low rumble as he takes a predatory step toward me. He's ostensibly letting a woman in a black suit and oversized handbag by, but I know better. Grant is an excellent tactician, and he's using his environment to manipulate the scene.

And me. Oh, how he loves to manipulate me, often in the best of ways.

"In fact," he continues, "I *promise* to do everything in my power to appreciate your legs to the fullest."

No, no, no. I refuse to be swayed by his hot, raking glances or the lulling heat of his proximity. Playing Grant's games—however much a thoroughly enjoyable staple of our marriage they may be—is not on the menu today, and none of the pistons firing between my thighs will change my mind.

I'm going to be strong. I'm going to prove my innocence. I'm going to show this man what I think about his underhanded tactics…by trying a few underhanded tactics of my own.

I'm not feeling particularly strong or innocent as he edges even closer with a determined gleam in his eye, so it's for the best that we're hit with a sudden blast of toxic air. My eyes sting and my lungs recoil and all thoughts of seduction reach an abrupt end.

Good old Riker. His timing hasn't always been impeccable, but he's managed it this go-around. That smell means one thing and one thing only.

It's showtime.

The smell of Liquid Evacuation (patent not pending) is difficult to nail down, but most people who encounter it say it smells like a deadly cocktail of a dozen different chemicals—a sulfurous tang you do *not* want anywhere near your lungs.

In reality, it's perfectly harmless…much like the group of thieves currently breaking into the FBI to have a look around.

The chemical made its way into the building thanks to the woman who slipped past on her way to Cheryl just moments ago. Riker planted a few drops in her bag while she snagged her daily coffee from the cart in front of the building. With a delayed reaction of about ten minutes, the timing of the chemical's release was perfectly planned to allow her inside and past all security checkpoints before it hit.

Grant smells it as quickly as I do. His first instinct, as always, is protective, and he propels me to the far side of the room so fast, I barely have time to register what's happening. His hand presses my head against his chest, where I feel his heartbeat pick up and his muscles coil in preparation to hoist me over his shoulder and carry me to safety, fireman-style.

My own body experiences something akin to a swoon. Oh, how I love this man. There's so much nobility in him, it scares me sometimes.

His next instinct isn't so sweet. It takes two seconds for the scent to register and two more for him to sift through his memories until he recalls where he's come across it before. His arms drop as suddenly as they came up.

"Oh, no. Oh, hell no. That better not be what I think it is."

"What do you think it is?" I ask all-too-innocently. "Is it anthrax?"

"Don't be ridiculous. Anthrax doesn't have a scent. That smells an awful lot like—"

Three agents burst through the back door, cutting Grant's sentence short. Not that I need to hear it to know what he's thinking. The way he looks at me—as if he'd like to tie me to the metal chair so I can't escape—says it all.

You did this. You're attacking the FBI.

Yes. Yes, I am, sweet husband. Deal with it.

"Emerson, there you are. We've shut down the ventilation system." The largest of the agents is clearly in charge, and he has the enormously wide chest to prove it. He looks like a Saint Bernard carrying a cask of ale around its neck. "We're isolating the floor and evacuating the rest of the building. Cheryl, make sure no one comes off those elevators."

He stops, as if only now noticing the diminutive woman Grant is inches away from murdering with his bare hands. "Is she with you?"

The *she* in question schools her features to give

nothing away. For all this man knows, I'm nothing more than an innocent bystander. A victim of bad timing. A poor, put-upon wife.

Hey, stranger things have happened.

"Don't evacuate." Grant's voice is tightly controlled, a slice of cold, hard steel coming to the surface. "Don't isolate the floor. Don't shut down the elevators."

"But they're saying it could be something lethal—"

He doesn't even blink. "Call it off, and call it off *now*."

"I don't think we can ignore—"

"I'm not asking you to think. I'm asking you to call it off. Anything that's standard protocol, any action we'd normally take. Don't do it." Grant turns to me, his dark eyes flashing. "And make sure you get those ventilation fans back on as fast as possible. We don't want anyone taking advantage of the downtime to sneak inside the ducts."

Please. As if FBI vents are big enough for that. Even the lowest-level thieves know they're impossible to navigate.

"I think the smell is already starting to go away," I point out—which, indeed, it is. Jordan, our chemist and explosives expert, worked out a new formula recently. This one has a delay activation of ten minutes, an active smell for half that, and then all trace of it disappears. It's a toxic smokescreen. *Poof* and then it's gone. "Maybe someone had gasoline on their clothes. That happened at a movie theater I went to once, in Jersey. Some lady spilled gas all over herself at the pump and had no idea she was carrying it around on her. We thought the entire place was going to blow."

Agent Barrel Chest listens to my story with interest, taking me for the innocent that I'm pretending to be.

Grant, however, grips me by the elbow, the clasp tight enough to warn me what thin ice I'm on.

The other agents sniff tentatively, noticing for themselves that the air is starting to clear.

"See?" I say. "It must have been an accident. Someone probably stepped in a weird puddle."

"It does seem unlikely…"

"I wonder if an air conditioning unit went out…"

"They're not reporting anything on the other floors…"

One by one, the agents begin doubting their senses. Their shoulders relax, and their guards lower inch by inch. Only Grant remains unconvinced, refusing to let go of my arm—bless his suspicious heart.

"Not good enough," he says. "I want to know if anyone's had any unusual visitors or received unexpected deliveries today." He glowers at me. "Also, the names and IDs of all independent contractors we've hired in the past three months. No job is too big or small—even some guy filling in for the window-washing staff. Got it? I'm especially interested in males between the ages of twenty-five and fifty, about five-eight, nondescript in every regard."

That would be Oz, the fourth member of our team. A master of disguise, he can sneak in anywhere undetected.

Well, anywhere except this building. We might be good, but we're not *that* good.

"There's no need," I tell Grant truthfully—knowing he won't believe me and loving the irony of it all. "He's not here."

Agent Barrel Chest perks up at that, but Grant draws me a few paces out of his range of hearing. "If you know what's good for you, you won't open your mouth again."

"But I have to breathe!"

"Not for much longer."

"Oh, dear. This is because I called you *my sweet darling*, isn't it?"

The stifled choke of his rage-fueled laughter is a sound I won't soon forget. It's like a werewolf being forced to swallow his howl and finding he rather likes the taste.

"Uh, Emerson?" Cheryl coughs discreetly, intervening before Grant can respond.

"Yes?"

"When you say you want to know about visitors, are you counting Blackrock?"

His head swivels in her direction so fast, it leaves *me* dizzy. "Blackrock is here? *Now?*"

She scans her computer before nodding. "Sterling had a meeting set up with him at two. I haven't checked him out yet, so I assume they're still back there. Do you want me to notify him?"

I could kiss Cheryl for her perfect timing, and I make a mental note to get her an even deadlier concealed weapon for next Christmas. Maybe a lipstick grenade or something.

"Goddammit!" Grant swears. "So that's what this is. Make sure Simon has backup, and get a man posted at every exit. Blackrock doesn't leave until I personally search him, got it?"

"Do you know what's going on?" Agent Barrel Chest asks as he steps forward, ready to set his impressive physique into action. "Who's Blackrock?"

"I don't know what's happening yet, but I'm going to find out," Grant says. He's careful to ignore the second half of the question, but I don't mind, because I already know the answer. Blackrock is the code name for Warren Blue, an infamous thief-turned-FBI-informant who's done miraculous things in helping my husband and his partner, Simon Sterling, put bad guys behind bars.

He's also my father, the man who taught me everything I know about breaking into highly secured government facilities. So you can imagine Grant's concern.

"As for you..." Grant finds himself at a loss, gazing around the lobby for the best place to stash me while he tends to his duties. From the look on his face, I get the feeling he'd like to knock me unconscious with a potted ficus, but that's frowned upon, even by the feds.

"Why don't I stay here?" I motion to the metal chair, knowing the mere fact that I'm suggesting it will force him to reject the idea out of hand. "Then I won't be in your way while you go about your business. It sounds *super important*."

"Oh no," he says, distracted enough to take the bait. "You're not going anywhere." He yanks me closer, holding me against the hard wall of his side. When the other agents look at him curiously, he adds a lackluster, "I want to be able to keep an eye on her until we know the danger is passed."

"Maybe you could leave me under Cheryl's protection," I suggest.

Cheryl lifts her hands. "No thanks. I'm not going anywhere near this one."

"I don't mind keeping an eye on her," Agent Barrel Chest says, but I can tell that option doesn't weigh much in Grant's opinion. There's no telling what I might get his coworker to do with a few smiles. Federal agents I'm *not* married to find me incredibly charming.

Time is ticking by, and Grant still has no idea what I'm up to, so he pulls me with him as he strides out of the room. "Fine. I guess you'll have to stay with me. Don't look at anyone, don't talk to anyone, and don't you dare try anything. Understand?"

"Yes, dear," I say meekly. I can't even pretend to be outraged, because I'm too busy keeping the smile from my face. In a few short steps, I've now breached the hallowed walls of the FBI—and with nary a handcuff in sight.

Of course, being manacled to Grant's side isn't conducive to finishing the job, especially since he doesn't slow down as he moves through the maze of hallways to the interview room where my father is being held.

We're halfway down a particularly gray corridor when Simon appears. A permanent frown carves into his face, his customary tie pulled so tight, it's a wonder his head doesn't pop and send gallons of shellac-like hair product flying. His frown only deepens when he spots me. Despite the fact that my father's capture has done great things for his career, Simon isn't much of a Penelope Blue fan.

"What are you doing?" Grant demands. "Why aren't you with Warren?"

"He's waiting for me in the interview room. I heard there was a breach?"

"Get back there immediately—and keep an eye out for anyone who might be Oz."

Simon turns to me and levels a knowing glare. "What did she do?"

"I don't know yet," Grant says grimly.

"Want me to beat it out of her?"

There's a long enough pause to cause me momentary concern. I mean, I know Grant and I have our problems, but there's a line between tricking a spouse and torturing one. It's thin, but it's there.

"Can I get a rain check on that?" Grant asks, his eyes fixed on me. "I'd like to keep the option open."

"Why, Grant Emerson, I think that might be the sweetest thing you've ever said." I nod back down the hallway. "I'll make this easy on both of you and go home. I know the way out."

"*No!*" both men yell at once. Grant releases a frustrated groan. "We don't have time for this. Simon, get back to Warren, and don't let him out of your sight. I'll take Penelope—"

He glances at the door we've stopped outside, which I now notice has his name engraved on a metal panel. My heart picks up speed as I realize it's his personal office. *Jackpot.*

I'm afraid my rapid pulse is going to give me away, so I pull my arms out of his grasp and pretend to rub the sore spots.

"Lock her inside," Simon suggests and pushes the door open. "You don't have any windows or vents, and we can post a man in the hallway to make sure she doesn't sneak out."

Grant grunts his agreement. "It isn't ideal, but there's not much damage she can do in there." He turns to me with an expression that's difficult to read. Determined and professional, yes, but also pained. "We *talked* about this, Pen. You're supposed to be keeping a low profile, remember? Head down, nose clean. There are people here who would like to see you—"

He shakes his head, cutting his own words short. He finishes instead with, "I'm sorry to do this to you, but I can't have you wandering around the building. Not until I know what you're up to."

"I can't believe you think me capable of such deception," I say, playing up the role of wounded wife. It's not a stretch. My profile has been nothing but low for months—and it hasn't been an easy thing to maintain. A little credit would be nice. "After all we've been through together."

He's not fooled for a second. "And I can't believe you'd use Jordan's chemical again. You should have known I'd recognize it." I *had* known; that was part of the plan. Thankfully, all the late nights and overworked hours have thrown my husband off his game—he doesn't yet realize I wanted to be caught. "Now get in there. We'll deal with this later."

He gently but firmly nudges me inside his office, offering a curt command to Simon before slamming the door and turning the key.

I hold my breath and count to ten before I look around, fearful this might be too good to be true—or perhaps Grant is toying with me, coming out on top in our endless game of cat-and-mouse. But as I turn to face those four white walls—Grant's home away from home, the place where he's leading an investigation that somehow pinpoints his *wife* as the Peep-Toe Prowler—the heady realization sinks in.

I did it. I'm in.

I guess infiltrating the FBI isn't so hard after all.

THE OFFICE 2

I start with Grant's desk, since that seems the likeliest place to find clues.

The exact shape and scope of what I'm looking for is hazy, and a surge of anxiety moves through me as I consider how much I've bitten off. Under normal circumstances—normal being premeditated theft—the target goal is clear. A two-million-dollar necklace. A shipment of uncut diamonds. A gilded statue in the shape of a horse's bottom half. These things are straightforward and tangible. Simple, if you will.

Oh, how different my life was when money was the motivating factor. Stealing hearts isn't nearly as easy as stealing valuables.

"All right," I mutter and survey the long wooden desk, taking in the vast stacks of paperwork with a sigh. "If I were highly classified information about the most important person in my life, where would I be?"

There is no easy answer to that question. For all his

highly professional ways, Grant has always been a bit of a pack rat. He loves antiques and collecting things, and he has a hard time throwing items away if he has any sort of sentimental attachment to them. Our home is a testament to this, filled to bursting with rickety chairs and colorful paintings, all of which are older than dirt and often smell like it.

It's sweet, his romantic attachment to things of the past, but it's hardly ideal when time isn't on my side. I have to shuffle through dozens of file folders, a framed photo of the two of us on our second honeymoon, and several antique paperweights before I even make it to the surface of the desk. There are plenty of serious-looking documents among the piles, but none that contain any mention of Penelope Blue, the Peep-Toe Prowler, or a code name he might be using to protect me.

Man, FBI agents have boring jobs. There's enough paperwork here to keep me busy forever—and that's with *reading* the reports, not writing them. It's hard to imagine a man as active and virile as Grant sitting stooped over this desk for hours at a time, but his dedication to the job is such that I don't doubt he does everything asked of him.

I'm not upset about the time he spends here, of course, and I would never ask him to give up something he loves solely because it conflicts with my own worldview. But, oh, how I miss having that same sense of purpose, that feeling of all-consuming passion for the job. Once upon a time, I too buried myself under plans and notes, got home late and left early, lost myself in the pursuit of something huge.

It's been a long time since I've had that in my life,

and I miss it more than I ever thought possible—so much, it's almost a physical ache. Everyone needs a reason to get out of bed in the morning.

Even a miserable thief like me.

As the desk is proving itself fruitless as a source of anything but morose self-reflection, I turn to the filing cabinets along the back of the office. There are five cabinets in all, a wall of information just waiting for me to jump in. If I were electronically inclined, I'd probably have more luck trying to crack the password on Grant's computer, but I have a hunch it's not my best bet. Having been personally investigated by this man in the past, I know for a fact that he's a hands-on investigator. He hits the streets, he watches and waits, he talks to people, and he follows paper trails.

He sometimes even marries his suspects. That's the level of dedication I'm talking about.

The filing cabinet isn't locked, and the top drawer pulls out smoothly, indicating it's well-oiled and probably used several times a day. It's also much better organized than his desk, and it doesn't take long to locate the bulging folder with my name on it. *Penelope Blue*. Right behind it, there's an even bigger one that reads *Warren Blue*. Two jewel thieves, connected by blood and talent, a menace to society and the world at large.

All I have to do is reach in and grab it. The beige folds practically flutter at me, encouraging me to spread their wings and unlock the secrets of my past. My adolescence, spent as an abandoned teen with only my friends for support. My list of past crimes, including the millions of dollars' worth of jewels that Riker and I stole over the years, with occasional help from Jordan and

Oz. My supposed current crimes, too—the work of a copycat who doesn't seem to mind that her thefts are being attributed to me.

If I were a betting woman, I'd also place a hefty wager that this file contains the courtship Grant and I shared, including our marriage—that rocky first year when neither of us knew how much love and trust we shared. Everything my husband ever thought or did in relation to me is a few inches away.

I take a deep breath and reach for the folder…and then drop my hand to my side.

To get what I want in this world, I've stolen precious heirlooms and priceless gifts, crawled into vents and climbed up elevator shafts. No job was too heinous to consider, no victim worthy enough to give me pause. I even married a man I knew to be my sworn enemy in an attempt to continue my criminal life without consequence.

But I can't do it. Even if Grant is seconds away from arresting me—either for being the Peep-Toe Prowler or because I tricked him into helping me break into the FBI—I can't betray the trust he put in me when he looked into my eyes and said *I do*. I guess some things are sacred, even to a woman like me.

Riker is going to be so pissed.

With a sigh, I shut the filing cabinet and sink into Grant's office chair to await the outcome of my day's work. The hiss of the hydraulics drops me further than I expect, and I flail against the backrest, which gives way behind me. Before I know it, I'm sprawled on the ground, the chair crashed to the floor and my head ringing as I stare up at the perforated drop ceiling.

Well, that was graceful.

At first, I think it's the head injury causing me to see things, because visions of one of the world's most handsome men start swimming in front of my face. There are three of him—three heads of golden hair glistening above three faces that form a triad of perfect symmetry. The man almost seems too good to be real, what with the three chins containing three clefts in the center, the three pairs of arched brows a few shades darker than the hair, the three dazzling white smiles that culminate in three dimples in three right cheeks.

I blink, and the images blur before coming together as one. The result is only more impressive, the power of triplicate combining to blind me with its brilliance.

"Well, well, what do we have here?" That cleft chin comes at me full force, and I find myself rolling to the side to dodge it. It's a useless maneuver underneath Grant's desk, where the heavy wooden legs and overflowing wastebasket impede my progress, so it's just as well that the man offers his hand instead. "You must be Emerson's wife. It's so great to finally meet you."

All I can do is blink at him as he pulls me to my feet. Still light-headed from the double impact of my fall and his dazzling beauty, I murmur a noncommittal response.

"I'm Christopher," he says. Booms, actually, his voice loud and full of the arrogant confidence I normally associate with investment bankers and men who tailgate. "Christopher Leon."

Of course he is. Leon the lion, roaring and golden and proud.

"I wouldn't go so far as to call myself proud, but thank you."

"Oh, God. Did I say that out loud?" I put my hand to my head, surprised when my fingers don't come away sticky with blood. I must have hit the ground harder than I thought if I'm blurting out random compliments. Women who break into the FBI should be a *little* more discreet than that.

"I won't tell anyone if you don't. I'm not sure anyone has called me a lion before."

"If it helps, I have nicknames for most of the agents Grant works with," I offer. "It's the only way I can keep you all straight."

Sterling Simon. Agent Barrel Chest. Before I got to know him, Grant was our Guard Dog—a great hairy beast of a threat to everything we held dear. Nicknaming people is a pretty handy trick when you have to meet a lot of dark suits who look at you with the same wary disdain.

"Then I accept," he says. Instead of wary disdain, he flashes his dimple at me. I can only assume it's the most powerful weapon in his arsenal, and that's saying a lot—I can tell from the familiar bulge at his side that he's packing. "Are you okay? That was some crash."

"I'll live. The chair was slippery."

Since I don't want to dwell on my other slippery movements around the office until I have a more accurate read on this guy, I attempt to deflect him with flattery.

"Thanks for coming in to make sure I was still breathing," I say. "Are you the one in charge of guarding—ah, I mean, protecting—me until this is all over?"

"No, Paulie's out there for that," he says. "I just wanted to come in and introduce myself while I had the chance. You don't mind, do you?"

Theoretically, I *don't* mind—I like meeting new

people, and I like meeting the people my husband works with in particular—but something about this overloud, overeager man feels off. I watch as he rights the office chair and holds it in place for me to take a seat. He doesn't move or speak until I lower myself into it.

"There's nothing to worry about," he adds with an uncomfortable laugh. "All signs indicate we're dealing with a false alarm. I'm sure you and your husband will be just fine."

"I know that," I say. "If there's one thing I've learned being married to Grant, it's that he can handle himself."

Too well, I want to add but don't. I sometimes feel my life would be much easier if my husband sucked at something for a change. He cooks, he cleans, he knows his way around the bedroom. He even remembers to call his mother every weekend. Independently, these things are great—*fantastic*, if we're dwelling on the sex—but together?

It's hard to compete with that kind of perfection is all I'm saying.

"Yeah, Emerson has never been one to rely on others. He'd take out a room of twenty men using nothing but a ballpoint pen before he'd consider calling for backup."

I groan, fully able to picture that exact scenario. In my imagination, he does it without a shirt on, too.

"Please tell me he's never had to take out a room of twenty men using nothing but a ballpoint pen," I say. "Can't you guys put a tracker on him or something?"

"I tried once. He found it within five minutes and threatened to extract my windpipe if I did it again." Christopher follows up this startling piece of news with a darkening look in his eyes, which are the same deep brown as Grant's. "He's not that violent at home, is he?"

I'm momentarily taken aback. "Um…no? Not usually. But he does sometimes throw cheese puffs at the TV when the Giants are losing."

I hope I sound convincing enough. Grant isn't a violent man—not to me, anyway—but if my presence at the FBI building today proves anything, it's that he *is* a tenacious one. Once he gets an idea in his head, he holds onto it like a—what else?—guard dog and his bone. Convincing him of one's innocence isn't so easy after that.

Although the two men share the same eye color, the similarities end there. Christopher takes a seat opposite me, nervously hitching his slacks before settling one long leg over the other. Like every other agent in this building, he's clad in a dark suit and dark tie, but I can tell from the way the fabric carries a slight sheen that his suit isn't the usual off-the-rack variety. Grant takes pride in his appearance but not so much that he's willing to drop a fourth figure on the clothes he wears when he shoots people.

"So, Mrs. Emerson," he says with a cough, "what do we have to thank for your presence here today?"

"Nothing, really," I say. There isn't time to come up with a more interesting lie, so I stick to the one I used with Cheryl. "I stopped by for a visit to see how my husband is doing. And I'm not Mrs. Emerson—I mean, I *am* married to Grant, but I didn't change my last name. Most people call me Pen."

There's a slight pause before the dimple appears in Christopher's cheek again. "Penelope the Pen. Mightier than the sword. To hold one is to be at war." He taps the cleft in his chin. "Hmm. I know I'm missing a few."

I'm forced into a laugh. "The war one might fit, but I don't know about the rest."

"I do. I've heard too many good things about you to believe otherwise."

Impossible. I'm pretty sure Simon uses my picture as a dartboard. "That's funny, when I've never heard about you. How long have you been with the Bureau?"

Immediately, a frown crosses his face, taking all traces of his dimple along with it. When he speaks again, his voice has lost its booming charm. Now it's merely loud. "Emerson has never mentioned me? Not even in passing?"

"Not that I can remember, but I'm sure it's nothing personal. Grant doesn't talk to me about work stuff."

Never about work stuff. Instead, he gives me shoes and waits for one of them to drop.

"Speaking of, he's been unusually preoccupied lately," I say, adopting an innocent smile. "I don't suppose you have any idea what that's about, do you? The case he's working on must be important to have him so wrapped up."

"It is." He blinks at me. "There are some pretty high stakes."

Now we're getting somewhere. "Oh, really? How exciting. Does that mean you're working on it, too?"

My sweetly feminine exhilaration is supposed to unwind him, but either my femininity needs improving or Christopher's flexibility does. He casts me a queer look that borders on suspicious, and I tuck my feet under the chair in hopes he won't notice my footwear. It's not that I'm *afraid* of the FBI—you have to be guilty of something for that—but I can't help recalling my husband's dire warnings that I'm one small slipup away from a life behind bars. I mean, I assume he's exaggerating most of the time, but even a broken clock is right twice a day. And if there *is* a case currently being mounted against me...

"You could say I'm working on it," he says carefully.

"Is that right? In what capacity?"

He leans closer. "Are you *sure* your husband hasn't said anything about me or this case?"

"Of course I'm sure."

"Not even in passing? Not even by accident?"

All of a sudden, the things I admired about this man seconds ago take on dangerous implications. His size, his charm, the gun at his side...just what is he implying?

"You obviously don't know my husband well, or you wouldn't ask me that," I say hotly. "Grant is the best and hardest-working agent in this place. He'd never do anything to jeopardize a case."

I know that's ironic coming from me, but it's the truth. Grant is everything I'm not—noble and honorable and righteous and *good*. I get to my feet and make as if to leave the office with all my dignity intact.

"What are you doing?" Christopher also rises, and since he's nearer the door, the movement transforms him into a human blockade. A very tall, very wide, very well-dressed human blockade. "I can't let you go. You haven't been given the all clear yet."

"Thank you, but I can make do without it. Now, if you'll excuse me..."

He doesn't. He grabs me by the upper arms before I take more than a few steps, his grip tight and his expression tense. I cry out, more from surprise than pain, but the damage has already been done. Before we can register the crash of the door being thrown open, Grant appears.

He fills the doorframe easily, all broad shoulders and stormy outrage, every sign of my beloved husband scratched from the surface. He's been replaced by a man who's one hundred percent business…and one hundred percent displeased to find me caught trying to escape.

My heart clenches. Of all the terrible things I've done to my husband—and there have been some doozies— he's never given me real cause for fear before.

And yet without waiting to hear my side of the story, he lunges into the room and heads straight for me.

THE LION

DESPITE MY CHECKERED PAST, FACING MY HUSBAND IN HIS full, federal agent fury isn't something I have much experience with. No sooner does Grant start charging than I find myself growing woozy. My head fills with a buzzing lightness as all the blood in my body is redirected elsewhere. Breaking into the FBI always carried a strong chance of upsetting Grant, but I never thought I'd see such loathing reflected in those soft brown eyes. I never thought he'd *hate* me.

Oh, God. I think I'm going to pass out.

"Grant, I can explain—" I begin, but I don't make it any further before Grant pounces.

"Get your hands off my wife," he growls.

But I am your wife, I think, confused.

It's only then that I realize he *isn't* heading toward me—he's angling himself so that Christopher is his target. And that lunge of Grant's, so frightening in its aggression, isn't to attack.

It's to protect. It's to protect *me*.

I yelp as Grant inserts his body between mine and Christopher's, my arm wrenched out of the latter's grasp in the process. Heat radiates off my husband—force and anxiety and anger mixing together in a mass of volcanic energy. Even though I'm not in need of his protection, I can't help but be flustered by his strength and his instincts, by the way those two things always seem to center on *me*.

He might think I'm a liar and a thief, but, dammit, he loves me. There's something to be said for devotion like that.

"Whoa, whoa." Christopher backs up a few steps, though I notice his hand goes down to his hip rather than up in a show of surrender. "Calm down, Emerson. I only stopped by to introduce myself."

Grant doesn't stand down, but a slight relaxation moves through him, water rolling over stone. "Right now? With the entire building on alert?"

"You told me you had it covered."

"What I told you was to stay out of it." Grant pauses, eyeing Christopher with what looks like lingering suspicion. "I put her in here for a reason—and that reason wasn't so you could manhandle her."

Manhandle seems a pretty strong word for what went on, but I know better than to speak up when two feral animals are locking horns. That's how lady animals get gouged.

"But she was trying to leave before it was safe!"

Grant's voice is a low growl. "As long as I'm breathing, she'll always be safe."

And that, my friends, is why lady animals don't necessarily mind.

"Of course she will be." Christopher backtracks with a light step. "No harm, no foul. I thought you might appreciate having extra eyes on her, that's all."

"Well, I don't. Not if they're your eyes."

"It won't happen again," Christopher says, though I notice he doesn't apologize.

"No, it won't," Grant agrees. He's also not very apologetic, and I have the feeling this is as close to a reconciliation as they're capable of getting. Which is odd, now that I think about it. My husband is the type of guy who gets along with *everyone*. Even the old man who lives across the street from our suburban house likes him, and Harold's idea of a good time is shooting squirrels out of his tree with a water gun.

"Then it's settled." Christopher nods as if everything has been arranged to his satisfaction. "Does this mean we're cleared to get back to work? There was no attack?"

Grant is careful not to look at me. "There was no attack. It was a false alarm."

"That's good news. We have enough to do today without a chemical spill on top of everything else. I left Doggart in temporary charge of the crime scene, but I'd like to oversee it myself. Would you rather head out to join me or interview witnesses back here?"

"I'd like a minute with my wife first, if you don't mind."

"Oh, sorry. Of course. I completely understand." Christopher claps a hand on Grant's back, a move even I—as the woman he pledged his life and love to—wouldn't have dared to attempt in his current mood. "Take all the time you need. I'll cover until you get her safely home."

"That won't be necessary. This won't take long."

That, at least, bodes well for my chances of survival. Smuggling my dead body out of here would take at least half an hour.

Christopher turns his false heartiness on me before he leaves, bending at the waist and pressing my hand warmly.

"It was lovely to meet you, Penelope," he says, oblivious to Grant's grunt of irritation. "I apologize if I startled you earlier. Working with your husband is something I'm keenly proud of, so it came as a surprise to discover he hadn't mentioned me. He's a pretty big deal around here. As soon as I found out we were assigned to the same case, I told everyone I knew."

Aw. Even though my adrenaline has yet to abate, my heartstrings give a gentle tug in his direction. The poor guy was probably feeling slighted earlier. I can hardly hold it against him. To be in Grant's inner circle, to matter to him, is the most glorious feeling in the world. It's like being the pope's confessor or knowing that James Bond keeps you on speed dial.

"It was nice to meet you, too, Christopher the Lion," I say. I withdraw my hand from his clasp, but only after giving his a squeeze in return. Solidarity among Grant Emerson aficionados and all that. "I hope we can try this again sometime soon. And don't worry—I'll have him back to you as quickly as possible."

He smiles and offers me a flash of those dimples before bowing himself out the door, leaving me all alone with my husband.

My justifiably angry, hulking husband.

My justifiably angry, hulking husband who may or may not be about to throw me into federal prison.

"Penelope," he says as soon as the door clicks to a close, "you've outdone yourself this time."

It's an encouraging start. "I know, right? This one might go under my greatest hits. It's even better than the time I took the place of that tranquilized panda being transported out of the zoo."

He takes a step back, and I realize I may have missed my mark. *Encouraging* isn't the word I'd use to describe his expression right now. I get the feeling I'd have better luck wrenching sympathy from Simon.

"Don't be cute with me. You shouldn't be here, and you know it. Not everyone in the FBI is as understanding as I am when it comes to your antics."

"They aren't *antics*," I protest. "Antics are for cartoon characters. I'm a professional, thank you very much."

He doesn't smile. "I doubt you'll notice the difference from the inside of a prison cell. I've told you a dozen times it's not safe for you in the city right now."

"Oh, yeah?" I ask. "Then where else should I be?"

"Staying home where no one's itching to add you to *their* list of greatest hits would be a start."

"Of course. Because that's where women belong. Should I be darning your socks and crocheting doilies while I'm at it?"

"Hardly. I wouldn't want you around any sharp objects. You'd probably stab one of the needles in my back when it was turned." He stops, eyes dark. "You're supposed to be honest with me now. You *promised*, Penelope."

There's a hint of real anguish in his voice. It stops the retort in my throat and my heart in my chest.

I was honest with him.

I am honest with him.

Sort of.

"Grant, I can explain—"

I expect him to launch into a list of my sins, highlighting all the ways I've ruined his life and career, but all he does is drop to his chair with his head in his hands, the weight of his worries crashing at once.

"What is it?" I ask, approaching him on suddenly wobbly legs. "What's wrong?"

He laughs. It's a hollow, bitter sound I've never heard from him before.

"It's not me, I swear!" My heart is in my throat. "I haven't lifted a single watch or looked sideways at anyone's jewelry in six months. I didn't even do anything today after taking all that trouble to get *in* here. I wanted to—I almost snooped through my files—but I couldn't bring myself to do that to you. Not after everything we've been through together." I pause and consider him. "Are you going to arrest me?"

He looks up. Lines of tenderness about those soulful eyes make my chest grow tight. "It's not *me* you should be worried about," he says. "So far as anyone except Simon and Cheryl know, it was nothing but a fluke, and I intend to keep it that way."

He's protecting me again, shielding me from harm.

"But *why* did you do it?" he adds, almost desperately. He rakes his hands through his hair. "That's what I can't figure out. What did you hope to gain by breaking in? There's nothing here to take. Nothing I wouldn't give you, if only you'd ask."

My heart snags. "I had to stop you."

"Stop me from what?"

Do I have to spell it out? The stupid shoes are starting

to pinch anyway, so I slip them off and set them in his lap. He looks at them and back at me, confused.

"I'm not the Peep-Toe Prowler," I explain. "I don't know who you've been talking to or what evidence you've discovered, but I didn't do it."

His confusion doesn't lift, which is strange for him. He's usually the first to pick up on clues, rushing forward ten steps ahead of the rest of the world. It's one of the most infuriating things about him.

"The only reason I'm here is to look at the case notes," I add. "I needed to know what I was up against, see what it is about the thefts that makes you suspect it's me. It could be a copycat—did you think about that? I have fans, you know. I got a letter once."

He sits up straighter. "What do you know about the Peep-Toe Prowler?"

I attempt to back away—my default reaction when anyone turns on the metaphorical spotlight—but I don't get far before Grant's hand grasps my wrist, the circle of his fingers serving less like a shackle and more as a—what else?—piece of jewelry.

"Penelope, tell me what you know about the Peep-Toe Prowler."

"I know she operates the same way my team and I used to," I say, meeting his gaze dead-on. He might have me at a disadvantage, but I'm not one to give in easily. "She only chooses wealthy targets, people who can afford to lose a few million without feeling the pinch. She gets in and out of the crime scene undetected— most likely through an open window or air vent. She only takes one item of jewelry at a time, and it's a show piece, something big and worth the risk."

He nods at each fact, adding to my feeling of sinking into quicksand.

"I also know that you think I'm her." There. It's out now. "And that you gave me these stupid shoes to try and trap me into confessing."

His response is a groan, which isn't helpful. Emotional outpourings like this aren't exactly easy.

"You accused me of not being honest with you, but that goes both ways," I say. "I thought we were on the same team now. No more tricks, no more lies. Remember?"

His groan deepens. "I remember. I only wish you had, too."

I glance up, surprised. He still looks as if he might enjoy hoisting me over his shoulder and hauling me out of the office caveman-style, but the lines around his eyes are the good kind. The crinkly kind.

"What are you talking about?" I ask.

"We *are* on the same team, Pen. Of course I don't think you're the Peep-Toe Prowler."

I blink. "You don't?"

"Okay, I will admit there were a few hours when it seemed like a possibility. And yes, I did have your friends tailed for a week to make sure. But even if I thought you were behind all this, I wouldn't have started investigating you again."

"You wouldn't?"

He lifts his hand to cup my cheek, a tender gesture that has always managed to break my defenses. This time is no exception. "I would have just asked you, Penelope Blue."

"But…" My head swirls from the combination of his

touch and the relief of hearing that rhyme back on his lips. "That doesn't make any sense. You've been treating me like a suspect for months."

"What are you talking about? I've been treating you the same as I always have. I mean, I've been working a lot of overtime, yes, but that's not anything new."

I stare at him, incredulous. Is he seriously going to pretend this is all in my head?

"Besides, everything else seems to be in working order." His voice drops to a sexy rumble over that *everything else*. "Just the other night, we did that thing…"

I know the thing he's referring to, and I'm not about to let him elaborate. We are, after all, in a professional setting.

"Exactly," I say.

"Exactly what?"

"You always get demanding and sexy when you think I'm stealing things. It's how you assert your dominance."

An enticing gleam sparks in his eye, and I can tell he wants to assert his dominance here, now, with his full dedication. Despite the thrill of desire that works through me at the thought of us tossing his desktop knickknacks to the floor and enjoying a full reconciliation, I'm determined to hold my ground.

"Sex has never been the issue, and you know it," I say sternly. The soft upturn of his lips indicates his agreement. Whatever else, we've always been great at that. "But you've been a walking, talking stranger for the past two months. You refuse to let me come to the office or even call in to say hello. The only time I see you is when you come home to sleep and shower and give me shoes…"

I trail off and let the footwear say the rest. Unfortunately, they aren't adept at communication, because he touches one with a puzzled furrow in his brow.

"What's wrong with them? You look sexy as hell when you have them on. I distinctly remember you wearing them when we did that thing—"

"Grant, if you so much as mention *that thing* one more time, we will never do it again."

"Never?"

"Not in a million years."

"A million years is an awfully long time." He caresses the shoe, his fingers trailing over the curves of the red patent leather in obscene and titillating ways. "And you seemed to enjoy yourself at the time. I know I did."

I snatch my shoes away and shove my sweaty, swollen feet back into them. It doesn't dampen his ardor as I'd hoped, so I have to resort to the obvious.

"They're peep-toes," I say and hold out a foot. "See my toes? Peeping out?"

He laughs, his voice crooning as he says, "It's just a shoe, Penelope Blue."

I look at him, waiting.

"I didn't mean anything by it. I was talking about them at work one day, for obvious reasons, and I thought…"

"…that you'd dress me up like a suspect in a federal investigation? And you didn't think I'd notice?"

He has the decency to look chagrined, and I fight the triumph rising to my throat. Sure, he's the picture-perfect FBI hero, swooping in and solving cases with his mighty powers of deduction, but I didn't get where I am today without *some* intelligence.

"Hmpf." The sound he makes is neither an admission of guilt nor a refusal of it, but I accept it like a trophy.

"Maybe I should have seen that one coming, but you could have asked me instead of going through all this trouble. I would have told you the truth."

He's not getting off the hook so easily.

"And you could have told me you have a new partner, but you didn't," I accuse. "I guess we both need to start sharing more."

My only intention is to remind him that there are *two* of us in this marriage of ours, but his whole body tenses, and the light in his eyes flickers off.

"Christopher Leon is *not* my partner."

"But he said—"

Grant gets to his feet. "Do us both a favor and forget anything and everything he said to you." Then, suspiciously, "What *did* he say to you?"

"Hello. How do you do. The usual."

"That's all? Are you sure?"

I spread my arms helplessly. "You can double-check with him if you don't trust me to tell you the truth."

That does the trick. Even though it's obvious from the way he's looming that he wants to shake more information from my parted lips, he restrains himself.

Well, almost.

"I'm sorry," he says. "I don't mean to be so overbearing, but you have to remember that as much as *I* love you, you're not a favorite with everyone at the Bureau."

"Give me time," I say. "I'm only one woman. It might take me a few years, but I'll get there."

His lips twitch. "Penelope…"

"And it's not as if he said or did anything bad," I add, eager to leverage that oh-so-promising break in his exterior. "We mostly talked about you. He seemed nice."

"That man is not nice. I don't want you to have anything to do with him or with this case from here on out. Promise me."

"I'll do no such thing," I scoff. "I'm not a child you can order around."

"Promise me," he repeats, firmer this time. He also takes an anticipatory step forward, though I'm not sure whether it's to kiss me or throttle me. "If there's any self-preservation in that crooked heart of yours, you'll swear not to have anything to do with Christopher Leon or the Peep-Toe Prowler."

As if I could promise that *now*.

"Why? What are you hiding from me?"

"I'm not hiding anything," he says too quickly, his normally implacable exterior slipping. "Could you please be conciliatory for once in your life and do as I ask?"

I think about it. I really do—for a whole two seconds and everything—but there's more to this situation than he's letting on. A man doesn't grow distant and moody from his loving wife for no reason. He doesn't throw around sex shoes unless he's trying to create a distraction. And most importantly, he doesn't lay down mysterious ultimatums without secretly wanting her to do everything in her power to determine the cause.

That one's plain common sense.

"I can promise to try not to get in the way," I hedge. *Trying* not to do something always makes for a good promise, since there's no real rubric for measurement. I *tried* not to steal things for years. I just wasn't any good at it. "But you can't ask me to pretend this whole conversation never happened—that these past few *months* haven't happened."

"This has nothing to do with you."

"Yeah, but I'm emotionally invested in the Peep-Toe Prowler now. I want to catch her as much as you do."

It's only through sheer force of will that Grant suppresses his smile in time. "Penelope, so help me…"

"Helping you is what I intend to do." I stand on my tiptoes to graze his jaw, rough in all the right ways. "I can, you know. I might be able to access information that's closed to you. Thieves talk."

"You aren't a thief anymore, remember?" He makes a vague gesture around the room. "The walls have ears."

"And you did want me to get a hobby…"

"Swimming is a hobby. Interfering in a federal investigation is obstruction."

"It's not obstruction if I help you solve the case," I point out. "Besides, didn't you just say you wouldn't arrest your own wife?"

His reluctant and groan-filled laugh is all the confirmation I need to know I've won this round. A nice side effect of having an important and busy husband is that he can't always spend as much time arguing as he'd like. He has a job to get back to.

Unlike me. I, unfortunately, have nothing to do and no one to do it with. I'm not one of the good guys, but I can no longer be one of the bad ones, either. I'm just a housewife with nothing but time on her hands and mischief on her mind.

"To be perfectly honest, my love," he says with a mock sigh, "the idea of putting you behind bars grows more appealing every day."

GRANT 4

(Two and a Half Years Ago)

THE FIRST TIME I WORKED ALONGSIDE CHRISTOPHER Leon, the bastard shot me in the back.

We were crouched behind a bullet-riddled 1950s Cadillac at the time, sweaty skin sticking to hot metal as shots peppered the dirt. The cloud of dust enveloping us obscured my vision, and I concentrated on attempting to count the number of gunmen firing at us.

Based on the smattering of shots to the left and the sparse but much more accurate shots to the right, I guessed there were at least six men in the warehouse and a sniper at the top of the tower overlooking the shipyard.

Not good numbers, but not bad ones, either. I'd faced worse, and if all accounts of the hotshot newbie by my side were to be trusted, he could handle himself.

"If we can make our way to the loading bay, we should be able to enter through the access port," I said as soon as the firing died down enough to allow for conversation. "I sure as hell hope you're lighter on your feet than you look."

Christopher Leon, hotshot newbie, glanced at me under lowered brows. I didn't know what worried him. By placing himself behind me, he'd secured himself a human shield.

"What access port?" he asked.

A burst of gunfire broke out again, forestalling my response.

"There is no access port," he said as soon as the air cleared. He looked every bit the new recruit in his sweat-soaked confusion. Getting paired with hot-off-the-presses agents from Quantico was never my favorite assignment, but I'd been asked to let him play along with me today. *This one is earmarked for the express elevator upstairs*, my section chief had said. *I need you to show him a good time before he gets on.*

Which was basically a bureaucratic way of saying Christopher had friends in high places. They wanted to promote him as quickly as possible, but they had to make a show of putting him through his paces first.

"We passed it on the way over the landing," I said and nodded in the direction we needed to head. "Blue door, probably rusted shut. Do you want to cover or make the run?"

"There is no access port there," he repeated, firmer this time. "It isn't in the schematics."

"Schematics can be wrong."

"These ones aren't. There's nothing there."

"Look, I saw it with my own two eyes. Besides, it could be a unicorn waiting to take us up on its back, and it would still be our best—no, our only—chance of making it inside. The other option is to sit here until one of their bullets hits its target. I don't know about you, but I'd prefer not to be that target."

Since Christopher gave every impression of continuing to argue, I made an executive decision. "I'll cover you by drawing the fire over to the right. Run like hell, newbie."

No sooner did I have my weapon ready, aimed toward the cluster of firepower doing the most damage, than I heard the sound of a trigger at my back. It was closely followed by an explosion of pain that spread like metal spikes.

"What the hell—" I cried, whirling.

Paintballs aren't deadly, but they hurt like a son of a bitch, especially when fired at close range. Even though the body shot meant I was officially out for the count, I fell back into position and gauged angles for the shooter's likeliest hiding spot. I acted on pure instinct at that point, and it was a good one: *never go down without a fight*.

"Where'd the lone gunman come from? I thought we had the rear perimeter secured."

I saw him then, the hotshot newbie, crouched where I'd left him. All that was missing was the smoke from the barrel of his paintball gun.

"Sorry, Emerson," he said and continued to level the firearm at me. "I can't let you go in."

"What are you talking about?" I asked. The pain he'd inflicted was a tight throb, hot and itchy as it spread upward. Giving him the satisfaction of seeing how much it hurt wasn't an option, so I resisted the urge to roll my shoulders. I was going to have a hell of a bruise tomorrow. "The entire purpose of this scenario is to breach the facility."

"And I will breach it—but I'll do it alone."

"Seriously?"

He stood and lifted his weapon in a gesture of surrender, arms up.

"He's dead," he shouted in the direction of the warehouse. "I upheld my end of the bargain."

"*Seriously?*" I repeated, louder that time. I stood up next to him, narrowing my eyes to bring the guys from the warehouse into focus. If Simon was in on this, I was going to kill him. "That's how you're playing this, Leon? On your first day?"

"No offense," he said, and had the audacity to smile as he holstered his weapon. "But there was no way you and I were going to make it in there alive. At least this way one of us still wins."

"I'd hardly call murdering your partner *winning*."

His smile lost some of its self-satisfied wattage. "It's not murder. They offered me an insurance plan before the game started, and I made the call to take it. Securing the cargo was more important than one agent's life. Besides, we lost six guys on the way in here already."

"Seven," I said. "We lost seven guys on the way in here."

His head tilted as he made the mental calculations, working his way through the paint-splattered bodies of our fallen brethren. "Oh, right. I guess you brought the total up to eight." He shrugged. "It's not an ideal outcome, but it's a positive one for the Bureau, and that's what counts."

I stared as if seeing him for the first time. Christopher Leon was an easy target for disdain and had been since the day he sauntered into the field office. Better dressed than every other agent in the place and on friendly terms with the higher ranks, Christopher wasn't a typical new recruit. He'd felt it; many a cold shoulder turned his way in the locker room. I was trying my best not to let myself fall under the same prejudices, but moments like these weren't making that task any easier.

As the warehouse group trotted over to join us—one of whom *was* Simon, the bastard—I lifted the shirt from my back. The paint stuck where it soaked through the fabric to my skin. I tossed the shirt at Christopher, letting him have it as a trophy.

"Congratulations on your success," I said dryly. "Remind me to watch my back the next time we get partnered up."

Christopher's mouth fell, and I felt a twinge of guilt for being so rough on the kid. It hadn't been that long since *I* was the hotshot newbie. I could still remember the painful earnestness of wanting to prove myself, to show I was capable of the job I'd been trusted to do.

"As promised, your delivery." Mariah Ying, a hacker-turned-IT specialist who had an alarming love of playing the bad guy in these training exercises, tossed a black duffel bag at Christopher's feet. "And congratulations. I don't think anyone has single-handedly won one of these things his first time out before."

"Except Emerson," Simon said with a rare grin. Few things in life got that man to smile, but seeing me beaten at my own game was one of them. "Remember, with the shoot-out in front of the baseball field?"

"I remember, thanks."

"That must burn, huh? Or should I say, it must *bruise*? Upstaged by an upstart."

I flipped him my middle finger. "I don't mind losing in a fair fight."

"The rules never said the mission had to be fair," Christopher said. He opened the duffel bag, disappointed when it revealed nothing but crumpled newspapers. What had he expected to be in there? Gold stars? "It only had to be successful. I made a professional judgment call, and I stand by it."

"Your professional judgment was that Emerson couldn't take down half a dozen guards led by No-Aim Mariah?" Paulie Jones, a robustly aggressive field agent I'd worked with a few times, laughed and slapped Christopher on the back. "You've clearly never seen him in action before."

"Or watched Mariah try to hit something that's moving," another agent added. "Unless it's encrypted in computer code, she's one hundred percent blind spot."

Simon also slapped Christopher on the back, hard, in the same spot where my own muscles still stung. His hand clamped long enough for me to make out the tight press of his fingers.

"Also, some friendly advice?" Simon said. "If you ever shoot my partner in cold judgment again, I'll kill you."

"Aw, shucks, Sterling," I said. "You're making me all gooey inside."

He flipped *me* off that time.

"I mean it," he added, directing his comments at Christopher. "I'm friends with the poison expert in forensics. Don't try me."

Ganging up on the new kid—even one who'd cheat to get a win under his belt—wasn't part of my job description, so I decided to take it easy on him. "According to the rules, winner buys the first round," I said. "I hope you came prepared."

Mariah picked up my cue without batting an eyelash. "And we don't come cheap. It's top-shelf scotch and Cristal all the way."

The relief that moved across Christopher's face was almost comical. "I don't mind," he said in a loud voice that seemed to be trying too hard. "I don't mind at all."

Another pang of sympathy hit me. "Then it's agreed. We'll meet at the Whiskey Room in an hour."

The prospect of free booze after a long day hunting an empty duffel bag was all we needed to start moving again. We broke to shower and nurse our wounds and/ or pride, depending on the situation.

My pride was mostly intact, but my back was complaining, and that shower sounded great. Unfortunately, even that small pleasure was denied me. Christopher jogged up before I made it to my car, still clutching my paint- and sweat-soaked T-shirt.

"Hey, no hard feelings?" he asked. His hand hovered as if he wanted to stop me from unlocking the door and driving away, but he didn't make contact. "I didn't mean to show you up back there."

"You didn't."

"Yeah, *I* know that, but I wanted to explain…"

"Look, Leon. I get it, okay?" I said as kindly as I could. "You wanted to put on a good show, prove to the powers that be that you have something to offer, and you did it. I might not approve of your methods, but I understand the motivation. Believe it or not, I was once young and eager to prove myself, too. And up until you shot me, I thought we were working pretty well together."

"Really?" His eyes lit up, and he reminded me of a kid getting a puppy for the first time. "I was afraid you might harbor a grudge."

"Nope. We're fine."

"I was hoping you'd say that. In fact, I was hoping we'd have a chance to talk. I've been doing some research into the case you're working, and I wanted to offer my assistance."

At that point in my career, I was working several cases—many of which would appeal to a man who was wet behind the ears and determined to prove himself—but I wasn't a professional investigator for nothing. I knew without a doubt which case he meant. It was the same one that everyone referred to in those hushed, reverential tones.

The Blue Fox. My white whale. The case that was going to make or break me.

"Thanks, but I have it under control," I said.

"Of course you do," he rushed on, oblivious to the warning in my voice. "I read the thesis you wrote on him, and I've been following your work since you joined the Bureau. It's amazing. If anyone can find that man, it's you."

His flattery was touching but unnecessary. Flagging confidence had never been a problem of mine, and I knew what I was up against. The Blue Fox, better known as Warren Blue, had gone missing eight years earlier. For the majority of that time, the FBI had operated under the assumption that the infamous jewel thief had died in the line of duty. It was only recently—when I forced the case open with a crowbar—that they started to take his possible return seriously. So seriously, in fact, that

I'd been given what amounted to a blank check to find him. The information that man carried in one fold of his brain was enough to close dozens of the organized art and jewelry rings currently littering my desk.

I *was* going to find him. It was only a matter of time.

"Thank you for the vote of confidence, but I already have all the support I need from Sterling." I turned to leave, hoping to cut the conversation short, but I underestimated the obstinacy of a young overachiever.

"Sterling is a great agent, of course, and I'm sure he's trying his best, but did you guys know that the Blue Fox has a daughter?" He waited for me to react, disappointed when all he got was a tilt of my head. "She's alive and in New York. I could tell you exactly where to find her."

That got a reaction, but probably not the one he was hoping for.

Of course I knew about Penelope Blue, the twenty-three-year-old daughter of my prey. Warren Blue was one of those rare criminals who'd kept his private life firmly *private*, but I hadn't spent most of my professional career digging into his secrets for nothing. There was a record of Penelope's birth and a few juvenile arrests, followed by years of nothing. It was as though she'd disappeared off the face of the earth with him.

But then a valuable necklace went missing from a hotel safe, and someone lifted half a dozen watches from a popular Wall Street hangout, and I found her. Or, more specifically, I found the pair of thieves responsible for those—and about ten similar—crimes. Luck wasn't something I believed in, not in this line of work, but I figured that was as close as I'd ever get to it.

I'd been following her for about three months, and

I'd yet to be disappointed. Tracking Penelope's movements was like tracking a cat. The petite strawberry blond slunk in and out of the most unlikely places, taking whatever she wanted, whenever she wanted it. She was indifferent to everything—especially the laws governing human society—but somehow kept her proud head erect as she moved silently through the night.

She was brazen.

She was determined.

She was *magnificent*.

She was also most valuable to me exactly where she was. I'd always considered myself more of a dog person than a cat person, but even I knew you couldn't tame a creature like that by putting her behind bars. She was much more useful running wild and free, the exact bait I needed to pull the Blue Fox out of his hole.

"I have reason to believe you could bring her in for questioning, possibly coerce her into helping you out," Christopher said. "Apparently, she didn't fall too far from the tree, if you know what I mean."

I didn't have to fake a cold, hard look at that. "I know what you mean, thanks."

"It'd be really easy to get a warrant out for her arrest," Christopher added. "I could call in a few favors for you, get the paperwork rolling within the hour. We could work the case together."

I would have liked to blame my reaction on the lingering tension of the training exercise, but that would have been unfair to both Christopher and me. Christopher, because he didn't know any better, and me, because I *did*. The reality is that federal agents are known to get a little territorial over their cases, and I was no exception—especially in this instance. Penelope Blue was mine. She'd become mine the day I caught her sliding down a rain gutter with a bejeweled machete between her teeth, unconcerned for her personal safety and oblivious to the fact that she was being watched.

"Knowing you, you'd shoot her before we had a chance to pursue any line of questioning," I said. My tight smile stretched my cheeks. "Forgive me if I'd rather not take that approach."

"But I could help," he insisted. "There's an angle you might not have considered—"

I tried, I honestly did. I breathed in and out, counted to ten, pictured the entire world in its underwear. None of it worked. The idea of this hothead rushing in and putting Penelope at risk for his own gain was too much.

"Thanks, but I've got it. I suggest you spend a little more time developing your own cases before you try taking over everyone else's. And Leon?" I didn't wait for a response. "Stop trying so hard. You need to lighten the fuck up, or this job is going to eat you alive."

I didn't catch everything he said as I opened the car door and slid behind the wheel, but judging from the way his face turned red, he wasn't happy with the way I handled the dismissal. I wasn't too happy with it myself, but what was done was done. And I couldn't regret the outcome. At least this way, he got the message. Under no circumstances was I going to hand Penelope Blue over to someone who turned on his own partner to win a training exercise.

A man who shot you in the back once was a man who'd shoot you in the back twenty times over.

THE 5 SUSPECT

(Present Day)

"Thank you for an interesting and highly invasive afternoon, Penelope." My dad is waiting for me at the door to his hotel room when I arrive, anticipating my movements, as usual. "Your little stunt at the Bureau put me back on at least twelve watch lists."

"Only twelve? You must be slipping."

I lean in to kiss him on the cheek before making my way inside, doing my best not to look as out of place as I feel. My father's current residence is none other than the Lombardy, an address he's called home since we reconnected six months ago. Living in one of the nicest hotels in the city seems extravagant, but he's always preferred it this way. Growing up, we lived in a series of rooms and suites that were easy to leave at a moment's notice. Some were like this one, ostentatious and grand. Others were less...shall we say, excessive? It all depended on which way the winds blew at the time.

Right now, the winds are blowing strongly in his favor. His suite isn't the penthouse, but it's the next best thing. The penultimatehouse, he likes to call it. Paying for the most expensive room in a building like this would raise red flags about his income. Second-best gets him the same amenities with half the scrutiny.

He's smart like that. You don't get to be a criminal kingpin and FBI informant any other way.

"You could have at least warned me," he says, a deep frown etched into his features. His face is a series of such etches and grooves. My memories of the handsome and powerful man he once was are now carved in stone. "I might have been able to provide assistance."

"There was no need," I say airily. I click over the marble floor tiles to one of several white couches in the main room.

Clicking is, unfortunately, the only way I know how to walk in these stupid shoes. I've had them on since I left the FBI building, and I'm going to wear them home later, too—I refuse to change as a matter of principle. Grant will have to look at them until he's sorry for what he did.

"You were our decoy," I explain when my dad stays silent. "We needed you to raise suspicions so I could get inside."

"And did you?"

"Of course."

"Take anything worthwhile?"

"Not anything of tangible value, if that's what you're asking," I say. I know he'll be disappointed by that—he considers an elaborate heist wasteful unless millions of dollars end up in his pockets—but he'll be disappointed no matter what I tell him. Although he supports my marriage, he doesn't understand it. Few people do. "But I got information, which is more important. What do you know about the Peep-Toe Prowler?"

A smoother, more elegant clicking sound fills the room, this time from the bedroom. I don't have to look up to know who it is. I can smell Tara Lewis coming from a mile away.

Well, not literally. A thief and con artist who *also* considers an elaborate heist wasteful unless millions of dollars end up in her pockets, Tara knows better than to wear perfume and risk detection. The smell is less a physical aroma and more like proof of the decay of her soul.

"Hello, Tara," I say blandly. Even though I haven't seen my stepmother in six months—not since she helped the FBI find my dad—I'm not surprised to see her. She has a way of disappearing and reappearing whenever it suits her. "I didn't know you were back in town."

She places one of her carefully sculpted fingernails against an even more carefully sculpted nose and winks. "And I'd appreciate it if you kept it that way. No running home to the man of the house full of news, okay?"

"Sorry, but I don't keep secrets from my husband anymore."

"That's nice. Also a lie. Any woman who wants to stay married for longer than a month has secrets." She turns to my father with a saccharine smile. "Isn't that right, Warren? I don't tell you anything, and look at how long we've been together."

My dad murmurs a noncommittal reply. Technically, the two of them will be celebrating their twelfth anniversary later this year. Even though Tara is only thirty-one—and a well-preserved, vibrantly blond thirty-one at that—she and my dad have quite the history together.

Of course, my dad was missing for most of that history, so it doesn't do to put much stock in her marital advice. Insight on how to abandon your young stepdaughter? She's your gal. Tips and tricks for incredible brassiere support? Absolutely. Her cleavage is nothing short of miraculous.

But the secrets of a happy marriage? Forgive me if I prefer my own approach, however unorthodox it may be.

"I doubt Grant cares whether you're in New York," I say, continuing with my bland smile. "He tends to focus on *important* criminals, and you haven't done much work lately, have you? I hope you're not losing your touch."

Satisfaction swells inside me at putting Tara in her place, but of course, she can't let me have that minor victory. She drops to the couch in a single elegant movement, crossing one leg over the other as she falls. It's only then that I note a peep-toe heel dangling playfully from the tip of her toes. My heart beats in an odd lurch.

Part of that lurch is jealousy—she looks fifty times better in these shoes than I do. Her toenails are painted to match the shiny red patent leather, and her calves are a sculpture worthy of museum space. But most of it is the realization that Tara's touch might be working perfectly fine. Those shoes are a dead giveaway.

"Are you kidding me?" I plop next to her, not caring

when she sinks so close, our thighs touch. "It's you, isn't it? This whole time, it's been you. I should have known. I should have guessed the second I heard about that size seven shoe."

"If you're going to be vague, please do it on a different chair."

"Scoot over if you don't like it. There's room for both of us." Scooting is beneath a woman of Tara's poise, so she remains in place as I add, "You know Grant's going to find you, right? Whether I tell him or someone else does, it's only a matter of time before he realizes you're in New York. And then?"

I make a series of hand motions to simulate her arrest, incarceration, and what I hope indicates a long celibacy behind bars. I can't say how much of that makes it through, but Tara's bright. She'll figure it out.

"All that time I wasted thinking *I* was the main suspect..." I say. I'm not supposed to meet my friends for a postmortem until tomorrow, as there's no take for us to divide up between us, but I'm dreading it already. How could I have not seen this coming?

Tara shows me the neat line of her profile as she faces my dad. "Do you have any idea what she's rambling about, Warren?"

My dad takes the stance he always has when Tara and I start bickering, which is to say he pretends nothing is amiss.

"I imagine it's the Peep-Toe Prowler," he says as he flips through a magazine. It looks to be about art museums, which means he's either thinking about investing in a piece or stealing one. "For the record, I would like to voice my objection to that name. So pedantic."

"Isn't it awful?" I agree. "If I take to a life of crime again, I'm going to make sure I leave a cool calling card, like titanium shavings or a bullet that's been bitten in half. Let's see what nickname I get for that one."

My dad looks at me over the top of his glasses. "If you start dropping clues at your crime scenes, I'm disowning you. Leaving anything behind is sloppy work, and calling cards smack of egoism."

"Yes, sir," I say meekly, though I can't help but grin at how stiff Tara grows next to me. She's always been a big fan of calling cards—her usual signature is a lipstick imprint on the mirror—but that's because she has the biggest ego known to mankind. She can't help herself. "Does that mean *you're* the one taking all those valuables?"

"I refuse to dignify that question with a response," my father says, still perusing his magazine. It's as much of a denial as I'm going to get, but he wasn't the most likely suspect in the room anyway.

"Well, Tara?" I glance at her expectantly. "Care to make a formal confession?"

"I don't care to do anything formally unless it includes an open bar. And if you want my opinion, those shoes look ridiculous on you. Your gait is too wobbly."

There's an element of truth to her insult, but one of my life goals has always been to ignore anything and everything my dear stepmother says, so I let it go.

"Come on, Tara. There's no way you just *happen* to be in New York while jewelry is going missing all across the Upper East Side. What do you know?"

She shares a look with my dad. Despite the mere five-year age gap between me and Tara, it's a parental look, and I don't like it. It's bad enough that she's in my father's hotel room in the middle of the day, acting like they're some power couple that has never been on the outs. Worse is the idea that they might be *communicating*. That's not the sort of family we are. We steal and lie and manipulate each other to achieve our own ends. We don't sit at the dinner table and talk about our day.

"I'm serious, you guys." I try for stern but end up sounding like the fifteen-year-old they once left behind. "Until two hours ago, I was pretty sure Grant was going to arrest me. Now I find out that not only am I *not* a suspect, but he's got a fancy new partner to help him solve the case—and he's forbidden me from having anything to do with it."

Tara lifts a perfectly arched brow. "He can forbid you from doing things?"

"Of course not," I say irritably. "That's not the point."

"Then what is?"

"Secrets." I let the word sit for a moment, but they don't seem to feel its weight the way I do. "He has secrets. You guys have secrets. I'm pretty sure his new partner has some, too. I know my being married to Grant puts everyone in an awkward position, but I'm not going to turn on you. I still want to be included."

I still want to matter.

It's almost desperate, that silent plea of mine, but I can't hold it back. Of all the changes I'd anticipated in marrying an FBI agent, this one never occurred to me. Less money flowing into my pockets? Of course. Fewer personal freedoms? I get it. It's not ideal, but being held accountable for your actions is part of any committed relationship.

Unfortunately, no one mentioned how untenable it would be to get caught between these two worlds of mine. The place where the good and the bad sides of the track meet isn't exactly a popular hangout spot.

My dad clears his throat and looks away, leaving Tara to fill in the gaps. She does this with wide eyes and an innocent, "Grant has a new partner?"

"Yeah, it's some guy named Christopher Leon. He's young. And cute. And loud. I think you'd like him, actually."

As I finish speaking, I'm struck by how true that is. Tara *would* like Christopher, even though he's closer to my age than hers. He's got the kind of outward appeal that would attract a woman of her…tastes.

Just as I'm about to explain how I came to meet him, Tara gives a peal of laughter. "Oh, sweetie. Is that what he told you? Christopher isn't Grant's partner."

"What? Of course he is. Grant said so himself." At least, I *think* he did. My memories of this afternoon are already growing hazy, misted over by relief at discovering my marriage isn't about to crack into a thousand pieces.

"Then your dear husband misled you, because he's no such thing."

"How do you know?"

My dad clears his throat again.

"You told *her* but not me?" I ask my dad, confused—and, to be honest, a little hurt. The sting of being an outsider looking in, of no longer fitting inside my own life, is magnified twenty times now. I look back and forth between them. "But if Christopher's not his partner, then who…"

"He's Grant's *boss*." Tara speaks with triumph, as if she's personally responsible. "I hate to be the one to tell you, but your poor, dedicated husband is no longer a rising star. He broke too many rules to keep your pretty little behind from incarceration, so they hired new blood to keep him in check. How does it feel to single-handedly ruin your husband's career?"

My first feeling isn't anger at Tara for being so snide, or even guilt for forcing Grant to break rules. Relief washes over me instead, and I take a moment to bask in it.

"So *that*'s why he's been acting so strange lately." My husband's behavior suddenly makes sense. The long hours, the unwillingness to discuss his work except to warn me away, the curt way he refused to refer to Christopher by anything but his last name... "And why he almost tackled the poor guy. It's not like him to be so aggressive."

Tara releases an incongruously elegant snort.

"I mean it's not like him to be so aggressive to regular people," I amend. "Obviously, he treats criminals like you differently."

"And what about criminals like *you*?"

"I don't count. He loves me."

Tara doesn't say anything, but her silence is voluble enough. Her silence is also kind of mean. Grant *does* love me. Even though I know it can't be easy to be married to me, his love is the one thing I can count on.

His love is enough. *Our* love is enough. I'm sure of it.

Most of the time.

"Well, there you have it, Penelope." My dad sets his magazine aside, closing it with a sense of purpose that also signals the end of the conversation. "The secret is revealed."

"Hardly." If anything, the vein of mystery has only proven deeper than I thought. Despite Tara's rude insinuations, my husband is exceptionally good at his job. They wouldn't have assigned someone to oversee him without a reason. "And you still haven't told me anything about the Peep-Toe Prowler. Do you know who it is?"

"If I knew who it was, I would have told Agent Sterling, per our arrangement," my dad says mildly.

"Don't look at me," Tara says. "I only got here a few days ago. But don't you worry—with Chris on the case, things are bound to get interesting soon."

Chris? When did they reach the nickname stage? Tara has worked with my husband in the past, so it's possible she's aligned herself with the FBI, but I doubt Grant would have brought her on again without telling me.

My eyes narrow in suspicion. "What do you know about him?"

"More than you, but that's not saying much." Tara gets to her feet. Like my father, she appears to be done entertaining me for the day. "Thanks ever so much for stopping by, but your father and I have some things to do."

"Like move a bunch of recently stolen jewelry out of the country?" I ask.

"Nice try. Things like a dinner reservation at Le Bernardin. Want to come?"

I most definitely do not. Rolling along as a third wheel on a date with these two isn't my idea of a good time.

Tara laughs at my expression. "I didn't think so. But if you're free next week, you and I should have lunch."

I look to my dad in alarm at this unprecedented offer, but there's an aura of contentment around him I don't quite like. He's watching the pair of us interact as if no time has passed since we all lived under the same roof. It's not a memory I'm particularly fond of. No one else seems to recall the less-than-happy times we shared or how irrational being around Tara makes me. Peep-Toe Prowler, FBI informant, general pain in my ass—she casts herself in the various roles on purpose, I swear. Nothing delights her more than casting suspicion and watching as I struggle to pick up the pieces.

"I'm going to figure out who the thief is," I warn as I rise to leave.

Tara sees me to the door, playing the gracious hostess to perfection. "You do that, sweetie."

"And I'm going to make them give all that stuff back."

"How noble. Your husband must be rubbing off on you."

She's obviously determined to withstand provocation, so I smile back and attack with the only thing I have left. "And I may take you up on that lunch offer, so you better start thinking of places you won't mind being seen in public with me."

It doesn't work. "Perfect. Give my love to Chris next time you see him, will you?"

My heart picks up as I try to read her, but Tara has me beat. The thick layers of makeup she wears make her appear effortlessly flawless as well as prevent actual human emotion from flickering on her face. It's not a bad trick, and I'm tempted to ask for a few pointers.

I don't, though. The mother-daughter ship has long since sailed. And sunk. And killed all marine life within a ten-mile radius.

"I was serious about us getting together, Pen," she says as a final parting shot. "I hope you know that. You make a terrible stepdaughter, but I can't help liking you anyway."

Her sudden lapse into kindness throws me off, and I can only reply with, "And you're a terrible stepmom, Tara, but I've never found any fault with your taste."

When I arrive at the home Grant and I share in the northern suburb of Rye a few hours later, the first thing I do is check my cell phone. I only take a burner when I'm on the job—old habits die hard—so the blinking light indicating I have messages comes as no surprise. Neither does the first message, since the house is dark save for the motion-sensor lights that switch on when I unlock the door.

"I know the timing is bad, but I'm not going to make it home until late," my husband's voice says. "Don't wait up for me, and please, please don't assume this means I'm going to handcuff you in your sleep. I promise to always give you a five-minute head start before I arrest you—you have my word on that."

Maybe it's the long day getting to me, but that strikes me as one of the sweetest things I've ever heard.

"And I'll make all these long nights up to you, I swear. It's just that—"

His message is broken by a loud male voice in the background, which Grant soon overrides with a string of low, muttered curses I plan on memorizing for future use. Nobody swears like an FBI agent. I think it's part of their training.

"Love you, gotta go, bye."

And they say romance is dead.

The second message is timestamped a few minutes later, and it's from a number I don't recognize. I'm about to pull cold Chinese food out of the fridge to enjoy a sad, lonely meal for one when a booming voice startles me into spilling chow mein all over the kitchen floor.

"Penelope. Penelope Blue."

I don't need to hear Christopher Leon identify himself to know who's responsible for that effusive volubility.

"I wanted to say again how nice it was to meet you today. I have nothing but respect for your husband and the work he does, and I'd love it if we could all get together sometime. Dinner, maybe?"

I abandon the noodles and stare at my phone in confusion. First Tara and now Christopher? Two unprecedented offers for a friendly meal in one day? Either I'm starting to look malnourished, or something strange is going on.

"Anyway, I promise to take good care of Grant out there. If you're ever worried or have questions about the case or even want to talk, I'm always available. I'm also discreet. So. Um. I better get going. It's going to be another long night. Sorry about that, by the way."

The call ends as abruptly as Grant's did, and it leaves me equally unsatisfied. Never, in all the time Simon and Grant have worked together, has Simon reached out to me in a gesture of friendliness. He treats me like a leper with dysentery and pink eye and maybe a touch of syphilis on the side.

Damn. I take a seat on the linoleum next to what was supposed to be my dinner, my head swirling with possibilities.

Tara was right. Now that Christopher's on the case, things are already getting interesting.

GRANT

(Two Years Ago)

As it turned out, Christopher Leon didn't improve with time.

"What do you mean, the DNA evidence got washed away?" asked the forensics tech working our case. "It hasn't rained in two weeks."

The case in question was the burglary of a small but valuable collection of Picasso drawings from a college library. It wasn't my usual fare, since I'd been spending most of my time in the jewel thief circuit lately, but I'd been called in to lend a hand to our hotshot newbie—now neither new nor hot.

"I mean that one of our agents accidentally spilled his coffee outside the broken window where the thief cut himself," I said with painstaking calm. "From the state of things, I'm guessing he must have been *very* thirsty."

The forensic tech groaned. "Oh, geez. You got partnered with Leon again, didn't you?"

A grim smile was my only response. A grim smile was generous, given the circumstances. Not only had I been pulled off my own case, which included a promising date with a certain strawberry blond, but I was being forced to clean up after a man who made Inspector Clouseau look like Sherlock Holmes. Some days, he seemed to be a perfectly capable investigator, dotting his i's and crossing his t's with all the efficiency one would expect from a man in his position. Other days... Well. Let's just say I wasn't the only agent who'd noticed how often an easy case went awry when Christopher Leon was on the job.

"Make do with what you have, but I doubt you'll find anything," I said. Just caffeine, milk, and the remnants of Christopher's ineptitude. Unfortunately, I'd learned the hard way that laying any of the blame on the man responsible would only result in a slap on my wrist and a threat to strip me of my badge. The man had friends in high places, as my wrist could attest. It still stung from the time I'd questioned his clearance to become a field agent. "And thanks."

The tech gave me a mock salute and went back to work.

I should have gone directly back to the crime scene after that to salvage what I could, but my phone buzzed with an incoming text.

I'm just sitting all alone at the café where you booked us a table, it read. Did you know you can see straight into Tiffany's from here?

I laughed out loud. Of course I knew the vantage

point from our proposed date. I'd chosen it—and paid off the manager—for the exact purpose of trying to get a reaction out of my quarry. True to form, Penelope hadn't shown any dismay at the last-minute cancellation, but I wouldn't be surprised to hear tomorrow that Tiffany's had suffered an overnight break-in. A woman scorned was capable of anything. And *that* woman scorned...

"What's so funny?" Christopher materialized in front of me, peering forward to get a look at my screen.

My instinct was to snatch the phone away and tell him to back off, but I forced a smile and flashed him the screen instead. "Just working the Blue case," I said as though it were a matter of supreme indifference. I wasn't giving this man any ammunition. *You remember? The one you tried to go over my head and take away from me?*

"Oh, yeah," he replied, casual to the point of suspicion. "How's that going?"

Two could play this game. "It's going as well as can be expected," I said. "I'm not going to wring any answers about her father's whereabouts overnight, but anything worth doing is worth doing well."

"You know, you *could* always bring her in—" He looked up, midsentence, to find me staring at him. He knew my cold look well enough by now. "Never mind. I'm sure you're handling it."

"Thank you," I said without emphasis. "I don't suppose you found any new leads?"

Before Christopher could open his mouth all the way, I added, "On the missing Picassos."

He hunched his shoulders and looked away. "No, not yet. I really am sorry about the coffee, by the way. I don't know what came over me."

There was something about a man so wholly out of his depth that I couldn't help but give him an out. "It's all right. I still like the security guard for it. He had access *and* opportunity—and unless I'm mistaken, he was also employed at the University of Maryland, where those Roman busts went missing last year."

Christopher looked interested. "Really?"

"Yes, really." I pushed off the wall and began covering the ground at a clipped pace. The sooner I could get this thing finished, the sooner I could get back to my own work. Until Christopher screwed up another case and I got called in to fix it, anyway. "Under a different name and social, of course. And he may have even gotten a nose job in between. I doubt I would have picked up on the link if it wasn't for the car."

Christopher kept easy pace with me. "The car?"

"Oh, yeah. He might have been willing to change his identity and undergo the knife for the sake of a few bucks, but he wouldn't let a '71 Hemi 'Cuda go. I mean, I've always been more of a Camaro SS man myself, but…" I released a low whistle. Owning any car in New York was ridiculous, but there were times when a man had to sit down and face the traffic. For me, it would have been a '69 Chevrolet Camaro SS—a lingering teenage fantasy and the one car I'd have sold my soul to own. For my suspect, it was a vintage Plymouth. I almost couldn't blame him for it. "He had to register the car at both schools to get a parking permit. I've already requested the VIN from both. We should have an answer in the next few hours."

Christopher stopped in his walk down the hallway. I turned back to look at him, unable to suppress a smug grin at the look of perplexity lowering his brow. "Does this mean you aren't going to look at other suspects?" he asked.

"If he's guilty?" I gave a short laugh. "No. That's usually how it works. You find the bad guy and move on. Was there someone else you wanted me to arrest?"

"No. No, of course not." He spoke quickly before checking his watch in a clumsy show. "I'm just relieved, that's all."

I didn't know why he was relieved. Any other agent who botched a job that bad might feel grateful at having been handed an easy win, but any other agent wasn't Christopher Leon. No fear of punishment ever crossed his mind. In fact, it was much more likely that *I'd* be the one to take the fall if the security guard theory didn't hold. He'd probably get a fucking promotion.

My phone buzzed again, and I glanced down to see another incoming text from Penelope. Interesting. Did you know that the guards at Tiffany's stagger their arrival times?

"Is that her again?" Christopher asked.

I bit back the chuckle that had risen to my lips. "Yes, it is," I said in a way that should have repressed further communication.

It didn't.

"You might want to be careful there, Emerson," he said, and in a warning tone I'd never heard from him before. "A woman like that isn't going to stick around for long. It won't do to get too attached."

"Then it's a good thing I'm not," I replied.

He didn't believe me any more than I believed myself, but short of calling me a liar and pulling me up in front of the ethics board, there wasn't much he could do about it.

"Was there anything else you wanted to add?" I asked.

He wanted to, that much was evident. But by that time, he was fast learning that there were some issues closed to negotiation, and Penelope Blue was one of them. *I* might not have the power to get him pulled from cases he was too inexperienced to lead, but *he* didn't have the power to take Penelope away from me.

Though not, I knew, from lack of trying.

"No, I'm good," he said.

I let it sit at that—and not only because I was done having a conversation that would lead nowhere. It was also because the sooner I called those colleges and saw about those VIN numbers, the sooner I could put a stakeout detail on Tiffany's. I could hardly wait.

Penelope might not have any long-term plans about sticking around, but I could at least enjoy the game while I was still in it.

THE
PARTNERSHIP

THERE'S AN APOLOGY GIFT WAITING ON THE KITCHEN COUN-
ter when I wake up the next morning. It's not a bouquet
of flowers (which I have little use for), and it's not jewelry (which, oddly enough, is something I don't wear
much of). The cobbler's children don't have any shoes,
and the jewel thief sticks to simple, understated pieces.
That's how I prefer it.

Grant knows this about me, which is why I'm delighted
to find a pink bakery box with my name scrawled across the
top instead. Doughnuts are a universal peace offering, and
they're one I gladly—and voraciously—accept. There's
nothing like criminal intrigue to get a girl's appetite going.

Going *too* well, apparently. I'm holding a half-empty
box and considering how to arrange the remaining pas-
tries to make it look like I only ate a dainty few when
Grant sneaks up behind me.

"Hello, wife," he murmurs into my neck. It's a smooth move rendered even smoother when he tightens his grip to catch my spasm of surprise. I seriously need to put a bell on that man one of these days. "Have I ever told you how much I enjoy waking up to your beautiful face?"

"Jesus, Grant. Were you hiding in a corner this whole time?"

His chuckle is a warm flutter of breath against my skin. "Do you mean did I witness you inhale those three maple bars? No. I was in the bedroom."

I bump him with my ass in mock annoyance, but his hands slide down to my hips and hold me there. It's the perfect position to have me pinned between a rock and a hard place—namely, him and the kitchen counter. Most of the rocks and hard places in my life include Grant in some form or another, but at least this one comes with a kiss that takes my breath away.

He starts, as he so often does, with my neck. I'll never know what it is about that part of a woman's anatomy that interests him so, but from the way he plants a line of soft kisses along the slope of my shoulder and up to my jawline, it's clear he intends to take his time—and enjoy himself in the process.

He's not the only one. Most of Grant's body is a solid wall of sinew and bone, difficult to break and hard to deny, but his lips have always been incredibly soft. They're also as insistent as the rest of him, growing increasingly demanding the further north he goes. By the time he reaches my lips, he's tilting my face to meet his mouth with my own.

"Mmm," he groans as his tongue sweeps against

mine. "You taste like maple and sugar. I should get you breakfast more often."

More arousing words have never been spoken, and I couldn't move now even if I wanted to. One of his hands holds me in place, grinding me against the counter. The other grips my chin so he can continue his assault unabated. His mouth is hot and demanding, his tongue stroking until I'm grateful that he's holding me up.

I might dissolve otherwise.

If this man ever learned how much power he has over me, I might be in real trouble. He breaks me down and holds me up at the same time. He makes it impossible for me to live with or without him.

I swear I'd hate him if his kisses didn't feel so damn *good*.

"How was your evening?" he asks. He spins me to face him, murmuring the question against my lips. "Did you discover any more crimes you'd like to convince me you didn't commit? Maybe you could break into a bank to try and prove it to me."

"Ha-ha. Very funny." I weave my fingers through the silky strands of his hair and nip playfully at his jawline. It's my favorite place to leave telltale marks of affection, since it forces him to keep his scruff a little scruffier than usual to hide it. "I'll have you know that sort of plan doesn't come up with itself. It took us a long time to decide on the best way to crack your office."

"You've always been good at your job." He speaks mostly to the slope of my shoulder, which he's exposing inch by careful inch. But his hands—and mouth—stop before he frees so much as the swell of a breast.

My breath catches with impatience and desire, my body straining for him to touch it again.

But of course, he doesn't.

"Wait a minute," he says. "Did you say the *best* way to crack my office?"

Despite the frustrated fizzle building between my legs, I have to laugh. "Well, you wouldn't want us to use the worst way, would you? Have some pride in our workmanship."

He grips me by my naked shoulders, the familiar look of exasperated amusement settling over his expression. "Like hell I will. How many ways are there?"

"Off the top of my head? I'd say about a dozen."

"Write them down," he says. Much to my dismay, he drops his seduction and snatches the pad of paper we use for grocery lists. "I want all twelve. In elaborate detail. Don't leave anything out."

"Hey, some of those are trade secrets."

"Not anymore." One hand steers me to a stool; the other grabs a pen and points it at me. It's not exactly how I wanted to spend my morning, but what's a girl to do? When Grant switches to business mode, there's not much in this world that can sway him.

Seriously. He'll stand there, aroused and with a look of intense longing in his eyes, frustrated and surly for hours, before he'll budge so much as an inch.

"You know I can't betray the team like that," I say, though I take the pen and nibble on the end with feigned thoughtfulness. I'm not about to tell him that preying on his natural suspicions was all we could come up with. Gotta keep the mystery alive. "Riker would kill me. He knows guys who would pay top dollar for this kind of information."

"You're not getting up from that chair until you start writing."

"Or you'll do what?" I ask archly.

"Never bring you baked goods again."

That's not a threat I take lightly. "Fine. If you're going to be mean about it…"

To assuage the domineering beast in my kitchen, I jot down random and wholly unlikely scenarios, like driving through the front glass of the building with the Batmobile or getting plastic surgery so I look identical to Cheryl. I cover the paper with my free hand so he can't see what I'm writing, hoping he'll take the hint.

When he doesn't move away, I turn to him with a glare. "I can't confess my sins while you're hovering over me. Get thee to the coffeemaker, husband, and make yourself useful."

He plants a kiss on the back of my neck and mutters something about ungrateful temptresses, but it does the trick. Mostly, anyway. Before he gets too involved in the process of transforming coffee beans into miracles, he pauses and watches me with an unreadable expression.

"You'll talk to me next time, right?" he asks. "Instead of going to Riker and Jordan to set up a mass-scale invasion? We'll have a good old-fashioned conversation between husband and wife?"

I'm reluctant to agree to those terms without an addendum, which says a lot more about me than it does him. That mass-scale invasion was the only interesting thing I've done in months.

"That depends," I say carefully. "Are you going to let me help catch the Peep-Toe Prowler?"

A perfectly readable expression comes over his face then.

"I saw my dad yesterday," I say in an attempt to stop his outburst before it begins. "I visited him at his hotel."

"Why do I get the feeling I'm not going to like where this is headed?"

"He wasn't there alone. He's got a roommate."

I pause and wrinkle my nose. Now that I think about it, there wasn't any sign of Tara putting down roots. She's not a messy person, at least not to my recollection, but I didn't see a single suitcase or article of her clothing. Not even a discarded glass with a lipstick print on the rim. There's always a chance she was there for a booty call—which, *gross*—but her stay didn't look like a prolonged one.

"At least, I *think* she's his roommate," I amend. "She could have been stopping by for a visit."

Grant is quick enough to catch the implication, and he releases a low whistle. "You're kidding. Tara's back in town?"

I nod, feeling smug and guilty at the same time. The former comes from a rare sense of euphoria at knowing something Grant doesn't, but I can't help feeling like I'm betraying Tara in the process.

Ugh. I hope this isn't going to be a thing—having actual human emotions for that woman.

"She didn't want me to say anything to you about it. But then, I'm a very loving and law-abiding wife, so what else could I do?" I'm not sure I care to hear his answer, as loving and law-abiding aren't two qualities anyone would accuse me of having in abundance, so I follow up with the part of my visit that's troubling me. "Is Christopher really your boss?"

The sharp turn of Grant's head my way is all the confirmation I need. "She told you that?"

"Among other things. She didn't confess to the crime, though, if that's what you're hoping. Of course, if you'd let me help with the investigation, I might be able to coerce more information out of her. She mentioned wanting to have lunch next week. What do you think that's about?"

I'm genuinely curious to hear Grant's answer, since he has experience dealing with Tara and might have insight into the dark and twisted inner workings of her mind. Unfortunately, he dismisses my question with a wave of his hand. As an only child who's the shining golden apple of his mother's eye, Grant doesn't understand the complex hate-hate relationship one can have with a close relative.

"Do you know how long she's been in town?" he asks.

"No, but I'd be happy to find out for you. Anything else you'd like while I'm at it? Her whereabouts last night? What size shoe she wears? Ooh, do you want us to sneak in and ransack my dad's place to find evidence? Riker has this new grappling hook he's been dying to try."

My offer goes unheeded. From the way Grant begins pacing across the kitchen floor, all thoughts of coffee forgotten, I get the feeling it's going to be another long-night-at-work sort of day.

"I don't think she's sloppy enough to show herself to you if she's the Prowler," he muses, mostly to himself. "She must have known you'd come to me, or at least that I'd find out through the grapevine. But then, that could have been her goal from the start—to throw me off balance. You Blue women have a tendency to do that."

"Excuse me. Don't lump me in the same category as that she-witch."

"We'll have to put a detail on her, of course, but if she's staying with Warren, that could be tricky. Dammit. He operates on a much bigger budget than we do. He'll pick up on any electronic surveillance the second it goes live, and there's no way we could get a guy placed on the hotel staff without him knowing about it."

I raise my hand. "Or—and I'm just throwing this out there—you could have me do it."

He stops pacing to stare at me. "You?"

"Yes, me. I don't know if you're aware of this, but I can come and go inside that hotel without raising any alarms." I drop my voice to a conspiratorial whisper. "Don't tell anyone at the Bureau, but Warren Blue is my father."

For the briefest moment, I think it's going to work. Grant rubs his jawline, head tilted as he works through the pros and cons of letting me play along.

Determined to see the pros win, I add, "Unless you're afraid Christopher won't allow it because of my past? I'm sure I could convince him I've changed. I could talk to him, tell him how much joy it would bring me to see Tara clapped in irons…"

At the mention of Christopher's name, the door is slammed shut with a metaphorical bang. "The less you have to do with that man, the better," Grant says. "The answer is no."

"No is such a strong word, don't you think?"

Even though it's wise to tread lightly, patriarchal decrees have never settled well with me. In fact, a large part of the reason I fell in love with Grant is because he's always treated me as an equal. An annoying, criminally minded equal he'd often like to strangle, but an equal nonetheless.

"There's this funny thing inside my skull called a brain, and it wants to do its own thing every now and then," I say. "Besides, it's not illegal for me to visit my father, is it?"

"Penelope…"

"And it's not out of the question that those visits might occasionally include my stepmother, right?"

"It's like you don't even hear me when I speak."

"Oh, I hear you all right. I just don't listen." I cross the kitchen to where he's standing and wrap my arms around his waist. It's like hugging a statue—an *angry* statue—but I stay in place until some of the stoniness crumbles away. "I won't do anything to jeopardize your case, I promise. I'll spend some time with her, ask a few questions, that sort of thing. If nothing else, it'll keep me out of trouble for a few days. Isn't that what you want?"

My light, teasing manner is intended to soothe the angry beast, bring out his playful side, but Grant's reaction is oddly serious.

"What I *want*, my love, is for you to be happy," he says.

I blink up at him, startled. "But I am happy."

"Are you? Are you really?"

My arms fall from his waist, and I step back as if struck. It's a simple question, and all it requires is a simple answer.

Yes. Absolutely. Couldn't be better, thanks.

But we promised to work on that honesty thing, and it seems like cheating to give up after less than twenty-four hours. I mean, I'm not *un*happy, but I'd be lying if I said I didn't miss the life I left behind. Sometimes, I'll see a piece of jewelry in a store window, catch sight of a gold watch glinting on someone's wrist, and the urge to take it is so strong, it overpowers everything I know and am. I miss the plotting and planning. I miss the adrenaline high. I miss feeling like I'm good at something.

No, scratch that. I miss feeling like I'm *great* at something.

There it is, that honesty he's asking for. It lands in the center of my chest with a soft *whump*.

I was great at being a jewel thief. I was great at it and I loved it and I'd give almost anything to feel that way again. Unfortunately, there's no way to tell Grant without breaking his heart. How do you admit to your husband that the thing you gave up for him, the part of yourself you buried and tucked away in order for your marriage to work, might be the only thing in the world that makes life worth living?

Easy. *You don't.*

"Of course I'm happy," I say, and it sounds so convincing, I almost believe it. "I have everything a girl could ask for—food, shelter, a husband who regularly brings home doughnuts. I'm just restless, that's all. It's hard work, sitting at home all day while you're out saving the world."

Grant's face is back to its usual handsome, unreadable facade, so I have no idea whether or not he buys it. He does, however, unbend. "I can't stop you from seeing Tara, but that doesn't mean I like it," he says.

"I'll be careful."

"And I'll have to start my own official investigation into her."

"Of course. But you should probably know—she

said something as I was leaving, something that felt off, even for her. She wanted me to give Chris her love the next time I see him. I thought she was just pretending to know him to get under my skin—you know how she is—but she *did* know he was your boss."

He doesn't respond. Silence isn't my favorite reaction from Grant, so I push harder. Thinking of last night's phone call from Christopher, of how odd it felt after spending so much time under the shadow of Simon's hatred, I joke, "There's not a chance he's working with Tara, is there? Like as a double agent?"

Grant finally reacts, and that spark of anger I saw in him before—that cold calculation as he prepared to take Christopher out—is back.

"Write down everything she said," he says, ripping off the list of breaking-into-the-FBI plans without even glancing at it. "Don't leave anything out."

My eyes widen as he once again thrusts the pen in my hand, this time without the sense of humor.

"Holy crap. He's a double agent, isn't he?"

Instead of answering, Grant makes an urgent scribbling motion, his lips pressed together.

With a face like that, there's nothing left for me to do but write—and, Lord help me, give in to a surge of excitement so strong, I have to suppress a smile for fear he'll think I've cracked. Forget loneliness. Forget boredom.

My husband is in trouble, and he needs my help. It's almost like being alive again.

GRANT

8

"So, I LIKED MEETING YOUR WIFE."

I don't glance away from the map of the Upper East Side I have tacked on my wall, a colorful array of pins indicating the locations of all the jewelry thefts over the past two months. We have a sophisticated computer program to look for patterns in location, but I've always preferred a more traditional method.

"Strange that she'd never heard of me before, though."

I stay silent, hoping Christopher will take the hint and go away.

Instead, I focus on a cluster of pins off to one side of the map, double-checking the dates as I do. Those were the sites of the first few crimes, which occurred over the span of several weeks. The thefts happen much more quickly now, which says two things: one, that the thief is gaining confidence after those initial hits, and two, that he's much more likely to make a mistake as a result of it.

"That's why I was thinking it might not be a bad idea to have you two over for dinner one night. So she can get to know me better."

"Do you mind, Leon?" I ask, indicating my map. "There's a jewel thief running through the streets of Manhattan. I know your social life is of paramount importance, but I, for one, would like to stop him sooner rather than later."

"Her."

I finally turn to look at him. "I beg your pardon?"

He's standing exactly as I expect him to, leaning against my desk with a fabricated air of nonchalance. His arms are crossed, and he assesses my map with a smirk, as if he can't believe agents still rely on things like hard work and experience to solve crimes.

"You called the Peep-Toe Prowler a him," he says. "According to our profiler, there's a ninety percent chance we're dealing with a female thief. Everything about the way she selects her targets—"

"Or the way *he* selects *his* targets," I interject, unwilling to play along.

"But the shoes," Christopher says. "You can't forget those. Between that and the profiler, you still think it might be a man?"

"I think it's a distinct possibility. The peep-toes could have easily been thrown in to divert suspicion." I allow my gaze to meet his, though I'm careful to keep the accusation out of it. It's one thing to suspect your direct superior of double-dealing; it's another to outright charge him with it. My suspicions are too new—and too dangerous—to be mishandled.

"The thief is getting overconfident," I add, watching

carefully for his response. "According to those same profilers, that's a male trait, not a female one. And he's moving from private residences to public venues, which makes me think he's working his way up to a larger heist."

"Really? How do you tell all that from a map?" Christopher pushes himself off the desk and joins me, his earlier conceit replaced by a note of earnest interest. He studies my pins and lines and theorized escape routes with a wrinkle in his brow. "What are you seeing here that I'm not?"

I sigh. The last thing I should have to explain to someone who is technically my boss is the basics of investigation. And the last thing I *want* to explain to someone who might be playing for both sides is how I plan to catch him.

But he's so damn persistent, so damn eager all the time. I can't decide if he's the trickiest criminal I've ever been up against—barring one very important woman in my life—or if he really is as stupid as he seems.

"Look, it's not that complicated," I say, giving in. It's not as if this stuff is top secret. Any agent in the place could tell him the same thing. "See how he started with one or two smaller jobs, all in private homes and with plenty of time between them?"

"Yeah."

"He was testing the field, pushing his boundaries. He'd steal something, wait a few days to see where suspicion fell, and then, when it didn't land on him, try again in a flashier, higher-risk setting. That means he's getting bolder. And he'll keep getting bolder until something or someone gets in his way. Most criminals are like toddlers that way."

Christopher shifts slightly, as if feeling the insult. *Good*.

But then he asks, "And that's something only male thieves do? Penelope didn't work that way?"

I stiffen. It's *not* something only male thieves do, and stereotypes of this kind can derail an investigation faster than cross-contamination in the lab, but I want him to know that I'm looking beyond the shoes—that I'm casting my net wide enough that even *he* could get tangled in it.

"I mean, she obviously operated on a higher level than our Peep-Toe Prowler, but generally speaking?" he adds.

Generally speaking, Penelope Blue is one of the best thieves this country has ever seen, and no one will ever come close to pulling off the kinds of jobs she did with the same savoir faire. But in a specific sense, no one— and I mean *no one*—is allowed to say that but me.

"My wife has nothing to do with this case."

"Of course," he says quickly. "I only meant hypothetically."

I refuse to dignify that with a response. Thanks to my involvement with the Blue case over the years, most of the agents I work with are aware of my wife's notoriety. They're also aware that it's a circumstance I neither regret nor care to discuss. Penelope's ability to break into the FBI building and run circles around every last one of them is my favorite thing about her.

It's also the thing that could land her in uncomfortably hot water, even if she refuses to see it.

Especially now that Christopher Leon has been put in charge of this case. It defies all reason and logic, but everything always has where he's concerned. He's the agent who gets regularly promoted despite a shocking lack of insight or skill. He's the agent who can shoot a partner in the back only to turn around and receive congratulations on his execution. He's also the agent who somehow gets Simon pulled off the Peep-Toe Prowler case so he can work by my side instead.

Either someone is pulling some serious strings for this guy, or his bumbling inefficacy is a cover for a deeper game—a game not dissimilar from the type Tara Lewis enjoys playing. Penelope's information about her stepmother's possible ties to Christopher has turned everything I know about this case upside down. After all, a guy like this shouldn't be allowed anywhere *near* a crime scene, let alone be running one.

Yet here we are. Once again.

"You know, it wouldn't be a bad idea to get her insight," Christopher says, his voice even. "Strictly as a consultant, you understand. I'd love to hear her thoughts about who might be behind all this."

"*No*." I can't temper the vehement protest that leaves my lips.

"It wouldn't have to be a formal agreement or anything. Like I said, I could have the two of you over for dinner one night…"

"She's really busy right now," I lie, and I feel a pang of guilt for how easily it comes out. Penelope would love a chance to sit opposite this man and try to trip him up. I can envision it already—she'd wear her peep-toe shoes and probably slip out during dessert to crawl up the fire escape and ransack his bedroom. She'd be good at it, too. "Another time."

Christopher hesitates, as if unsure whether it's safe to continue along these lines. It's not, but I go ahead and let him speak anyway. Maybe he'll dig his own grave and make this easy on all of us.

"I think it's great, what she's done," he says carefully. "What you've both done."

The words are out before I can stop them. "Not as great as it would be if you brought her in, though, huh?"

His startled eyes meet mine, but I don't give anything away. I don't even blink. Of all the tricks I've developed over the years, wiping my face of emotion is the one that most often comes in handy. You'd be surprised what people admit to when they don't know what you're thinking.

My wife, for example, says more to me when she's curled up in a ball on the other side of the couch, leafing listlessly through a magazine, than she does during a dozen conversations about our plans for the future. According to what comes out of her mouth, she's happy, she's fine, she's living the dream. According to the way her eyes take on a distant wistfulness when she thinks I'm not looking, I know she's lying.

The problem, you see, is that I knew her when she *was* happy.

The Penelope Blue of a few years ago was a bright, brilliant, buoyant creature. She'd rob a man blind and then laugh in his face when he got upset about it. She'd turn a corner and disappear, only to show up again scaling a building ten miles away. She'd amass a small fortune and then walk around in the same black leggings she wore ragged, as if she had five dollars in her pocket instead of five million. She was a thief and a rogue, and she had a brass-faced audacity that should have made her a villain.

But she's not. She's one of the best people I know, but men like Christopher would be much happier seeing her behind bars.

Over my dead body.

"Look, I'm sorry you don't want to work with me, but if you have a problem with it, you'll have to take it up with the associate deputy director," Christopher blusters. "He's the one who gave the orders, not me. And he happens to like the way I'm handling things so far."

Which probably means the ADD is in his back pocket on top of everything else. *Fan-fucking-tastic.*

"So if you'd like to change your mind about bringing your wife in to consult on this case..."

No. I most definitely do not. It pains me to keep her at an arm's length like this, to ask her to subdue the natural spirit that could have her skewering a man like Christopher Leon for breakfast and making a meal of his bones, but I don't know what else to do. Her safety comes first—before my own career, even before our marriage. It has to.

Penelope is too good at what she does. And Christopher, unfortunately, seems to know it.

"I could force you to bring her in, you know," he adds, his voice low. "All it would take is one phone call."

I snap. One of the things I've always prided myself on is my ability to maintain an implacable calm in the face of danger, but that was when the danger only extended to *me*. I'm quickly coming to learn that my own safety means nothing compared to hers.

I thought, the day I married Penelope Blue, that I was protecting her. Unfortunately, I'm only just now starting to realize that I may have done her a disservice by slipping that ring on her finger. Every day she comes under the attention of men like Christopher, the target on her back gets a little bit bigger, a little more obvious.

And it's my fault. I'm the one who brought her into this. I'm the one who put that target on her back in the first place.

"You are not to go anywhere near my wife, do you understand?" I warn. "Believe me when I say you don't want to find out what will happen if you so much as touch a hair on her head."

I draw forward, not stopping until my toes touch Christopher's, until he can feel the anger coming off of me in waves. Penelope would hate to hear me laying decrees on her behalf, hate even more to know that I'm cutting off her opportunity to interfere at its source.

To protect her means I have to keep killing that sparkle in her eyes, day by day. And be know that there's nothing I can do to stop it.

It's her life or her happiness. *Our* life or her happiness.

"I didn't say—" Christopher begins.

"You said enough. You might have been able to steal my partner away from this case, and that's fine, but I will do everything in my power to make sure you can *never* touch Penelope Blue."

I expect him to push back, to force the issue, but all he does is draw a deep breath and step down.

"She could prove helpful, Emerson. That's all I'm saying." Christopher waits a moment before adding, "She was a thief, after all."

Yeah, well, if Tara's insinuations are to be believed, you might be one, too, I think, deliberately turning my back on him and returning my attention to the map. *At least Penelope never tried to hide it.*

THE 9 CREW

"I COME BEARING GOOD NEWS. GRANT DOESN'T THINK I'm the Peep-Toe Prowler after all."

The chorus of groans that greets me at the door to Jordan's apartment is offered in a perfect pitch of exasperation. Without waiting to hear what I have to say in my defense, my three best friends scramble to their feet, knocking aside a set of blueprints as they do. Even from this distance, I can make out the plans and access points to an unmarked building.

Oh, man. I love unmarked buildings. They're my favorite kind.

"What are we breaking into?" I peer closer to see if I can discern the details, but Riker inserts himself between me and the table before I have a chance. He's not a large man, but he jolts around to make himself appear bigger, like a crow protecting its nest. I can't see around him. "Would you please stop moving for a second? I just want to take a peek."

"No way, Pen," he says as Jordan rolls up the plans. "We don't want you giving your husband any funny ideas."

His words sting the tender area where my pride used to be. "Come on. I'm not going to tell Grant anything."

"We talked about this. Plausible deniability, remember?"

I remember, all right. It's the same conversation I had with my father yesterday and with Grant this morning. No one wants to talk to the monkey in the middle for fear she'll give something away to the other side. Considering that I *have* given something away and that I'm currently operating as a not-exactly-sanctioned-but-not-*not*-sanctioned operative investigating my stepmother, I can maybe see their point.

"Give me something," I beg. "To whet my appetite. Is it diamonds?"

Riker remains unmoved, not even sweeping away the swatch of dark hair that falls over one eye. Jordan is equally impassive as she puts a lock—a *lock*, of all things—on the chest where she's tucked the blueprints. Like everything else about her, the chest is neat and chic, with cute, hand-scrolled gold swirls painted on the outside. Also like everything else about her, I don't let its appearance deceive me. That sucker is as secure as Cheryl's gun safe.

Oz is the only one to take pity on me, shaking his head as I turn my pained plea on him.

"Really?" I ask. "But if it's not diamonds, what are you after?"

Riker whirls on him. "Goddammit, Oz! Can't you keep your mouth shut for five minutes?"

I laugh. Oz can, when spurred, keep his mouth shut

for five *months*, but that wouldn't stop him from saying everything he needs to through alternate means. In addition to relying on a bizarre version of sign language developed between him and Jordan when they were foster kids together, his nonverbal skills are top-notch.

So are mine, and I land a sloppy kiss on his cheek before settling onto the couch. "Well, that's something, at least. I don't think I could handle it if you guys were after a big take without me."

The pang near my heart indicates I'm not too great at handling it, even if it's *not* a big take they're after. I force a smile anyway.

"Guess what, Oz?" I say brightly. "You'll be happy to hear you're developing quite a reputation over at the Bureau. As soon as Grant smelled the Liquid Evacuation, he put out a call looking for anyone of your vague description. He suspected you'd gotten hired on as a window washer."

"I did, once."

"Pretend to be a window washer? I know. We've taken that approach a few times."

"No, get hired at the FBI," he says.

He doesn't elaborate, and as intrigued as I am, I don't bother asking him to. Although Riker and I have known Oz and Jordan since we were teenagers, we haven't always acted as a unified crew. Some of the things Oz has seen and done could make it into the annals of history, but he won't be the one to talk about it. I doubt even the best interrogators at the FBI could force him to do that.

"Not that it matters where you get hired," I say with a sigh. "Breaking in was a complete waste of our time. Sorry, guys. That was about a month of planning for nothing."

I expect there to be outrage, annoyance, even an avowal never to assist me in my schemes again. Instead, Riker holds out his hand and waits patiently as Jordan fishes a handful of bills out of her purse.

"That's five hundred bucks to me. Easiest money I ever earned."

"Riker!" I snap.

"What? I still helped you, didn't I?"

He did, and without hesitation, but—"That's not what I'm mad about," I say. "Now that I'm retired and we don't have a regular revenue stream, you promised to lay off the gambling."

"This *is* me laying off," he replies. "We knew Grant's suspicions only existed in your head. We were just playing along for the fun of it."

First of all, that's not true. When I initially voiced my worry, Riker offered to (a) murder Grant and hide the body, and (b) do whatever it took to clear my name, *including* murdering Grant and hiding the body. He'd do it, too. He's happy that I've found true love, but fierce loyalties die hard.

Secondly, betting on a sure thing still counts as betting—especially if it's Riker. For as long as I've known him, he's had a fondness for all things chance. When he's on his best behavior, he'll stick to casinos and the occasional scratch ticket like any normal gambler. In the throes of a binge, he's been known to bet on everything from raindrops racing down a window to a pair of toms fighting over a female cat in a back alley.

The binges *sound* entertaining, but they're mostly scary. A man sizing up cat testicles isn't a man who's capable of making healthy life choices.

"Besides," Riker continues, "if I lost, Jordan was going to make me clean her bathroom. There was no financial risk on my side whatsoever."

Jordan shoots me an apologetic look. "It's true. Sorry. I had a bottle of bleach ready and everything."

The financial risk of Riker's gambling addiction is only part of the problem, and I'm about to say so when Riker and Jordan share a look of playful understanding. It's the type of look Riker and I used to share all the time, a look born of years of friendship and dependence on each other for survival.

My heart sinks, cementing itself even deeper in the pit of my stomach. There's no denying the meaning of that look. It says that this conversation, like so many others these days, has already been had. *Jordan* is the person Riker turns to for help in planning his next big heist. *Jordan* is the person in charge of keeping him out of trouble. In this, as in all things, I've become superfluous.

"Not that cleaning her bathroom would have been hard. It's so sanitized, you could eat off the floor in there." The left side of Riker's mouth lifts in a smile. He has a lot of easily recognizable looks—including his dark, broody eyes and the sharply molded features of his face—but it's the half grimace, half grin that truly characterizes him.

"Please don't do that," Jordan says. "I'd prefer if you ate in the living room like normal people. Which reminds me..."

In picture-perfect-hostess fashion, she reveals a plate of chocolate chip cookies from the kitchen and hands it to Riker. He takes a cookie for himself before tossing one to me.

"Since you're not in prison, I assume your dear husband didn't mind the minor trespass," he says with another of those half grins.

I catch the cookie but don't bring it to my lips right away. This, more than anything else, is a sign of how drastically our relationship has changed. Back in the old days, Riker's favorite hobby was policing my diet with an iron hand. In his mind, every cookie that touched my lips was an extra five pounds that would prevent me from squeezing into the next tight space. I still have PTSD from the amount of vegetables I consumed under his dictatorship.

"Of course he didn't," I say tartly. "I'll have you know we had a nice, healthy discussion about our differences and settled on mutually agreeable terms."

Riker snorts. "Bullshit."

"We did! Just because you can't fathom treating a woman as an equal doesn't mean all men are walking around scraping the skin from their knuckles. In fact, I've been given an assignment."

Riker might still be mocking me with his chiseled smirk, but Jordan perks up at that. "Really? What kind of assignment?"

"Intelligence gathering."

Okay, so it's a slight misrepresentation of the truth, but the idea is basically the same. Grant may not have used the terms *assignment* and *intelligence*, but I feel sure he would have if he hadn't been so caught up with the smoke billowing out of his ears.

"He's got a prime suspect, and it's my job to tail her," I elaborate.

"*Her?*" Riker laughs. "That's not a real assignment, Pen. He just wants you to spy on Tara."

"How did you already know she's back in town?" I cry, mostly outraged at having my thunder stolen. It's not like I'm rolling in the stuff to begin with. "I only found out yesterday."

"Deduction, my dear Blue. There are only three women in the world capable of pulling off the Peep-Toe Prowler heists, and two of them are in this room. I assumed it was Tara from the start."

"You did not. You never even mentioned her name until two seconds ago."

"So? I don't tell you everything. I've got a whole life going on you know nothing about."

Jordan sends him a rebuking look.

"It's true," Riker protests, flushing mildly. "Only last week, I was approached by a talent agent who thinks I could become an underwear model. I'm thinking about making a career change."

"Oh, please. You're just trying to distract me from the fact that you guys don't include me in anything anymore—which hurts, by the way. After I let you help me break into the FBI building and everything."

"But you said that was a complete waste of time," Jordan points out with both of her eyebrows perfectly arched. Like Riker, she's also got model-level good looks, most of which can be credited to the deep ocher of her skin and those selfsame brows. They're thick and expressive and so unlike my own blondish wisps that I feel an unholy amount of jealousy just looking at her.

"That's why I want to make it up to you with this Tara assignment," I say. "There's no promise of payout at the end, but we'd be assisting the FBI. Think of what you could do with that gold pass in your pocket."

"Grant really wants our help?" Jordan asks, only one brow arched now.

"He doesn't *not* want it," I reply, wondering how much I should tell them about my husband's true suspicions. Part of me wants to spill the gritty details—Christopher and Tara and the treacherous intrigue of it all—but a bigger part of me hesitates. Grant didn't give me the go-ahead to tell anyone about Christopher, and I doubt it's standard protocol for an FBI agent to let his wife help with investigations of this sort. Having me for a wife is a trial for him, I know, but I would never purposely jeopardize his job or put his life in danger.

I mean, I trust my friends with my life—I really do. I'm just not sure I trust anyone with Grant's.

"Won't you indulge me this once?" I beg. "It's the first real job I've had in ages, and it'll give us a chance to work together again. You guys never call, you don't write…"

It's an underhanded tactic, and it's beneath me, but it works. The three of them share a look of guilt and understanding, and there's no need for Jordan's eyebrows or Oz's sign language to communicate between them.

Poor Pen. We'd better indulge her. We're all she has.

Sadder, truer words have never been left unspoken.

Riker takes a bite of his cookie and sighs. "You know you can count on me for anything."

"Me too," Jordan agrees with only a slight hesitation. "If it'll make you happy."

"It will," I say before I realize the implication of her statement. That sentence is almost exactly the same as what Grant said to me earlier—a plea for my mental state, a desire to indulge me in anything if it will fill the gaping maw of my current life—and I'm not sure what to make of it. It's not as if I'm wandering around in the depths of despair all day. I do things. I stay busy.

Oz rubs his hands together. "So what's the plan?"

Since I haven't made any plans beyond recruiting my nearest and dearest, all I can do is shrug. "Well, I obviously need to get close to Tara by gaining her trust and affection, so let's start there. What do ordinary daughters do with their stepmothers?"

What ensues is a long, painfully drawn-out moment of silence. Jordan covers it by making another attempt to pass around the plate of cookies, Riker recounts the five hundred dollars in his wallet as if it's the most interesting thing in the world, and Oz sits there looking confused.

That's all they give me.

With a sigh, I realize I may have overestimated my team's ability to pull this one off. We don't exactly have experience with healthy parental relationships.

With our backgrounds, we barely have experience with any relationships at all.

Jordan waits until after Riker leaves to pull me aside.

Despite our slow start, we managed to come up with a plan of attack, one that involves the time-honored tradition of women bonding over commercialism. In other words, I'm going to ask Tara to take me shopping.

Hey, I didn't say it was a *good* plan of attack.

I'm prepared to leave and get things underway, but Jordan gestures for me to take a seat on her couch first. Like a psychologist's leather recliner, there's something about the combination of floral linen and knitted afghan that invites confession. So when she asks, "How many times did you bail Riker out of trouble?" I'm only partially taken aback.

"Um, in his entire lifetime? Probably close to a million, give or take a couple of zeroes."

"Do you have a more accurate count than that?"

"Oh, God." I groan, interpreting her serious look in the worst possible way. "What did he bet on? Who did he bet on it with? And how much money does he owe?"

She shakes her head, and my sense of foreboding increases.

"We always knew that a lot of the money you guys stole ended up in the hands of Riker's bookie, but how often would you say that happened?" she asks. "Monthly? Weekly?"

"Not weekly, that's for sure. I mean, he had his slip-ups, but it was never so bad I couldn't cover it with what I had saved. We always managed to make it out okay."

Jordan chews on her lower lip, causing me to turn an anxious look at Oz standing nearby. I might as well not be in the room for all the attention he's paying me. His gaze is fixed on Jordan's frown, his own lips mirroring the sentiment. As Oz isn't one to show concern—part of his incredible ability to blend into any environment is his own lack of outward emotion—I can tell this is a big deal. Jordan once told me that Oz's impassivity was the only thing that helped him survive their childhood together. If no one knew when you were happy or sad, they couldn't turn around and use those feelings against you.

Alarmed now, I grab Jordan's hand.

"What's going on? Is he in serious trouble?" I try to recall the last time I gave Riker money, but it's been so long, I can't remember. "You should have let me know earlier. I have money tucked away. Gobs of it—some even Grant doesn't know about. Riker can have it all."

"That's sweet of you, Pen, but he doesn't need it."

I start. "He doesn't?"

"No. And that's what worries me."

My relief comes out as a shaky laugh. "You're worried that he's *not* drowning in debt for the first time in his life? No offense, but maybe he's finally cleaned up his act and given up gambling for good. Lord knows I've begged him enough times."

"Maybe." Jordan doesn't appear convinced. "Oz and I assumed that with you out of the picture, we'd need to pick up where you left off. You know, help him out here and there, maybe keep an eye on his finances. But he's never asked us for anything."

I can't help growing prickly at the sound of those words, which hit too close to home. "For crying out loud, *I'm not out of the picture*. I swear, you guys are acting like I'm dead and buried. I know things are different now, but I'm still the same Penelope Blue who used to steal change from the Bryant Park fountain with you."

"Of course you are," Jordan says quickly.

"I'm still the same Penelope Blue who'd steal the whole fountain if you wanted it. In fact, I'll do it right now. I'll take it apart stone by stone."

"Please don't. It's really not necessary."

Maybe not, but I'm tempted to do it all the same—if only to prove that I still can, to prove that somewhere deep inside, I'm still *me*.

"If Riker did need help, you guys would come to me, right?" I ask. "You'd make sure I'm in on it?"

She hesitates a split second too long. "Absolutely."

I want to believe her, and I really try, but the damage of that split second has been done. When it comes to my friends—my *family*—I'm no longer a first responder. I've become an afterthought in the life we all used to share.

"I'm sorry." Jordan presses my hand warmly, but it doesn't cut the pain. "I didn't mean to worry you about Riker. He's probably fine, and I'm creating worries out of nothing. I'm sure he'd talk to you if there was a problem. You're his best friend, his rock."

I don't feel very much like a rock. Or if I am, I'm one slowly sinking to the bottom of the ocean.

"About that blueprint you guys were looking over before…" I say.

She gives an elegant shrug. "It was nothing. I thought I could tempt him with a jewelry store that recently upgraded its security system, that's all. Get him to open up about his troubles."

"And he didn't take the bait?" I find that hard to believe. Jewelry stores with upgraded security systems are Riker's catnip. Technological glitches as they get the system settled into place are the perfect thief loopholes.

"He still might. You came in before he could give me a firm answer."

Which is a nice way of saying I ruined things simply by walking through the door.

"Keep me posted on what he says?" I ask. "And if you do end up deciding to break into that jewelry store…"

The look Jordan gives me is full of pity. Friendly

pity, but pity all the same. "You'll what, Pen? Break your promise to Grant and give us a hand?"

"You never know," I say, my shoulders falling. "Stranger things have happened."

If nothing else, my life is ironclad proof of that.

THE **10** OUTING

Much to my relief, Tara isn't staying in the same room as my father.

"She's on the sixth floor in one of the regular suites," Grant says with a mixture of efficiency and regret as he pulls his sleek, FBI-issued car into a nonparking spot next to a mailbox. He's dropping me off a few blocks away from the Lombardy—we're a husband and wife carpooling to work today—and since his job requires him to use one of their cars, they soften the inconvenience by letting him park wherever he damn well pleases. In Manhattan, that's a pretty amazing perk. "Payment for the room seems to be routed through an account under the name of Bella Donna."

"Cute," I murmur. "And fitting."

"That's all I've been able to get without raising any red flags."

"That's all I need." To be honest, I didn't even need that much. Tara isn't an inconspicuous person. I could walk into any shop on this block, and I'm sure the clerks would remember precisely how many times she'd walked by their window and how little she was wearing at the time. "And stop acting so worried. I'm just going to ruffle her feathers, see what shakes out. I'll report back at oh-five-hundred hours."

"Do you know what oh-five-hundred hours means?"

"No, but it sounds cool. Did I sound cool when I said it?"

"It's five o'clock in the morning."

I make a horrified face. "Oh. Never mind. I'll report back at that plus about twelve more."

Grant is trying hard to play it cool, but he kisses the top of my head in a worried, possessive way that makes me feel like a breakable doll instead of the highly bendable human being that I am.

"I don't know why you're being so weird," I grumble, but I kind of like it when he's weird. Being cherished is still new enough to appeal to my romantic senses. "Riker and Oz will be watching me the entire time. We have a plan."

"That shouldn't comfort me, but it does."

"That's because you don't have any other choice. There's no one you can trust inside the Bureau, so you have to turn to your dark, seedy connections for the inside track."

"If you don't stop talking like you're in a gangster movie, I'm not going to let you help anymore."

"You can borrow Oz later, if you want," I offer. "You could use him to investigate Christopher on the sly—maybe set him up as his new hedge fund manager or something. Christopher looks like the type of guy who has one of those."

Grant shakes his head. "It wouldn't work. Leon's known about Oz for years."

"Really? For years?" It doesn't take much of a mental calculation to reach the next part. "Wait a minute—does that mean Christopher has known about *me* for years?"

My jewel thief senses start tingling, and I don't mean in a good way. Nothing about Christopher's actions that day at the FBI indicated he thought of me as anything other than the sweet, docile wife of a coworker. One who needed protecting, no less. He even called again yesterday to remind me of his phone number, in case I didn't write it down the first time around.

Highly suspicious. But then, that's what you'd expect from a double agent.

"Yeah, he knows," Grant says.

"So he also knows I'm a jewel thief?"

Grant groans. "When we're sitting inside government property, could you please use the past tense? I swear, it's like you're *trying* to get the FBI to keep investigating you."

I ignore him. I know for a fact my husband checks his vehicle for bugs on the regular. "How long have you known him?"

"Long enough not to trust him."

"Does he know our personal story?"

"Most of it, yes."

"But that doesn't make sense! He was so nice to me at your office—not at all like Cheryl or Simon. They treat me like I'm going to steal your soul if they take their eyes off me for one second. He actually seemed pleased to meet me."

"Yeah, well." Grant casts me a speaking glance. "As

I've said about a dozen times already, Leon's motives aren't exactly pure where you're concerned. You'd almost think there was a reason I told you to stay away from him."

Not good enough. Grant has never warmed up to Riker, not really, and he'd gladly sit here for the next half hour and share a litany of reasons why. In fact, I suspect he'd enjoy himself in the process. If he has nothing to say about Christopher except *stay away*, I can only assume he's gone well beyond dislike. We're talking out-and-out hatred here.

I cast him my most alluring smile. "But if I'm going to try and weasel information out of Tara about this guy, don't you think you should give me some insight into his background? It's not good to send a fellow agent in blind."

He groans again, this time passing a hand over his eyes. "For the love of all that's holy, you are *not* to go around claiming you're a federal agent now," he says. "And you're not going to weasel information about him out of Tara. You're going to see what she's up to, remember? Chat about hairstyles and diamonds. Normal stuff."

"You're deranged if you think anything Tara and I do together is normal."

The deep, laughing breath he draws at that is a clear sign he's aware of that fact and is doing his best not to dwell on it.

"Forget Leon," he says. "Forget the double agent theory. I'm sorry I mentioned it in the first place. This is just you spending some time with your family…and if you happen to come across helpful information in the process, you can pass that information along to me. But there's no pressure whatsoever to make that happen."

"Geez. You make it sound so boring."

"Good." His laughter drops at the same time his hand comes up to cup my face, the pad of his thumb tracing my lips. The rough texture causes a shudder to move through me, the pressure of his skin on mine more intimate than a kiss. "Boring is safe, Penelope. Please remember that."

I *do* remember it, but I also know, deep down, that safe is boring. And if that's what my husband wants in a wife, I'm afraid our troubles have only just begun.

"Penelope!" Tara pulls open the door to her hotel room with delighted surprise—or, at the very least, a convincing approximation of delighted surprise. "I didn't expect to see you so soon. What are you doing here?"

"I went to visit my dad, but he's not in his room," I lie, and then, because it's a lie she could easily verify for herself, I add, "Either that, or he's hiding from me. I think he sometimes bribes the bellhop when he doesn't want company."

"Yeah, I've thought the same thing myself a few times." Tara pulls the door open, inviting me in. "Makes us seem pathetic, doesn't it? Clamoring for a man's attention rarely looks good on a lady."

I'm so taken aback by her friendly overture, I don't step over the threshold right away. This feels suspiciously like a trap.

"Can I get you a drink?" she asks. If she notices my hesitation, it doesn't show as she waves over the modest accommodations. And by modest, I mean it still costs at least a thousand bucks a night. "I know you're more of an eater than a drinker, but I don't have any food except what's in the minibar. You're welcome to it."

As tempting as an eight-dollar Toblerone that Tara has to pay for sounds, I pass. "Water is good, thanks."

While her back is turned, I peek around the hotel room, which has much more of that lived-in feeling than my father's. Like I said before, my dad likes to be able to pack up and leave without a trace at a moment's notice. With this much stuff lying around, Tara wouldn't be able to get rid of her traces in a moment—probably not even five moments. In addition to overflowing garbage cans, there are more than a few discarded outfits draped on the bed and a stack of books on the coffee table. I tilt my head to try and make out the titles, but Tara interrupts me by handing me a glass of water.

Huh. I never thought of my stepmother as a reader before. I'm not a reader, either—you can't eat books or hawk them at pawn shops, so they didn't figure much in my adolescence—but libraries have always had a special place in my heart. You could say Grant and I fell in love in one.

"So, what's up?"

I stare at Tara for a second before I realize she's posed a question and is waiting for my answer. "Oh. Um. Shopping."

The plan—so far as we have one—is to get Tara into as public a place as possible so Oz can cause a distraction while I rummage through her purse for clues. Breaking into her hotel room is out for the same reason Grant and his team can't gain access—it's not just bellhops being bribed by my father around here—and there's a limit to how much information I can glean through cunning alone.

I mean, I'm good at cunning, but I'm not without my limits.

"You want to go shopping?" Tara asks, slightly perplexed.

"Yes."

"With me?"

"Yes."

"On purpose?"

She's making this much more difficult than it needs to be. "Yes. You *did* say you wanted to maybe grab lunch with me sometime soon. Or were you showing off because my dad was in the room at the time?"

It's not the nicest thing I've ever said to Tara, but it's not the meanest, either, and she takes the challenge as intended. One thing that's great about only knowing conniving, egotistical thieves is we're easy to manipulate. Few of us can resist a dare.

"Of course not," she says, proving my point to perfection. "I'll get my purse."

"But I want to go to Barneys."

I follow Tara's breakneck speed down the sidewalk with a hitch in my step and a stitch in my side. It's been too long since I adhered to Riker's strict exercise regimen, and the speed at which that woman moves in high heels is nothing short of miraculous. If I'd had any doubts about the likelihood of her being the Peep-Toe Prowler before—or about the ability of *any* thief to manage million-dollar heists in those monstrosities—those doubts are shot, buried, and long since decomposed. She could hike the moon in stilettos and not miss a step.

"I have a whole list of things I need to get," I say

with a pant. "I counted, and it's been at least four years since I bought a new bra. I can't decide if that makes me ecologically responsible or just gross."

"I hate those big stores. They have too many floors and way too many hiding places. You never know who could be in there, waiting for a chance to pounce."

I can't argue with that logic. That's why we picked it—and why Oz is lying in wait near the sprinkler system. The forecast inside that building is looking very cloudy indeed.

"But you love Barneys," I protest.

"And it's gross, Pen. Really gross. You should get a new bra at least every six months."

Oh, sure. Now she's full of motherly advice. "You used to go there all the time without any complaints," I say. "I remember you dragging me along and making me pretend to raid the makeup counter so you could hit the designer purse section."

There's a slight halt in her step. "That was over a decade ago. It doesn't count."

"Easy for you to say. You didn't get felt up by that creepy security guard in the holding room. He never pressed charges against teenage girls on purpose. He wanted us to come back and try again."

"I know." She pauses. "For what it's worth, I feel terrible about it now. I shouldn't have asked you to do that."

Her apology is so sudden and unexpected, I almost topple on a sidewalk crack. I'm also startled into offering a piece of solace in return.

"It wasn't too bad." I hurry to catch up, and when she slows her pace to match mine, it almost feels as though we're purposely walking side by side. "I was ready for it the second time he tried. I bit his hand. Drew blood, too."

"Good girl."

A surge of pride fills me, followed shortly by another surge I strongly suspect is guilt. Both feelings are foreign to me, and I'm not sure where I'm supposed to put them. Tara's approbation has never been something I've sought or desired, and to receive it now—eleven years too late and from a woman I consider a peer rather than a mentor—is absurd. Guilt is equally unwelcome, because it's not like I'm doing anything to her that she wouldn't do right back, were our positions reversed.

It would serve me well to remember the facts. Jewels are missing. Tara is in town. There's pretty much a straight line connecting those two things. She might feel remorse for subjecting me to the wandering hands of a scumbag department store security guard oh-so-many years ago, but her human emotions don't run deeper than that.

"It's only fair that you return the favor now," I say, doing my best to wheedle her into compliance. "I'll even be magnanimous and pay for everything so you don't have to resort to biting strangers."

My wheedling may have gone a touch too far, because she halts on the sidewalk and studies me, her perfectly red bow lips pursed. "You suggested we go shopping today because you want to spend time with me." It's not a question.

"I do."

"You made it sound like this was some spur-of-the-moment idea."

"It *was*."

She's not buying it. "Why did you want to come out with me today, Penelope?"

Direct questions have never been Tara's style, and my mind races as I try to come up with a way to deflect. I could play the woebegone daughter card, claiming a wish to be nice for the sake of my aging father, but there's no way she'd believe me. My dad has never been in better health, and I doubt he loses much sleep over my feelings for Tara. He seems to regard the pair of us more like bickering sisters than anything else.

I could also come back with my own direct approach, telling her straight-out that I suspect she's behind the thefts and will do everything I can to bring her to justice. By now, she has to realize I've told Grant about her being in town and that she's their number one suspect. For all she knows, there's a whole team of FBI agents waiting inside the department store to arrest her as soon as she crosses the threshold.

That's when it dawns on me.

"Oh my God. You *can't* go to Barneys, can you?" I laugh out loud, drawing the attention of several people streaming past us. Their jostling bodies remind me that standing still on a New York sidewalk isn't the best way to make friends.

"I'm sure I don't know what you're talking about," Tara says without meeting my gaze.

The truth is sealed after that. Tara isn't being direct because she wants to unsettle me or because she's trying out a new intimidation tactic. She's trapped, and there's no other way for her to get out of this.

"It's not that you don't *want* to go. It's that you're afraid of what will happen if you do." I laugh again when I see the flash of irritation that mars her otherwise perfect exterior. "What happened? Do they have your picture posted at all the emergency exits? Did you try to steal one too many pairs of earrings from the jewelry counter? No, don't tell me. You slept with the manager to get the security codes, and now he's a gentleman scorned?"

Tara starts walk-running again, but this time, I find it an absolute pleasure to keep up.

"It's not funny," she mutters.

"Are there any other places you're banned from that I should know about?" I persist. "Maybe we should put you in a trench coat and a mustache before we go out in public. Or only hit the bargain basements from here on out. Do you even know how to find a bargain basement?"

"I'm glad you're enjoying yourself," she says. "I'm taking a risk being in New York, let alone shopping for underwear with you, but of course, it's a huge joke."

I slow my steps. "Hey."

"No, it's fine. I get it. I probably even deserve it. I'm a horrible person who only looks out for herself."

I wait for her to elaborate, to confess to also being a horrible person who is currently stealing rich people's jewelry, but all she does is shake her head and sigh.

"The place I'm taking you isn't bad, Pen, I promise. You might even like it. It's got lots of quirky pieces— stuff like chandeliers crafted from animal skulls and underwear made from bioluminescent materials. I saw it a few days ago and immediately thought of you."

That is, bizarrely, one of the nicest things Tara has ever said to me. I'd love a bioluminescent bra.

"Okay," I say and wind my arm through hers. "I like the sound of that. Let's go there."

Her eyes narrow in quick suspicion, but she doesn't pull away. Our bodies feel strange so close to one another, but we continue that way, the overwhelming cacophony of the city serving as our soundtrack, until we arrive at the storefront in question.

"Well?" she asks at the door, which is painted black and has a pair of lion's mouth knockers attached to the front. I can already tell her shopping instincts—or dare I call them mothering instincts?—are dead-on. I adore it.

"You head in," I say and pull out my phone to send a change-of-plans text. The team is going to be annoyed to have all their plotting brought to a sudden halt, but there's not much more I can do without raising her suspicion. "I'll join you in a sec."

I expect Riker to reply with a string of expletives—or even cold, stony silence—but no sooner have I alerted him to the situation than he texts back, No worries. Moving on to plan B.

No worries? Never in his life has Riker strung those two words together into a single sentence. He worries about anything and everything—his way of interacting with other human beings is to assume them incapable of solving problems on their own. It makes him happy.

I think, uneasily, of Jordan's concerns about Riker—of this new venture into self-sufficiency where he doesn't need money for his gaming debts and he's crafting alternate plans out of thin air. Pride should be my default reaction, but I can't help but feel something bigger is going on than Riker reaching maturity.

But we don't have a plan B, I reply.

Oh, Pen, he texts back, and I can almost see him grimacing at me from afar. You might be surprised to hear this, but I always have a plan B.

PLAN B

11

"YOU'RE KIDDING. YOU WERE THERE? IN PERSON? YOU actually saw him walk the wire between buildings?"

Tara places a hand over her heart. "On my honor. To this day, it remains the best escape I've ever seen. The police didn't have the heart to chase him down after that. He got away with all ten million."

Riker releases a low whistle and continues perusing the collection of handcrafted porcelain doorknobs he's ostensibly helping me select. Riker's interest in ceramics is about equal to his interest in musical theater, which is why his presence should be setting off every alarm Tara possesses.

Should be, but isn't. Tara leans across him to pull out a knob in the shape of a giant squid, and he stands there, basking in the full-bodied press of her.

"Maybe we should take up bank robbery, too," Riker says with a laugh. He eyes me sideways, and I immediately distrust the playful look I see there. Of all his moods, playfulness is the rarest and most concerning. "What do you say, Pen? Ready to take to the skies as a tightrope walker? Think of all the ways we could expand our market."

"Sure thing. Let me put circus training on my to-do list for next week, right after grocery shopping."

"Oh, no. Not Pen." Tara's voice drips with faux innocence. "She doesn't do that sort of thing anymore. Not now that she's found true love."

It's hardly a statement I can argue with—I *did* find true love, and I *don't* do that sort of thing anymore— but I still don't care for her implication. Retirement is a perfectly acceptable alternative to theft.

Or it would be, if I could get used to the hollow feeling that seems to come with it.

"Yeah, she's pretty much useless to us these days," Riker agrees. "She used to be game for anything, but now it's all 'Grant wouldn't like that,' and 'I don't think that's such a good idea.'"

I open my mouth to object, as most of Riker's ideas have never been any good, but he's not done.

"In fact, it's been a lot more difficult than we thought to keep a steady influx of funds without her, if you know what I mean. Turns out she and her light fingers are damn near irreplaceable."

"Aw, Riker," I say. "That's so sweet. I had no idea—"

"I said *damn near* irreplaceable." He turns that playful gaze on Tara, and I recoil when I see not only a cunning gleam in his eye, but a carnal one, too.

Gross. That woman once had sex with my dad. There has to be a best friend rule about that sort of thing.

"What we need is a professional who can squeeze

into tight places. Someone flexible. Someone willing. Someone who doesn't get so unnecessarily freaked out by claustrophobia."

"I was never *unnecessarily* freaked out," I say, stung. "That fear was highly necessary. It kept me on my game so I wouldn't be sucked into ventilation fans and crushed by slowly moving walls."

I snatch the squid out of Tara's hands and put it back on the shelf. The rational half of my brain knows that this is part of Riker's plan B, a ritual of distraction-laden flirtation that Tara seems to be lapping up like it's the blood of diamonds, but it hits too close to home for comfort. There are a lot of things I'm willing to overlook where Riker is concerned, but an alliance with this woman isn't one of them.

"I'm sorry, but I don't really squeeze." Tara sidles closer and squeezes Riker's arm as if to prove it, failing to note that his other hand starts snaking toward her purse in the process. "I'm more of a saunter in and out with my head held high sort of girl. You'd be surprised what you can get away with by acting like you belong somewhere. People rarely question the confident."

"Is that how you've been doing it?" I ask. The question slips out before I can help myself. "You walk into those fancy parties and pretend like you belong?"

Although Riker shoots me a look of irritation as he's forced to snatch his hand back, Tara just laughs.

"Penelope is operating under the delusion that I'm the Peep-Toe Prowler," she explains. "She's convinced I'm the one sneaking into all those parties and stealing jewels from the wealthy. It'd be cute if it wasn't so misguided."

"It's not misguided," I say. "It's logic. If you're

not in New York to rake in a fortune, what's keeping you here?"

"You."

"Oh, really? You're risking your personal freedom for the sole benefit of my sparkling company?"

"Well, not the *sole* benefit. I multitask."

As far as I'm concerned, that's as good as a confession.

"I don't know why you're so fixated on this Prowler of yours, anyway," Tara continues in what I can only assume is an attempt to throw me off her scent. "Does Grant share the glory if you catch the criminals for him?"

"Of course not. It's a matter of principle, that's all."

"You have principles?"

"No, but I have pride. It's basically the same thing."

"I told you—she's useless to us now," Riker chimes in with a sad shake of his head.

Tara clucks in sympathy, but she keeps her attention on me. "If you want my opinion, you're going about this all wrong. If you want to find out who's behind all these thefts, you need to get closer to the source."

"The source?"

"The rich. The robbed. The Republican." She waves her hand, as if tired of the topic already. "If it was *me* trying to find the culprit, I'd get on the next guest list and see for myself what's going on behind those closed, gilded doors. A seasoned pro like you could probably pick out a thief in minutes."

"Right. Because an ex-jewel-thief-turned-housewife is at the top of every high-profile party invite. Why didn't I think of that before?"

Tara's brow comes up in a way that would make Jordan proud. "Doesn't your grandmother go to a lot of those functions? Strange. I'd have thought she'd be dying to show you off to her friends by now. You must be less fit for society than I thought."

I blink at her in bemusement, watching as she crosses the shop to investigate a dress that looks as if it's woven from a spider's gossamer threads. Riker goes with her, and I can't even rouse myself long enough to warn him to stop being so heavy-handed with both his flirtation and his pickpocketing.

Because Tara's idea is, frankly, genius.

Oh, she's still my number one suspect, no question. And I'm ninety-nine percent sure she's saying all this to make a game out of me. That's why I'm not going to stop Riker from digging around in her purse.

She's right, though. It *wouldn't* hurt to start sniffing around the upper echelons to see what people on the inside are saying. In my experience, rich people tend to avoid authority figures just as much as poor people do—it's usually only the middle class that has nothing to hide. Chances are they know something about the thefts they aren't sharing with the feds.

That would make me, granddaughter to a wealthy socialite, the ideal person to sneak in and find out what that something is.

And the best part is that Grant can't protest, because I'll be doing exactly what he told me to. Just hanging out with my family and reporting back on my findings. Living the happy, carefree life of a retiree.

"Can I help you with something?" a clerk asks, approaching me. She notices me staring at Tara and adds, "Or your friend?"

"Oh, she's not my friend," I say, the words spouting

unthinkingly from my lips. I can't help it. Denying kinship with that woman is such an ingrained part of me, it functions on autopilot.

I am, however, developing a grudging respect for the convolutions of her intellect—and an admiration for the way she wields it. She sees a problem, she finds a solution, and she puts those two things together, consequences and the feelings of other people be damned. Especially if the feelings in question are mine. I only wish I had half her resolve. The longer *I* spend trying to connect my problems to solutions, the more I flounder.

"Your…sister, then?" the clerks suggests.

I laugh out loud at that. I doubt the clerk would believe me if I told her the truth of our relationship. "She's not that, either," I say by way of explanation. "Tara defies labels, unfortunately."

And as I'm rapidly coming to learn, I do, too. I'm not a jewel thief anymore, and as my stalking Tara while Riker's hand is in her purse attests, I'm not a normal person, either. I'm just this weird, useless lump of a human being who used to steal things for a living.

I'm also a human being who needs to keep the clerk busy so Riker can finish his fishing expedition. I ask the clerk a series of pointed questions about a wooden goat sculpture, but it's to no avail. When Riker finally removes his hand from Tara's purse, he comes out empty, shaking his head at me with a frown.

I bite back my disappointment. It was a long shot to think Tara walked around with stolen jewels in her purse in the first place. If she has them, they're either well hidden or already on their way to a third-party buyer.

I'm going to need to catch her in the act if I want to learn the truth.

"You ready, Pen?" Tara calls, oblivious to our efforts.

"Almost. Gimme a minute." I give the clerk my brightest smile. "I'll take the scorpion serving spoon and the glow-in-the-dark underwear, please."

"Excellent choices," she agrees and leads the way to the register. That's her first mistake—and my tenth or eleventh. I should know better than to trust a hardened thief. Tara uses the distraction I provide as an opportunity to slip a silver candlestick down the front of her dress.

Sighing, I place a few extra bills near the cash register to cover the cost. No way am I getting felt up in a back room for this one.

12

GRANT

SHOOTING PAPER TARGETS ISN'T AS SATISFYING AS shooting double-crossing federal agents, but it does the job in a pinch.

The cavernous echo of Simon's shots peeling off beside me come to a halt, and I glance around the partition wall to see how our results compare. As usual, they're easy enough to distinguish. We might have trained at the same facility and taken aim at the same silhouette, but while my shots are dead center in the man's chest, Simon has systematically outlined the shape of the man's brain.

He can be a bit dark sometimes, that Sterling. Anger issues, mostly.

"You better not let the office psychologist see that. They're already concerned with your lack of a social life." I watch as Simon unclips the target and folds it, tucking it carefully in his messenger bag. I've never asked what he does with them, but Penelope likes to think he stuffs them in his mattress and floats off to bed every night on a sea of fond, bullet-fueled memories.

"I won't tell them if you don't." He indicates the earmuffs around my neck with a nod. "Another round?"

As tempting as it is to spend the rest of my day demolishing invisible demons, I shake my head. "Can't. I have to meet with the detail I'm putting on Lewis. Wanna guess how many of my guys volunteered for the job?"

Simon releases a short, barking laugh. "All of them?"

"Just about." It was impossible to get clearance for a full team to watch Penelope's stepmom without Christopher finding out about it, so I had to go through less formal channels. And by less formal channels, I mean I asked the small team of agents I've come to know and trust during my time at the Bureau. Paulie Jones, who was there at the first Christopher Leon paintball betrayal, an information technology specialist named Nathan who owes me a few favors, and a handful of other agents I know can be counted on to keep things quiet. All I had to do was say the name *Tara Lewis*, and the hands shot up.

Not that I blame them. Having spent a hefty portion of my own career investigating a highly attractive jewel thief, I can understand the appeal.

"No one volunteered to help me watch the guy Blackrock has me tailing," Simon grumbles. "He only has one ear."

Considering the quality of people Penelope's dad associates with, I don't find this surprising. I know she looks back on the time she and her father were apart with regret, but it's a sentiment I can't share. Riker and I don't always see eye to eye, but I know he did his best to keep her away from those kinds of criminals, to shield her from the less savory aspects of the world they both inhabited. I'll always be grateful to him for that.

"What happened to the other ear?" I ask.

"He cut it off to prove that he could." Simon pauses. "And then he ate it."

I grimace. *Yeah*. Riker's definitely not looking so bad these days.

I'm in the middle of unrolling my shirtsleeves when there's a loud outburst of voices at the door. Outbursts and shooting ranges rarely make for a happy combination, and it takes all of two seconds for Simon and me to have our stances secured, every possible angle covered as we approach to discover the cause.

Damn, but I miss working with this guy. One more point to stack up against Christopher—anyone in a position of authority who would purposely break up a smoothly working team is an idiot. I don't care how happy the ADD is with his performance. I'm much happier with a partner who has my back.

As if to prove me right, we move as one around the partition, heading toward the raised voices in a semi-crouch. Simon gets there a few seconds before me, giving me enough time to hear the sharp intake of his breath before I see the cause of the commotion.

Of course. Christopher Leon, leaning on the front desk and booming at the assembled crowd as if he owns the place. Which, given his track record to date, isn't an outrageous idea. I expect him to be pronounced president any goddamned day now.

With considerable regret, I relax my guard.

"Hello, Leon," I say, fighting back a sigh. The man

can't go anywhere without making a disturbance. "Here to brush up on your target practice?"

I mean the comment benignly enough, but he must take it as a reference to our first training exercise together, because he loses the self-satisfied smile for a fraction of a second.

"Not today," he says before slapping his smile back into place. "I came looking for you. There's been a development in the case."

My professional interest picks up almost immediately—and not just because I left Penelope out there in the field today, lurking around with Tara and her ilk. "Has the Prowler hit again?" I ask. I shrug into my jacket. The burglaries are definitely coming faster and closer together now. "What's the address?"

"No, no, it's nothing like that," Christopher says quickly. An almost guilty flush washes over him as he adds, "But the forensics report is finally in, and I thought you might want to take a look."

I blink at him, waiting for the rest, but apparently, that's all he has. The desire to inform him of this great invention called the telephone—or better yet, email—is strong, but there are several people milling around the desk, watching our interaction. Despite my suspicion of the guy, I don't want to diminish his position any more than I already have. I may not respect Christopher's authority, but I tend to respect authority in general.

"Did they find anything?" I ask instead.

"Nothing conclusive, but there may be a partial fingerprint worth running."

One partial at a crime scene where at least a dozen people had been present is hardly a break worth getting excited over, but it's more than we've had in a while. Usually, all they get is evidence of Christopher's shoddy investigative work. The man leaves footprints everywhere. Literally.

"All right. I'll head in and look it over. Anything else?"

"Oh, there's something else," says the agent working the front desk, a paper-pushing lackey named Justin who, by my reckoning, has never taken a day off. "You obviously didn't notice what Christopher rolled up in."

"I'll work free overtime for a month if you let me take her for a spin," another field agent adds. "Two months if I can floor it."

"What are you talking about?" I ask, but that's when I glance out the front window and see it, double-parked on the street and cutting off a major stream of backed-up traffic.

To anyone else, it would be nothing more than a sweet ride, the type of car that men with big dreams and small lives buy as soon as their bank account tips into the black. To me, the '69 Camaro SS parked a few feet away, gleaming with its sleek black body and freshly polished chrome wheels, is more.

A *hell* of a lot more.

"What is that?" I ask, even though I know down to the three-speed transmission what I'm looking at.

Christopher's beaming face breaks into an even bigger smile. "Do you like it? I picked her up today. You wouldn't believe the power she's got under that hood."

I *would* believe it if I wasn't having such a hard time wrapping my head around the fact that this man could be so cunning and so fucking stupid at the same time. A car in that condition is worth a quarter of a million dollars, and that's a modest estimate. I used to fantasize about all the things I might have to do to come up with that exact amount of money.

Marrying a jewel thief who I *know* has a secret reserve of cash she's not telling me about wasn't on that list, but that's about as close as I've been able to get. Mostly because FBI agents don't have that kind of income. Believe me, anyone getting into this rig for the money is setting themselves up for disappointment.

Unless, of course, he has major income beyond what comes with the job. The guy has always worn nicer suits than any other agent, but this is a whole different playing field.

"That's some car," I say neutrally.

"Way above my pay grade, though," Justin puts in. It's what we're all thinking, and we're all grateful he's the one to voice it. "And a pain in the ass to own unless you're a Jersey boy like Christopher. I guess that promotion must have come with a few extra perks, huh?"

Christopher has the decency—or stupidity—to look guilty. "Well, not exactly. I've been saving up for a while. I've wanted one ever since I was a kid."

I don't move, not even to glance at Simon, who I know is paying as much attention as me. Besides my mom, he's the only other person who knows how prominently this particular car figured in my adolescent dreams. I've never mentioned the vehicle to anyone else at the Bureau. Except, of course, during the Picasso college bust Christopher and I worked on a few years ago. But that had just been a throwaway line, a casual comment that could be interchanged with any number of similar ones throughout the years.

"Now that's interesting," Simon says, his lips thinning in a poor attempt at a smile. "I'd have taken you for a Lamborghini sort of guy."

"Or a Bentley," Justin puts in.

Before they launch into a list of all the traditional status cars, Christopher shakes his head. "Nah. My dad always had a thing for the classics."

This time, glancing at Simon isn't optional. I'm fairly sure I've said that exact same sentence before. Granted, I never knew my father, given that he bailed on me and my mom when I was five years old, but pieces of memory remain. One such piece includes the glossy black '69 Camaro SS he always dreamed of having.

What. The. Actual. Fuck.

"Do you want a lift?" Christopher asks me with a tilt of his head. I'm tempted to say yes, but Simon clears his throat significantly, stopping me short.

I'm grateful for his intervention. I don't think of myself as an overly sentimental man or even that much of a car guy anymore, but seeing that model up close and personal hits me harder than I expect. It's too strong a reminder that relationships end and people leave, regardless of who gets hurt in the process.

Sometimes, three thousand pounds of steel is all that's left behind.

"No, thanks," I say and turn away from the car. "I'll head back to the office in a few."

The agent who offered free overtime gladly claims my spot. I try not to watch as Christopher revs the engine before lurching into traffic, but I can't seem to help myself. He cuts off at least three cabs in a cloud of exhaust. I'm left with my memories and, as much as I hate to admit it, a healthy twinge of jealousy.

Damn. Maybe taking up a life of crime isn't such a bad idea after all.

"Emerson." Simon's voice indicates he knows what I'm thinking.

"What? I was just looking."

"Emerson."

"I know, I know."

"I don't think you do know." His voice drops to a hiss. "This is fucked up. That's *your* car he's driving away in—the one you used to talk about, the one you've always wanted. You never told him about that, did you?"

"I mentioned the car in passing once." More to convince myself than Simon, I add, "It could just be a coincidence."

"And you don't have that stuff about your dad written down anywhere?"

"What, like in my diary?" I tap my temple. "No, Sterling. I keep my feelings locked up in here."

"Joke all you want, but I smell something off. Between the way he's been gunning for your cases and his obsession with Penelope…"

"What about her?"

"Oh, nothing," Simon says. "Only that Christopher Leon seems to be trying to take over your life, one detail at a time. I hate to say it, man, but I think you're being single white femaled."

My first reaction is to laugh—a person doesn't just take over someone else's life. Especially not when one of them is well armed and good with his fists.

But a feeling of cold anxiety builds in my gut as

the clues line up. Christopher's questions and constant interest in what I'm doing. The way he always pops up when he should be handling his own shit. His refusal to accept that I neither need nor want him around. It was weird before, but this car thing pushes it into out-and-out batshit territory.

"He wouldn't dare," I say.

"You said that exact thing when he tried to toe in on your Warren Blue case. You also said it when the order came in for me to step off the Peep-Toe investigation. And God knows he's always been a little too interested in your wife. Not a good track record, wouldn't you say?"

It's a terrible track record, and if I didn't think it would get me kicked out of the Bureau, I'd say it to anyone willing to listen. Unfortunately, all I have to go on so far are theories and suspicions. Proof, that ever-elusive mistress, is nowhere to be seen.

Or is she? As my success record with the Bureau attests, proof is usually just several hundred man-hours of due diligence away. My mistake has been shouldering those man-hours on my own. Two things I've learned from tracking my wife's brilliant but less-than-ethical career: one, blithe unconcern for your own safety is a must, and two, the *real* secret to success is having a strong team at your back.

"You're right." I make a decision on the spot. "I've had just about enough of this bullshit."

"Wait, where are you going?" Simon asks, his tone worried.

"I'm tired of letting a few bureaucratic reprimands stop me from figuring out what that man's up to," I say.

That overeager desire to please, the systematic theft of cases from more experienced agents, hell, even trying to arrest Penelope so he can pretend he actually solved a crime on his own—I understand them all. I don't *like* them, but I can understand them.

This, however? Single white-femaling my life? *My wife?*

"I'm heading back to the office," I say. "I've got someone I need to talk to."

"Emerson…" Simon calls after me, but there's nothing he can say at this point to stop me. I'm already out the door.

"You're sure about that? Leon has no personal data listed whatsoever?"

I don't move from my position behind No-Aim Mariah, who's in her element hunched behind a panel of flat, glowing screens. It's not the wisest place for me to stand, since peering at a tech expert's monitor and questioning her findings is like holding a field agent's gun for them to make sure it's steady, but there's nowhere for me to sit. Mariah doesn't like people hanging around while she works, a circumstance she avoids by refusing to keep any chairs in her office.

It's not a bad idea. The spiky-haired computing genius might not be able to hit moving targets, but she's not without her insights.

"Well, the basics are here, of course. Date of birth, height, weight, the usual. But it's wiped of any personality, which is odd."

"Since when does an employee database have personality?"

"I'm not saying the FBI includes biography-level insight, but they tend to keep pretty close tabs on their people. Want to see yours?"

"No. Absolutely not."

She ignores me with the rapid-fire movement of her fingers over the keyboard, and I use the moment to gently shut her door. The information she's digging up for me isn't illegal, per se, but her backdoor access to it is.

Her fingers stop, and she leans close to the screen for a few seconds before releasing a low whistle. "Damn, Emerson. You've been busy."

"I told you not to look at my page."

"Pages."

"What?"

"Pages. Plural." She angles the screen so I can get a better view. I try not to look, but the word *Blue* pops up enough times that my profile looks like it belongs to a Smurf. "Hot damn. Did you really threaten to bury all your case notes and contacts if they gave Warren Blue to another agent?"

"Yes."

"And that worked?"

"I was very convincing."

Her shoulders shake with laughter. "I'm guessing these marksmanship scores had something to do with that. You have some interesting skills listed here. I'm a little scared to be looking at this right now."

"Liar. You love this. It makes you feel alive."

Mariah was a hacker before switching teams, which makes her an invaluable—if sketchy—asset in the Bureau. She's also a hell of a personal liability, since

I'm the one who got her the job after I busted her for breaking into the servers at the Treasury.

I have what some people have called a bad habit of transforming the criminal world's sketchy assets into my own sketchy assets. Personally, I find it to be a *great* habit. The best people I know are the ones who have to make a conscious decision every day to do the right thing. Give me someone capable of evil but willing to toe the line over someone inherently good every time.

I don't trust inherent goodness. I never have. Until someone knows what it's like to walk on the dark side, has faced the blackest temptation and emerged triumphant, it's impossible to learn the true measure of their soul.

I've measured a lot of souls in my lifetime, and few of them are as blindingly brilliant as the one belonging to my wife. I'd do anything for her, even —*especially*— risk my job by investigating the FBI's inexplicable golden boy.

"Could he have wiped his own profile?" I ask.

"Yeah, but he wouldn't have made it this clean. Not unless he wanted to be caught."

"So someone else has to have been in on it? Someone higher up?"

"You mean, like part of a government conspiracy? Sure." Mariah shrugs. "But I doubt it's the case here— cool things like uncovering a ring of high-ranking officials working together to overthrow the government never happen to me. Chances are your man is either boring as toast or he's got a dark past someone buried in the name of the greater good."

Oh, he's no piece of toast. There was yet another Penelope summons from him in my inbox when I returned to the office, this time with the ADD on copy and a thinly veiled warning that the next request will be an order. It's just like the man to go over my head instead of confronting me with the message face-to-face.

"What would it take to have you run a few off-the-books scans into his background?" I ask, thinking of both that email and the car, of the increasing suspicion that Christopher isn't a man I should underestimate. "Hypothetically speaking?"

"You want me to illegally investigate a fellow agent, thereby jeopardizing my entire career and my position as a law-abiding, free-to-roam U.S. citizen?"

"Yes, please."

She laughs so hard, it's a cackle. "Only for you, Emerson. And only if you promise to introduce me to that wife of yours when I'm done. Cheryl says she gives the best Christmas presents."

I groan. The last thing I need right now is those two women in a room together. I can all too easily imagine Penelope wrapping Mariah around her little finger the same way she does everyone else, calling her up for a chat and a quick hack into the White House mainframe. "That's a terrible idea."

"Maybe, but it just so happens I love terrible ideas. Do we have a deal?"

I don't see any way around it, so I stick out my hand with a sigh. "Fine. But I'd really like to know why all the women in my life have to turn everything into a twisted game."

She pumps my hand once and turns her focus back to the screen. "That's easy. It's because you make it such a joy to win."

I stare at the back of her head, seeing but not seeing the dark strands of her hair. "That was supposed to be a rhetorical question."

She looks over her shoulder long enough to laugh at my expression. "Only because you didn't realize the answer was right there. I'm sorry to admit it, Emerson, but most days, beating you at your own game is the only fun to be had around here. Nothing keeps a girl on her toes like a good challenge and an even better adversary."

"A good challenge and an even better adversary," I echo. That sounds an awful lot like Penelope's idea of heaven. In fact, it's the only way I got her to go out with me in the first place. She never would have given me the time of day if I hadn't turned our courtship into a dare. I can still see her standing on the sidewalk, laughter in her sparkling blue eyes as she wove an intricate web of lies and truth to ensnare me.

As if I ever had a chance of escaping. As if I wasn't hers the moment she tossed down the gauntlet.

Mariah's head bobs in a nod. "If you ask me, those are getting harder and harder to find these days. You're a diamond in the rough, boss man. No wonder we criminals flock to you."

THE LUNCHEON

In the end, I decide it's best *not* to tell Grant about my plans to infiltrate the Upper East Side.

"You look awfully fancy today," he says as I root through the closet in nothing but a black pencil skirt and my new bioluminescent bra. As my wardrobe is ninety percent cat-burglar chic, the glow-in-the-dark flashes of my breasts are the only color to be seen.

"That's because I'm having lunch with my grand-mother. Aha!" I hold up a not-black tank top in triumph. It's dark gray, but it still counts. "Do you know if Café Boulud has a dress code?"

Grant doesn't answer right away. Thinking he's left the room, I turn around to find him standing with his arms crossed and a darkly suspicious look on his face.

"They do, don't they?" I sigh. "Great. I knew I should have tried to talk her into ordering pizza instead."

"Good try. Where are you going?"

"Um. I just said. Café Boulud. *Not* my choice, in

case it gives you ideas about where to take me for our next anniversary."

He continues that disconcerting stare.

"What?" I ask. "You know how awkward I get at those fancy places."

He clears his throat. "The last time you said you were having lunch with your grandmother, you broke about fifteen federal laws."

I don't manage to suppress the laughter that bubbles in my throat. I'd already forgotten about my cover story the day of the FBI break-in—my conscience never holds on to things for long. It's an occupational necessity.

"I know, but I mean it this time."

I saunter over to him and run my hands up his sides, slipping them under his suit jacket to finger the outline of his holster. There's leather and metal and cotton and skin—all of it warm to the touch and capable of sending my pulse skittering. It's perverse to find the law-abiding side of him so attractive, but I can't help myself. The man knows his way around a pair of handcuffs.

"Penelope…" he warns.

"It's true!" I protest even as I continue fingering his badge. "I don't make enough of an effort. I want to start trying harder to get to know her."

He hesitates but lets the lie pass. I suspect the only reason I get away with it is because it technically *isn't* a lie. When I first discovered I had a grandmother—an event that not-so-coincidentally aligned with the redis-covery of my father—I'd been elated to think I had a maternal relative within city limits. My emotional world was suddenly full of possibilities. The two of us could hang out, catch up on our lives, and, most importantly, talk about my mother. There were so many things I wanted to know about the woman who gave her life to bring me into this world and so few people willing or able to tell me.

Unfortunately, Grandma Dupont—or Erica, as she demands I call her—was another dead end. No sooner would I mention my mother's name than she'd ask me where I picked up so much street slang or command me to adjust my posture.

"She seemed really surprised to hear from me when I called," I add. "She also offered me money, which is weird. Is she afraid I'm going to rob her if she doesn't pay me off ahead of time?"

"Of course not."

"Then what does it mean?" I wrinkle my nose, remembering the way she'd couched the offer, without kindness or preamble. *Okay, Penelope. How much do you need?* "It almost felt like she was bribing me to go away."

Grant's expression gentles. "I'm sure that wasn't her intention."

"Then what was?"

"My guess?" He lifts a hand to my face and runs the back of his fingers against my cheek. It's a tender gesture at odds with his words. "You scare the shit out of her."

I'm startled into another laugh, though this one feels rougher around the edges. "Very funny. The only thing that woman is scared of is her accountant. Well, and maybe the lady who cleans her house. I bet she knows where all the expensive stuff is hidden."

He presses a soft kiss to my forehead. "You have no idea, do you?"

"You think she keeps her valuables somewhere else? That's smart, given that the Blue Fox is her son-in-law. It can't be easy, marrying into my family."

"Truer words have never been spoken, but that's not what I meant," he says. Taking the gray tank top from my hand, he motions for me to lift my arms. With painstaking care, he slips the fabric over my head and shoulders, taking his time as he tucks it into place. If he were serious about seduction, he'd caress the swell of my breasts and grip the curve of my waist, his fingers pressing a familiar pattern.

This morning, however, his thoughts are elsewhere. Instead of taking my arched back as an invitation to linger, he trails his fingers up the line of my spine and pulls me into his embrace. He dips his head to kiss the sensitive spot below my ear, his lips moving against my skin as he adds, "You scare the shit out of everyone."

A shiver runs through me. "That's not true."

He pauses, as if choosing his next words carefully. "She offered you money because she doesn't know what else to do."

"That's not true," I protest again. "She probably offers everyone money. That way she can yell at them to sit up straighter, and they can't complain."

"Or—and I'm just throwing this out there—she doesn't know what else she can give you. She *wants* to make up for the past, and she *wants* you to feel supported, but trying to do anything for someone as willfully self-sufficient as you requires three layers of armor and a nerve of iron."

I strongly suspect him of mocking me. "A Hallmark card would do the trick."

"Only if she held it against your neck and threatened to slit your throat with it." He releases his grip on me, his gaze clouded as his eyes meet mine. "You don't make it easy, Penelope. You know that, right?"

I don't, actually, and I'm not sure I want him to continue. A difficult wife sounds an awful lot like a disposable one.

"Are you saying I should take the money?" I ask.

"I'm saying you should be gentle with her, that's all. Like the rest of us, she only wants to make you happy. She just doesn't know how to do it." He looks at me as if searching for something. I don't think he finds whatever it is, because he shakes his head. "A good challenge and a better adversary. That's all you want out of life, isn't it?"

I have no idea what he's talking about, but both of those things sound lovely.

"Just…" He shakes his head again. "Be nice to her today, okay? And for the love of everything that's holy, promise me you won't take any unnecessary risks."

Now he's not mocking so much as insulting me. "All the risks I take are necessary ones, thank you very much."

"Why do I get the feeling this isn't a regular lunch date?"

"Because you're a highly suspicious and untrusting man," I say and then laugh. There's no real use in trying with him. "And because you have the annoying tendency to be right about these things."

His eyes flash. "Penelope, so help me…"

I get up on my tiptoes to kiss his nose before ducking under his arm and out of his reach. Being quick on my feet sure comes in handy sometimes. "Don't worry so much. It's lunch at an upscale French restaurant. What could go wrong?"

His reply is a loud curse I won't bother repeating. Ladies who lunch at Café Boulud would never repeat *that* sort of profanity.

"Penelope, I know you're flexible, but please tell me there's a spine somewhere inside that body of yours."

I shoot up so quickly, I almost drop my spoon into the bowl of beef-flavored water. According to my grandmother's impeccably accented French, the soup is called consommé, but I'm pretty sure it's a long con that France has been playing on the world for centuries. Twenty dollars a bowl for *this*?

"Sorry," I say with a sheepish wince. "It's habit."

"Not a very good one."

"Sorry," I say again—my fifth apology in as many minutes and, if things keep progressing like this, not even close to my last. I'm not sure what distorted view Grant has of my relationship with this woman, but I seriously doubt *she's* the one in need of three layers of armor. "I've never been very good at sitting up straight. Or sitting still, for that matter."

My grandmother blinks at me slowly. Well, maybe not slowly so much as purposefully. All of her movements are like that. She's languid in a way that screams elegance and power, as if she possesses the ability to control time itself. The urge to emulate her is strong, but I get the feeling I'd end up looking like a sloth.

"How on earth did you sit inside air vents for hours if you can't be still?"

I laugh. That's the other thing I admire about my grandmother. She's not one to tiptoe around the truth.

"It wasn't easy; I can tell you that. I also get claustrophobic in tight spaces. I had to teach myself to breathe through it."

She pats the edges of her shell-pink mouth with her napkin. "Well, no one can say you aren't committed to your chosen profession. You got that from your grandfather."

"Actually, I think I got it from—"

She blinks at me again. "He had a great work ethic, your grandfather."

"Yes, ma'am." Arguing with her would be futile. So far, she's been pretty accepting of the fact that her granddaughter is a criminal, which says a lot, considering Erica disowned my mom the day she married my dad. This is a woman who has convictions and sticks to them. "I'm sorry I never got a chance to meet Grandfather. What was he like?"

It's the wrong question. That same shell-pink mouth—which matches the pantsuit she's wearing to perfection—purses tightly. "You know I don't like dwelling on the dead."

I do know. I also know that what she's really saying is under no circumstances should I mention my mom or try to introduce her into the conversation. It's the same whenever I try to talk to my dad about her—something I learned as a child and had to rediscover a few short months ago. *Not now, maybe later, why don't you run along and play.* Twenty-six years have passed, and the pain of my mother's loss is still so strong that neither one of them can even say her name out loud.

She must have been something special to foster that

kind of love and devotion. And they both had to trade her in for *me*.

"Maybe another time." I manage a small smile. "That's not what I'm here for anyway."

"Ah. Now we get to the heart of the matter. I thought there might be a reason for this unprecedented event. What's the amount?"

I can't decide whether or not to be insulted. After a moment's reflection, I decide there's no point. It's no different than me offering Riker my life's savings to bail him out of trouble. I *want* to do more for him—so much more—but I can only reach out so far on my own. At some point, he's going to have to reach back.

Oh, geez. Was Grant right? Am I that hard to help?

"It's not money." I trail my spoon through the pretend soup, which has now gone cold. "I was, um, sort of hoping you might take me to some events over the next few weeks."

"Events." There's nothing in her tone to make this easier.

"Yeah. I know I'm not exactly the debutante type, and you probably aren't eager to trot me out and show me off to all your friends, but—"

"You mean *social* events? Charity functions?"

I look up, hoping her face might show a glimpse of the humanity her voice is lacking.

It doesn't. My grandmother is beautiful—well preserved, with a classic look that time can't touch—but she's not what you'd call *approachable*. Then again, I'm not what you'd call squeamish.

"Charity functions, parties, dinners…" I leave the list open-ended. "I'm not picky. What sorts of things do you and your friends normally do?"

There's a shrewd look to her narrowed eyes that makes me think she knows what I'm really asking— *where do all the rich people congregate?*—but her shrewdness goes deep enough that she doesn't voice her suspicions. Instead, she says, "Most of the time, I hide from charity functions, parties, and dinners because they're mind-numbingly dull and frequented by self-indulgent egoists."

I release a shout of laughter. It's hardly a ladylike response in a setting like this one, and I draw the attention of several diners seated around us. Most of the couples dismiss me as quickly as I do them, but one woman seated on the other side of the bar does a double take.

There's only enough time for me to take note of her smooth black bob and catlike eyes before I turn my head the opposite direction. *Please, please don't let that be someone I've robbed in the past. Please, please say she's merely admiring my tinkling laughter and air of natural grace.*

I turn my laugh into a discreet cough. "Does that mean you won't take me anywhere?"

"Of course not," my grandmother says crisply. "They're only dull because I don't have anyone to show off. I haven't had anyone to show off in a long time."

My brow wrinkles in confusion, but I don't have an opportunity to ask her to elaborate, because the waiter returns to remove our soup and present us with an artfully arranged pile of weeds. Oh, I'm sorry. *Salad.*

I use the distraction to sneak a peek at the bobcat across the bar and immediately wish I hadn't. Her eyes—even from this distance, I can see that they're dark and sharp—have focused on me with an intensity

I know from long experience doesn't bode well. I want to ask my grandmother who the woman is, but by the time the waiter leaves, she's already launched into a plan of action.

"It's better to ease you in gently, so we'll start with a tea party meeting next week," she says without room for question—not my question, not hers, and not, apparently, the bobcat's, because her attention finally turns away.

I guess a ferocious grandparent who doesn't take crap from anyone comes in handy sometimes.

"A tea party meeting?" I ask. "What does that mean?"

"It means you don't need to worry about the details—the Ladies' Society needs to finalize plans for our annual Black and White Ball, and Millie Ralph has been trying to find a way into my house for years. A tea party is the way to do it. She'll jump at the chance to snoop around, and where Millie goes, the rest will follow."

"Who's Millie Ralph?"

She waves her hand. "A terrible woman. Meddlesome and loud. You needn't worry about her." But then she leans over the table, her fork poised as if to stab. "But I'd appreciate it if you made an effort to at least *look* the part when you arrive. That'll show her."

I'm almost scared to ask. "Show her what?"

"That there's some fight in the Duponts yet. We never stay down for long."

"But I'm not a—"

The fork remains firmly in place. "You *are* a Dupont, and it will behoove you to remember that. You might think your courage comes from that crook of a man you call father, but I know better. No one except *my* granddaughter could have pulled off half the things you've done in your lifetime."

I have no response to that, which is just as well, because she's not done yet.

"Now. Eat your salad, and try not to shovel it all in as if you've never seen food before. Honestly, Penelope, didn't anyone teach you to use a fork?"

THE 14 DEAL

I KNOW SOMETHING IS UP THE MOMENT I GET HOME.

In the general way of things, it's not uncommon for me to enter a scene of domesticity as soon as I walk through the front door. Grant *enjoys* activities like cooking and cleaning, which makes no sense to me, but I know better than to complain. Fresh sheets and regular meals are quite nice once you get used to them, and there's something comforting about having a husband who can don a frilly pink apron and make it look like a loincloth skinned fresh from the kill.

However, when that same husband rounds the corner wearing not an apron, but a towel that slings low on his hips, the rest of his body a bare showcase of masculinity, it's taking things a step too far. Talk about throwing a girl in unprepared.

I drop my bag in the doorway. "Um. Hi. Hey. Hello."

He grins and leans against the wall, fully aware of how he looks and what he's doing to me. "Hello yourself. How'd it go with your grandmother?"

Coherent thoughts aren't within my current range of capabilities, which means full sentences are out. I grunt instead. You'd think that regularly sharing a bed with this man would inure me to the sight of him without any clothes on, but you'd be wrong. *So very wrong*. Not even the most jaded visitor tires of the Sistine Chapel that quickly.

"I take that to mean you didn't get what you were looking for?" He tsks, which makes his entire torso flex, including those enticing hip muscles peeking over the top of his towel. "Pity. After all your careful plotting and everything."

I'm instantly on alert. "What do you know about my plotting?"

"Did she refuse to help you? Tell you to turn your attention to something more productive? I've always liked Erica."

Fortunately for me, half-naked taunting will only get a handsome man so far.

"Actually, she promised to throw a tea party in my honor," I say. "She's going to introduce me to some people so I can start mingling with the victims of the Peep-Toe Prowler and get the inside track."

He pushes himself off the wall. "She didn't."

"Oh, she's excited about it," I reply with a smirk, but then I catch sight of the dark gleam in his eyes. "It wasn't my idea, I swear! I was just planning on feeling her out—I didn't expect her to take me under her wing like this. Tara's the one who suggested it."

"Since when are you taking Tara's advice? She's under investigation."

"I know, but you have to admit she has a point. It's a

perfect way to keep an eye on things. If I'm at the parties the Prowler is targeting, then I can watch everyone who comes and goes, and no one will think anything of it."

"Except Tara and anyone she happens to be working with." He rakes a hand through his still-damp curls, causing a few of them to stand on end. "Goddammit— did it ever occur to you to wonder *why* she suggested such a thing?"

"Of course it did."

He stares at me expectantly. "And?"

"And it doesn't matter. She probably wants me there to witness her triumph. In case you hadn't noticed, she's kind of a narcissist."

Grant groans in a way that doesn't bode well for the rest of the conversation. In the interest of our future life's happiness together, I decide to stop him before he says something we're both going to regret. Risking life and limb, I lift my hands to the hard slabs of his shoulders and force his dark, glittering gaze to meet mine.

"Is it my intelligence you underrate or my ability to defend myself?" I ask.

"Penelope, you know it's neither of those things…"

"Or is it my courage? Because, so help me, if you think for one second that I'm not willing—"

Grant releases a short laugh. "I doubt anyone can accuse *you* of cowardice. No, it's not you I'm worried about so much as everyone else who's involved."

That's almost as bad, and I say so. "If Tara's so dangerous, why don't you arrest her? I'm sure you have enough information on her past activities to make it believable. Get her off the streets and save us all the trouble."

"I'm not talking about Tara, either," Grant says.

"Then who—"

"It's Leon." He says the name like he's biting it off. "I was hoping it wouldn't come to this, but I can see now that I don't have any other choice. He's asked me to bring you in."

"He wants you to bring me in?" I echo, my voice hollow. To the FBI building? To the place where I might be able to sneak my way in, but getting out is virtually impossible?

At first, I think he's joking, his twisted sense of humor getting the best of him, but his perfectly rigid stance is a dead giveaway. Tense muscles rarely mean happy things where this man is concerned. It's usually an indication he's about to strike.

"Unfortunately, yes," he says and takes a dangerous first step toward me. "I don't like it any more than you do."

I somehow doubt that. He wouldn't be standing there half-naked otherwise, flashing his bare torso at me so he can clap me in irons while I'm distracted by the glory of each chiseled plane.

"As my direct superior, it's within his ability to insist," Grant adds.

The devil it is. "And as your wife, it's within my ability to respectfully decline," I state, my words wavering only slightly. "Which, for the record, I do. Vehemently."

"Noted, vehemently."

He takes another one of those predatory steps, and every natural instinct I have to flee in the face of authority leaps to the surface. I'm usually able to subdue that part of myself around Grant—since he's all authority, all the time, I don't have much choice—but something about the combination of *his* nudity and *my* vulnerability breaks down all those barriers.

After all I've given up, all the compromises forged in the name of love, *this* is where it leads us. Not the lifelong battle of wills we once pledged one another but the need for a hasty and not-so-strategic retreat.

Starting…*now*.

"But you said you'd give me a five-minute warning first!" I accuse, giving his chest a shove.

Startled, he actually takes a few steps back.

"You promised, Grant."

"What? Penelope, I'm not—"

I don't wait for him to finish, too eager to capitalize on the element of surprise. I'm out the front door and half-way down the front steps before he realizes I've bolted.

Unfortunately, halfway is as far as I get. I blame the stupid shoes I wore to lunch to impress my grandmother. In flats, my smaller size and catlike agility make me able to dart around my husband as much as my heart desires. But I'm no Tara Lewis, and the precarious heels cause me to falter on the bottom stair. I prepare to fall into a tuck and roll to safety, but I have to regain my balance first.

That precious second of hesitation is my undoing.

Grant is suddenly behind me. He wraps his arms around my waist, his body still slippery from the shower. I give my legs a hearty kick, but it's no use. Not only is his body damp, but it's incredibly strong, and he's not afraid to fight dirty. With bare muscles rippling, he lifts me off the ground and pulls me back into the house. The picture is as undignified as it sounds, especially when I notice Harold across the street staring at us out his front window.

Of course, it doesn't help that Grant appears to be taking pleasure from my struggle. His arms tighten, his body shaking with what I presume is laughter as he pulls me back inside and slams the door.

"Enjoying yourself, are you?" I grumble.

"More than you realize."

Oh, I realize it, all right. A towel isn't a very thick barrier, and the evidence of his enjoyment isn't long in making itself known against my backside.

I stop struggling at once. "You're sick, you know that? Do you get aroused every time you arrest a woman?"

"Only the ones I'm married to."

His lips are right next to my ear, blowing warm air over the sensitive lobe. There's this trick he knows how to do against the side of my neck that damn near renders me unconscious with desire, and he pulls it out in full force.

"And only when she's trying to wriggle away," he adds with a low rumble. "Don't forget, you've tried to escape me before. There's a lot more teeth and a lot less ass involved when you're really trying."

First of all, that's not true. I *always* use my ass to try and get my way. It's one of my best features. And second of all...

"Okay, okay. I get the point." I relax in his arms, not pushing him away so much as melting into his pecs. "You're the master, and I'm the weak, swooning female you can reduce to a pool of desire with your tongue. Congratulations."

His eyes crinkle in a self-satisfied—and ridiculously alluring—smile. "Really?"

"Yes, really." I force myself away from the warm

protection of his body and hold out my wrists. "You can take comfort in that while I sit in a cold, sterile cell surrounded by hardened criminals. Don't get mad if I come home with all kinds of new tricks. I intend to use my time in the clink wisely."

His laugh is half groan. "For Christ's sake, Penelope. I'm not arresting you."

"But you said—"

"That Leon *asked* me to bring you in, not that I'm going to. Why do you have to make things so goddamned difficult all the time?"

"Because I married a goddamned difficult man. Funny how these things work out." I drop my wrists. "You really aren't going to haul me in?"

"Why is it that *I'm* the only FBI agent you consider a viable threat?"

I can tell, from the way his lips quiver between amusement and a deep-seated urge to strangle me, that we're on safe ground again. Also that I might have over-reacted a little.

Oops.

"Because," I say, flashing him my most mischievous smile, "you're the only FBI agent who can catch me."

With such flattery as that up for grabs, he has no choice but to blow out a long breath—the breath of a man goaded to his limit. I take advantage of the moment to press my case.

"And I don't understand," I add. "If you're not put-ting me under arrest, what are you trying to do? What does Christopher want from me?"

"It doesn't matter. He's not getting it," is all the answer Grant provides.

"Come on—you have to give me more than that," I say.

"I can't."

"Why? Because I can't handle the truth?"

"No. Because I don't *know* the truth."

"Then you better make something up. Something convincing, because I'll take *myself* in if you don't start giving me some answers."

Grant's eyes flash. "Christopher Leon is obsessed with you and has been for years. I don't know why, but by the way he's been acting lately, I'm half convinced he plans to kidnap you, lock you in an abandoned warehouse somewhere, and extract your family's secrets fingernail by fingernail."

I throw up my hands. This is what happens when you try to talk rationally to an overbearing FBI agent who also shares your bed. "You were supposed to tell me something convincing, not the plot of a B horror movie," I accuse.

"I can't help it if truth is stranger than fiction. I already told you that he's been angling for your arrest. You chose not to believe me. You thought I was being overprotective."

"You *are* being overprotective."

"I'm being the exact amount of protective I need to be," he says with a growl. It's a good opportunity for him to open up and elaborate, but all he does is pause, his hard gaze gentling as he reaches out to take my hand. "If I asked you to go out of town, no questions asked, until this case is over and Christopher Leon has moved on, would you do it? Would you let me keep you safe the best way I know how?"

I want to say yes—I really do. Few things in life make

me happier than pleasing my husband. I love seeing his lips spread in a smile of fondness and affection; I love even more that I have the ability to elicit that response whenever I want. That's a heady power few people can boast of possessing.

And if it were anything else he was asking me for, I might do it.

"No." I see the pain in his eyes and wince. "I'm sorry, but that's not how this works."

"I know it's not." However promising his words, the sigh that follows is about a thousand years old. "I haven't been fair to you lately, have I, my love?"

My heart clenches. There aren't many people who could look at the life Grant and I share and think *he's* the one who's being unfair.

"I'm onto something here, Grant," I say, my voice wavering only slightly. "This stuff with my grandmother means I have a good opportunity to dig deeper. I can go places and talk to people you can't, attend parties, and keep my eyes open. Who knows? I might end up being good at this undercover criminal investigation stuff. It's…fun."

There are a dozen more reasons I could give him for letting me in—my connections and my ability to hide in small spaces, the fact that I'm willing to work for free. But none of them are as important as that one simple fact: *it's fun*.

These past few days have given me more pleasure and purpose than the entire past six months combined. These past few days, I've been happy.

I pause, desperate to say those words aloud but unable to, knowing how much pain they would cause him. I can only watch and wait, my heart thumping in my chest.

Grant pauses with me, his eyes dark and searching. I swear that he can see the rapid beat of my pulse, that he knows how much hinges on these next moments, but I don't back down.

Neither does he, and I have no idea how long we stand there before he finally nods and says, "Okay."

I'm not sure if I heard him correctly. "Okay?"

Both his nod and his voice gain strength the second time around. "Okay. I wouldn't want to stand in the way of your exciting new career."

"Bullshit. You want to stand in my way so bad, you can taste it."

He laughs at that, though there's a tense undercurrent he can't fully hide. "I want to do a lot of things to you, Penelope Blue, but I usually find a way to restrain myself. I don't think I get nearly enough credit for that." He draws a deep breath, his chest expanding until it seems twice its normal size. "If there's nothing I can say or do to stop you..."

I shake my head.

"Then you have my full support. I told you the other day that I want you to be happy, and I meant it. If meddling in a federal investigation at the risk of your own safety is what makes you happy, then I'll move the sky and earth to make it happen. And I will do everything in my power to keep Leon at bay while you do it."

I wait patiently for the bricks to start falling.

"But..."

Ah. There they are.

"I want something from you in return."

"I'm listening," I say, and I *am* listening—so hard you could hear a grenade pin drop.

"The deal is simple. When the case is solved and everything is over, you have to promise me you'll find a safe, sane occupation as far away from the FBI as you can get."

I blink a few times, waiting for the rest—the catch or the ultimatum, an indication that my husband is playing a deeper game. The silence with which he greets me doesn't make me feel confident it's coming any time soon.

"Um. Are you joking?"

"No. You're asking me to set aside my better judgment for something you want. It's only fair that I get the same consideration from you." The only thing flatter than his tone is the hard press of his lips. From the look of him, you'd think he just asked me to stop murdering people and burying them in the basement. "No more moonlighting as a federal agent after this, I'm begging you. Find something else you can enjoy. I don't like—"

He doesn't finish. A curt shake of his head and a deep breath are all he gives me, and I gotta say—they're not making me feel much better. What doesn't he like? That I'm trying to help him? That I'm a drain on society and the world at large? That it turns out I'm no good at anything other than stealing jewels?

The last one makes my blood run cold, the truth of it too blaring to ignore. It's exactly what I've feared since the day I gave up my life of crime. As a jewel thief, I was pretty decent. As a law-abiding human being, I'm barely mediocre. I always knew Grant would realize it someday.

I just didn't expect it to happen so soon.

"I don't like seeing you so miserable," he finally finishes, but it's a case of too little, too late. The damage has been done, the cold weight of reality wedged between us. I'm not the wife he thought he was getting the day he married me.

"I don't understand," I say. "Earlier, you said Christopher wants to lock me in a warehouse."

"He probably does."

"You said he wants to pull out my fingernails."

"I wouldn't put it past him."

"And you don't care? You'll let that happen as long as I find myself a nice, ordinary job like a nice, ordinary person?"

He sighs and rubs a hand on the back of his neck, a picture of masculine perfection. "Of course I care. If I had my way, I'd have kept you out of this entire case—out of the entire FBI database—from the start. But that's not possible now, and more than anything, I want you to be…"

I wait, my chest tight as he struggles to suppress another sigh. His gaze catches mine and holds. I can see that there's more going on behind those dark eyes, but he doesn't let anything go.

"You know your own limits, Penelope—better than Christopher does, better than I do. That's why I've decided to stop trying to stand in your way and take an alternate route." His lips turn up in a slight smile—his first since this conversation started. "A dangerous, misguided route, yes, but when have we ever walked anything else? If there aren't underhanded deals and convoluted bargains required to get there, you aren't interested."

"That's not true!" I protest, but it totally is. A flicker of excitement has already begun heating the soles of my feet. Not about finding a safe, sane occupation, obviously, but the rest of it—the opportunity to meet this man on the battlefield once again, the sense of danger and intrigue involved in a case of this magnitude.

In other words, all those things a decent human being would balk at but that I can't seem to live without.

"What's the catch?" I ask, still suspicious. I can't help thinking there's more to this plan than Grant is sharing.

If there is, he's not going to open up about it today. "You mean other than the possibility of you falling under the power of a dangerous man? Nothing. I don't love this idea, but I do love *you*, so those are my terms. You're free to take them or leave them as you see fit."

He turns and saunters down the hall before I can do much more than open and close my mouth in disbelief, his ass a vision of perfection wrapped up in white terry cloth.

"That's all you're going to say?" I call after that perfection.

"Yes." But he pauses at our bedroom door. "Oh, and I'd appreciate it if you'd invest in a different pair of shoes before you decide. If you're going to be running for your life, I'd feel a lot better knowing you're doing it in flats."

THE 15 ALLY

THE FIRST PERSON I TURN TO FOR ADVICE ISN'T THE MAN you'd expect.

"So you're okay with me investigating Tara on the sly?" I pass my dad his stethoscope and watch as he hangs it over his neck, looking very much like a nice, ordinary doctor. The effect is ruined when he heads straight to the safe hidden in the wall of his closet. "It's not only me who thinks she might be the Peep-Toe Prowler. Grant also suspects she's involved."

"I'll tell you exactly what I told her," my father says calmly. "What you do with your free time is of no concern to me, and I refuse to get involved. Have lunch. Go shopping. Break into rich people's homes and steal their valuables. I don't care. I'm just glad the two of you are spending time together."

"Dad, *I'm* not the one stealing—" I begin, but he slips the stethoscope into his ears, and I give up. Explaining to my father that I'm with the good guys for once is useless. Equally useless is getting him to believe that he—or anyone he cares about—is in danger from the law. Like most great men, he has an ironclad belief in his own infallibility.

Which, given his current arrest record, is a touch ironic.

I watch as he places the chestpiece near the safe's dial and makes a few twists and turns. His brow furrows as he listens for the telltale click of the drive pins falling into place. Childhood memories of this exact scenario remind me that he requires complete silence to get the job done. There's no playing, no talking, no fun. Just watching and learning from the best.

Despite my early exposure, cracking safes is a task I never mastered. Neither is being quiet and unobtrusive, but I slow my breathing and prepare not to make any sudden movements for as long as it takes him to gain entrance.

Fortunately for us both, less than sixty seconds pass before my father swings the safe door open in triumph.

Or, rather, as much triumph as you can expect from a man as cool and collected as my father. Even in moments of victory, he's like Clint Eastwood getting his man.

"Fifteen and *then* seven." My dad slips the stethoscope off with a shake of his head. "I had it backward. Take my advice, baby doll: never get old."

I blink at him. "Couldn't you have called down to the front desk and asked them for the combination?"

"I'm going to pretend you didn't ask me that." He extracts an envelope from the safe and hands it to me. "And I hope this little ruse of yours is worth it. I was saving this for a rainy day."

A knock prevents me from showing my appreciation in full, but I manage to brush a quick kiss on his cheek before he goes to open the door.

"Ah, Agent Sterling. Right on time. Your punctuality is always a delight."

Simon cracks a smile—an actual *smile*—before he notices me standing in the middle of the room. Then he can't drop the joy fast enough.

"Hello," I call cheerfully. I also wave the envelope, since there's a good chance he might turn tail and flee otherwise. "My dad entrusted his deepest, darkest secrets to me, so you might as well come in. I'm not giving them up easily."

He doesn't cross the threshold, opting instead to look between me and my father with a confused purse to his brow. "What is this?"

"Don't ask me. I'm merely a vessel." My dad pauses. "But you'll find that the list is fully intact. Don't make me regret my decision to share it with you, yes?"

And with that, my dad walks to his bedroom, pulling the wide French doors closed behind him. It's a grand exit, the only kind he's capable of, and I sigh at how neatly he pulls it off. My dad sure kept all the suave genes for himself.

"Stop gawking at me, and get inside already," I say to Simon irritably. "I'm not going to hurt you. This isn't what you think."

"You have no idea what I think," Simon says. He takes a step and shuts the door but refuses to move beyond the threshold. His already uptight posture is so tense, it's a wonder he can move his legs.

Good thing I know how to get them going again.

"Are these really the secret locations of all the lost Fabergé eggs?" I ask as I pretend to open the envelope. Predictably, Simon lunges across the room before I manage to crack the seal.

He's fast, but I'm faster, and I hold the envelope just out of his reach. "How much money do you think I'd get if I took the grand tour and recovered them for myself?" I add in a teasing voice. "They've only been missing for, what, a hundred years?"

"Give it to me."

"Not until you do something for me first."

"This isn't funny." He swipes again, but he's reluctant to get close enough to make physical contact. In all the time I've known Simon, I don't think he's willingly touched me a single time. It's almost as if he's afraid I've got FBI-agent-turning powers at the tips of my fingers. "The only reason I came here today is because your father said it's important."

"It *is* important." I stop the game as quickly as I started it and press the envelope into his hand. I also seat myself on the couch while he's still staring perplexedly at it. "Sit down, Simon. I promise this won't take long."

I've never considered Simon a particularly handsome man, especially not when set against the brawny, all-American charm my husband oozes in abundance, but he has a straitlaced attractiveness I imagine might appeal to women who don't mind cozying up to blocks of ice. His chilly exterior remains in place as he seats himself across from me, careful not to let our knees bump.

Eventually, he thaws. "Is this about you trying to catch the Peep-Toe Prowler on your own?" he asks.

I'm less surprised by the fact that he knows about my

efforts and more surprised that he doesn't seem to be censuring me for it. Talk about unprecedented behavior. Warily, I reply, "I'm not doing it on my own. My friends are helping."

"Huh."

Not *You guys are a menace to society*. No *Stay out of it or else*. Just huh.

In Simon terms, that's as good as an invitation, and it's one I don't neglect to take him up on. "I need you to tell me everything you know about Christopher Leon," I say. "Especially as it relates to him being a potential double agent."

Simon's glittering blue eyes meet mine in a moment of rare understanding, and I'm grateful, for what might be the first time in my life, that FBI agents don't have to be spoon-fed the details. It's no accident that I chose my father's hotel room as the location of our tête-à-tête today, and Simon knows it. As Grant was all too quick to point out when I first told him about Tara being in town, neither friend nor foe nor FBI mole can get inside this room without my father knowing about it. It's the only truly secure place in the city, the only place a man—or woman—can feel free to talk without fear of being overheard.

Simon wouldn't have been willing to speak to me under any other circumstances. But now that we're both here...

He holds my gaze for another long moment before releasing all of his anxious, uneasy energy in a long breath. He even leans back against the seat, his tight-pinched nostrils taking on a normal human shape for once.

"I guess you're better than nothing," he decides. "How much do you know?"

"Very little, unfortunately. Despite your fears to the contrary, Grant doesn't come home every night and tell me all the FBI's secrets. Getting information out of him is like pulling a falcon's teeth—and yes, I'm aware that birds don't have teeth. That's why my metaphor works."

"No." His face is perfectly grave. "It still doesn't work."

That Simon. Always a barrel of laughs.

"All I know is that after I told Grant about Tara being back in New York and about how she and Agent Leon seem to be on a first-name basis, he reacted like I'd punched him in the face," I say. "Then, yesterday…"

I stop, unsure how to frame this next part. Simon and Grant are best friends, and I'm sure they have some kind of bro-camaraderie in which conversations about our life together take place, but I like to think our marital problems aren't part of them.

He doesn't need to know that Grant backed me into a corner or that I spent the better part of last night figuring out how to wriggle my way out of it. After all, I may not be a great wife, but I *am* good at extricating myself from tight spots. My husband wants me to promise to lead a clean, happy existence for the rest of our days together. In exchange, I get one last opportunity to be an active part of his life.

At first glance, it looks like a bad deal—a *terrible* deal—trading one moment of glory for a lifetime of the opposite. I'd have to be a fool to take it. But there's more at stake here than the state of my fingernails, I'm sure of it.

I just need to find out what.

"Yesterday…" Simon prods.

"So I came up with this plan for going undercover

with my grandmother, right?" I say, leaning forward with an eagerness that takes him aback. "It's not much, but she's going to show me around, take me to parties— the normal society stuff she's done her whole life, only this time, she's doing it with her favorite granddaughter in tow. It'll allow me to keep an eye on things from the inside without drawing anyone's suspicions."

Simon nods as if that makes perfect sense, and I have to prevent myself from swelling in triumph. I *knew* it was a good idea.

"But when I mentioned the plan to Grant, he freaked out. He told me it's not safe because Christopher wants to cut me up and store the pieces of my body in his freezer—or, you know, something along those lines. I'm paraphrasing."

He nods again, and a frisson of alarm moves through me. *Wait*—that's a real possibility?

"Leon has always shown an unhealthy amount of interest in you," Simon says. "You and Grant both."

"What? So there really is a crazed, rogue FBI agent out for my blood? Why has no one mentioned this before?"

"Oh, calm down," he says with an air of disgust. "I'm sure you're not in any real danger. If that were the case, Grant would pack you up and ship you out at the first opportunity."

I swallow heavily. He would certainly try.

"And if anything, it's Grant who's in trouble, not you. I never had many personal dealings with Leon, and I was moved off the Peep-Toe Prowler case early on, but something about that guy doesn't fit."

"He was nice to me," I venture optimistically.

Simon quells that optimism with a glance at the

envelope in his hand. "Most people are, when they want something."

I can't argue with that. "So what does he want?"

"Your contacts? Leverage over Grant? Who knows?" He shrugs. "I won't go so far as to call him a double agent, but I can say for sure that Leon attempted— unsuccessfully—to get access to you when Grant first started investigating your father. From the looks of it, he's attempting the same thing now. He's a brave soul for trying, I'll give him that much. I can't imagine you're worth that much trouble."

"Maybe he has a crush on me."

The scorn with which Simon refuses to answer that says it all. "Look, I wish I could be more help, but my hands are tied by bureaucracy. I've already been reprimanded for fighting the reassignment, and I've been warned against trying again. Pushing too hard now could end up hurting Grant more than it helps him."

"So that's it? You're going to let him move forward with this on his own?"

He releases a sound that's a borderline snort. "If I were capable of stopping Grant once he gets an idea in his head, you and I wouldn't be sitting here."

There's no mistaking his meaning. If Simon were capable of stopping Grant once he gets an idea in his head, I would have been removed from the picture—and Grant's life—years ago.

There's a finality to that truth that clatters hard in my chest. I've never made any secret of the fact that I don't care for Simon's stringent personality, but I've always felt confident knowing he'll protect Grant in the field— even if it means doing so with his life. But he couldn't protect Grant from me, and he can't protect him from Christopher Leon.

We bad guys can't be trusted. There's no telling to what depths we'll plunge to get our way.

My heart sinks. "How much danger is he in?"

Simon doesn't have to ask what I mean. "Some. Enough. More than I care for. When it comes to finding answers, you know how little he cares for his personal safety."

"And there's really nothing you can do?"

"Officially? No. It's out of my jurisdiction. But if you want my opinion, the sooner this case is wrapped up and Leon moves on, the better it will be for all of us. If history has proven anything, it's that Grant won't take Leon's interference lying down."

I believe him. Grant's tenacity is a thing to be feared and admired. Witness the lengths he's willing to go to reform his criminally minded wife.

"As much as I hate to say this, you and your friends might be the best chance we have of settling things quickly. You have access we don't—both legal and illegal." Simon shudders, as if even saying the word *illegal* causes him pain. "Do your thing, Blue, and do it fast."

Any thrill I might have felt at being imbued with such responsibility—especially from Simon—is cut short by his next words.

"Oh, and one more thing?"

It's almost too much to bear. What's next? An offer to crown me queen?

"If there's anything I can do to help—unofficially, I mean—all you have to do is ask."

GRANT

"TELL ME HE'S A KNOWN TERRORIST. TELL ME HE'S ROBBED six banks. Give me anything I can use to get that man out of my life for good."

The empty café where Mariah waits for me isn't one I normally frequent, but I drop into the seat opposite her knowing full well not to order coffee. The brew they serve here tastes like black tar steeped in horse shit. Most of New York knows it and avoids the place accordingly.

In other words, it's a great place for a clandestine meeting between friends.

"Hello to you too, Emerson. I see you're feeling particularly vengeful this morning. Bad night?"

She has no idea. It's not every evening you spend bargaining for your future with the love of your life. "Let's say it was interesting."

"I like interesting things."

"So do I," I say, not falling for it. I *like* Mariah, would even call her my friend, but I'm not about to explain the subtle nuances of my marriage to her. Some things are best kept between spouses—especially when those things involve blackmail and life-or-death ultimatums. Or, as we call it, a regular Tuesday. "What do you have for me on Leon?"

"You're no fun, you know that?" she grumbles. She turns her attention to the laptop screen in front of her. "Most agents who ask me for risky and highly illegal favors give me at least a little entertainment in exchange. I don't leave the office very often. If I want to live at all, I have to do it vicariously."

"You're out of the office now, aren't you?"

"Only because I didn't want anyone to hear your screams when I show you what I found."

It's preamble enough for the both of us, and she angles the screen so I can see what she's pulled up. It's not, as I expect, the most up-to-date record of events. The words on the scanned article are almost impossible to read, a newspaper story that was poorly printed to begin with.

"Is that Leon?" I lean forward, doing my best to make out the picture at the top, which looks to be around a dozen years old. In it, a grainy youth hangs his head, his arms behind his back in a telltale gesture of defeat. "Is that Leon...getting arrested?"

"Sure is, boss man. And for armed robbery, no less."

Holy shit. I lean closer, but proximity doesn't change the facts.

Armed robbery is big—it's something not even Penelope and her friends can lay claim to. It's also something I rarely deal with, as most of my criminals use brains rather than brawn to achieve their ends. Even in my wife's heyday, she never used anything more dangerous than a lighter and whatever chemicals Jordan happened to be carrying in her purse at the time.

"I don't understand. It took you all of twenty-four hours to uncover this information. How can the FBI not know?"

"What makes you think they don't? It wouldn't be the first time they overlooked a few criminal details in the name of justice."

She doesn't have to say the rest—that she's a prime example of a record being expunged by the powers that be, that my own marriage skirts the line of *reasonable personal risk*. The longer I work for this organization, the more I'm coming to learn that we all have something to hide—and the things we hide might be what make us so valuable.

"Fuck, fuck, fuck," I mutter. "I knew there was a reason I didn't like that guy."

"And here I thought you were jealous because he's better looking than you."

I casually flip Mariah off, but my insides aren't so dismissive. I couldn't give a rat's ass whether or not Christopher Leon is the world's most handsome man— but whether or not he's the world's most *dangerous* man is particularly relevant. Especially since I may have willingly sicced my wife on him.

"How much time did he serve?" I ask.

"Uh..." She scans her screen. "It looks like a hundred hours of community service. He was only seventeen at the time, and he pled out, so he was never officially charged. The two guys who were with him got five years each."

"Of course they did. Was he the one who turned them in?"

Mariah nods with a wince. I don't know why she feels bad about it. It's all too easy to picture a fresh-faced Christopher Leon smiling as he sent two men to do the time for a crime he committed.

"So what else did he do?" I ask. "Skin animals? Throw rocks at toddlers on the playground? On a scale of one to serial killer, how bad is he?"

"A negative three? Sorry, Emerson—that one brush with the law is all he's got. From there, his record is nothing but awards and accolades and ass-kissing of a magnitude I've never seen before."

"Tease."

"I don't create the facts. I find them."

"So that's the whole story? He was a little shit of a kid who made a mistake, turned his friends in, and became one of the good guys to make up for it?" I shake my head. "No, that doesn't fit." It doesn't explain why he's acting so suspiciously toward me—*toward Penelope*—now.

"Don't lose heart. There's an interesting pattern to his behavior you might want to take a look at."

"You *are* a tease!" I push my chair closer to hers. "What'd you find?"

"The police never recovered the jewelry he and his friends took. Don't get too excited—it wasn't anything noteworthy, just some necklaces and rings worth around ten grand—but if there's a plea bargain involved, it usually means the items are returned." She pulls up another screen, this one showcasing two columns of addresses. "I thought that was strange, especially since he and his mom moved into a pretty nice apartment after that."

I sit up. "How nice?"

"Nicer than a waitress and a juvenile delinquent can usually afford. About ten thousand dollars nicer, if you ask me. And there's no father listed on his birth certificate, so I'm guessing it's not delayed child support kicking in."

I sit up even straighter. The tale of a low-income woman raising a son on her own isn't foreign to me, nor does it lower Christopher in my eyes. If anything, it brings him up a few pegs. My own mother worked countless double nursing shifts to make sure my childhood wasn't lacking. From the day my dad walked out on us, she became everything to me—mother, father, financier, friend. Our home had also been a modest one, more comfortable than grand.

Of course, I was always up front about that fact. And I didn't wave a gun at innocent people when things got tough.

I think about the suits Christopher wears, the names he drops, the car of my adolescent dreams he's driving around town as we speak, and say, "Well, that's interesting. He's always made it seem like he comes from money."

"I'm starting to wonder if that's only what he *wants* us to think." Mariah scrolls down, pointing out the similarities between the two columns. "Look here. The addresses on the left are all the places he lived over the next two years until he went to college—without a scholarship or loan package, I might add. The man paid cash for an Ivy League education. The addresses on the right are unsolved home invasion cases over the same period of time. Notice anything interesting?"

I do. Not one of the addresses is situated more than a few miles away from the other; most share a zip code. It's hardly enough to convict a man, but if that map hanging on my office wall means anything, it's that proximity and opportunity are usually related.

"So we think he made his journey up the Bureau ladder the easy way?" I'd always assumed his personal connections were the cause, but there are a few of our good leaders I can imagine being open to a friendly bribe. Considering how bad Christopher is at his job, it would make sense if he greased the way with stolen money.

"If you call a life of crime easy, sure." Mariah's tone indicates that she disagrees, but that's an argument for another day. "It might even explain why he entered law enforcement in the first place. Getting away with theft is a hell of a lot easier when you lead the investigation yourself."

And there it is. The clincher. Everything I need to convince me that I'm on the right path, that Christopher Leon *is* the Peep-Toe Prowler, despite the fact that he wears size eleven wingtips. He's got access and information to pull off the jobs in the first place, resources and connections to cover up his tracks afterward. It would even explain why he's so sloppy at the crime scenes—he's purposely confusing the evidence.

But… "All right, if we go with that theory, it doesn't explain why he wants Penelope to be involved," I say, brow furrowed. "Unless he's stuck and wants her help, but she would never do that."

"No?" Again, Mariah's tone is less than conciliatory,

but I ignore her. Not because my wife is fully reformed—far from it—but because she would never lower herself to be someone else's sidekick. Christopher might need her, but she definitely doesn't need him.

"Of course, *he* might not know she's unwilling," Mariah muses. "Or he might have other plans for her, like needing another close friend to take the fall."

I push my chair out with a start, heart leaden. "Fuck me."

"No, thanks. You're not my type."

I kick the leg of Mariah's chair, but it does little to alleviate my feelings. I'd need to smash about fifty such chairs to do that. "It wasn't an offer. It was an observation. That's not a bad theory—it fits almost everything."

She makes a slight bow from her seated position. "Thank you. I'll be here all week."

"Do you happen to know what other cases he's worked since he started at the FBI?"

"No, but I could find out for you. Why?"

Because if Mariah is right about Christopher—if *I'm* right about Christopher—then I may have stumbled onto something huge. A powerful man who takes what he wants, when he wants it, and then sets up other criminals to do the time for him. No one is in a better position to pull that off than a federal agent, a man whose crime spree has gone unchecked for years, a man who's growing bolder and braver with each passing success.

Like I said before—he's nothing more than a toddler pushing his boundaries.

Too bad *this* boundary has every intention of pushing back. I told him before that he'd put Penelope behind bars over my dead body, but that wasn't wholly accurate.

If he's trying to pin these thefts on my wife, it's not *my* death he should be worried about.

It's his.

"Just get me a list and case details," I say. Since my voice is hard enough to scare the café waitress into hurrying back behind the counter, I amend it with, "Please. If that's something you can do."

"I can pull that up in my sleep. Next time, you should try and get me a real challenge."

"I'll see what I can do. And Ying?"

"Yeah?"

"Don't mention this to anyone, okay? No need to start blowing smoke before we're sure there's a fire."

"Sure thing, boss." She sends me off with a wink. "But what are you going to do if the flame catches?"

That's easy. I'm going to burn this whole operation down.

"I put you in an untenable position."

My wife looks at me through perfectly round, accusing eyes. "Yes, you did."

"It was wrong of me, and I admit that."

"That's very big of you, thanks."

Her words are conciliating to the extreme. From the moment I got home, full of apologies and regrets about the deal I offered her yesterday, she's been nothing but gracious in her acceptance of them.

The brat. She's always been a terrible liar. Those perfectly round, accusing eyes are a dead giveaway.

"Then you'll forget everything, and we can go back to normal?" I ask. It's a long shot, but I have to make the attempt. Now that I have a real idea about what Christopher Leon is up to, the risk of letting Penelope play investigator is too high. He's been waiting for his chance to get her involved, and I practically handed her over on a silver platter. "We can pretend it never happened?"

She blinks at me, her face a beautiful mask of innocence and devilry. It's the exact look that got us where we are today, the look that captures everything I adore about this woman.

"Not on your life, Grant dear. I've done some hard thinking, and I'd like to formally accept your offer."

I groan. Of course she would.

"I *am* going to keep investigating the Peep-Toe Prowler by whatever means necessary, and there's nothing you can do to stop me." Her eyes meet mine in a clear challenge, and I'll be damned if that challenge doesn't spike straight to my groin. "I'm not afraid of Christopher Leon—and even more importantly, I'm not afraid of you."

"I know you aren't. You never have been. It's the best and the worst thing about you." In case she takes this as a compliment, I add, "Mostly the worst."

She flashes a smile at me, and I recognize it at once—it's that bright, brilliant smile of old, the smile I wasn't sure I'd ever see again. I'm unprepared for how strongly the sight of it affects me, like a cannonball shot into my chest.

This woman, I think, *will someday be the death of me*.

If I'm lucky. If she lets me. If she doesn't come to the same realization I have—that this staid, ordinary life we share is all I have to offer—and runs away as fast as her feet will take her.

"You should know that I have reason to believe Christopher Leon is using the FBI as a cover for his own crime ring," I say in the absence of more appropriate sentiment. "He has a history of armed robbery and turning on his accomplices so they take the fall in his place. I think that's why he's been so interested in us, why the Peep-Toe thefts are so similar to yours." I give her the details.

Penelope's eyes widen in a combination of excitement and alarm, and I know she understands. All the things I want to say, all the things I can't—she apprehends them as easily as if I'd said them all aloud.

"He wants to set me up?" She throws herself onto the couch and waits until I settle into my favorite armchair before continuing. "That's why he's being so nice and making all these overtures? To get me on his side?"

"That's my theory, yes. He's pretending he wants to set you up as a consultant for the case so you're directly involved. He also wanted to get his hands on you years ago, back when I was starting the investigation on you and your dad, but he couldn't get the access he needed."

"Why's that?"

I set my jaw. "Because I wouldn't let him."

Her lips turn up in a gentle smile. "Aw. Agent Emerson. Always my guard dog."

"Yeah, well." I take a deep breath in an attempt to balance myself. When she looks at me like that, mocking me with her nicknames and insinuations, it's all I can do not to pick her up and haul her off to the bedroom. "Either he's getting desperate, or he's come up with a new plan to involve you, because he's even more determined this time around."

"So that's it, then." She speaks with the finality I've come to know and fear. "I have to accept his offer. There's no better way to find out what he's up to than to get as close as possible."

"No."

"But you said—"

"No."

"We could set up a trap—"

"No." I'm prepared to sit here and continue my flat denial for hours, but I realize her request to be involved includes more give-and-take than that. And I want her to be involved—I do. In this and in everything. "I know it's not what you want to hear, but the less you have to do with that man, the better. Until we know for sure what his plan involving you is, we can't counteract it."

She opens her mouth to argue, but I forestall her.

"I think your plan to spend more time with your grandmother is a good one. You'll be able to see if Christopher shows up anywhere he's not supposed to, ask around if anyone can recall seeing him at any of the parties where jewels went missing. I can't take my suspicions to the FBI yet, which means having you work undercover is the most ideal course of action."

She nods. "Okay. I can accept that. I don't like it, but I can accept it."

The amount of relief I feel equals the size of a mountain. "And you can also keep feeling Tara out, if you want. I have a few guys keeping an eye on her movements, but she's not easy to track, since they lose eyes every time she goes into the hotel. Your extra surveillance will help."

She bolts upright in her seat, eyes wide. "Oh, no! Tara."

"She spent a few hours this morning getting her hair and nails done at a Gramercy salon, according to Paulie," I offer. I don't add the colorful list of adjectives Paulie used to describe how she looked when she finally emerged. He always did have a thing for the high-maintenance ones.

"No, I mean *Tara*. Knowing Christopher. Working with Christopher."

"Yeah, we already suspected that. That's why we're watching her."

"But what if *she's* his backup plan?" Penelope asks. She makes a grunt of irritation when I don't immediately respond. "Last year, when you tried to get me to steal the necklace out of our safe and I didn't take the bait, what did you do?"

"I used Tara," I say, realization settling in. "She was my backup plan."

"Exactly!" Her triumph is a beautiful thing, flushing her with color and energy. "If they're working together, it can only be because Christopher is planning on making her take the fall if I don't pan out. He's using her."

"Huh. You might be on to something. That would fit the narrative."

"Oh, geez. Do you want to be the one to warn her, or should I go do it?"

I struggle to keep a laugh from springing to my lips. The reluctance in my wife's voice isn't hard to miss. "I'm sure Tara's fine. She's not a woman to get caught unaware."

"I know, but she could be in trouble."

"No offense to your stepmother, but I'd much rather Leon pin it on her than you. And so, I might add, would you. Just yesterday, you wanted me to arrest her on any pretext I could find."

"Yes, but that's when I thought it was *fair*."

I can't help it—the laugh escapes. I doubt I'll ever be able to fully understand the moral code under which my wife operates, but the one thing I can count on is that her own convoluted sense of right and wrong will always come out on top.

"I'll have my guys step up their surveillance," I promise. "And don't forget she also has your dad looking out for her. She's not without protection. The best thing we can do for her is find a way to get the evidence we need on Leon."

"She doesn't have my dad."

"I beg your pardon?"

Penelope looks up at me, nose wrinkled. "She doesn't have my dad. I don't think they're together—at least, not in a Biblical way. They're just friends. He doesn't feel that way about her anymore."

Knowing what I do about sexy jewel thieves and the men who marry them, I very much doubt it, but I don't say so. "Even if they aren't sleeping together, I promise he still cares enough to protect her. He always will."

"That's awfully sentimental of you."

"Yeah, well. I've got some experience in this area."

Her response to that bit of truth is to rub up against me like a cat, her lithe, compact body doing its best to make me forget everything else. For a woman whose job is predicated on sitting perfectly still for hours on end, she has a remarkable talent for constant movement. She slinks and slides and presses her breasts against me until I can't think of anything but how much I want to take them in hand.

As punishment—both mine and hers—I don't.

As proof that punishment—both mine and hers—is something I will never control, she yanks me by the belt buckle and grinds her hips against mine. I feel the sweet, unyielding pressure rocket through me.

"I'll stop by the hotel later to warn her anyway," she says, as though unaware of how much the touch of her body affects me. "I might not like her, but I know she'd do the same for me."

Ah, jewel thieves. Why did I ever think I could figure them out?

"So does this mean we have a deal?" A smile plays on her lips as she continues her full-bodied assault on my sanity. I find out why when she lowers her voice to a purr and adds, "Partner?"

"Yes, Penelope," I say, liking the sound of that word on her lips more than I thought I would. A partner implies longevity. A partner promises forever. The thought of losing her to Christopher's machinations causes a visceral reaction, but losing her in *any* capacity does that. "This means we have a deal."

The full implication of what I've done is borne on me when she jumps back, releasing a delighted squeal and clapping her hands. The coy temptress is gone as quickly as she came, replaced by the resilient, mischievous woman I first fell in love with.

Damn, but it feels good to see her again. I only wish it was *me* and not the promise of life-threatening danger that drew her out.

I groan. "What did I do in a past life to deserve you in this one?"

"You probably started a school for underprivileged

youth," she replies with a laugh. "No—a dozen schools for underprivileged youth. And an orphanage to match each one. I bet you even won a Nobel Peace Prize."

"Either that or I was a mass murderer."

"Yeah. That too." She grins. "Should we seal this thing with a kiss or a handshake?"

I reach for her. "Oh, I'm definitely picking the first one."

It's not the most official way for an FBI agent to contract with an independent investigator, but I don't care. It's how *this* FBI agent and *this* independent investigator are going to do things.

She tastes, as she almost always does, of cotton candy. I never know if it's her terrible diet that causes spun sugar to spout from her mouth, or if it's part of her bewitching charm, but kissing her is always a feast for my senses. If she'd let me, I'd hold her here and keep kissing her until she begged me for mercy. Each curve of her body is worthy of hours of exploration, and hours of exploration in her arms are exactly what I need right now.

But of course, Penelope refuses to play along. She *always* refuses to play along.

"Don't you dare try to keep me vertical right now," she says and grabs my tie. Wrapping it around her fist, she tugs until I can feel the choke hold around my neck. "We're taking this thing horizontal immediately."

"Or what?" I ask, my voice strained—and not because of the tie. "You'll strangle me?"

"It's what you deserve," she says and tugs again. This time, she brings my face level to hers and nips playfully at the side of my mouth. "No taking your time today, Grant Emerson. I need this to be fast and hard."

I don't bother asking why. For me, sex with Penelope has always been a transcendental experience; so much more than the fusing of two bodies, I like to think it's the fusing of two souls. Unfortunately, she doesn't see it the same way. For her, sex is more like a game—a power play that usually finds her coming out way ahead. In this, as in all things, she likes there to be a fight.

Which is fine in theory. Fighting this woman is easy. Fighting this woman is fun. *Winning* against her? That's a different story.

"Fast and hard, huh?" I ask.

"Unless you think you can't handle it?" she asks archly. "I wouldn't want to force you to do anything you're not capable of."

"Brat," I growl and close the distance between us.

Fast and hard isn't a challenge where this woman is concerned, not by a long shot. If I gave in to my baser instincts, fast and hard is the only way we'd ever make love. It's so easy for me to push her to the couch, catching her *whoosh* of surprise with my mouth. It's even easier for me to bypass her black miniskirt to slip my hand between her soft, parted legs.

Penelope's legs have always been one of my favorite parts of her, mostly because I know what they're capable of. Their feats of endurance and flexibility are second only to how they feel under my hands.

Still, I move quickly over the silken skin, feeling her quiver as I reach the eager heat at the apex of her thighs. Her excitement is no surprise, nor is the way I react to it. If, at any point in our relationship, she'd shown the least reluctance to welcome me into her arms or into her bed, our story might have had a different ending. Fortunately, she's always been consistent in this regard. I might not know what's going on inside her head or heart, but her body has always been an open book. She wants me.

She wants me fast, and she wants me hard.

And I, weak bastard that I am, give her exactly that.

We don't bother removing all our clothes. There's no need. All it takes is a bit of kissing and a tilt of her hips before we're both primed and ready.

There is no finesse. I don't get to run my tongue and teeth over her body or finger the supple rise of her breasts. The way she arches against me demands that I thrust inside her without affection or regard.

I do, but I can't help feeling both affection and regard. With this woman, there always will be. I pause at the entrance to her body, gazing down at her flushed skin, at the frustration of her lip sucked up and chewed between her teeth, and tell her how much I love her—the best way I know how.

"I don't know what I'm going to do with you, Penelope Blue," I say, my breathing hard. "Just when I think I've got the upper hand, you turn everything upside down."

"I'm going to turn *you* upside down if you don't hurry up," she retorts.

"Now that's something I'd like to see," I say.

The tussle lasts for all of five seconds. She's pinned underneath me on the couch, her clothes so wound up and askew, they bind her limbs. I outweigh her by at least seventy pounds, and my arms are braced on either side of her head. In no way, shape, or form should she win this match.

But she smiles up at me, a calculating gleam in her

eyes. I'm so distracted by how beautiful she looks like that, her lips swollen and her game face on, that I don't notice her hands snaking down between us. A thief's hands always move faster than you'd expect.

Her grip on my hard length is both sudden and excruciating. It's not a *painful* excruciation, though. This is the opposite of that; it's pleasure in its purest form, a woman who knows how to drive a man to distraction with a few expert flicks of her wrist.

There's no pretending I'm in charge anymore. While I'm busy trying to keep myself from losing control, she manages to wriggle out from beneath me. She pushes me to my back and climbs astride, pausing only long enough to fit our bodies neatly together.

"You cheated," I say, but I can't find it in me to care.

"I always do," she says and begins moving again. "I always will."

In true Penelope Blue fashion, her movements are not simple ones. She squirms and undulates and holds nothing back. No matter what task she takes it upon herself to do, she's always like that—dedicated and uninhibited. It's one of the things I love most about her. The sky could fall around us, but still, she'd sit astride and scream my name, refusing to acknowledge anything until she's damn well good and ready.

The waves of her pleasure tug at me with their familiar insistent pull. The result is a rushed but powerful orgasm, the shudder of our release difficult to hear over the pounding of blood in my ears.

I'd like to do more to her—so much more, and for so much longer—but I know better than to push my luck. Especially since we stay on the couch, horizontal together, until the sun starts to set outside. We don't talk, but her head nestles perfectly in the crook of my neck, our limbs intertwined and our hearts beating in sync in a rare moment of unity. With each gentle stroke of my fingers down her spine, I can't help but recite the same two sentences over and over in my head.

She's my wife. She's my partner.

And for now, she's safe in my arms.

THE
BLUEPRINTS

THE FIRST THING I DO AS A SECRET OPERATIVE OF THE FBI
is tell my friends about it.

"Riker?"

I open the front door to his apartment without preamble or even a polite knock—a force of habit. Riker took
over the apartment that was mine when I got married, so
it's second nature to walk right in. I sometimes forget
I don't live here anymore, that I'm not the string-free
jewel thief of years past.

I pause on the threshold, adjusting myself to Riker's
shiny black furniture and glossy stolen electronics—to
a life that feels unfamiliar—before speaking.

"Guess what happened to me last night?" I ask.
"You'll never get it right, but I want you to try anyway."

"You were abducted by aliens, and now you have
to relive the same day over and over again for the rest
of your life." Even though Riker is sitting on one of
the aforementioned black couches, he shrugs out of his

leather jacket and tosses it on the coffee table, almost as if he's just arrived home. "In fact, this is the fiftieth time we've had this conversation."

"Close. Try again."

"Um... You've decided to go to college to become a marine biologist."

"What? That's less realistic than the alien one. I don't even have a high school diploma." I flop onto the seat next to him, the cushion deflating underneath me with a squeak. Shiny black furniture is rarely as comfortable as it looks. "Think more along the lines of my actual skill set."

"You're tired of playing investigator and have decided to leave the poor Peep-Toe Prowler alone so she can get some actual work done."

With a suddenly stiffened spine, I turn my attention to the voice emanating from the kitchen. I suppose I should be grateful that Tara and Riker have their clothes on, but the fact that she has an apron over her skintight dress and a mixing bowl under one arm is just as bad.

Sex with Tara is something I understand. I don't condone it, but I understand it. The domestic arts? I smell something funny...and I don't mean the delicious scent of cinnamon wafting from her direction. She never used to bake for *me* like that.

"Goddammit, Tara. What are you doing here?" I ask.

She gives a half shrug, causing the strap of her dress to fall over one shoulder in a move clearly calculated to get Riker's attention. It does, too. "Same as you. Hanging out, killing time. Was my guess close?"

"Not remotely. I've almost got this thing solved already."

It's a lie, obviously, and not a very good one, but it's the only thing I can come up with on such short notice.

"You might show more concern, you know," I add. "If I so much as see you sniffing around where you shouldn't be, I'll hand you over to the authorities so fast, you won't be able to pack a clean pair of underwear. And I doubt your new friend *Chris* will bail you out. He wants to see you behind bars just as much as I do. Don't be surprised if he tries framing you for the whole thing. Grant says that's probably been his plan from the start."

That piece of news doesn't cause so much as a blink. "Uh-oh. Turning tattletale on us?"

"Of course not. Things are more complicated than that."

I don't mention *how* complicated things are or what promises have been made in the name of duty, but that's more out of a sense of self-preservation than strategy. A good criminal never thinks too hard about her future. Therein only lies heartbreak.

"Does this mean your grandmother took the bait?" Tara asks. "Did you make it into the upper echelons?"

"Not that I should be telling you anything, but yes. I'm in."

"Good for you."

"But not so good for you, huh?"

"Oh, I'm not worried. I'm a big girl. I can take care of myself."

Riker apparently disagrees, because he coughs and inserts himself between us—linguistically speaking, that is. "Pen, you know Tara has nothing to do with those thefts, right?"

"I'm not ruling anything out."

"Well, you should. You're being stupid."

One of us is being stupid, but it's not me. Like it or not, Tara is tangled up in this mess somehow. I'm not saying she's *for sure* the Peep-Toe Prowler, but I'm not saying she didn't do it, either. Her presence in New York is too coincidental, her insistence on popping up everywhere I go too convenient. As our history together attests, she loves toying with me like that.

I turn to my stepmother with a forced smile. "Tara, could you give us a second?"

"Sure thing. Take as many seconds as you need." With a wave of her spoon, she disappears into the relative seclusion of the kitchen. It's not the most discreet distance, but it's not as if I'm going to say anything I wouldn't willingly—gleefully, even—say to her face.

Still, I drop my voice to a near whisper. "What's the matter with you lately? Why are you on her side?"

"I'm not on her side."

"It looks an awful lot like her side from where I'm sitting. Did you forget that she's a suspect in a federal case—and a primary one, too? If you look out the window, you'll probably see the detail of men Grant has watching her."

Riker snorts. "Oh, don't worry. She says she lost them hours ago. They think she's shopping for yachts."

"What?" I go to the window in hopes of catching sight of a dark suit or pair of binoculars pointed our way, but there's nothing besides the usual neighborhood riffraff selling drugs and scraping registration numbers off bicycles. "Crap! I thought they were supposed to be trained for this sort of thing."

"And I thought *I* was the one keeping an eye on her."

"You can't watch her all the time," I retort. Based on the cozy domestic scene I entered, it seems more of a possibility than I would have thought yesterday, but even Riker has to sleep sometimes. "Besides, opening your home to her is hardly a good idea. In case you've forgotten, she's the enemy. The idea is to get her to move on, not move in."

"Maybe I don't want her to move on."

I turn away from the window. "I'm sorry, could you repeat that? I thought I heard you say you *want* her to stick around."

He shrugs. "Would it be so terrible? I've been doing everything you asked me—hanging out with her, following her around, making nice. She's not bad, once you get to know her. Did you know she speaks fluent French?"

"Knowing all the dirty words does not make her fluent."

He ignores me. "And I haven't seen or heard her do anything that would indicate she's on a million-dollar crime spree."

"Well, obviously. Because she knows you're watching her. That's what she *wants* you to believe."

Riker doesn't respond right away, and that's when I know we're in trouble. No matter what life has thrown at the two of us, Riker has *always* had something to say. He lectures and argues and keeps going until the last word is his.

My heart sinks. This new responsible independence of his isn't just a fluke. Something about him really *is* changing—and if Tara's involved, it's not for the better.

"We used to joke about her being a black widow for a reason," I say, almost pleading. "She uses people for her own benefit and then walks away. She did it when I was fifteen and had no one else in the whole world to turn to. She did it again six months ago when my dad came back. Be careful not to eat anything she cooks, or you might wake up the next day in a bathtub full of ice with your kidneys missing. How do you say *dialysis* in French?"

Riker's only answer is a glower.

I assume this means our conversation is over. My intention in coming over today was to get an update and see if he had any ideas about how to utilize my time with my grandmother, but if he's fallen under Tara's top-heavy spell, he won't be a reliable source. Once again, it's starting to look like I'm on my own.

That's when I notice the piece of paper rolled out on the coffee table, hastily covered by the sliding corner of Riker's signature leather jacket.

Without giving him a chance to intervene, I push his jacket away. The slump of fabric hitting the floor seems much louder than it should be, but that's probably because my attention has reached superhero levels of concentration.

That's not just any piece of paper. Those are blueprints. Those are blueprints that look awfully similar to the ones he tried to hide from me once before, the ones Jordan assured me were being used solely for bait.

"Riker, no."

"I can explain—"

"Does Jordan know you have those?"

"She's the one who gave them to me, but—"

"What? She did? Does she know you're sharing them with Tara?"

"The only person she made me promise not to show them to is you, so—"

I turn away before he can finish. My friends and I share a complicated relationship, especially now that I'm retired, and I know Riker hinted that they needed a replacement for me when he was buttering Tara up to rummage around in her purse. But they'd never actually take on someone like her.

Would they?

I grab the blueprints from Riker and roll them up, tucking them securely under one arm. I can think of only one reason they'd resort to such extreme measures as allying themselves with Tara Lewis.

"Okay, spill," I say. "How much do you need?"

Riker sets his jaw.

"And you might as well tell me the full amount. There's no use asking for half and trying to recoup your own losses on a sure thing. It always costs more that way."

He has the audacity to look affronted. "I don't want your stupid money."

"It's technically your stupid money as much as it is mine. I saved it from my pre-Grant days."

"I don't want your stupid money," he repeats.

"Fine. Then plan the heist with Jordan and Oz. Plan fifty heists with Jordan and Oz. I couldn't care less. Just don't…"

The rest lodges in my throat, oddly sharp.

Like the true friend he is, Riker sees it. And like the true friend he'll always be, he calls me on it. "Don't what, Pen?"

Don't replace me with her. Losing one man and ten

years of my life to that woman's greed was enough. I don't think I can go through that kind of pain again.

But all I say is, "Don't suffer in silence. I know you don't like talking about your gambling problem, and we don't have to after this, but I want you to know that everything I have is yours. It always has been. Grant doesn't know about the money, so if you need it…"

"For the last time, I don't need it."

"Okay, but at least let me tell you where it's hidden."

His jaw ticks angrily. "Would you listen for once in your stupid, stubborn life? I'm *fine*, Pen. Stop worrying so much about me, and take care of your own shit for a change. I promise—of the two of us, you're much more miserable. Just look at you. You can't even be in the same room as your stepmother without having an emotional breakdown."

The blueprints crunch under my arm. I am *not* having an emotional breakdown over Tara. I'm having one because in Riker's eyes, Tara and I are interchangeable, even though the woman has all the trustworthiness of a snake. Twelve years of solidarity mean less to him than one stupid jewelry heist—a heist he wouldn't even need if he'd just take the money I'm offering.

"I'm not miserable," I say through gritted teeth, but his look of disbelief speaks volumes. "I'm *not*. I'm just going through a transition period, that's all."

Tara's reappearance in the living room stops Riker from responding. Even though she's the last person I want to see right now, I can't help but be grateful for the interruption. It was inevitable anyway. She probably noticed the heat of drama and was drawn to it like a moth to a bonfire.

When she speaks, though, it has nothing to do with

our argument. "I've been thinking about your plans with your grandmother, Pen, and I'd like to help."

Riker and I turn to goggle at her.

"I don't know how much time you've spent in that sort of company before, but there's no way you'll pass for Erica Dupont's granddaughter."

"I don't need to pass for her granddaughter. I *am* her granddaughter."

"Not in that outfit, you're not. You look like a juvenile delinquent, not an upscale debutante."

I look down at my black leggings and oversized T-shirt with a frown. I thought I was looking rather cute today. Slouchy chic is all the rage.

"I wore a skirt to lunch the other day," I say in my defense. "I'm not totally without resources."

"What material was it?"

"The skirt? I don't know. Cotton?"

She shakes her head with a sigh that would have done my grandmother proud. "When's she staging the grand unveiling?"

"The day after tomorrow—but it's not that big of a deal. She's having a tea party at her house so I can meet a few of her friends. She said it would be casual."

"Yeah, *casual* as in don't wear your best ball gown. Second-best will be fine." She places her hands on my shoulders and gives me a contemplative whirl, ignoring the blueprints under my arm. "I wish you said something sooner. We don't have much time."

"Oh, sorry. Does my being on top of things get in the way of your plans?"

"Yes, actually. It does. I don't know what Grant is thinking, sending you in unpainted and untrained."

"He was probably thinking he *likes* the way I look."

"Either that, or he wants you to fail before you get started."

"Of course he doesn't—" I begin, but I stop myself short. *Damn*. That sounds like something he would do, the sneak. Call me his partner and smile his crinkly eyed smile. Screw me senseless then hold me in his arms for hours. He knows all the surefire tricks to lower my defenses.

Still, "I'm sure he's not that underhanded," I say loyally.

"All men are that underhanded. They can't help themselves." Tara's lips spread in a grin, not unlike a cartoon evil stepmother about to get her way. "But it's okay. Don't you worry your little head over it. I have just the thing."

I gulp. Nothing good can come of the patent joy on Tara's face.

"Penelope Blue, it's about time I introduced you to the wonders of cashmere."

"How good are you at reading blueprints?"

I walk through the door straight to the kitchen, a woman on a mission. It would be easy to let Tara's insinuations about Grant trying to sabotage me get in the way of our fledgling partnership, but I'm determined to uphold my end of the bargain we struck last night.

"I'm no architect, but I can tell an emergency exit from a window," Grant says. He looks up from the table, where a slew of papers are spread out in front of him. I assume it's work he's brought home, work he'd usually finish at the office away from my prying eyes. I slow my steps at the sight of it.

If this is his way of being open and honest with me, it's not a bad start. He's making sacrifices, showing his willingness to change. He's *trying*. So far, all I've done is warn Tara about Christopher's intentions—and even that didn't go as planned.

"Why?" he asks. "What do you have?"

"The plans for a jewelry store." I wait for him to move a few of his neat stacks aside before uncrinkling the stolen blueprints on the antique slab of wood that serves as our dining table. "I need you to tell me which one."

He glances up sharply. "Why?"

Because I need to stop my friends from making a terrible mistake, I think but don't say. Instead, I offer, "It doesn't have anything to do with the Peep-Toe case, if that's what you're worried about."

"Penelope… Where did these come from?"

I hold my hands up. "It doesn't matter. Just trust me, okay? No one is going to steal anything from it—you have my word."

He watches me carefully—looking, I know, for those oh-so-familiar signs of untruthfulness. But my breathing is even, and my eyes aren't the least bit dilated. No one *is* going to steal anything from this jewelry store—not Riker, not me, and certainly not Tara. The monkey in the middle is putting her foot down on this one.

"I need to figure out where it is, that's all. You can even put a detail on it if that'll make you feel better."

"When has a detail ever stopped you before?"

"Never." I give a wry grimace, thinking of Tara and

her lost FBI tail. You have to admire the woman's inno-
vation. "Pretty please? I tried looking them over myself,
but something doesn't make sense. It's not like any jewelry store I've seen."

"All right." He sighs. "Let's take a look."

It says a lot about Grant that he only wears his frown
for the first ten seconds. At ten and a half, his expression
fills with the little-boy excitement he always gets when
presented with a challenge. Our roles might be carefully
delineated—good and bad, lawman and outlaw—and I
respect that, but in another lifetime, he'd have made a
hell of a jewel thief.

The drawing is crude, a hastily scribbled reproduction
of real blueprints, lacking in identifying marks should it
fall into the wrong hands. It also has swirled notations
around most of the entry and exit areas, indecipherable
to anyone but my crew. The notations are a trade secret
of ours, which is why I know this thing is serious.

Bait, my ass. This may have started as an attempt
to help Riker out of his financial troubles, but they've
been working hard on this. There's real intention here,
real possibility. I'd be thrilled if I didn't feel like it was
cracking me in two.

Grant runs his finger along a few of the lines. "I
see what you mean. It's not like any jewelry store I've
seen, either."

"Right?" I lean over his shoulder to get a better look.
"It's too open in the center area, and there's a bathroom
on either side of the building—I'm guessing men's over
here and women's here. No jewelry store would separate
the restrooms that way. They'd want to keep an eye on
everyone coming and going."

"There's also this second floor." He taps the page. "Offhand, I know of three freestanding jewelry stores in the city with an upstairs, and it's not any of those. Are you sure it's local?"

"No, I'm not." It would make total sense for my friends to strike outside the tristate area, especially if they didn't want me to get wind of what was happening. In the past, we always stayed pretty close to home; a new operation might bring new geographical limits. "Isn't there a database or something you could run this through?"

"A mysterious blueprint identification database?" His breath comes out in a soft chuckle. "Unfortunately, no. We don't have one of those."

"You laugh, but if I were in charge of the FBI, that's the first thing I'd create. I'd get a whole team of blueprint experts. I'd head up the blueprint division."

"Actually, I *might* know someone..." He glances sideways at me. "How urgent is this?"

Not very, not when compared to all the other investigations I'm supposed to be working on, but I hold my hands up in a wide gesture anyway. I *need* these answers, even if I'm having a hard time articulating why.

To be fair, my friends and I never had a serious discussion about what the future would hold for us after Grant and I decided to make a real go of our marriage. Part of me has always known it would be difficult—I mean, my friends still have to earn a living, and *they're* not the ones who pledged themselves to an FBI agent—but I don't think I realized how difficult it would be. I can't help them without betraying Grant, and I can't betray them without betraying a part of myself.

I bite back a sigh. Maybe Jordan was right to hide these blueprints from me, keeping the glitter and lure as far away as possible. Plausible deniability might be the only chance I have.

"It's not a matter of life and death, if that's what you're asking. But it would really help me out."

"I'll need a few days, but you can consider it done." Grant rolls up the blueprints with a neat efficiency. "I have a hacker friend who might be able to help. She loves this type of thing."

I perk up. "A hacker friend? How come I've never met her before? I love hacker friends."

"Funny, that's exactly what she said about you. Except what she loves are thieving wives." Grant turns to me, his dark eyes glittering. "Speaking of, what *did* you get Cheryl for Christmas last year?"

THE TEA 18 PARTY

IN MY HEAD, TEA PARTIES HAVE ALWAYS EXISTED AS AN *Alice in Wonderland* affair, where everyone wears crazy hats as they sit around a long table, with saucers and cartoon mice flying. In reality, hats have been eschewed in favor of lustrous, fresh-from-the-salon locks, and no one seems to think a table is necessary at all. Instead, we're lounging inside a color-coordinated room poured directly out of a magazine, perched on the ends of chairs that look great but feel like they're made of concrete. My poor legs are bound so tightly together in the cream-colored pencil skirt Tara loaned me, you couldn't fit a dime up there. To top it all off, I have a teacup balanced in my lap and a smile plastered on my face.

In other words, I'm miserable. I'm miserable and out of place and have no one to blame but myself.

"I love the Adirondacks this time of year, but Vincent prefers the beach, so it's off to Martha's yet again," says a statuesque woman to my left. Her tendency to gesture with her hands while holding her cup makes me nervous. "It'll be the third time we've gone this year. I'm starting to loathe the sight of cedar shake."

"You could always come to Milan with me instead," the woman on my right replies. She's not nearly as statuesque, and she has to lean halfway over my lap to converse with her friend. "There's plenty of room on George's private jet."

"Don't tempt me. You know I can't leave Vincent alone for five minutes. Especially not at the beach."

I'm about to open my mouth and offer my opinion—that she should go wherever she wants, with or without Vincent—but a warning look from my grandmother stops me before I begin.

I flush guiltily and slump in my chair. I'd been prepared to be out of my element among these women, but this is above and beyond my worst expectations. I mean, I could probably purchase a vacation house in the Adirondacks and Martha's Vineyard *and* have money to spare, but that's not the point. No amount of stolen diamonds can buy class.

Fortunately for my dwindling sense of self-worth, a commotion at the door draws my attention. I'm hoping for a guest closer to my own age or someone's sullen teenage daughter I can commiserate with, but what I get is a familiar-looking woman with a smooth black bob and catlike eyes that set my heart racing.

"Oh, Jane. I'm so glad you could make it." My grandmother gestures for the woman to come in and make herself comfortable. "You know everyone here, I believe, with the exception of my granddaughter. Allow me to present you to Penelope. Penelope, this is Jane Bartlett."

An imploring look from my grandmother has me getting to my feet—no easy task in this skirt—and offering Jane my seat. As was the case at the lunch date last week, she stares at me much longer than politeness dictates. I *still* can't remember if she's a past victim or not, and since my last meeting with Riker ended with an argument and me confiscating his blueprints, I never had a chance to ask him.

"Um, you can sit here," I say, in case my gesture wasn't obvious enough.

"Thank you, but I wouldn't want you to give up your seat." She speaks kindly enough, but then she turns and stares at the nonstatuesque woman on my right. Without a word of communication between them, Jane somehow conveys a direct order for the woman to give up *her* seat instead, which she does with alacrity.

Oh, dear. I cover my racing pulse by attempting to sit with a semblance of grace. Jane is going to confront me right here in front of my grandmother. She's going to tell all these women that I stole her favorite necklace/watch/tiara/firstborn child, and I'll be out on my ass before I make any headway with the case.

"So what organizations do you belong to, Penelope?" Jane asks. She accepts a cup of tea and takes a drink, the smooth lines of her neck undulating as she swallows. My bobcat comparison suddenly feels off. This woman is much more like a jaguar with her shiny black hair and lean, muscled body.

"Organizations?" I echo, thinking fast. "Um, I think my husband signed us up for AAA, but I usually take the subway, so I've never had to use it."

The Adirondacks women release an uncomfortable titter, but Jane's lips lift in a genuine smile.

"No doubt the AAA will come in handy someday," she says, not unkindly. "But since we're supposed to be deciding which charity we want to benefit from the annual Black and White Ball, I wondered if there was any group near and dear to your heart you wanted to put on the short list."

Ah, yes. That makes more sense. It's also more difficult to answer, since my knowledge of global charities is limited. I probably *should* give my bus station locker full of cash to one of those instead of the Riker Has a Gambling Addiction Fund, but old habits die hard.

"Oh, you know—they're all so worthy." I wave my hand airily, hoping to emulate my grandmother's breezy elegance. But instead, I almost tip the contents of my cup all over my lap. Gulping down the rest of the tea seems like the best way to stay dry, so I do that before returning my attention to Jane. The liquid burns my esophagus and tastes like feet—two things I'm unable to hide from my face.

"I hate teas like this, too." Jane drops her voice and shoots me a laughing look that lifts the catlike corners of her eyes. Now that I'm seeing her at close range, I notice the effect is accomplished by a perfect sweep of eyeliner. "So much fuss, when all we really want is a tumbler of gin, yoga pants, and a dark room somewhere. But it's nice of you to play along for your grandmother's sake."

With the exception of the gin—I don't drink, having spent far too much of my wayward youth under the influence of stolen bottom-shelf alcohol—the rest of her plan sounds wonderful. Wearing yoga pants in total darkness is my idea of a fantastic time.

"I'm afraid I'm not living up to her expectations," I admit. "I'm supposed to make a good impression on her friends, not spill tea and expose my blue collar roots. She wanted to show me off."

"You're doing fine." She reaches over and takes my teacup, effortlessly setting it aside. "Besides, most of the women here have nothing to brag about when it comes to their offspring. See that woman in purple hogging all the cream cake?"

I do. It's Millie Ralph, the reason we're all here today. As my grandmother predicted, she's already made several trips to the restroom to try and peek around the house. I followed her the second time, as it occurred to me that a middle-aged snoop would make a wonderful Peep-Toe Prowler, but all she did was rummage through the medicine cabinet and steal some Vicodin. She left fingerprints everywhere, too.

"Her only son, Richard, is one of the wealthiest men in America," Jane continues in a low voice. "He's also a Madoff-level scam artist who would cry if a clown jumped out and said *boo*, so believe me when I say you have him beat."

"I don't know. If a clown jumped out at me, I might cry, too."

Her sudden laugh causes several of the other women to look up, and my grandmother beams at me as if I'd managed to entertain a particularly reluctant pope.

"I knew you and Penelope would get along," she says to Jane.

"She's delightful." Jane doesn't lower herself to wink, but the twinkle in her near-black eyes is close enough. "Although I don't see how she could be anything else."

"What are you two talking about?" my grandmother asks.

Jane answers for us both. "Clowns."

Millie, who had been holding court on the other side of the tea service tray, lights up. "Oh, how lovely. They were Richard's favorite — we always used to hire one for his birthday. He'd sob and sob when they left."

This proves too much for me, and I dissolve into a giggle that sounds more like a deranged hiccup. I'm afraid I'm going to have to exit the room to get control of myself, but Jane is every inch the lady I'm not, and she asks a few loud questions until my breathing resumes a normal pattern.

It's nice of her to do, which only casts me into further confusion. If she isn't a wronged victim out for my blood, then what does she want from me?

"To be honest, that isn't a terrible idea," my grandmother muses as soon as there's a lull in the conversation. "Of course, clowns themselves are awful, but circus animals... I don't think we've done an animal charity in a few years, have we?"

The woman seated next to her, poised with a pen and the only one treating this party as an actual business function, shakes her head. "We did service dogs back in '08, but nothing more recently than that."

"I like it." My grandmother nods, and as if attached on connected strings, all the heads around her start bobbing in tandem. "The fair treatment of performing animals. I'm sure there's a national group that would love to hear from us. Good job, Penelope."

I'm much more pleased by that small piece of praise than I should be. Of all the things I'm capable of, helping pick a charity is hardly up there in terms of complexity. I once stole a gold watch off a man *while he was wearing it*, for crying out loud. Yet here I am, as beaming and flustered as if I stole the crown jewels.

Talk turns to things like caterers and fire safety inspections for the ball, so there's not a lot for me to do after that. My attention—always short of social norms—starts to wander, and I find myself mentally appraising the jewels on display instead.

Rope chain necklace, solid gold, at least three thousand.

Drop earrings, pearl, probably only a few hundred each, and only if they're not freshwater.

Hideous peacock brooch, sapphire and—

"Of course, they're not going to let us access the collection on the night of the ball, but the Starbrite Necklace alone is worth a separate trip. Have you seen it yet?"

My head jerks back.

"No, but I've heard wonderful things. It's supposed to be one of the best examples of mid-century modern jewelry in the world."

My spine straightens.

"I heard them say it's worth at least ten million. The rest of the display is extraordinary, but can you imagine the size of those diamond spikes?"

My feet plant more firmly on the floor.

"I have to stop by the museum tomorrow to drop off the guest list. Maybe I'll take a look while I'm there."

"Um, what are you talking about?" I ask, trying not to sound as interested as I feel. *Diamond spikes* and *ten million dollars* happen to be two of my favorite things. "What museum?"

It's Jane who answers, which she does with a warm

smile in my direction. "The venue where we're holding the Black and White Ball this year," she says. "It's a lovely little space uptown. The Conrad Museum. Have you been?"

"No, but I love jewelry from the fifties." And from, you know, the forties. The thirties. The twenties. Any decade, really. I'm not picky.

"Oh, then you'd adore this collection."

She has no idea. "I bet I would."

Now that I've shown an interest in something relatable, the statuesque woman turns to me with a smile. I bite back a laugh—if I'd known a few diamonds were all it took to get these women to like me, I'd have opened with my highly educated opinion on carat weight versus cut. A hint: for resale value, always go for weight.

"I believe you can only see it by appointment right now, but I'm sure your grandmother could get you in," the statuesque woman says. "They've been rather tight with their security since…well, you know."

I don't know, but I can make an educated guess. "Since the Peep-Toe Prowler burglaries?"

A hush falls over the assembled crowd. Apparently, admitting my familiarity with the case is one of those faux pas my grandmother encouraged me to avoid.

"Based on my very slight understanding of what I've read in the newspapers," I backtrack. "Is it even peep-toes? Maybe they said stilettos."

The shocked looks dissipate only slightly, and it's up to Jane to come to my rescue once again.

"We don't like to talk too much about it," she says. "A few of the women here have lost some of their most valuable pieces. You understand."

"Oh, I'm so sorry. I didn't know."

For a moment, I think I've blown it. They can sense that my apology isn't heartfelt, that a large part of me isn't sorry at all, since each and every one of them probably had a hefty insurance policy to make up for their loss.

I mean, it's not like I think someone like Tara or Christopher *deserves* the jewelry any more than these women, but if you think about it, they probably did earn it. High-quality, seamless heists aren't easy to pull off. Most people don't realize how much legwork and planning go into stealing things of that magnitude.

"I'm sure you didn't." The statuesque woman smiles tightly at me. "The point is, we're very grateful to the Conrad Museum. They've been more than generous in allowing us to host the ball at their facility, all things considered."

I nod. Generous is one word to describe it. Anything that valuable on display is a security risk, no matter what. But right now? With a prowler on the loose and no sign of an arrest on the horizon? This Black and White Ball is practically an open invitation.

"I'd love to see that necklace," I say with complete honesty. "It sounds right up my alley."

My acceptance or nonacceptance in this crowd teeters for a moment, balanced as if on the edge of a diamond spike. I hold my breath, waiting to see which way I'll fall, when my grandmother intervenes with a request that everyone drink up their tea before it gets cold. The reminder of her existence—of her natural authority—is enough to secure my place for at least another day.

Cold sweat seems to have broken out on my upper

lip, so I use the distraction of a quick trip to the powder room to regain my composure. The woman staring back at me in the mirror is one I recognize well. Oh, she's dressed up in cream-colored cashmere, and her hair is pulled back in a loose and elegant braid, but there's no mistaking that greedy glint in her eye.

It's being around these jewels on display, all this talk of diamond collections, that does it. Riker's not the only one with a problem controlling his impulses.

"You will *not* think about stealing the Starbrite Necklace," I command in a harsh whisper, chastising the woman looking back at me. "You made a deal with Grant to catch a thief, not slip back into becoming one. You're reformed. Clean. One of the good guys."

I'm so convincing, I almost believe it.

By the time I return to the party, the crowd has departed. All that remain are Jane, my grandmother, and one weary-looking maid appraising the mess of plates and cups on every surface.

"There now. That wasn't so terrible, was it?" Jane asks. "I think they liked you."

"Are you kidding? I almost blew it there at the end. I had no idea I wasn't supposed to talk about... certain things."

"No need to tiptoe around me. *I* haven't been robbed. I keep all my valuables in a safe deposit box for a reason."

Safe deposit boxes aren't that hard to get into, not if you time things right, but I decide to save that tip for when we know each other better.

"Let that be a lesson to you in behaving like a lady," my grandmother says. "When in doubt, speak less, and smile more. Believe me when I tell you that these women aren't afraid of passing judgment—and acting on it."

"Yeah," I say. "I picked up on that."

"On the bright side, you already have the approval that matters most," Jane says. She tilts her head toward my grandmother. "No one is tougher on new recruits than this woman right here."

I cast Jane's severe cheekbones and cold eyes a doubtful look, which only causes her to smile. "I know, I know. I come across as mean, but don't hold it against me. That's what decades of functioning as a woman in a man's world looks like. It's my resting I-can-fire-you-and-cancel-your-pension-so-don't-even-try face."

I can sympathize. My own expression tends to fall into a resting I'm-totally-innocent-and-in-no-way-did-I-steal-that face. Occupational hazards are a real thing.

"Your grandmother is the true dragon," Jane adds. "I can't tell you how hard I shook the first time we met. Knees knocking, teeth chattering, the whole show. And *I* had the advantage of being your mother's best friend, so you can imagine how scary her reputation must be."

My grandmother breaks into a laugh at that, but I don't hear it. I can only see it—her mouth open, lips moving, all of it happening as if from a distance. I think, at first, that something must be wrong with my hearing, but the sudden sound of blood rushing to my ears and thrumming in my head is loud enough to convince me I'll be fine.

Though *fine* might be pushing it.

"You were my mom's best friend?" I blink at her. "But I don't... But you can't..."

Jane waits patiently for me to finish, but I have no

idea how either one of those sentences ends. "But you're so young" is the best I can come up with.

"The magic of good skin care products, Penelope," my grandmother says with a snap. "It's never too early to start."

"Not that you'll need them, I'm sure," Jane says warmly—as if I'm not standing there marveling at her, close to falling at her feet. "That gorgeous hair will keep you ageless. Hers was that exact shade. Does yours turn almost blond in the summer, too?"

Nodding, I reach up and touch the fine, thin strands. My hair has always been a burden to me, quick to tangle and difficult to style, but in this moment, I wouldn't trade it for anything.

"We'll get together soon and have a nice long chat, okay? She and I…" Her smile wavers, my own not too far behind. "There's so much I want to tell you about her, so much I want to know."

I nod again, unable to say more for fear of choking on my own tongue. Not only does this woman claim to have known my mother, but she's willing to talk about her. *Wants to*, in fact.

No one ever wants to talk about her.

"I'll be in touch then," Jane says. "Good-bye, Mrs. Dupont, and thank you for inviting me. Ever since I saw the two of you at lunch, I've been wracking my brain for ways to wrangle an introduction. Seeing your granddaughter was like looking back in time."

"So *that's* why you kept staring at me!"

Jane laughs at my outburst, but my poor grandmother releases a long-suffering sigh. "As you can see, it's not only her looks she shares with Liliana. She's just as impetuous and uncontrollable."

I take that insult to my breast and hold it there long after Jane and my grandmother exit the room, leaving me alone to help load teacups onto the maid's tray. I don't even care. My grandmother has no idea how much of a gift she has given me.

My mother—*my mother*—was impetuous and uncontrollable. And I, for one, love her for it.

GRANT

"It is with deep regret and profound reluctance that I present to you Mariah Ying."

I watch, that deep regret and profound reluctance spilling over, as Penelope approaches the table where Mariah sits, working. We're once again in the Café du Black Tar, once again meeting for not-coffee and back-channel talk. Penelope took one look at this place's peeling linoleum interior and declared herself enchanted.

"Agent Ying is the hacker friend I was telling you about," I add. "Mariah, this is my wife, Penelope Blue."

I'm not sure what I expect from these two women being in the same room together, but neither one is known to be shy around strangers—or around me. I'll be lucky to walk out of this café with my dignity intact.

"Did you really hide inside a safe as it was being transported on an armored truck?" Mariah asks. She forgoes the traditional handshake—physical contact, like people lingering in her office, has always been something she strives to avoid—and squints at Penelope from behind a pair of dark-rimmed glasses. "And for the full eight hours it made its route?"

"Technically, it was closer to nine hours. The driver got stuck in traffic." My wife gives a delicate shudder at the memory of those four metal walls and a dwindling oxygen tank. It's amazing to think about how successful a greaseman she was, given her fear of tight spaces. Amazing and frightening. She's not a woman to balk at a challenge, no matter how foolish it might be.

As our current situation attests.

"Hot damn," Mariah says, summing up my feelings. "You're hardcore."

"And did *you* really hack in to the Treasury and change the serial numbers on all the five-dollar bills printed in the United States for three whole months?" Penelope asks.

Mariah turns to me with a grin. "Aw, Emerson. You told her about me?"

Flipping her off is useless. By this time, Mariah and Penelope have forged an unbreakable bond of questionable ethics and mutual admiration. I *knew* this was a bad idea.

"Sorry I had to ask you to meet me here," Mariah says and gestures for Penelope to take a seat. There's only one other chair at the table, so I'm left to stand. "The coffee is terrible, and the food is worse, but this is one of the most secure places to talk in the city."

"Oh, we can totally meet at my dad's place next time," Penelope offers. "It's equally secure, and it comes with room service."

"Absolutely not," I say. "I may have allowed you two

to drag my morals this low, but I draw the line at using Blackrock's hideout. We'll say what we need to right here."

My tone of authority can make at least half a dozen agents in the New York field office cry, but of course, it has no power here. Penelope shrugs with a calm, "Suit your stubborn self," and Mariah laughs to see my wife put me so neatly in my place.

I know better than to pitch myself into a fight tipped so far out of my favor, so I pull the blueprints out of my interior jacket pocket and hand them to Mariah. I spent a few hours this morning trying to decipher the markings, but I didn't get any closer than I did with Penelope a few days ago.

Much to my dismay. Part of me wanted to figure out what the schematics are for and why my wife is so keen on locating them—without her knowing about it. But I didn't, and I promised to trust her, so here we are. In a secret meeting to beg more favors from a hacker who knows enough about my activities to hand me over to her superiors and have me stripped of my badge within minutes.

Trust is hard.

"We were hoping you could find out what type of building this is and where it's located," I begin. "I know it's not much to go on, but—"

"Of course." Mariah lifts her glasses to the top of her head and skims the blueprints. "Is it here in the city?"

"I think so, but I can't say for sure." Penelope's tone is anxious. "I have reason to believe it's a jewelry store, but Grant and I both feel like it might be something else."

"That's because it is something else," Mariah says.

Penelope and I exchange a glance.

"What kind of something else?" I ask.

"My best guess?" Mariah hands the blueprints to Penelope. "An art gallery. Either that or a museum. In my experience, they're almost interchangeable."

"But you barely looked at it," I protest.

Beside me, Penelope echoes, "A museum?"

"It's big for a gallery but small for a museum, which means if it's local, it's either the Youngtown Gallery in SoHo or the Conrad Museum uptown. I haven't been to either of those, or I'd be able to confirm it for you."

Penelope holds the blueprints, staring at them as if seeing them for the first time. I'm as impressed as she is by how quickly Mariah placed them, but I set my wonder aside in favor of more concrete answers.

"How can you be so sure?" I ask.

"Please. You've hacked into one museum building plan, you've hacked into them all. Rooms that size almost always mean someone is showing something off, and there's electrical wiring between every stud. You need that if you want alarms on each display item."

Damn. She's good. I'm glad—and not for the first time—that she's on my side.

"Of course, if it's in another city, your guess is as good as mine," she says. "Did you want me to double-check? If you give me a few minutes, I can pull up both Youngtown and Conrad."

I'm about to ask her to do it, but my wife interrupts. "No, that's okay. You've been a big help."

I lift a brow. "You sure? We came all this way…"

"There's no need." A smile, quick and fleeting, crosses her face. "I got the information I wanted. I'm good."

"That's it?" That seems easy. Too easy.

She nods and begins another intense perusal of the blueprints, her brow furrowed and eyes averted from mine. This would ordinarily be a loud warning that now is a good time to demand answers—who gave them to her, why they have her in such a worry—but Mariah draws my attention.

"I also have some information on that other thing you asked me to look into," she says.

I don't miss a beat. "Leon's past caseload?"

"Yeah, but you're not going to like it."

My heartbeat picks up. I lean down to get a look at her screen, but she closes the laptop and hands me a sheet of paper instead.

"What's this?" I hold the page at arm's length. "There are only six names listed—and one of them's the Picasso case I solved for him."

"Those are the only six cases he's worked on in the three years he's been with the Bureau," she says.

A quick mental calculation of my own workload hands me roughly twelve times that amount in the same window—and that's with the Warren and Penelope Blue investigation taking up most of my efforts. We're known for moving slow in the Major Thefts department, thanks to the scope and scale of the rings we uncover, but six cases is ludicrous.

"How is that possible? Even if he'd arrested the entire crew for the Harry Winston heist of '08, there's no way they'd let him get away with a track record that bad, much less *reward* it." I scan the list. In addition to the Picasso bust, three of the names are small-time retail jobs, but I don't know the other two, which isn't a point in his favor. Ours is a field where celebrity matters. "I don't understand. What's he been doing all this time?"

"According to what I found?" Mariah shrugs. "Not much. In fact, he took an extended leave of absence last year. Ten months of it, to be exact."

"Maybe he was working undercover," Penelope offers.

"As what?" I ask. "A bumbling, ineffective criminal mastermind?"

"Maybe he's working undercover now," she amends.

"As what? A bumbling, ineffective criminal mastermind?" I rub my hand along the back of my neck, feeling tense. Nothing about this man makes sense, and it's starting to seriously piss me off. Either he's obsessed with my wife, or he's not. Either he uses his position as a cover for theft, or he doesn't. Just once, I'd like him to show me his true face. "At least tell me this much. Those three retail cases…were the items recovered?"

"Yeah, they were—in full and without a fuss. There's no way he could have kept them for himself. Sorry, Emerson. Looks like he might not be the bad guy you were hoping for."

"I don't *hope* anyone is a bad guy," I say, shaking my head at this well-matched pair of miscreants. "I only *hope* to catch them before they do too much damage."

"I'm with Mariah on this one." Penelope casts an anxious look at her blueprints again before whisking them off the table and out of sight. "Maybe it's not Christopher. Maybe the Peep-Toe Prowler is someone else."

"You mean Tara?"

"Yes," she says quickly. "I mean Tara. I never could picture him in heels anyway."

I grunt my dislike of that theory. Tara would make a

neat and tidy answer, but I know the way that woman operates, and this isn't her style. She likes to make a mark, leave a trail. For her, fame is half the goal—and if I can believe my guys tailing her, she's become a model citizen as of late.

I'm missing a step, not seeing something that's right in front of my face.

"Well, I'm not giving up that easily," I say. Taking Penelope's hand, I pull her to her feet. Her fingers feel small and cold inside mine, and I give them a reassuring squeeze. "One closed door doesn't mean anything except that it's time to open a window."

"What are you going to do?" Mariah asks.

"Find a window."

"How was your tea party, by the way?"

I escort Penelope out of the café with a hand on the small of her back, aware of how tense she feels under my fingers. Her body has always been a great means of communication—as a contortionist and the most beautiful woman I've ever laid eyes on, her body is one of her best tools of the trade—and I've learned to read every inch of her skin.

"Oh!" A round-eyed, startled gaze flies up to mine. "Good. It was good. Fancy."

"Good and fancy. Why do I get the feeling you're not telling me everything?"

"Because I'm not telling you everything," she says promptly and then pauses. I know enough to see that pause to its natural conclusion, so I wait. "I, um, met a woman there."

"I was under the impression you were going to meet several of them. Any likely suspects? We've interviewed everyone who was at the parties where the thefts occurred—multiple times—but we haven't found any patterns worth following up on."

"No, no. It's nothing like that. They were all pretty normal—well, one of them might be addicted to pain pills, but she left fingerprints all over the medicine cabinet, so I doubt she's a suspect."

My lips twitch as I struggle to suppress a laugh. I'm not going to ask how she knows that.

"This was a woman named Jane. Jane Bartlett."

She sounds familiar, but not in a way that raises alarms. In fact, the only thing remotely alarming is the way Penelope sighs over her name, her gentle exhalation full of longing and admiration.

She's never sighed over me like that.

"She's amazing. Beautiful and funny and nice..." Her voice takes on a wistful note. "I saw her at lunch with my grandmother the other day, too, but I didn't know who she was. She kept staring at me, so I figured she was someone I stole from once."

Again, it's with considerable effort that I keep from laughing. Only my wife wouldn't remember all her past marks, and only my wife would brazen it out when potentially confronted with one. Every other thief I've known—and I've known my fair share—would have fled at the first sign of recognition.

"I take it she turned out to be a friend rather than foe?"

Penelope releases another of those sighs. "She knew my mom, Grant. She was her best friend growing up."

I stop in the middle of the sidewalk, my hand around

her waist compelling her to do the same. Some conversations require a complete suspension of time and movement, and this is one of them. "Oh, Penelope."

"I know." Her lips lift in a wistful smile. "She said I remind her of my mom. She even promised to tell me stories about their childhood together."

"I'm so glad," I say, and I mean it.

This hole in Penelope's life has been a painful one. When she was young, her dad gave her an education and a roof over her head, but he's hardly what I'd call a *soft* man. No one kissed her knees when she scraped them jumping out of three-story buildings; no one sang her back to sleep when nightmares came. She was pitched into adulthood way too young and under circumstances I shudder to think about.

Yet she still managed to grow into this warm, funny, vibrant human being everyone can't help but love—and she did it on her own.

"How does Erica feel about it?" I ask.

"That's the weird thing," Penelope says. "She didn't seem to care. You know how she always changes the subject whenever I mention my mom? Well, it didn't happen this time. With Jane there, she actually opened up for once."

"Yeah? What did you find out about her?"

"Mostly that she was a pain in everyone's ass."

I don't bother suppressing my laugh this time. "Why am I not surprised?"

She draws a deep, contented breath. "I don't mind being so lost now, you know? It's weird. Knowing that one tiny thing about her is like finding the door to a whole new side to myself. For the first time in my life,

I get to be more than just Warren Blue's daughter. I get to be part of her, too."

My heart gives a painful lurch. *You're not lost*, I want to say. *Not when you're with me.*

"I'm so happy for you," I say instead. I pull her into my arms and kiss the top of her head, her hair sending up the familiar scent of citrus shampoo. "This Jane person sounds like just what you need."

"I think she will be," Penelope says, but as soon as I release her, a troubled look descends. "At least, I *hope* she will be."

My instincts kick in. She's not telling me something.

"And you're sure there isn't anything else?" I ask as gently as I can. I watch and wait, hoping she'll give me more.

She forces a smile. "I'm sure."

THE 20 MIDDLE

I'M GOING TO KILL THEM.

I'm going to round them up, tie them together, and force them to watch bad action movies. I'm going to break into their homes and take their most valued possessions. I'm going to tell Grant about everything I've discovered and let him handle it.

Okay, I'm not going to do that last one. But the other three are definite possibilities.

There aren't many places I can go in this city to be alone with my thoughts, which is why it's no surprise I've ended up in the rare books room at the library. I sit in my usual seat, munching on a candy bar I smuggled in inside the leg of my pants. My dad used to come here when I was a kid, citing the restful atmosphere and absence of his young daughter as two very good reasons for retreat. I sort of picked up the practice when he was gone. Many a heist has been plotted here, many a problem solved.

It's difficult for me to see a way out of this one, though. The Conrad Museum. The Starbrite Necklace. My friends and Tara in possession of the blueprints that provide access to both.

I tip back on two chair legs, staring at the ceiling as I try to wrap my brain around everything I know. Grant always says that new agents spend too much time acting and not enough time thinking. Even though I'm not a *real* agent, this is probably as close as I'll get, so the advice holds.

He also says to take emotions out of the equation, but I doubt that's going to happen anytime soon. I'd like to be the hard-headed, efficient machine he so often becomes in times like these, but I can't. I *can't*.

My friends and I have done a lot of unsavory things in our lifetimes, but the one thing I could always count on was our commitment to one another. I don't love all of Riker's life choices, and he definitely doesn't love all of mine, but the unspoken rule is that nothing—*nothing*—can break the bond we share.

But they broke it. I broke it. It's broken.

Not only is the Conrad Museum *not* a jewelry store like Jordan said, but the target has always been diamonds. Sure, there's a chance they're after an emerald necklace instead of a diamond one, but I highly doubt it. The Starbrite Necklace is too ideal a target for that.

My instincts wouldn't lie—it's everything we love in a take. It's big and flashy and valuable enough to be worth the risk. Ten million times valuable enough, in fact. Security is tight, and access is limited most of the time, but a fancy setup like the ball opens up all kinds of possibilities. Next to jewelry stores upgrading their systems, it's our favorite setup.

There's no other way to look at this situation. I can't be the only one getting excited about that necklace sitting in a museum, just waiting to be taken. My friends obviously heard about it and didn't want me to know about their interest, so they lied about the blueprints. All of them, including Oz. I didn't think it possible.

As if that isn't bad enough, there's also Tara to consider. Back when I was part of the team, I was the one responsible for the actual *stealing*. In order to pull off the same caliber of job as before—which the Starbrite Necklace obviously is—they'd have to find a replacement. Tara showing her face at just the right moment would have clinched the deal.

They disregarded what that woman did to me. They cast aside my pleas not to be forgotten, buried, left behind. They proved that when it comes to our history together, the next big take matters more than everything we've shared.

Despite all that, I can almost forgive them for it. Stealing things, planning heists—it's the only thing we know how to do. If the past six months of my own struggles are any indication, it's also who we are. If letting go of that hurts *me* this much, with Grant as the prize waiting for me at the end of each day, then I can hardly fault them for not following suit.

But.

I rock my chair down on four legs, hitting the carpet with a dull thud.

But.

There's more to this situation than just a shiny necklace in a museum—and if I hadn't been so caught up in my own affairs, I might have recognized it earlier. The truth is, the Peep-Toe Prowler operates too close to my methods to be a coincidence. It's what made me think I was a suspect in the first place, what makes me so determined to uncover the truth now. Whoever this thief is, she's got a serious Penelope Blue vibe.

And my Penelope Blue vibes? They're feeling very, very excited about this Starbrite thing. If I hadn't made a commitment to Grant—if I wasn't determined to make a go of this honesty nonsense—I would be *all* over that necklace. Which means there's a good chance that the Peep-Toe Prowler will be all over that necklace, too.

So either my friends are planning a heist to steal a necklace that the Peep-Toe Prowler is *also* planning to steal, or…

"Oh, no." I groan, letting my head drop to the table. It shakes, but the wood is heavy enough to hold my many burdens. "It's them, isn't it? It's been them all along."

All their meetings without me. Their willingness to help me break into the FBI despite having already decided I wasn't a suspect. Even their willingness to help me out now, obfuscating the truth at every turn. There's no other way to take it: they've been using my proximity to Grant—using *me*—to get away with it this whole time.

The empty room doesn't answer. Thousands of years of knowledge are trapped inside these rare books and manuscripts, and they have no advice for an ex-criminal whose federal agent husband is letting her help catch a group of thieves who also happen to be her best friends.

Whose side are you on, little monkey? the books ask mockingly. *Good or bad? Right or wrong? Your husband's or your friends'?*

Stupid books. They've never been much use to me in the past, and they're certainly not helping now. What I should do is burn the lot to the ground and fake my own death to go along with it. Short of breaking into the Conrad Museum and taking the damn necklace for myself, it's the only exit strategy no one would see coming.

My breath catches, and I sit up straight.

No, Penelope, I think. *You can't. You promised Grant that no one would steal from there.*

I did promise, comes the faintly mocking reply. *But I never said I wouldn't look around…*

"Uh, ma'am?" The security guard at the door pokes his head in. "Is everything okay in here?"

"No, everything is *not* okay. I've been betrayed."

He blinks. "I'm sorry, but you'll have to leave. We don't allow that in here."

"Betrayal?" I laugh. "That's what *you* think. It's everywhere."

"I was actually talking about the candy bar." He points at the table. "There's no food in the rare books room."

I get to my feet, tucking the crumpled wrapper in my pocket as I do. "Fine. I'll leave, but only because this place is useless to me now. It's been tainted."

"Do you need me to call someone?"

"No, thanks. I'm good."

It's a bald-faced lie. I'm not good—I'm not even okay. But if history has proven one thing, it's that Penelope Blue doesn't stay down for long. My heart might be breaking and my marriage stumbling, but for the first time in a long time, I have a plan. There's not much to it yet, but I need to see that necklace and witness for myself what kind of security protocols are in place. Not to steal it, of course. This is to solve a case, help my husband, get my life on track.

And if I find a few of my friends wandering around the building while I do? I tuck my wobbling lower lip between my teeth. Well. That's a road I'll cross when I come to it.

THE NECKLACE

IT TAKES SEVERAL CASUAL PHONE CALLS AND A CHANCE meeting at my grandmother's, but I manage to convince Jane to meet me at the Conrad Museum for a private tour.

The museum isn't very tall, but it takes up half a block, signaling its importance to the city's cultural backdrop. The people passing by—mostly dog walkers and au pairs—also indicate the wealth of the area, as does the valet parking out front. If those signs weren't enough to indicate that this bland, unassuming building holds a necklace worth ten million dollars, then the security features I immediately pick out would do the job.

Take that small doorway at the front, for example. There's nothing about the single frosted glass door that inspires awe, but it's a good deterrent for the theft of large-scale items—specifically, framed art and sculpture installations. If the item won't fit, it's not coming out that way. Similarly, the lack of windows across the front means outdoor surveillance is impossible. You have to get inside to survey the building, which comes with a higher risk of detection. And one of the large skyscrapers next door houses a bank on the bottom floor—complete with an ATM outside—which means there's an external video surveillance feed to worry about.

I might not know as much about museum architecture as Grant's friend Mariah, but I can tell you this much—breaking into the Conrad isn't for the faint of heart. These people are good at security. There's a reason my friends and I avoided places like this for most of our career.

Jane pulls back from the airy kiss she lands on my cheek and gestures at the museum, seeing none of the same details. She's here as a favor to an old friend, her errand pure and simple, and I can't help but envy her for it.

"I'm so glad you asked me to show you the collection," she says warmly. "I've been dying for an excuse to see it again."

"No, thank *you* for making it so easy to get in."

She looks stunning in flowing black pants and a black blouse that billows all the way down her arms. Repeating Tara's cream-colored skirt risked exposing myself as the fashionless hack I am, so I stopped at the bioluminescent store on the way here. The wood pulp tunic the sales clerk suggested is a lot less weird than it sounds.

"I was under the impression it was almost impossible to see," I say.

"Ah, that's because you don't have my connections. Welcome to a whole new world of inside access." Jane winks and leads the way into the museum with a sure-footed speed even Tara would be forced to admire.

At first glance, I don't see any major security features other than the traditional electronic system at the front door and individual triggers on each of the displays. Unfortunately, I don't have a chance to look deeper before a dapper, mustachioed museum curator greets us with outstretched hands.

"Pierre, so lovely of you to squeeze us in." Jane leans in to Pierre to plant another of her airy kisses. "This is the girl I was telling you about, Penelope Blue. She's Lily's daughter."

He turns to me with alarm. "What? Impossible! This is no girl. She's too old."

I guess maybe the wood pulp isn't as flattering as I'd hoped.

"I expected a baby, a child. If Liliana's daughter is this old, then we're…"

"Ancient," Jane says wryly.

Pierre laughs and extends his hand. It's surprisingly soft. "I refuse to accept it. You're not her daughter; you're her spirit reincarnated."

"Um. Thank you?"

"You're welcome. I liked Liliana. A wild thing, but always good for a laugh. I was sorry to hear of her passing."

My chest gives a painful squeeze. He's not the only one. "How did you know her? Were you two friends?"

Pierre shakes his head, his mustache twitching. "Oh, no. She was quite above my touch."

Jane interprets for me. "Nonsense. When we first met, Pierre was an art tutor, and we were his wayward pupils—I never could get the hang of watercolors, even at his exorbitant rates. It didn't take long for him to surpass me in this world. As you can see, he now holds the keys to some of the most beautiful art collections in the world."

I perk up at the picture thus conjured. "My mom was an artist?"

"Not at all. She was worse at watercolors than me." Jane speaks in a friendly way that robs her words of any offense. "She mostly came along to keep me company."

"You mean cause mischief," Pierre suggests. "She once switched the lids on my oil paints when I wasn't looking. My next pupil gave his Mona Lisa purple skin."

That picture causes me to perk up even more. The idea of a serene mother figure painting watercolors is fine and all, but I can identify much more strongly with this delinquent version of her.

But Jane quickly corrects that assumption. "That was my idea, I'm afraid, Pierre." She turns to me with a warm smile. "Don't believe a word either he or your grandmother says about your mother—she was an angel."

Although I'm dying to hear more, Pierre shows himself ready to move on. He nods once and ushers us through the rest of museum, showing it off with a proud, almost paternal air.

Poor man. If only he knew what kinds of plots are underway.

As expected—and as the blueprints indicated—the museum's main area is cavernous, lofty and wide with a few displays artfully arranged to make it appear even larger. Residing as I do in Grant's *living* museum, every nook and cranny filled with memories and treasures, this waste of space alarms me.

Equally alarming is the blasé way Pierre leads us into

an elevator at the back of the museum. The metal doors open to reveal a space so small, it sets my heart racing to look at it. I know, on a cognitive level, that it's another security feature to limit access to the second floor, but that knowledge doesn't make me feel better about stepping inside.

In an attempt to distract myself from the familiar signs of claustrophobia—heart pounding and breath coming faster—I decide to get to work.

"I was just thanking Jane for bringing me to see this collection before it's gone," I say. "I understand it's pretty exclusive."

Pierre's mustache twitches, but I can't make out the full expression of his lips underneath. "A financial necessity, unfortunately. The display was open to the public when we first opened, but our insurance company decided they didn't care for that. We had to move the collection upstairs to a more secure location, and access is by appointment only. To be honest, I'll be glad when it's no longer my responsibility."

The elevator shudders. Almost by impulse, my hand shoots out and grasps Jane by the arm. She feels tense, and I wonder if she, too, gets nervous in spaces like this.

"Sorry about that," Pierre says as we finally reach the upper floor. "We have someone coming out to look at it tomorrow."

My step wavers as I get off the elevator—and not only because I'm grateful to be in the open air again. Elevator repairs are one of Oz's specialties. He looks incredibly convincing in coveralls and can also install an override chip to control the movements from afar.

In other words, things are looking very good for my friends…and very bad for me.

In the twenty seconds it takes to get to the collection door and wait for Pierre to swipe his key card and enter the access code—it starts with a two, but I don't see anything beyond that—I make a quick survey of the scene. In addition to elevator access, there's an emergency stairwell exit on one side. It's protected by an alarm system, but those can be bypassed, so it's a possible way in. The vents are small, though—almost as small as the ones at the FBI—so those are probably out.

Which is no real surprise, to be honest. If my friends don't have me to fold up like a pretzel, they'll need to get in a different way.

"And here it is!" Pierre opens the door to the display room, but I notice that before the overhead lamps turn on, he issues a voice command to disengage a blinking red light off to one side.

I know what that blinking red light is. It might not look like much, but should one of us light up a cigarette and start puffing, the answer would be clear.

Lasers.

Oh, God. They're going to try and get past lasers. Riker must be in his element—he's been preparing for lasers his whole life. I know him well enough to assume he'll try using mirrors—something that only works in the movies, and even then only with perfect timing and expert intervention. If he wants an actual chance of getting through, the system will have to be electronically disabled, which isn't nearly as much fun but just as risky.

"Oh, and I'll need you both to sign in." Pierre hands Jane a clipboard and apologizes as he asks to check our

IDs. Under normal circumstances, I wouldn't have a problem with his request—there are no fewer than three fake driver's licenses in my wallet at all times—but with Jane watching and the introductions already made, I'm forced to pull out the real deal.

Jane smiles as she passes me the clipboard. "This is so they know who to blame if anything goes missing. Better keep your hands in your pockets."

I finish signing my name with mixed emotions, my presence here sealed and delivered. Whether I like it or not, there's no way I can take the necklace for myself now, and I'm equally committed to stopping my friends—and/or the Peep-Toe Prowler—from making the attempt. Grant will never forgive me if he shows up to investigate a burglary only to find his wife listed smack in the middle of the suspect list.

I guess this is what I get for letting my interest in this case get the better of me. *Curiosity killed the cat burglar*.

"I'll do that," I manage, and I sneak a quick glance at the other names before Pierre takes the clipboard back. Nothing pops out as an alias my friends have used in the past, and I don't see any mention of Christopher Leon or Tara Lewis, but that doesn't mean much. "So do we just walk around?"

"Take all the time you want. I'm merely the gate-keeper." Pierre takes a post near the door. It's the only way in or out of the room, but that doesn't mean a crafty thief couldn't cut in through the walls from the outside, assuming they disabled that ATM camera next door. "And let me know if you have any questions."

I do have questions—hundreds of them—but I keep my thoughts to myself as Jane and I work our way clockwise through the room, admiring the fifties- and sixties-era jewelry displays secured behind thick glass cases. Ornate flower brooches inlaid with mother-of-pearl, square-cut emeralds and jade layered into chunky necklaces, diamond cuff bracelets... It's quite a collection, and I can understand why the Peep-Toe Prowler—or Prowler*s*, as the case may be—are looking here next.

"And here it is," Jane says, pulling my attention to the piece in the center of the room. A large pedestal case draws the eye, but not nearly as much as the promised diamond spikes contained within. "What do you think?"

Oh, man. What do I think?

It's *hideous*. Starbrite is an accurate description for the starburst pattern with its round center and radiating spikes, but I don't know anyone—short of a medieval torture mistress—who would want protruding shards of the world's hardest gem that close to her jugular. Not to mention the yellow gold so typical of this era is off-putting in a setting that size.

But.

Diamonds.

Really big diamonds.

"I love it," I say.

She laughs. "It's beastly, isn't it? There are all of five women in this world who could pull it off, and not a single one of them is under the age of seventy."

My grandmother, for example, could totally make it work. But I'm determined to be polite and uninterested, so I say, "That's not true. You could probably wear anything and look great."

"You think?" she asks and indicates her barren neck

with a raised brow. Like her slender, ringless fingers, the lack of jewelry suits her, gives her a hard edge I find appealing and intimidating at the same time. "You're sweet, but I don't wear much in the way of jewelry. The things I *like* are soft and feminine—two things I can't pull off, no matter how hard I try, so I gave up years ago. A small, delicate thing like you, however…"

She makes a sweeping perusal of my own minimal adornment, but I don't, as I expect, feel uncomfortable about it. "Hmm," she continues. "I see you're like me. You aren't wearing anything other than your wedding band and that single chain."

Both were gifts from my husband, and I love them because of their simplicity. The infinity knot around my neck might not be worth much from a financial stand-point, but it is, without question, the most valuable piece of jewelry I've ever owned.

Fingering the delicate chain, I think of the man who gave it to me—along with his promises of fidelity and affection. I don't know what I've done to deserve either, especially since a part of me is standing here contemplating major theft, preparing to stab one of those diamond spikes in his back.

"Yeah," I say and sigh. "I'm a minimalist."

"That's an area where you and your mother don't align. She loved jewelry of all varieties, diamonds especially."

I latch on to the change of topic like it's oxygen. "Tell me your favorite memory of her," I beg, turning my back on the Starbrite Necklace with a pivot of my heel.

Jane's brows raise a fraction. She seems surprised by how easily I'm able to dismiss ten million dollars on display, but there's no way to explain without giving myself away. *Diamonds are easy. Relationships are hard.*

"There are so many to choose from," she says carefully. "What do you want to know?"

Everything. All of it. What she was like as a child, what her hopes and dreams for the future held, why she gave up her whole life to marry a man who was her exact opposite.

How she gave up her whole life to marry a man who was her exact opposite.

I settle for, "Were you there when she met my dad?"

"No, I wasn't. I'm sorry. I wish I *had* been—when we were teenagers, all we could talk about was our future careers, husbands, children…" As she trails off, her eyes turn mistily to mine. "The career I managed, but the family side of things has always eluded me. She did a lot better at that than me."

I don't yet trust myself to speak, so it's just as well that Jane keeps going.

"Lily and I had a falling out a few months before she met your father, and we never got a chance to reconcile before she became pregnant with you and… Well, you know the rest."

Yes. I'm familiar with the details. That's when I was born, when she died—when I stole the one thing my dad cared about most in this world. It will forever be my greatest take.

"We had a fight about something stupid, a dress I borrowed and didn't return, and that was the last I ever saw of her. I tried to stay in contact—several times, I tried—but she didn't need me anymore. Not when she had your father."

I don't like the way this conversation is going, the idea that friends and husbands are mutually exclusive, so I attempt to turn her thoughts. "What about the thing you and Pierre were talking about before?" I ask. "The switching paint lids and stuff? Did you guys pull a lot of pranks like that?"

Jane turns her head as if to avert my gaze, the sharp line of her hair cutting across her cheek. "Not really, no. Don't get me wrong—we *could* have gotten away with that and much more. We were young and wealthy and, in your mother's case at least, breathtakingly gorgeous."

I nod, unwilling to say anything aloud for fear Jane might remember where we are and stop.

"It would have been so easy for your mom to become spoiled by it all, but she didn't." An almost perplexed line folds her brow. "I don't know how she managed it, to be honest. Everything in the world was hers for the taking, but she still managed to be kind to everyone—it didn't matter who they were or where they came from. I've never known anyone with such a good heart."

I nod again, except this time it's to keep myself from bursting into tears. Jane's description of my mother is everything I'd hoped and feared it would be. Her beauty, her virtue, her nobility—and *me*, standing in a museum with her oldest friend, casing ten-million-dollar jewels and scanning for exits.

"What else can you tell me about her?" I ask, afraid to learn more but unable to stop now. "Did she have any fears, any bad habits? What sorts of things made her cry? What did her laugh sound like?"

Instead of answering, Jane shakes her sleek black bob. "So many questions. She was never very patient, either. Don't be angry if I don't give you all my stories at once, okay? I like having an excuse to keep seeing you. Let's go look at the hammered gold bracelet again, shall we?"

I agree, pleased with the distraction this suggestion affords. I'm also grateful to return to my survey of the second floor, since I still have a job to do, little though I like it. I make one last circle of the room, committing its dimensions and layout to memory. I'd also like to nail down details about the event while I have Jane on hand, but she takes a few furtive glances at her watch, and I realize I'm probably keeping her from more important places.

"Thank you, Pierre, for letting us see this," I say as we make our way out. He doesn't frisk us or anything, but he does make us sign the paper again. "The collection is stunning—it really is. I assume this will be closed on the night of the ball?"

"Without a doubt," he replies and commands the lasers to go back up again. He also locks up behind us, the lights plunging as he once again enters the key code. "We've even hired an outside security company to add to our numbers. It never hurts to be careful."

I don't disagree. Extra security is exactly what this facility needs. Except that Oz is on the payroll of half the security companies in the area. And the other half?

Well, they've never stopped us before.

As we leave the Conrad behind us, I detain Jane long enough to ask her one more question. "You know, with all the extra security needed, did you guys ever think it would be easier to hold the ball somewhere else?"

She casts me a curious, searching look. *Crap.* I glance

away and focus on a nearby pigeon's attempt to steal a sandwich. Did I push too hard? Make my interest in the collection too obvious? Riker and Oz are so much better at reconnaissance than me—they both have a subtlety I lack.

"Moving the event was discussed," Jane replies, still watching me. "But in the end, we decided it was worth the risk. The best things in life usually are, don't you think?"

I swallow and nod, feeling the full weight of those words. She might be talking about high-end charity events and diamond collections, but I know better.

The best things in life are the riskiest of all.

I stop by Jordan's apartment on the way home. The set of blueprints, which are beginning to show serious signs of wear and tear, are tucked under my arm.

"You might want to look into your home security system," I say as she pulls open the door to reveal the beckoning scent of vanilla and ammonia—a clear sign she's either cleaning or working on a new chemical formula. "You've been burgled."

She blinks at me. "But I don't have a home security system. I have an Oz."

I give the papers a shake. "Then you might want to look into Oz, because he's slipping. Is he here?"

"Uh, no. He's at work."

Work. Right. Ten million bucks says he's wearing a security guard's uniform and training up on museum protocol. Either that or he's setting appointments for elevator repair. We're not a hold-a-real-job sort of people. I did a lengthy stint as a volunteer dance instructor last year, but that ended along with my deception of Grant.

I shake the blueprints again. Jordan takes them this time, her brow furrowed as she unrolls them and registers the familiar sight. "Where did you get these?"

"Riker had them. I'm surprised he didn't tell you. He somehow managed to extract them from your high-security chest without your knowing about it. I think he was using them to woo Tara."

"Oh. Um. About that."

"About him wooing Tara? I know—it's gross, right? Do you think she chains him up? Do you think he likes it?"

"Actually, Pen…"

"I know, I know," I say. "It's my fault. I'm the one who asked him to keep an eye on her. But of all the people in the world who could withstand her lures, I thought for sure he'd be one of them. He knows what that woman is to me. He knows how much it would hurt me to see them working together."

I'd intended to play this light and breezy, leaping over the emotional hurdles with sure-footed grace, but I'm unable to keep the bitterness out of my tone at that last part. Jordan notices, and her voice goes flat. "You found out."

"That these blueprints aren't for a jewelry store?" I nod, not waiting for her confirmation. I don't trust what will happen if I hear her say the words out loud.

Yes, Penelope, we lied. Yes, Penelope, we're moving on without you. It's been fun. See you in the next life.

Jordan bites her lower lip. "Does that mean you know—"

"That they're for the Conrad Museum? Yeah. That too."

She pushes open the door, inviting me in with one wordless gesture. I almost take her up on the offer, falling into the vanilla chemical lab that feels so much like home.

But it's not my home. Not anymore.

"No, thanks," I say. My voice is harsher than I intend it to be, but I blame it on the emotion I'm struggling to keep at bay. "I only came by to let you know that I jeopardized your take today. Not on purpose—I stopped by to see the collection with a friend of my grandmother's, so I had to sign the visitor's list with my real name. I'll be the first one they haul in for questioning if anything goes missing."

"You did *what*?" Jordan asks. "Pen, how could you? What were you thinking?"

That's it. No apologies. No excuses. Just a reminder that by standing alone in the middle, I'm in everybody's way.

My eyes sting. "I don't care what else you guys do. Just don't steal the Starbrite, okay? It's too hot."

"But—"

I fling up a hand. "Don't worry. I'll stay out of your way from here on out, and I won't turn you in for this or any other crimes." Despite everything Grant and I promised each other, despite the fact that Simon all but begged for me to solve the Peep-Toe case, my FBI investigating career is over before it began. *And so is everything else.* "You might think I'm not much of a friend anymore, but I promise I'm good for that much."

I turn to leave, unwilling and unable to face that silent, fixed look on Jordan's face any longer. I might not be as good as Oz at nonverbal communication, but I know what that look says: I'm not part of the team anymore, and telling me anything while I'm so close to Grant is dangerous.

Which is fine. Really. I would never put my friends in a position where they feel like they have to choose between me and the job.

Mostly because I know all too well how that feels. It's an awful lot like getting ripped in half.

THE PHOTO

THE NEXT DAY DAWNS BRIGHT AND CLEAR — WHAT JORDAN would call ideal conditions for scientific experimentation; what Riker would consider a blight on all attempts at secretive reconnaissance.

"Every goddamn person in the city comes out at the first sign of sunshine," is his most common complaint on days like these. "Don't they know I'm trying to monitor the deliveryman's movements?"

I'm not trying to monitor anyone's movements today — or ever again, apparently — so the world is free to come and go as it pleases. Instead, I find myself elbows deep in a pile of dirt, cursing so loud that even squirrel-hating Harold across the street starts to look worried.

"So *that's* where you hide your money. I've been wondering."

A shadow crosses my path, literally and figuratively. I look up, the sun beaming in my eyes, and indulge in one last curse for good measure. There are several people I have no wish to see today, and Tara Lewis is at the top of the list.

"You'll have to keep wondering, then," I say, unable to keep the pique out of my voice. "It's not here. Who would keep millions of dollars under a rhododendron?"

Tara tilts her head. "*Is* that a rhododendron?"

"Of course it's a rhododendron." I rock back on my heels and stab my spade in the dirt. It's only my second choice for the sharp metal tip, but there are witnesses around. "You're being contrary on purpose."

"No, I dated a florist once. I'm pretty sure that's an azalea."

"You mean you *conned* a florist once. I think I know my own garden better than you do."

"That's what she said."

I try not to laugh. I don't *want* to laugh. It's not a good joke, and the last thing I want to do is encourage Tara to stick around. But an hour of hunching in one place and the realization that I couldn't tell the difference between a rhododendron and an azalea if the fate of the world hung in the balance is enough to tip me over the edge.

"Help me up," I grumble and take a small amount of satisfaction from slipping my dirt-covered hand into hers. "It's the least you can do after all the problems you've caused."

She ignores me, staring at her dirty palm in confusion. "Are you really gardening?"

"You can't tell?" I glance over the small patch of land where I've spent the better part of my morning, scraping dirt and pulling weeds, and realize I can't tell either. Stupid gardening. Why is this even a thing people do? "Damn. I was trying to be normal."

She laughs outright. "I'm sorry, what?"

"Normal. Ordinary. The kind of person who takes delight in making green things poke up out of the earth."

"Why?"

That's a good question, but I don't have a good answer. *Because this is my life now* feels as pathetic as it sounds, and *because the alternative is to steal someone else's identity and practice being normal that way* has a decidedly disturbing ring to it.

"It's something I'm trying out," I say.

"And?"

I sigh. "I'd rather sit inside an empty box for fifteen hours with only a single air hole poked in the side."

Her sympathetic wince shows how much she understands my feelings. There is no such thing as *normal* for women like us. At least Tara has the good sense not to try.

"What are you doing all the way in Rye anyway?" I ask sullenly. "I don't remember inviting you."

She gestures at the sidewalk behind her, where a flashy suitcase with a rose-gold shell rests. "If you're going to keep spending time with your grandmother, I figured you'd need to supplement your wardrobe with more than one skirt. I brought supplies."

"Oh." I'm taken aback by the straightforward—and generous—answer. "That was nice of you."

"Yeah, well. I guess I'm not the monster you always make me out to be. Can I come in?"

I give in with a shrug and head for the door. I could use the company now that I've confirmed my inefficacy at gardening, along with everything else. Nothing would have been solved if I discovered a green thumb and a passion for horticulture, but at least it would have been *something*. Penelope Blue: motherless, jobless, and friendless, but quite handy with a hoe.

"There are some casual dresses in there and some slacks that might fit if you have them hemmed." Tara drags the suitcase into the house behind me, thumping it on each step. We don't get any farther than the living room, though, as I'm disinclined to be hospitable.

"Good to know."

"I also have a few formal gowns you might need for things like gala events, but you should stop by and try them on first, see which ones you like."

Gala events sounds awfully suspect, considering how I spent my day yesterday, but as much as I'd like to shut this woman down and escort her out of my life, curiosity gets the better of me.

It always does, the cheeky bastard.

"That would be great, thanks. I have a thing next week that I'll need a gown for, so you have good timing."

"The Black and White Ball?" Tara picks the dirt out of her nails with feigned interest. "Yes, I remember reading about that. You'll hate it, but the guests are guaranteed to arrive dripping in diamonds. If I were the Peep-Toe Prowler, I wouldn't miss it."

"If you were the Peep-Toe Prowler," I reply as calmly as I can, "missing it would be the only thing keeping you out of federal prison."

She *wants* to take the bait, I'm sure of it. I recognize the glittering look in her eyes as she tries to figure out how much I know.

I hold her gaze steady. *All of it, Tara. I know it all. And I know my friends sent you here to confirm it.*

"I guess it's a good thing I'm not the Prowler, then," she says.

"I guess so."

This could go on for hours, but Tara clears her throat and forces us to continue playing nice. "Does that mean you're not going to the ball?"

Oh, I'm going. I don't see what other choice I have. The old Penelope would have rested easy after she warned her friends away, but the new Penelope isn't so sure. I need to be there to make sure they don't try to sneak in behind my back. I made a promise to Grant, and I intend to keep it.

"I have to," I reply. "I already said I'd be there. People are counting on me."

"You mean people like Jane Bartlett?"

By now, Tara should no longer be able to shock me. Ever since she sashayed back into my life in her stupid peep-toe shoes, she's been at least two steps ahead of me and unafraid to show it. No matter what I seem to accomplish in this world, she's always been a shinier, more put-together version of myself.

Still. Just once, it would be nice to have something untainted by her hand—to have something for my very own.

"You know her?" I ask.

"I know *of* her," Tara replies and sighs when I don't reply right away. "She owns one of the biggest cosmetics lines in the world, Pen. In fact, I'm wearing her lipstick right now. Of course I'm aware of your family's connection to hers. I always have been."

For most of my life, I've assumed that my father is the omniscient one in the family, manipulating the people around him like pawns on a chessboard. It's the way he shows his power, his status, and as much as I wish he would stop playing every now and then to simply be my *dad*, I understand his nature well enough to accept reality. To love my dad is to be bested by him, every time.

I'm starting to wonder, though, if Tara isn't his master.

Love her or hate her, the reality is that she knows people. She knows their relationships. She knows who they care about and who they're related to and how she can use that to her own advantage. This stuff with Christopher Leon is a prime example. Is he really a secret double agent she's working with on the side? Does he somehow tie into her plans with my friends to infiltrate the Conrad Museum under the guise of the Peep-Toe Prowler? Is it all a smokescreen to cover some other, deeper truth?

To be honest, I have no freaking clue anymore. But *she* knows enough about the strained professional relationship between Grant and Christopher, the strained relationship between me and my friends, that it doesn't matter. She dropped a single name in my ear and shifted the entire course of an FBI investigation. She dropped a single name in my ear and derailed my entire life.

That's power, right there.

I draw a deep breath and square to face her. "You knew I might meet her at my grandmother's?"

She nods.

"You knew she was my mom's best friend?"

She nods again.

"And this whole time, you never told me? *You never thought I might want to know about her?*"

"I wasn't aware you were interested in her...or, as long as we're on the subject, her in *you*." She watches me for a suspended second, but I'm not sure what reaction she expects.

"Why wouldn't she be interested in me?" I ask, my hackles up. "Maybe she likes me. Maybe she thinks I'm nice. Maybe she loved my mom so much, she's even willing to put up with *me* for a chance to feel close to her again."

"Don't get angry. I was just asking. It seemed awfully sudden, that's all."

"You weren't just asking." I try to lose the juvenile, peevish note to my voice, but it's hard. "You never just ask. There's a double meaning to everything you say."

I expect Tara to retaliate with a taunt or a sneer, mocking me for my excess of emotion, but she doesn't. Instead, she turns to me, her mouth drawn tight—actual lines of age showing around the curve of her lips—and asks, "Have I ever told you about my mom?"

"Um. No?" I step back and nudge my calves against the couch, startled by the sudden topic change. To be perfectly honest, it never occurred to me before that Tara *had* a mother. I'd always assumed she sprang into the world fully formed.

"She was a beautiful woman, probably the most beautiful I've ever seen. The most beautiful *anyone* has ever seen." This, coming from the lips of the most beautiful woman *I've* ever seen, is a tad surreal. "Watching her get dressed in the morning was a spiritual awakening. The way she moved in a slip, like she knew the whole world was watching—I can tell you this much, you've never met anyone so magnificent."

"Why are you telling me this?" I ask. "So I can be jealous of your great relationship with your mother?"

Tara's eyes snap dangerously. "She was magnificent around everyone except *me*. To this day, I couldn't tell you why she kept me or why she had me in the first place. I knew what I was to her before I could even walk. Her burden, her shame, the one thing she owned that didn't make her look good."

"That sounds familiar."

Tara ignores me. "I hated her. I've met a lot of terrible people in my lifetime, but I've never hated anyone as much as I did her."

"So does that."

The look she gives me is her most maternal to date, and I promptly clamp my lips shut. Perhaps this is more of a listening moment than a back-talking one.

"I know you think I'm this horrible, evil stepmother, Pen—and that's on me. I messed up, and there's nothing I can do to make up for my past mistakes. But you have to understand the situation I was coming from. My mom…" She opens her mouth as if waiting for truth and sentiment to pour out, but when nothing but a heavy sigh comes, she shakes her head and tries again. "She could barely muster up enough enthusiasm to feed me, let alone care about me. And don't give me that shocked look. I don't mean I starved. It was more like our life was a stasis between men. When she had a man—which was most of the time— she was this gorgeous, enchanting creature who would cover me with fake kisses and send me to bed while her lover admired the picture it made. Those times were fine. Lonely, but fine. But when she didn't have someone…"

I wait, unmoving, but all Tara does is shrug.

"Let's say I learned to take care of myself pretty early on."

Those stupid feelings of guilt and sympathy return, and I wish I could pluck them from my stomach and shove them under the couch cushions. I'm not *supposed* to feel sorry for her. She's using my father, my friends, and my husband to line her own pockets, consequences to the people I love be damned.

But the words still form before I can stop them. "I'm sorry."

"Don't be. I learned a lot about how to handle men from that woman. More than most girls learn their entire lives." With a lick of her lips and a toss of her long platinum hair, I know I'm witnessing one of those tips firsthand. "When I married your dad, I didn't know how mothers were supposed to act—and it didn't occur to me that you might want one in the first place. I was so glad to finally be rid of mine that I assumed everyone else felt the same way."

"I never expected you to be my mother."

"And I never planned on being it. Not then, and definitely not now." She reaches into her purse and extracts a scrap of folded paper, which she extends in my direction. "It's not much, but your father used to carry it around in his wallet. I, uh—well, I was only nineteen at the time. Don't hate me too much for asking him to get rid of it."

The scrap of paper turns out to be a photograph, heavily creased from being folded all these years. It's also grainy and in the faded yellow typical of late eighties photography. The woman in it is yellow, too, her hair the same color as the exposure, her details difficult to make out.

But her details don't interest me. I don't care where

she is or what she's holding in her hand, don't need to know what the print on her shirt says. All that matters is the smile on her face, as recognizable to me as my own.

Because it *is* my own.

"I think she's about six months pregnant with you in that photo. See? It's hard to tell from the way she's standing, but you're there all the same."

Me and my mom. *Together*. I open my mouth and close it again. "My dad carried this around with him?" I ask.

"Everywhere he went. It was the only thing I remember us fighting about. Well, except you, of course. I told him I wasn't willing to compete with a perfect dead woman he all but erected a diamond pedestal for, and that if he didn't get rid of the picture, he could get rid of me instead." She casts me an anxious look. "Remember the part about me being nineteen?"

"You were a very old nineteen."

"I was a very experienced nineteen. It's not the same thing." She pauses. "My plan was to burn the picture and remove all traces of her for good, but you and I had a huge fight right before I was going to do it. I decided to keep the photo around in case I needed leverage."

I'd done a decent job of keeping the swell of emotion inside my throat from erupting, but at that, it starts to leak. "Leverage?" I echo. "You were going to use the only picture that exists of my mom and me together as *leverage*?"

"Yes. But I didn't, and now I'm giving it to you instead—along with a piece of advice." Her voice drops. "Don't forget who your real friends are, Pen."

It's more threat than advice, and I treat it as such. "What are you talking about?"

"I've been spending a lot of time with Riker lately, and he's much more vulnerable than you realize. You have this great new life now—with your husband and your grandmother and Jane Bartlett—and that's fine, but all he has is a void where you used to be. Don't punish him for not knowing how to fill it."

In other words, don't turn him in to the FBI. Don't ban him from the Conrad Museum. Let him try for the Starbrite Necklace as payment for abandoning him when he needed me most.

I can't believe it. After all this, they still want my permission to go through with the museum heist.

Except I *can* believe it, and I glance down at the picture in my hand with a laugh. It's a bizarre reaction, I know, but this is a bizarre situation. It was generous of Tara to give me this piece of my mother, and I don't know that I'll ever be able to repay her—but if this isn't emotional leverage, I don't know what else is. She basically walked in here, admitted she kept this picture as a means to play me, and then played me so hard, I almost didn't see it.

I laugh louder.

Tara looks at me with a carefully arched brow. "I'm sorry. Did I miss something?"

"No, and I'm beginning to think you never do." I swear, if I didn't dislike this woman so much, I'd adore her. "Thank you for the picture, Tara, and for the clothes, but I think you should go now."

She doesn't argue as she heads for the door. "You are some kind of messed up, Pen, you know that?"

"What can I say? I learned from the best."

"And you'll keep in mind what I said? Especially

about Jane Bartlett? In our line of work, it's never a good idea to trust someone you barely know."

I don't answer as I close the door behind her. In our line of work, I'm coming to learn that it's the people I know best who pose the real problem.

THE SOCIALITE

THE NEXT WEEK IS A BLUR OF SOCIAL ACTIVITY AND TRYING to figure out what I'm going to do about the Peep-Toe Prowler—in other words, business as usual.

Tea parties give way to cocktail hours, which soon transform into brunches where the women drink copious amounts of gin and complain about their husbands. Every time I turn around, my grandmother is admonishing me to *make an effort, for heaven's sake* or *at least put on an interested face*. Which is why, at one such brunch hosted by Millie Ralph, I find myself discussing my married life with virtual strangers.

"That makes three times he's stood me up for our anniversary," says the statuesque woman from the tea party—her name, I've since learned, is Olivia Newton, absolutely no John. "Each year, he promises to make it up to me, and each year, I get the same tennis bracelet two days later."

I pray she's not wearing one of those tennis bracelets

now, because the flash of those rocks is one hundred percent cubic zirconia. Her husband sounds worse with each passing day.

"You're married, right?" she asks me earnestly.

"Ye-es," I reply.

Olivia and the nonstatuesque woman, whose name I still haven't learned, look down at my plain band in clear judgment. I immediately bristle.

I might not wear flashy jewels or have a private jet, but I *could* tell them all about how Grant woke me up this morning. His method was slow and careful and included a lot of tongue—so much of it, in fact, that I'm still struggling to stand on solid ground.

I don't mention it, though. No one likes a show-off.

Besides, there's that minor problem where I have yet to tell him that I'm pretty sure I know who the Peep-Toe Prowler is. He spent his entire day yesterday at Otisville Federal Correctional Institution, interviewing the criminals Christopher Leon put away in hopes they might admit to working in league with him.

It was a waste of twelve hours and of Grant's talents as a federal agent, and he has no one to blame for it but me.

"What's your husband like?" Olivia asks.

I doubt she's asking about his weight and height, but my grandmother gives me another one of those steely try-to-fit-in looks, so I offer a tentative, "Um, he can be overprotective sometimes?"

"Overprotective?"

"Yeah, he's an FBI agent, so he gets really worried about the things he can't control. Including me." *Especially me.* "Like, I know he loves me and everything, but I can't help thinking he'd rather have a different version sometimes. A quieter, softer one, you know?"

"A quiet one?" the nonstatuesque woman echoes.

"I know, right?" I grab a crab-filled pastry from a passing tray and shove it in my mouth. "You might as well bury me in a box for the rest of my life as ask me to be quiet, but he won't listen. He just wants me to be safe and happy."

From the look on Olivia's face, it's obvious she finds the box part alarming, but the nonstatuesque woman nods. "Safe and happy sounds nice, if you ask me," she says.

I turn to her eagerly. Pouring out my heart and soul to a woman whose name I don't know reeks of desperation, but that's what I am—desperate. I can't talk to my friends, and talking to Grant is obviously not an option, but I need to get this out to *someone*. The only alternative is to call Simon and get his thoughts on the subject, but I doubt that's what he meant when he said I could turn to him for help.

"That's the problem," I say. "Safe and happy sounds nice to ninety-nine percent of the population. I know it's what I'm *supposed* to want, but it feels like a death sentence. Oh, not the sharing my life with him part— he's pretty great, actually."

More than great, but that right there is a big part of the problem. He's everything I'm not. He always will be.

"It's all the stuff that comes with being safe that freaks me out," I explain. "Following rules and obeying, um, traffic laws and playing nice… If that's the kind of person my husband expects me to be, if that's what he wants out of our relationship, then I'm starting to wonder if we're doomed. How can two people be so different and still be so much in love?"

"Are you sure you're all that different?" the nonstatuesque woman asks. "There must be a common ground somewhere."

"Not a very big one," I say. "Sometimes it feels like we're killing time until one of us is willing to admit we made a mistake."

"Honey, you just described every marriage in this room," Olivia says.

"Get a counselor or get a lawyer, that's what I always say," puts in another woman lingering at the edge of our group. "I'm on my third husband already."

Although I get a sympathetic smile from the nonstatuesque woman, she also shrugs and holds up two fingers, indicating her own marital status. In other words, I'm screwed.

There's not much to hold my interest in the gathering after that. I wouldn't have come at all except I need to pretend to be investigating this case for a while longer. How *much* longer, I can't say, but I hope my part ends soon. I like my grandmother, I really do, but it's possible to have too much of a good thing—especially when that good thing is as strong and willful as her. I'm starting to see why she and my mother might not have always gotten along.

In an effort to curtail some of that togetherness while I can, I approach the corner where my grandmother and Jane stand politely chatting. "If you don't mind my leaving early, I think I'm going to head out," I say.

"Uh-oh." Jane gives a maternal cluck. "So soon?"

"Yeah, I'm not feeling well."

She reaches out and presses her palm against my forehead, her fingers cool on my skin. It's silly, this time-honored test of illness being conducted between grown women, but it's nice, too. I don't think anyone has checked my temperature before.

"You do feel warm, poor thing. We've been trotting her too hard, Erica. Do you want to go upstairs and lie down for a spell?"

My grandmother's eyes narrow in what feels to me like a much more normal reaction to feigned illness— doubt and suspicion. "Of course she doesn't want to lie down. Duponts don't get sick."

It's true. I can't recall the last time I had a cold, but it's too late for me to pretend I have a family emergency instead.

"Don't forget I'm half Blue," I say. "We're a frail, sickly people."

My grandmother sets her champagne glass aside. "I guess there's no reason for us to linger on. Millie always overdoes these things. I've never known such a woman for showing off. Did you notice the entertainment she has planned for later? Belly dancers. How ghastly. I'd rather she bring out Richard's clowns again."

"Oh, don't worry," I say, struggling to hide my laugh. "You can stay. I'll just take the subway to Grand Central and get home that way."

"Are you sure?"

I'm sure. The last thing I need is to spend the next hour in my grandmother's town car while she lectures me on my slovenliness. I *am* slovenly, even in this sequined jersey dress of Tara's, but I'm not up to the task of hearing about it.

If Jane offered me a ride, however...

I look at her expectantly, but she only repeats her offer to find me a dark, quiet place to rest upstairs. "Millie has plenty of space. You won't be interrupted up there, I promise."

As much fun as crashing at a virtual stranger's house for a postbrunch nap sounds, I pass. "That's okay. You two have a good afternoon. I'll be fine. And I'll plan on seeing you both for the Black and White Ball this weekend."

"Yes," Jane agrees with a smile. "It promises to be a good time."

"I only hope you found something appropriate to wear," my grandmother adds.

I haven't, but I assume Tara's offer to try gowns on still stands, so I'm not too worried about it. With a polite murmur to a few familiar faces on the way out—I'm getting good at this—I make my grateful escape. Blue skies above and the pristine sidewalks of the Upper East Side below change my mind about the subway, so I head out in favor of a nice, long walk to clear my head.

I don't get far.

Under normal circumstances, the sights and sounds of incessant New York traffic only interest me insofar as they can be used to help or hinder a quick getaway. That's my excuse, anyway, for why I almost miss sight of the glossy black muscle car that veers sharply around the corner. I'm alone in the intersection when it does, my attention focused on my own whirling thoughts rather than the road around me. More out of instinct than reason, I leap toward the sidewalk and out of the path of danger, heedless of gravity. The gravel digging into my knees as I come to a stop a few feet away indicates my success at this maneuver.

For a dizzy second, my legs sprawled and my heart fluttering wildly, I think the car is going to ignore me and pull away. It's an extremely rude thing to do—for all the driver knows, I could be dead down here—so I get to my feet and glare as best I can in a spangled dress and banged knees.

That's when I catch sight of the driver. A full head of leonine hair. Dark, inscrutable eyes. A cleft chin to make Roman statuaries rise up in jealousy.

Christopher Leon.

Before I can react to the sight of him, the driver's side door swings open, and his booming voice assails my ears. "Oh, God. Penelope Blue. Are you hurt? Did I hit you? Should I call an ambulance?"

"No, no, and no." I answer his questions in the order they were received. "I'm fine, just startled. You were driving really fast."

He winces. "Sorry. I didn't mean to veer so far to the right—I saw you there and panicked. I'm not used to this car's power yet. Did Grant tell you about it?"

About his car? We've spent quite a bit of time discussing Christopher lately, but his preferred mode of transportation has never come up.

"Uh, no," I say, wondering if I should apologize for the oversight. "Was he supposed to?"

His crestfallen look is almost comical. "No, of course not. I thought he might have mentioned it, that's all. Can I give you a lift somewhere?"

I hesitate. Grant's worries about this man's intentions toward me are difficult to silence, even in the broad light of day. I highly doubt he's the Peep-Toe

Prowler—especially now that I know who's *really* behind things—but it's hard to let the idea of extracted fingernails go once it's gotten a firm grip on your subconscious.

"I'm not going to kidnap you or anything, if that's what you're afraid of."

He laughs, and his overloud voice carries over the honking of stalled traffic to the sidewalk behind me, where a few passersby halt and take note. Shouting the word *kidnap* has a tendency to do that, though none of them pause long enough to memorize our details. If my body washes up on the Jersey shore next week, I doubt any of them would be able to identify me.

"I was looking forward to the walk, actually," I begin.

"Nonsense, I don't mind. In fact, I've been hoping to get a chance to—" He cuts himself short and releases another one of those loud, nervous laughs. "To, ah, talk to you. I feel bad for how we left things last time."

Seeing the look of eager anticipation on his face, I do a quick statistical calculation before agreeing to get in—and by statistical calculation, I mean I determine the odds of my body washing up on the Jersey shore next week. In the end, I decide the odds are pretty low.

It's not that I don't believe Grant when he says Christopher Leon is dangerous, of course, and it's not that I don't trust my husband's judgment as a man of the law. But I know criminals, and I know my own value. I mean, I'm related to some ridiculously powerful people. If the threat of Grant's vengeance isn't enough to scare this man, then my father's vast network of underworld criminals should be. My disappearance isn't one that would go down easy—and if Christopher is as devious as Grant thinks he is, then he knows it.

"My dad is expecting me," I say in clear warning.

"Perfect," he says. "I'll take you to him."

The speed of his reply settles it. I get in.

The car is as nice on the inside as it is on the exterior, shiny and new in the way only refinished old classics can manage.

"He's at the Lombardy, right?" Christopher asks as he pulls jerkily into the street, the engine revving much harder than it needs to. He seems nervous, though I can't tell why. Of the two of us, *I'm* the one most likely to end up dead. "Does he like it there? I've only been inside the lobby and bar before, but it seems like the rooms must be nice."

This is an odd line of questioning, but I go along with it, hoping he'll lead us somewhere more interesting. "Yeah, he's comfortable enough, or so I assume. My dad's not one to stick around if he's not happy."

"But he wouldn't go far, would he?" He flips on the blinker and turns left—two actions that put me at ease. For one, this is the correct way to get to the hotel. For another, I doubt a kidnapper would bother with turn signals. "If he wasn't happy at the hotel, I mean. He wouldn't leave New York. He'll stay wherever you are."

"Actually, I don't know if that's true. I mean, he loves me—and he'll protect me no matter what—but as much as I wish I was the reason he's sticking around, I don't think I am. We don't have that sort of relationship."

He frowns. "Yeah. I know how you feel."

"Oh? Is your father a highly capable jewel thief wanted in fifteen different countries, too?"

"Well, no." He turns to me with a grin, his dark eyes flashing with laughter in a way that reminds me so much of Grant. "I don't know much about my dad, to be honest. He left when I was really young."

"That's too bad," I say, and I mean it. Grant isn't one to dwell on his own childhood disappointments, but I know his story is a similar one. "Are you close to your mom?"

"I was." His gaze returns to the road. "She passed away not too long ago."

"I'm so sorry. That's hard." It's not my best consolation, but I hope he can feel my sincerity. If anyone knows about surviving after the loss of both parents, it's me. After my dad left, I wouldn't have made it without Riker's support. Sure, we were juvenile delinquents, and we stole most of the things we needed to survive, but we were juvenile delinquents stealing *together*.

The knife in my back twists a little deeper.

"At least you have your work to keep you busy," I say. "You enjoy being an FBI agent, right?"

"Um. It's okay, I guess."

Only okay? So far, I've never met an agent who wasn't willing to live and die for the job. "You don't like it?" I venture. "Why not?"

"It's hard to say." He hunches his shoulders. "The work is interesting, and I like being part of something bigger than myself, but…"

"But?" I prompt.

He casts me a quick, rueful smile. "It's not easy, fitting in with those guys. They've got their own brotherhood with their own set of rules to guide it. It's pretty tight-knit. No matter how hard I try, I always seem to be on the outside looking in."

Oh, man. I know how *that* feels, too.

"That's part of why I wanted you to know you could

reach out to me…for anything. Anything at all. I'm on your side, Penelope. I hope you know that."

It's a sweet offer, but *I* don't even know what side I'm on anymore.

"And you could always put in a good word for me, too," he adds. "You know, if you wanted. Grant trusts your opinion more than anyone's. You could get him to do anything you want."

Although I try to hide my sharp look of surprise, I don't think I do a good job of it. Of course, I can't get Grant to bend to my will—believe me, I've tried—and anyone who knows him the slightest bit would be aware of that fact. That Christopher Leon isn't aware of it, and that he'd try to manipulate my husband by going through me…

Well. Let's just say it's a good thing I look out the car window to find the familiar facade of my father's hotel rolling up. Part of me wants to find an excuse for Christopher to keep driving me around so I can pump him for information, but another part feels suddenly shaky.

Maybe getting in this man's car wasn't the best idea I've ever had.

I slide out the passenger door before he can make a grab for my fingernails. "Thank you for the ride, Christopher," I say, forcing a smile. "It was nice running into you today."

"You too, Penelope. I'm sorry for almost hitting you earlier."

"No problem. I bounce back pretty fast." I pause, wondering if I should add something about how difficult I am to kill, but he speaks up before I get a chance.

"We'll chat again soon, yeah?"

I nod, unsure how else to respond. He takes it as an assent and waves as he pulls away. I watch him go with mixed feelings, though I mostly feel grateful to have escaped the car. What a strange, confusing man. Whatever he's up to, I definitely don't want to be a part of it.

I guess this is what I get for interfering. A smart woman would bow out of this game while she still has a chance. A *smarter* woman would have never started playing in the first place.

And the smartest woman of all?

I sigh. If I find her, I'll be sure to ask.

GRANT

IT'S NOT MY PROUDEST MOMENT WHEN THE CALL COMES IN notifying us that the Peep-Toe Prowler has struck again.

"Oh, thank fuck." I hang up the phone and reach for my jacket, pausing to make sure my gun is secure in its holster before I slip my arms through. "It's about time."

"Good news?" Mariah asks from where she stands in the doorway. She stopped by to update me on her continued efforts to uncover something shady in Christopher's past, which is a nice way of saying she stopped by for no reason at all.

I've never had a case stall so hard before. The boys following Tara lose sight of her half the time, Christopher is keeping his nose squeaky clean and out of my way, and even Penelope hasn't come across anything strange with her grandmother.

The calm before the storm always makes me uneasy. I like to know what kind of damage is headed my way.

"Technically? It's bad news," I say. "That was the

NYPD. They got reports of another break-in this afternoon, and it might be the work of our prettily shod friend."

Mariah doesn't have to be told twice. "Where's Tara?"

"According to Paulie's latest report, shopping on Fifth."

"And Leon?"

"That one I don't know. I haven't seen him all day. An interesting coincidence, don't you think?"

"Do you want me to get a copy of today's entry and exit logs from Cheryl?"

"Yes, please. Print it out, and get her to confirm it in case he decides to go in later and update the records to give himself an alibi. I'm heading to the crime scene now. I want to be there before he arrives, make sure the evidence isn't damaged this time. I might even have a chance to ask a few questions."

"You mean, did anyone see a man matching his description in the area? Please. What do you think this is, your birthday?"

I grin. "You never know—it could happen. I've never credited him with much in the way of intelligence."

"Well, good luck." Mariah offers me a mock salute. "Where did the Prowler hit, anyway?"

I'm already halfway out the door. "I don't know. The home of some woman named Millie Ralph."

"Emerson! You're here!"

Damn. Not only has Christopher beaten me to the crime scene, but he's elbows deep in his shoddy investigation work, leaving finger- and footprints all over the place. The victim's house has been roped off, and a forensics team is inside snapping photos—but while they're wearing paper booties over their shoes and gloves on their hands, Christopher is walking around at large and booming orders that have nothing to do with anything.

Covering his tracks, most likely.

"Leon." I pause on the threshold and nod, waiting to see how he plans to play this. "What's the story here?"

He shakes his head quickly, as though to stop me from saying more. He also gestures for me to follow him away from the building's facade.

Intrigued and on alert, I follow.

Like most of the homes the Peep-Toe Prowler has hit, this one is impressive. The freestanding structure is rare, even for this part of town, and every detail speaks of wealth, from the wrought iron fence around the grounds to the decorative brackets along the roofline. It also appears secure, with reinforced windows and what looks like an external video feed routed through a hidden surveillance system.

Of course, none of that means anything if you know what you're doing. Penelope could stand in this exact spot and list every access point without blinking.

We stop as soon as we reach a garden path along the north side, which I note with interest isn't visible from the street or from the house itself. Large, leafy trees provide a secluded overhang, and at this time of day, a calm silence settles the farther along the path we go.

"Did you find footprints back here?" I ask, careful to position myself in the middle of the path. If he thinks he's escaping here without first tackling me, he's way off the mark. "It's not like our Prowler to be so sloppy."

"The perimeter has been secured," he says. "I saw to it myself."

"What's been reported missing?"

"Two rings. One brooch in the shape of a peacock."
His voice is as loud as always, but there's a clipped
terseness to it that feels off. I look at him curiously. He's
not normally one for brevity. It takes him five inanities
and three non sequiturs to order lunch.

"That's new," I say. "He usually only takes one item
at a time. Estimated value?"

"The homeowner says around two hundred thousand,
but that's not what I want to talk to you about."

"Too bad. It's what I want to talk about." Especially
since that's a much smaller dollar value than the last few
thefts. It may be that residents are starting to take better
steps to secure their valuable belongings, so he had to
grab anything and everything he could get his hands on,
but any variation in pattern is worth looking into. "What
else do you know?"

"No sign of a break-in. No forced access. Once again,
it looks like a professional job." He's still acting odd,
and this time, he lowers his voice to a discreet murmur.
"Listen, have you seen your wife today?"

All thoughts of investigation stop, anger taking over
before I have a chance to control it. My jaw clenches so
tightly, it could crack, and my right hand forms a natural
fist at my side, but I'm happy to find that my voice is
level as I ask, "I beg your pardon?"

"Penelope. Your wife. Have you seen or talked to her?"

That's none of his goddamned business, and I tell
him in the most polite terms I'm able to muster. So...
not polite at all.

"I often see her and talk to her. That's the point of
being married." Since he doesn't look convinced, I add,

"And she's spending the day with her grandmother, in case you're wondering about her whereabouts. She has nothing to do with this."

He forces a laugh that feels tense and uncomfortable even from my distance. "Of course not. If you say she's trustworthy, she's trustworthy. One hundred percent."

My other hand curls into a fist, too. "Before you take another step down that road, let me remind you that any attempts you make to get to my wife will have to go through *me* first."

I mean it as nothing more than a warning, some friendly advice that any plans he has to involve Penelope will be met with extreme and unyielding force, but he doesn't back down. He does put his hands up in conciliation, though.

"I know you ignored my email to the ADD," he says. "And I know you don't like the idea. It's just that…"

I wait, watching as Christopher swallows heavily and tries again.

"We may need to start *considering* the possibility that she has information that could help our case. Out of respect for you, I could do it off the books, meet her somewhere later tonight. At this point, no one needs to know she's involved."

Every muscle in my body tenses. So this is it, then. Late-night, clandestine meetings and threats of exposure, a plan to pull her in without the protection of regular FBI protocol.

"No," I say, for what I hope will be the final time. "And if you know what's good for you, you won't ask again."

I prepare to return to the house.

"Wait, where are you going?" Christopher calls after me.

"To the crime scene. I'd like to take a look at the video surveillance while the burglar might still be in the immediate area."

"The video?" he echoes. "Emerson, wait a second. How do you know there's video?"

Because, unlike him, I noticed the electrical box on the exterior panel near the side window as I approached. Except homes like these don't have visible electrical boxes—not if they can help it. They pay a lot of money for the power companies to hide them. My guess is it's not electric at all, and that there's a series of wireless cameras all over the grounds transmitting to that box.

Surveillance footage is the one thing we've been missing since the start. And based on the panic in Christopher's voice, it sounds as though my fearless leader had no idea this house was being watched.

"Emerson. *Stop*. How do you know there's video?"

My heartbeat kicks up a notch. In fact, it sounds as though my fearless leader knows he's about to be caught red-handed. This could finally be it—the break I've been waiting for.

Unfortunately, the telltale swish of a gun being pulled from its holster causes my accelerated heart rate to stop cold. "Don't take another step," Christopher says, his voice not panicked now so much as on the edge. "I mean it."

Even though I know it behooves me to tread warily, I can't help laughing at the sight of his gun pointed straight at me. *He wouldn't dare*. In the broad light of day? With a full team of agents standing a few feet away?

"I mean it, Emerson," Christopher says. His words are even, but I notice the tip of his gun shake. "You can't pull that video feed."

"Or what?" I ask. "You'll kill me?"

"Just head back to the field office, okay? I'll handle things from here. That's an order."

I laugh again, but there's no humor in it. No way am I walking away from this now, not when he's all but admitted I'm going to find his face on that surveillance camera. Finally—*finally*—I've got the proof I need to put a stop to this thing.

"Put the gun away," I say coldly and turn on my heel. "You can't shoot me; the house is full of agents. You've been caught. It's time you faced up to the consequences of your actions."

I'll never know which part of that decision was my biggest mistake—taunting him or turning away—but I have a strong suspicion it's the latter. *I showed him my back. Never show a coward your back.*

"Emerson, you can't—"

Either he doesn't finish that statement or the blast of gunpowder covers the sound, because I don't hear it. My senses are too tied up in the blinding pain of a bullet—a *real* one this time—tearing through my torso at lightning speed, searing me from the inside out.

Christopher fucking Leon.

As my body seizes up in pain and I'm sent sprawling to the dirt, my only thought is that I can't believe I didn't see this one coming.

THE CALL

25

"I'd like to report a crime."

Cheryl looks at me over the top of her glasses, unimpressed and unmoved by my confession—which is a little rude, if you ask me. Coming up with the resolve to do this wasn't easy. "You're too late. It's already been called in."

"What?" I ask. "That's impossible. It hasn't been committed yet."

"Then how can you report it?"

"I'd like to report a *potential* crime. I know where the Peep-Toe Prowler is going to hit next."

Cheryl's lack of interest, apparent in the dry disbelief of her tone, remains firmly in place. "Oh? Do tell."

I shift from one foot to the other. "Well, the thing is, there's a stipulation."

"Of course there is."

"I need a promise that no one will be arrested."

"Of course you do."

"But people cut deals with the FBI all the time!" I

protest. "That's what I want to do. Cut a deal. And I'd like to do it anonymously. Also without Grant knowing about my involvement. On a scale of one to a weekend trip to Mars, how impossible are we talking?"

Her glance is full of Mars. "It doesn't matter. Like I said, you're too late. It's already been done."

"But that's impossible!" I cry. There's *no way* the Conrad Museum heist is set for any time before the night of the ball. I know how my friends operate, and we never do anything without a crowd. Sneaking into an empty museum is virtually impossible, since every alteration of regular protocol is noticeable in a big way. Lots of people around means lots of opportunities to blend in. "There must be a mistake."

"I don't make mistakes. As much as I'm sure we would have loved your anonymous and highly suspect tip, you missed your window by"—she checks her watch—"about one and a half hours. The Peep-Toe Prowler has already hit."

So much for my good intentions. "Shit. Did they take the whole collection or just the necklace?"

She glances at me over the top of those glasses again, ignoring my question. "You don't sound very upset."

I try again, this time picturing my friends sitting over a pile of the jewelry I begged them not to take. "*Shit*. Did they take the whole collection or just the necklace?"

"Much better, but I don't have the specifics yet. I'm sure Agent Emerson will file a full report when he gets back from the house, and you can talk to him then."

It's as good as a dismissal. I'm fully willing to take it as such, but I stop before I turn all the way around. "Wait, did you say *house*?" I ask.

She blinks at me. "No. I said the scene of the crime. I'd never give away unnecessary specifics."

"You did! You said house!"

"Sorry, Penelope. You must be imagining things."

"After all we've been through together, Cheryl, you can't lie now. Whose house?"

She presses her lips together in a firm line of refusal.

"I'm not leaving this desk until you tell me," I warn. "And believe me when I say I can wait all day. I literally have nowhere else to go and nothing else to do. Do you have solitaire on your computer?"

Her lips crack enough to allow a sigh to escape. "It was in the usual spot," she says. "Private residence, upscale address. From what I gather, the most valuable thing taken was a peacock brooch."

That's funny—I remember seeing a peacock brooch the other day, at my grandmother's first tea party. It had been a heavy thing, pulling at Millie's blouse so that it sagged in tandem with her breast.

I halt.

"Not Millie Ralph's house?" I don't wait for a response. It *is* her house, I'm sure of it. Usual spot, private residence, a party this morning. All the signs are there. "You don't have to say anything. Look at me disapprovingly if I'm right."

Her eyes, already full of disdain, don't so much as flicker.

"But that doesn't make any sense! I was there today— and let me tell you, there was *no one* suspicious at that party. No dark figures, no weaselly-eyed deliverymen. Not even a rogue butler."

That's when the pieces click. There may have not been any of the usual suspects, but there was a chauffeur. Well, a sort-of chauffeur. A man speeding away from the scene so fast, he almost hit an innocent bystander; a man visibly nervous as he drove me to my father's; a man Grant has spent weeks trying to convince me is a villain.

"Oh, no," I blurt.

"Uh…are you okay?"

"This is bad."

"You look awfully pale."

"I must be the worst investigator of all time."

"Do you want to sit down?"

I stare at Cheryl, her question barely registering. "I think I need to sit down."

I don't wait for her to offer me a chair, opting instead for one of my favorite austere metal seats by the wall. Cheryl watches me without a word, though I notice she discreetly picks up the phone. Calling security, most likely. Either that or someone to come tranquilize me.

Not that I'd stop them if they tried. Numbness is taking over, my body on hold while my brain grapples to figure out what happened this afternoon. I was present at the scene of a theft, obviously, but more than that, I solved this case.

For the second time.

My friends. Not my friends. Christopher Leon. Not Christopher Leon.

I don't know what's going on anymore, but the thing I can say for sure is that I saw Christopher fleeing under highly suspicious circumstances. Which is great. Which is fantastic.

Except that if *I* saw Christopher at the scene of the crime, that means he also saw *me*. And there's no denying I was present at that party today. The witnesses number in the dozens.

Oh, hell no. I am not taking the fall for this. Not for some chintzy peacock brooch.

"I need to talk to him," I announce to no one in particular.

"Penelope, hon, is there something I can get you? A glass of water, maybe?" Cheryl starts to look genuinely concerned, which isn't good news from a woman whose primary worry in life is whether she's carrying enough weapons on her body at any given time.

"I need to talk to Grant," I repeat. "If you can't get him on the phone, then I need a radio. Or a car to take me over there. Please. It's important."

"Penelope?"

Cheryl and I both turn at the sound of Simon's voice. I never thought I'd be so relieved to see his pinched face and tightly buttoned shirt, but these are strange times.

"Thanks for coming so quickly," Cheryl says in a low voice. "I didn't know who else to call. It's not like her to freak out. She's usually so blasé."

"You did the right thing." He moves across the room with two long strides before shoving me back down in my seat. As if that physical contact isn't unprecedented enough, he squats in front of me and clasps my hands in his. Of course, he then counteracts the gesture with a sharp, "Stop with the hysterics, Blue. You're making a scene. Take a deep breath, and tell me what's going on."

The breathing part I can do, but—"I'm not sure I know... I can't figure out..."

"Yes, you can. Tell me."

Simon might be a dick, but he's effective. I try again.

"Okay, so in order to work on that…thing we talked about, I've been spending a lot of time with my grandmother, right? Nothing big, just keeping my eyes peeled and poking around to see what people know. On the down-low, of course."

A jerky gesture of his hand tells me to hurry up, so I do.

"Well, I was with my grandmother this morning."

"So?"

"We were at a brunch together. A brunch at Millie Ralph's house."

He snaps to attention, dropping my hands with a start. "You mean you saw it happen?"

"Unfortunately, no. But when I was leaving…" I can see that Cheryl is doing her best to appear occupied and uninterested in our conversation, but she's been stapling the same sheet of paper for a full minute now. I drop my voice. "Simon, he was there. He was speeding away in a black muscle car."

"Who was? Oh." The full meaning of my confession takes hold. "*Oh*."

My sentiments exactly. "He almost ran me down a block away, but I didn't think anything of it at the time," I say. "I mean, I was hesitant at first, but once I got over the initial shock, he drove me back to my dad's hotel like it was no big deal."

"*You got in his car?*"

"It seemed like a good idea at the time," is all I say. It's going to be enough of a challenge trying to explain it to my husband.

"But if he knows you were there, if he knows you can place him at the scene of the crime…"

Our eyes meet.

"I'm worried about Grant," I say, my voice high.

"I'm sure he's fine. Emerson can take care of himself. The more important thing to do in this situation is make sure *you're* fine. You're not going to like this next part, but I'm going to have to place you in protective custody."

"Wait, what?" I spring to my feet, angling my body for a clear path to the stairwell. "Simon, have you lost your mind? You can't lock me up. I didn't take anything. You have to believe me."

"I do believe you, but I have no other choice. He'll never forgive me if I let anything happen to you, and you may have just become the material witness in this case." The handcuffs come out, and I swear there's a glint of pure joy in his eyes. "It's for your own good, Blue."

"I'll witness your dead body at my feet before I let you handcuff me again."

The fear of knowing that Grant is out there with Christopher imbues me with a strength I didn't know I had, because I feel fully capable of seeing that threat through to the end. Simon must recognize it, too, because he pauses.

For a moment, I think that pause is going to stretch into infinity. We're locked in stalemate, he and I, united in our loyalty to Grant but somehow always finding ourselves on opposite sides.

It's only when Cheryl breaks the silence—her voice a flat monotone I know I'll hear in nightmares for the rest of my life—that we're able to start moving again.

"I just got a call. They're reporting shots fired at the crime scene. Sterling, they're saying we've got a man down. They're saying it's Emerson."

THE
26 AFTERMATH

Despite a lifetime spent bending society's rules and treating government regulations more like guidelines than requirements, I'm a fairly peaceable person. My friends and I don't carry firearms on the job, and we operate under the premise that no prize is worth harming another human being. We deal in commodities, in replaceables—in the things in life that shouldn't matter but that people tend to pin their hopes and dreams on anyway.

That being said…

"I'll kill him." Even though Simon's car has stopped, the locks are still activated, so I start rolling down the window. "I'll wrap my hands around his neck and squeeze until there's nothing left. I'll stab him with a pen until he's more blood than skin. I'll rip out his fin-gernails *and* his teeth *and* his testicles until he begs me to send him off into the sweet bliss of death."

The locks pop open. "Don't forget the eyes," Simon says. "Everyone always forgets the eyes."

My laugh is shaky, but not as shaky as my legs as I climb out of Simon's car and dash toward the emergency room doors. "You don't think he's here, do you?"

"Who? Leon?" Simon is barely half a step behind me. "No, they'll have taken him into custody by now."

"Damn."

"Don't worry, Blue. We'll get our chance. He can't stay locked up forever."

It's a strange moment of solidarity, the pair of us standing on the threshold of New York-Presbyterian Hospital as we picture various ways in which to end Christopher Leon's life, but the blood-soaked thirst of my rage has been the only thing keeping my other emotions at bay. Now that we're here, with the bright lights of the hospital overhead and the efficient movements of the medical staff around us, it's difficult to keep a grip on my anger. I'm slipping, swirling, sinking—and the one man I can count on to pull me back up is bleeding out on a gurney somewhere inside.

"He's going to be okay, right?" I ask, unable to take that first step inside.

"I don't know." Simon's face is a hard mask as he pushes me through the doors. "All they would tell me is that Leon shot him in the back."

I don't know enough about anatomy or modern medical care to know what that means, but the pit of my stomach doesn't like the way it sounds.

"Excuse me," I say to the first person I see in scrubs. "My husband was brought in for a gunshot wound. How do I—"

The look on the young man's face confirms my worst fears and adds a few more on top. "You'll need to take a seat in the waiting room. Someone will be with you shortly."

"Yes, but I need to see him."

"I'm sorry. It's standard protocol. I'm not allowed to tell you anything more."

"Because he's dead?"

He neither confirms nor denies it. "Have a seat. I'm sure the surgeon will be out to speak with you as soon as he can."

Surgeon? The closest I've ever come to a surgeon was the time Riker got a bad stomachache when we were seventeen. We thought it was appendicitis and came up with a plan to discreetly leave him at the hospital doors under an alias, but it ended up being nothing more than a twenty-four-hour flu. And a good thing, too, because Riker was trying to convince Jordan to remove his appendix so he could avoid being put in the system.

The second medical professional in scrubs is equally unhelpful. "I'll tell you exactly what the last person told you—you have to take a seat and wait. I'm sorry. We'll give you more information as soon as we have it."

Simon and I have no choice but to comply, if only because the woman firms her stance and glares until we choose a pair of plastic waiting room chairs. I force a deep breath even though the constriction of my lungs sends me into a whirl of panic. The smallest crawl spaces in the dingiest holes have nothing on this moment.

He's dead, he's shot, he's gone.

All Grant wanted was for me to be safe and happy, but instead of giving him that, I forced him to let me interfere. I put that bullet in his back—as neatly as if I'd pulled the trigger myself. I'm the worst wife a person could ask for.

"Okay, Blue." Simon's crisp voice is like a slap to my cheek. "How do you want to play this?"

"Play what?"

The look he gives me conveys his opinion on my intellect. "You broke into the Federal Bureau of Investigations because you felt like looking at a case file, but you're going to take a nurse's word for it that you can't go any farther than a hospital waiting room?" He blows out a puff of air. "I repeat, how do you want to play this?"

Even with my heart struggling to beat in its constricted knot, a smile lifts the edge of my mouth. *Of course.* When have I ever let an authority figure stop me from doing exactly what I want?

I hadn't been aware of casing the room when we walked in, but it appears my instincts took on the task for me, because I have the hospital security figured out almost instantly. "Okay, did you notice that the nurse had to use her badge to get past those double doors over there?"

"Yeah."

"That's where we need to go."

"Thank you. I figured that much. Did you have an actual plan for getting through them?"

No, but I've always been good at thinking on my feet. And since the alternative is to sit here in the agony of the unknown with Simon for company, I don't hesitate to do just that.

"This man has a gun!" I cry, pointing an accusing finger at Simon. "He brought a gun into the hospital!"

It takes a second for the people around me to respond and a second longer for Simon to realize what I've done. Despite an initial indignant outburst, he proves himself a good sport and lifts his jacket to flash his holster—as well as the fully legal firearm carried within it. A few panicked screams confirm my accusation, and much to the hospital's credit, a security guard appears out of nowhere to take him down.

Simon commands the guard's full attention as he shows his credentials, pausing only to make sure I successfully lift the man's badge before I go. My pickpocket skills are a little rusty, but I manage to unclip it and push through the dispersing crowd before anyone is the wiser. A quick swipe of the card and a slip through the door later, and I'm on my way.

It's not as triumphant a success as I hope, and the buoyancy of sneaking past armed officials doesn't last longer than the first nurses' station. There's something about hospital professionals, with their hushed tones and the knowing glances, that turns me into a blubbering child.

"Excuse me, can I help you?" The nurse who catches me sidling down one of the hallways speaks in the requisite hushed tone, which doesn't do much to bolster my confidence. "Are you looking for someone?"

Since it's not likely I'm going to find Grant in this maze of clinical fluorescence on my own, I aim for a friendly smile. I miss.

"An FBI agent was brought in for a gunshot wound," I say through quivering lips. "Do you know where I can find him?"

The nurse looks carefully for someone to share a

knowing glance with, and I can tell I'm about to be escorted back to the waiting room. I take her hand and squeeze it. "Please. I know you're just doing your job, and there are a lot of people here who need you, but the man—Grant, Grant Emerson—he's my husband. No one will tell me anything, and I need to know…"

My voice cracks, and I don't finish. *I need to know if he's dead. I need to know if I've killed him.*

Human kindness isn't something I'm so accustomed to that I can always recognize it at a glance, but I see something close to absolution in the sympathetic flash of her eyes.

"Sure thing, hon," she says and squeezes my hand back. She doesn't let go, either, leading me around to the side of the desk so she can punch a few keys on the computer and look him up.

"Okay, it says here he's out of surgery, so that's a good sign. Gunshot wound to the right flank, clean entry and exit, no organ perforations. Those are also good signs. Oh dear, let's see…"

I don't breathe, waiting for the bad news to hit.

"Ah! There he is. They took him down to recovery a few minutes ago. You should be able to see him shortly."

I blink, dazed. "That's it?"

"That's it." She releases my hand, shaking hers to get the blood flowing back to it. "And if he's half as strong as you are, I wouldn't be surprised to find him up and walking by tomorrow. Come on. I'll take you."

If someone asked me to retrace my steps through the maze of that hospital at a later date, I doubt I could do it. The journey only takes five minutes, but my relief and anxiety swirl together in such an overwhelming mass of emotion, I see nothing but a blur of eternal gray and white.

"Here we are," the nurse says kindly as we approach a door marked *Recovery*. "They don't usually let spouses in there, but I assume you'll find a way in no matter what."

I'm confused until she gently lifts the security guard's badge from my hand. In my rush to find out what happened, I forgot I still had it clutched in my fingers.

I don't have a chance to thank her, because my husband—my poor, bandaged, hooked-up-to-a-monitor husband—chooses that moment to blink blearily up at the doorway.

"Penelope?" he asks. His voice is slurred and his eyes—those sharp, dark eyes that see everything—are impossible to read, as always.

I've never seen him so vulnerable, and it almost shatters me. Grant is the strong one, the good one, the dependable one. It's the foundation on which our entire relationship rests, the truth that drives me crazy and anchors me at the same time. He can't break, because I need him to keep me whole.

"He shot me," Grant mutters. "The bastard actually shot me."

"I know," I say and rush to his side. "I heard."

And then I promptly burst into tears.

THE REVENGE

27

IT'S NOT LONG BEFORE I FIND MYSELF WISHING Christopher Leon had better aim.

"I swear to everything you love and cherish, Grant, if you don't stop trying to get out of this bed, I'm going to tie you to it," I warn.

"And I'll help her with the knots, so you know they'll hold," Simon adds.

Grant looks at Simon and back at me, his eyes returned to their normal eagle state thanks to his refusal to take narcotics in any dosage. *Lucky to be alive*, the surgeon said. *Less than an inch from hitting his spine*, he vowed. And Grant won't even take a stupid Vicodin to relieve the pain.

"I don't believe you," he says as he struggles to sit up.

With a sigh of exasperation, I leap onto his bed—as gently as a human being *can* leap—and pin his legs to the mattress using the entirety of my body weight. The action is enough to give him a moment's pause, but a moment is all we get. Simon lunges to move the lunch tray out of Grant's reach so he can't use it as a weapon, something he tried with some success this morning. Simon gets to it, but barely, and the plastic cup of gelatin ends up on the once-spotless sleeve of his steely gray suit.

Had Simon asked *my* opinion, I could have told him how to dress for a day at Grant's bedside. Suits and nice slacks won't do the trick. What he needs is chain mail.

"Dammit, Emerson, look what you did! This is my favorite suit."

"Yeah, well. This was my favorite back. Look what happens when you grow too attached to something."

I press harder on Grant's thighs. From the way he winces, the added pressure isn't doing anything for the gaping hole where metal tore through flesh, but I don't care. If he wants me to treat him like someone who was shot, then he needs to start acting like one.

"Even if you could get on your feet and start walking," I begin, "which, for the record, you *can't*, there's nothing for you to do about Christopher. Simon and I are handling it."

"That's what I'm afraid of." Grant grunts and makes a renewed effort to get out of bed. I asked the hospital for restraints like they use on death row prisoners, but they refused to indulge me. I think it's mostly because they're as eager to see him leave as he is. Grant is not what they call an *ideal patient*. "As long as Leon is alive and I'm stuck in this bed where I can't guard you, it's too dangerous to have you walking around. You should be in protective custody."

Right. As if me sitting in a room with a pack of armed FBI agents is going to help any of us.

"What are they saying about Leon's release?"

Simon and I exchange a careful look. We haven't told Grant yet, but Christopher was released on suspension late yesterday afternoon. The review board found no evidence of intent—they're saying it was an accidental misfire—which means he's a free man.

For now.

"Don't worry about it," I say quickly, at the same time as Simon offers, "You know how these things work."

How he and I manage to keep Grant in bed after that is nothing short of miraculous.

"They let him go? How? Why? He shot me on purpose to keep me from seeing that video!"

"I know he did, and I'm going to do everything I can to make sure it doesn't happen again." I use my most soothing voice, but it only makes Grant tense up, which of course means he winces. He's not supposed to move this much—or, you know, at all. There are a lot of stitches in his body right now, and even though he'll never admit it, he came awfully close to dying on that operating table. "But I can't do that if I have to sit on your legs all day."

"If you're sitting on my legs, at least I know where you are. At least I know you're safe."

"I don't want to hear that stupid word out of your mouth again."

"What? *Safe?*" He says it almost triumphantly. "I'm sorry, my love, but I was right about Leon all along."

Forty-eight hours ago, I would have given anything to hear my husband baiting me from his hospital bed. Forty-eight hours ago, his triumphant smile was the only thing in the world I craved.

Funny how quickly things change.

"Yes, dear. You *were* right," I say, still in that sooth-ing voice. "He's a big, bad man, and he needs to be stopped. Unfortunately, it looks like his friends in the Bureau don't agree—which is why I've come up with an alternate plan."

He doesn't ask what that plan is, but one of the vir-tues of strictly enforced bed rest is that he has to listen—whether he likes it or not.

"The external video feed came back empty, which means it's my word against Christopher's that he was at Millie Ralph's house earlier that day," I say, ignoring the dark look that crosses Grant's face.

I know he'd been counting on that video to close the case, but it had shown nothing but an unending stream of static. According to the official FBI report, the thief used some kind of electronic jammer to keep it from recording anything. According to Simon, Christopher Leon was a sneaking bastard who probably wiped it in the mass confusion following the gunshot. Either way, it was an official dead end.

"Even if I *did* make a formal statement that he was in the area, which I haven't, it wouldn't be enough to get him arrested," I add. "I'm not what they consider a reliable witness."

"I consider you reliable. That should be enough to get you on the witness stand and under protection."

I don't tell him that Simon already made the offer—or that I refused it. This next part will be a hard enough sell as it is. "Simon and I have talked about it, and we believe that unless we can catch Christopher with his hand in the cookie jar, the authorities are going to con-tinue to turn a blind eye."

"I'll *make* them see," he grumbles, but by this point, it's the pain talking. If he was capable of making them see anything, he'd have done it by now.

"The way I figure it, the only thing to do is hand him a cookie jar," I continue. "But it needs to be a *big* cookie jar—so big, he won't have any choice but to dig in. Since I know what the next target is—or, at least, what the most logical next target is—I intend to start there."

"Start where?" he asks. "What target are you talking about?"

I firm my position on Grant's legs in anticipation of what I'm about to say. "I, um, believe he has his sights set on the Conrad Museum."

As expected, his whole body jerks in reaction to my confession. I wince, thinking of the newly changed dressing on his flank.

"I didn't know!" I cry, hoping he can hear me over the rush of pain that follows his sudden movement. "When I first showed you the blueprints, I didn't know what they were for. It was only after Mariah suggested it might be the Conrad that I put the pieces together."

"Penelope, you little—"

I hold up my hand to stop him before he says something we'll both regret. "It was wrong of me to keep it from you, but I had my reasons." Three reasons, to be exact, each bearing the name of a dear friend of mine. "I can't tell you everything, but what I can say for sure is that the Black and White Ball—that big charity event I was telling you about—is happening there in two days. And there's a necklace on display, this ugly piece from the fifties, worth about ten million dollars. It's the perfect opportunity."

"Opportunity for what?" Grant asks. When I don't respond right away, he practically roars. "*Opportunity for what?*"

I'm hoping Simon will jump in and save me, but his mouth is a firm line not even a crowbar could crack. With the proper amount of trepidation, I take a deep breath and—

—am saved by a familiar voice in the hallway. "I don't care when visiting hours are or who you intend to call to stop me. I'm going in there to see my son, and I doubt you want to see what happens to anyone who gets in my way."

"Oh, thank God." I heave a sigh of relief and climb off Grant's legs. The move may be a trifle premature, however, because he *also* recognizes that voice. His startled movement to remove himself out the nearest window looks to have ripped at least five stitches.

"Penelope Blue," he says, his voice dangerous. "What did you do?"

I'm not scared of that voice. I'm horrified by the IV still dripping in his arm, and I'm terrified of what might have happened if Christopher had shot slightly to the left, but Grant's anger means nothing. Not when I'm doing what I know is right.

"This is your own fault," I accuse, but I run a hand across his forehead in an attempt to get him to lie back down. It doesn't work, but I don't need it to, because his mom chooses that moment to saunter through the door.

"Oh, Grant," she says with an exasperated sigh. "I always knew it was a matter of time before you got yourself shot. I just assumed it would be one of the bad guys who did it."

"It *was* a bad guy—" Grant begins, but he doesn't have a chance to finish. His mom is too busy pulling off his blankets and making tsks of annoyance at what she finds.

The action isn't as strange as it seems, especially for anyone who's met Myrna Emerson before. For starters, she's an ER nurse, so she has heaps of experience with this sort of thing. She's seen more than her fair share of gunshot wounds, and her capable efficiency prevents her from turning maudlin at seeing her son fall victim to one. Myrna is also Grant's mom, and if that sounds obvious, too bad. There's no other way to describe her. Imagine someone like Grant—stubborn and capable and gentle and proud—and then imagine the kind of woman it would take to raise that man on her own.

It's why I called her in for reinforcement. She'll succeed where I failed, keep him subdued until the healing starts. She's halfway there already.

Sensing the moment is right for retreat, I back up to where Simon hovers in the doorway, looking relaxed for the first time since we got the news. He and Grant grew up together, so he knows how effective the Myrna method will be. In the two minutes she's been here, she's somehow gotten Grant on his back, covered him with blankets, *and* forced him to take a drink of water. I couldn't get him to drink even when I threatened to drown him in the cup.

Despite his mother's capable ministrations, however, Grant sees me edging toward the door and releases a low growl of discontent—my guard dog issuing a clear warning. *Stay where I can see you.*

"Stop that right now." Myrna snaps the blanket she's

in the middle of folding. "Your poor wife looks like
she hasn't gotten a wink of sleep in two days. Or taken
a shower. Or eaten anything that hasn't come out of a
vending machine."

All of these things are true, but I had no idea it was
so apparent. Tucking a strand of greasy hair behind my
ear, I try not to look as chastened as I feel.

"She's not going to be any good to you if she's
dead on her feet, which is why I'm sending her home
to get some rest and clean up. She can come back later
this evening."

Confronted with his mother's good common sense,
Grant can't do anything more than nod. The motion
doesn't come easy, though, and I can see the agony it
causes him to let me go. My wifely instincts urge me to
lavish him with kisses and promises to give up the whole
scheme, shackle myself to his side until he's ready
to confront the enemy on his own. But my criminal
instincts are there, too, and they're not as sentimental.

This sneaking around and setting traps and coming
up with underhanded plans? I'm good at this part. No,
scratch that. I'm *great* at it.

"Before you go, I'd like to have a word with Simon."
Grant looks at his mom with a belligerent air. "If that's
all right with you?"

She laughs. "Don't take your bad mood out on me.
I'm not the one who shot you. Speaking of bad moods,
do you know if this hospital gets cable? I love you, but
I'm not missing my shows because you can't be bothered to wear a bulletproof vest."

Grant opens his mouth to protest but decides against
it as his mom settles herself near the foot of his bed and

fiddles with the remote control. He learned the art of picking his battles from the best.

While the men have their super important conversation without me, I take a moment to thank Myrna for coming all the way from West Virginia to lend a hand. I do it quickly, though, because she appears to have found her favorite soap opera, which features a similar scene to the one we're living in, though with more bandages and better hair.

"Just make sure he doesn't do anything stupid while I'm gone," I say in an urgent undertone. My voice borders on desperation. "The doctors keep telling us what a close call it was and that he needs to reconcile himself to a few weeks in bed before a long and painful rehabilitation, but he won't listen. He thinks…"

I'm not sure how to continue. Myrna doesn't know all the details of the case, and I doubt she would care even if I was at liberty to tell her, but we owe her *some* explanation.

"He thinks he's indestructible and that it's his job to take care of everything and everyone all the time?" She laughs when she sees my expression. "Believe it or not, I'm fully aware of my son's flaws. I'll keep him here as long as I can, but there are limits to my capabilities. Whatever you need to do, I suggest you do it quickly."

Grant has finished issuing his instructions and glares at us from his position in bed, ready to issue a few more. "Simon is going to stay at the house with you," he says. "You're not to go anywhere without him."

"Lovely. He can help me take showers and everything. Did you tell him how I like to be loofahed?"

"Not funny." Grant points at me. "And whatever it is

you think you're planning, it's not happening. There's no way I'm allowing—"

"Christopher won't hurt me."

"You don't know that."

He's right—I *don't* know that. If Christopher was willing to shoot a fellow federal agent in order to access the video feed and get away with his crimes, there's no telling what he'll do to a pesky jewel thief like me.

Too bad this pesky jewel thief doesn't care.

"Then I'll stop him before he gets a chance," I retort. "I'll take precautions. I'll watch my back. I know it's hard for you to accept, but I've *got* this."

He sets his lips in a firm line. "No, you don't. You can't."

"Why not? I already fooled the FBI once. I'm sure I can do it again."

"Dammit, Penelope, would you stop and think for five seconds? You have no idea how dangerous this has become."

I snap. Maybe it's the long hours of vigilance at his bedside or maybe it's that I *am* terrified of what I'm purporting to do, but I can't take this a second longer.

"Oh, really? I don't understand what's at risk? I don't understand how close I came to losing you?" I face him head-on, noting out of the corner of my eye that Simon and Myrna have quietly left the room. Grant struggles to sit up, but he gives up with one quelling look from me.

Hmm. There may be a little Myrna in me yet.

"You don't get to tell me what to do, and you definitely don't get to tell me how to feel," I say. "When we made our deal—"

"The hell with that deal!"

"When we made our deal," I repeat firmly, "it was a

partnership. A give-and-take. We both assessed the risks and accepted them. You can't unaccept them halfway through because you don't like the way things are turning out."

"Penelope…"

"I'm sorry, but if the situation were reversed, you know you'd do the same. If there was a man out there who shot me in the back, who almost took my life, would you sit by my bed and hold my hand while he roamed free?"

If the dark look in his eyes is anything to go by, he knows I have him, and he's not happy about it. I'm sorry to say it, but neither am I.

"You think the only way to get me to agree to anything is to offer me convoluted deals, to turn things into a complicated and twisted maze, but that's not it. That's not it at all." I lean down and brush the hair from his forehead, dropping a gentle kiss on the heat of his brow. "I enjoy the challenge, you know I do. But what I love most is that when you offer me a back-alley bargain— however much you dislike it—what you're really doing is treating me like a partner. You're offering me a position as your equal."

"Of course you're my equal," he says gruffly. "I've never seen you as anything less than that."

Not yet he hasn't. But the more time I spend drifting aimlessly through my life, wondering where I belong, the more I realize how tentative our relationship is—how difficult it is to keep up with this man I married. Grant is unquestionably the master of his own universe. He knows where he fits and what he wants, perfect in the precision of his certainty. And I—adrift and unsure—am in danger of becoming nothing more than his satellite.

I refuse to let that happen. I love my husband, I respect my husband, and every time I think about him lying in a pool of his own blood, my entire body grows numb.

But I'm no one's satellite.

"Then don't insult me by treating me any different now," I say and force myself away from his bed. If I don't get out of here soon, I'm afraid I might lose the strength to leave his side. "You're not always going to like the choices I make, Grant, and I'm coming to realize there's nothing I can do about that. I'm a thief." He opens his mouth to protest, but I cut him off. "No, don't argue. I don't care if the entire FBI overhears me. I *am* a thief. It's what I've always been, and it's what I'll always be, even if I never steal anything again. I sneak around. I hide things from you. I make decisions you don't—or can't—approve of. But guess what? That's Penelope Blue. That's what you signed up for. And if that's not good enough for you anymore, then I'm not so sure this marriage of ours is going to work."

His shocked, hurt expression makes me feel like a monster. He's already suffered so much. It's cruel to add this on top of everything else.

But it had to be said, and it had to be said before I head out that door and make a dangerous situation even worse.

"I'm going now. I'll report back when I have something concrete to tell you."

I stand, waiting for his hurt expression to set into something harder. I'm unsurprised when he closes off altogether.

"If you get yourself killed," he says coldly, "I'll never forgive you."

"If I get myself killed," I reply, "I'll deserve it."

"Well, that was a disaster. I hope you know what you're doing, Blue."

Simon waits until we've exited the hospital before he transitions back to asshole mode. For a few hours there, when we sat side by side waiting for Grant to gain his full bearing after the surgery, there had been something like kinship between us. For a few hours more, as we attempted to keep Grant in bed and on the mend, I like to think we'd been friends.

Oh, well. Some things weren't made to last.

"Yes, actually, I do know what I'm doing," I say, and it's not a complete lie. I might not have all the details ironed out yet, but the hazy shapes of an idea are there, lodged in the back of my brain.

So far, they look an awful lot like the blueprints to the Conrad Museum.

I turn to him with shoulders squared. "What are your thoughts on stealing a ten-million-dollar necklace out from under the noses of roughly five hundred of New York's rich and famous?"

"I'd rather go back inside and help Mrs. Emerson chain Grant to his hospital bed."

"Too bad." A sympathetic listener I'm not. I'm still too raw from the confrontation with Grant, too aware of what's at risk if this mission fails. "I need you to head back to the office and grab me a few things."

He's instantly wary. "What kind of things?"

"Mariah Ying and Cheryl Brownstein."

He does a double take.

"Don't worry, they'll come," I assure him. "Bring them to the Lombardy, twenty-first floor."

His double take doubles down. "Your dad's suite?"

"The very one. I can't think of a better place to plan a multimillion dollar heist, can you?"

"Jesus. You weren't kidding about that?"

"Pulling off a heist like this is the only thing I'm good at, Simon. It's the only thing I can do. If I can use those skills to catch Christopher Leon red-handed and put him away so he doesn't set foot near my husband ever again, then that's what I'm going to do."

For the longest moment, I think he's going to refuse. The look he gives me, drawn thin and painful, is full of all the things he wants to say but won't. He can't. Not when I was so nearly a widow.

"If you think heists are the only thing you're good at, you're a bigger fool than I took you for." He pulls his car keys from his pocket. "Don't worry. We'll be there. I just hope we won't live to regret it."

He's not the only one.

THE TEAM

28

I start at Jordan's apartment.

"So, funny story," I begin as soon as she opens the door. She looks understandably wary—brows lowered over dark eyes, her hand paused on the knob. "Remember that time I told you that under no circumstances should you guys break into the Conrad Museum?"

"Pen—"

"I might have changed my mind about that. Can I come in?"

It says a lot about the shift in our relationship that she hesitates, checking over her shoulder to run it by Oz before she allows me in. It also says a lot that I'm slow to follow her through the door, unsure of my own actions. Do I wait to be asked to sit? Take my usual place on the couch? Fall on my knees and beg for the help I need?

Jordan cuts my worries short. "You look terrible. Sit down, and I'll get you something to eat. And a first aid kid. Is that *blood* on your arm?"

I glance down to find a rust-colored smear along the underside of my forearm.

"It's not mine," I say wearily. Now that I'm seated— and on Jordan's magical couch, no less—the sleep-lessness of the last two nights hits me like a ton of mattresses. "I was trying to hold Grant down."

Oz appears with a washcloth to wipe the blood away, leaving Jordan to decipher my meaning.

"Um, is that a sex thing?" she asks.

"No, it's a hospital thing. He was shot."

My confession causes the expected reaction. Oz applies the washcloth with renewed fervor while Jordan peppers me with questions: *What happened? Who did it? Is he okay? Are you?*

It's difficult to handle this much sensory overload at once, so I ignore the bulk of her questions and focus on the ones that matter most.

"He's fine, Jordan. He's going to live. And so will I."

Putting it into words—*I will live*—gives me renewed strength. That belief, the idea that I can sur-vive this period in my life the same way I've survived all the rest, is a luxury I haven't allowed myself in a long time.

With a deep breath, I tell the rest of the story—or as much of it as I can recall at the moment. Grant, the Peep-Toe Prowler, Christopher, the bullet… I get most of the details out, barely noticing when a sandwich and cup of coffee appear at my elbow, though that doesn't stop me from consuming both.

"So there it is," I say when I'm through. "The whole sorry mess of it. I know I have no right to ask for your help after the way we left things, but I need to know what kind of plans you guys made for the Conrad Museum—and whether those plans are still in place."

Jordan's expression is softer than when I first arrived, but it hasn't reached her usual friendly levels yet. "I'm confused. Does this mean you thought *we* were the Peep-Toe Prowler?"

"Of course not!"

In my desperation to secure their assistance, the lie pops out without my permission. I have to force myself to retract it and try again. If I'm going to do this, I'm going to do it right. I take another breath.

"Actually, that's not true," I admit. "I *did* have you guys fingered as the culprits. The style fit, and you guys were getting along so well with Tara…"

I glance up, heart heavy, to find they've arrayed themselves side by side, mirrored frowns on their faces. I shouldn't be surprised; with Jordan and Oz, you never hurt just one of them.

"You have to admit it makes sense," I add defensively. "You guys had the blueprints to the museum this whole time, *and* you lied that it was a jewelry store. And when I came over the other day, you didn't deny that you were going to try and break in to steal the Starbrite Necklace."

"Yeah, steal the *necklace*," Jordan says. "It's everything we love in a take—but the rest of that stuff? Pen, we helped you break into the FBI to prove that you weren't the Peep-Toe Prowler."

I flush. "I know, but you also told me the blueprints are nothing more than Riker bait, and that's obviously not the case."

"They *are* Riker bait. Or they *were*, rather." Jordan

finally relaxes, dropping elegantly to the chair across from me. She looks as sorry as I feel, so I think we might be making headway. "I lied about them being a jewelry store because I didn't want you to get suspicious."

"Because I'd tell Grant."

"Because there was a possibility, however remote, that you might accidentally let something slip to him. You're not a good liar, Pen. You never have been. Especially where Grant is concerned."

I sigh. It's true. It's what makes leaving him at the hospital the way I did so hard. He knows I meant every word I said.

"I wasn't kidding about Riker not taking the bait, either," Jordan continues. "He didn't show any interest in the job at first, and we had every intention of letting it go. But then Tara showed up and..."

Oz gently takes the empty coffee cup from my hand. I guess heavy projectiles aren't something he wants near me right now.

"And all of a sudden, the doors miraculously opened," I say in a flat voice.

"She's good at that sort of thing. I know you dislike her, but even you have to recognize that she has her uses."

Oh, Tara's good. I never denied that. I couldn't hand-select a better replacement if I tried.

"I wish I'd known about your plans, that's all," I say. "I understand you guys still have to make a living, and I know I'm not the most ideal confidante anymore, but I hate being banished like this. I feel like I'm being punished for making the decision to stay with Grant."

Jordan takes my hand and presses it. "This is a lot harder than we thought it would be, huh?"

I nod, unsure of my ability to speak. It's so much harder—and for so many reasons I never thought about before.

"If it's any consolation, we dropped the museum heist as soon as you warned us away," she says. "We wouldn't do anything that's in direct conflict with Grant's interests. I hope you know that. All you have to do is ask."

I groan, thinking back to the real reason for my visit today—not a long-overdue chat about our circumstances, but the hole in Grant's side. "Actually, that's not a consolation at all. In fact, I was hoping you would help me break in."

Oz returns the coffee cup to me. I'm not sure what he's doing at first, but when he goes to the chest and pulls out the familiar crumpled blueprints, the message comes through loud and clear.

These two have my back. *Always*. I'm ashamed of myself for forgetting that, but when I took to doubting myself, I started doubting them, too.

"You guys are the best," I say, trying hard to keep it together. "I'm sorry I got so upset. From now on, we'll do better at finding a way for us—for all of us—to move forward together."

Jordan nods her agreement. "That sounds great, but I wouldn't get too excited yet. You still have to get Riker on board."

I'm halfway hoping Riker won't be home when I arrive, or that he'll take one look at me standing in the hallway and slam the door in my face, but of course, neither of those things happen. In his role as the injured party, he takes the magnanimous route, which means he lets me in with a cool, "So you've decided to start talking to me again. How nice."

Tara isn't anywhere to be seen, which doesn't mean much except that Jordan probably called ahead of time and warned Riker to clear the apartment before my arrival. But magnanimity goes both ways, so I don't mention it.

"I brought you something." I hold out a duffel bag, heavy and stiff with the telltale sign of hundred-dollar bills in banded stacks. "Here. Take it."

He doesn't. He remains standing immobile, his arms firmly crossed. "I told you I don't want your stupid money."

"I know, but I'm giving it to you anyway." I set the bag on the ground next to him and leave it there, determined not to give it another thought. If he doesn't want the cash, he can flush it down the toilet after I leave. "It's your half. I should have given it to you months ago, but I wanted you to have to come to me for it."

"Well, that was a shitty thing to do."

"I know." While Jordan's anger made me hesitant and unsure, Riker's is familiar ground, and I saunter comfortably into his living room. "But it was the only way I could be sure you'd still have a reason to talk to me."

He stares. "I talk to you. I talk to you all the time."

"Not like you used to."

"Maybe you've become a bad conversationalist. Maybe I ran out of things to say." When his provocation doesn't work, the right-side scowl on his face deepens, and he gives up his motionless stance. His movements are jerky as he enters the room behind me, but there's no menace in him.

Only anger. Only pain.

"Fine," he says. "You want to talk? Go ahead. I won't stop you."

So I do.

"I hate Tara Lewis," I say. "I hate what she did to me, I hate what she did to my father, and I hate what she's doing to you."

His head jerks back in surprise at my bluntness, his anger dissolving to sarcasm instead. "Gee, don't hold back on my account."

So I don't.

"I wanted her to be the Peep-Toe Prowler so badly, I looked for any excuse I could find to cast her in the role," I say, gaining momentum. "It's not that I want her to go to prison or anything, but her guilt would have confirmed everything I know about her being unscrupulous and evil. And I needed that. I needed it so much. I swear, Riker, I hate her a little bit less every time I see her, and it scares the crap out of me."

"She's not the Prowler."

Well, obviously. I realize that *now*.

"I know it's not fair for me to blame her for everything bad that's happened in my life, but you have to remember that she's been the villain of my story for just about ever," I say. "It's not easy to flip a switch and turn that off."

"Yeah, well." He sniffs. "You're always on my case about getting my shit together, and that's exactly what I'm trying to do—changing my bad behaviors, flipping those switches off even when it's hard. Maybe it's time you start doing the same."

Ah, yes. Here he is. The new, responsible Riker. The Riker who doesn't need gambling money and can stand on his own two feet. My instinct is to remind him how easy it's always been for him to slip back into his self-destructive patterns, but I recall the photo Tara gave me of my mother, remember our conversation that day at the house, and I soften.

All he has is a void where you used to be. Don't punish him for not knowing how to fill it.

"Do you really like her?" I ask, watching carefully to see his reaction. "Like…in a gross way?"

All he gives me is a one-shouldered shrug. "I don't know yet. Maybe. Would it be so bad if I did?"

Yes, it would. I can't picture the two of them locking lips without wanting to throw myself over a bridge. But if Tara is going to—ew—fill his void, then it's not my place to interfere. Our friendship has shifted. Our lives have shifted. Instead of fighting it, the best thing I can do is try to shift with them.

"I guess not," I concede. "You're both consenting adults."

He glances up through that wayward lock of hair in his eyes. "Seriously?"

Now it's my turn for the lopsided shrug. "I'm not overjoyed at the prospect, but I guess that's how you felt about me and Grant."

"Tell me about it. I fucking hate that guy."

I laugh—I can't help it. Riker can stand there on the opposite side of the room, staring me down with equal proportions of antagonism and irritation, and still make me laugh.

My laugh turns into a hiccup. "Then you'll be happy

to know he's currently tied to a hospital bed with an enormous hole in his side."

"What?" He drops his pose and reaches for me, but the move is an abortive one, his uncertainty getting the better of his reflexes. "Pen, *what*?"

There's nothing for it after that but to tell him the whole story, which I do more neatly and succinctly than I did at Jordan's. The story loses some of its pain in the retelling, but I suspect that might have more to do with me pushing my feelings down as far as they'll go. It's the only thing I can do—I can't handle them right now. Not if I want to see this thing through.

"Jesus fucking Christ." Riker sums up the situation quite nicely. He also finishes crossing the room so that we're side by side once again. No more distance, no more walls. "Are you okay? That's some serious damage."

"Serious is right. And you can imagine how happy he feels about being incapacitated while I head out and save the day for him."

The first real smile I've seen in a while spreads across Riker's face. "Yeah. I'll have to go visit him later and rub it in."

A feeling of hope floods through me at the sight of that evil grin. God, I forgot what this felt like. To be part of a team. To know I'm not alone.

"Does that mean you'll help? You'll sign on for one last heist with me?"

"You know you don't have to ask," he says roughly and pulls me in for a brief and angular hug. "If I know you, Pen—and I think I do—this isn't our last heist. Not by a long shot."

THE COUNCIL 29

With the arrival of three federal agents and four newly reunited jewel thieves, my father's once-spacious hotel room shrinks to the size of my first apartment.

"I am *not* sitting next to the one who keeps smiling at me like the Joker."

"Well, I'm not sitting next to the one who looks like someone's soccer mom."

"Is there a reason my Wi-Fi keeps cutting out in here?"

"What do you mean, all communications are jammed? How am I supposed to work?"

"Are you sure that one is an agent? She looks like she's twelve."

Since I don't have the power to whistle commandingly and bring everyone's chatter to a close, I do the next best thing: I wheel out the dry erase board my dad had the bellhop bring up from one of the conference rooms. I noticed earlier that the back wheel squeaks, and the screech of rubber against metal does the trick.

This must be what power feels like.

"Okay, everyone. Quiet down. We have a lot of work to do and not a whole lot of time to do it." I slap a picture of the Starbrite Necklace in the middle of the board to motivate them. It was either that or the gruesome picture I took of the exit wound on Grant's stomach, but I wasn't sure how squeamish some of them might be. "As most of you already know, Grant was shot in the back two days ago by Christopher Leon, a man he's long suspected of double-dealing. Since the federal authorities have seen fit *not* to hold that agent accountable for his actions"—the criminal side of the room casts an accusing glance at the noncriminal side—"I've decided to take matters into my own hands. Namely, this."

The two-dimensional necklace doesn't make as profound a statement as I'd like, but the message gets across.

"It's my belief that the Starbrite Necklace is too strong a lure for the Peep-Toe Prowler to resist, especially now that his continued federal career is in question. Regardless of whether or not he has any current plans to take it, I intend to make access so easy, he'll have no choice but to go for it." And, in so doing, get caught with the diamonds literally on his person. I defy any federal agency to clear him after that. "Which means that in the next two days, we need to come up with a surefire way to break into the Conrad Museum during a gala ball. Plans have already been partially laid by Riker, Oz, and Jordan over here on my right. Wave, guys."

Oz lifts his hand and offers a cheerful wave. Jordan does, too, much more daintily, but all I can get out of Riker is a vague flap. I don't blame him. This much authority in one room is a tad overwhelming.

"They'll be able to fill you in on their details in a moment, but for now, it's enough to know that the necklace is located on a heavily guarded second-floor gallery, complete with a laser security system and alarmed doors."

Mariah, sitting crisscross on the floor with her computer in her lap, raises her hand. "So what you're saying is, it'll be a piece of cake?"

The room gives a reluctant chuckle.

"I know it sounds intimidating, but we've got seven of the best, most devious minds in this room right now. Eight, if you count my dad in the back."

"Oh, don't count me." My dad doesn't move from where he's leaning on the doorframe to his bedroom. "It would break the conditions of my agreement with the FBI. I'm merely a spectator."

Simon grunts in what could either be approval or condemnation.

"I've broken you into groups based on what I consider your strengths, but don't feel like you have to stick to them," I continue. "Remember, the goal here is to streamline our entry as much as possible. We want to grease the wheels so well that Christopher won't be able to pass up the opportunity to lift the necklace. He's probably scared right now—understandably—so there can be no errors."

Picking up the whiteboard marker, I scrawl out the basics. "Okay, Mariah and Oz, you two are our hackers, which means you're in charge of finding a way past the laser system."

"No need, Pen," Riker puts in. "I was already planning—"

"Riker, if you so much as say the word *smoke* or *mirror*, I'm kicking you out of this room."

"But we had that part covered!" he protests. "It doesn't make any sense to start from scratch now."

I offer my best withering stare. "Oh, yeah? What were you going to use to get in?"

"Sm—" He slumps in his seat. "Never mind."

Since I'm sure we could waste the next eight hours arguing over it, I decide to move on. "Oz, I believe you already found a way to take over the elevator to get us upstairs, yes?"

He nods. "I can control it remotely."

Mariah, who had been eyeing Oz as competition, turns to him with interest. "Really? How? Did you have to hack into the elevator company's security override system, or was it in the museum's local controls?"

He ducks his head in a move I recognize as professional modesty. "Neither."

Jordan fills in the rest. "He installed a communication box in the interior panel when they called him out to repair the elevator last week. It's a mechanical override, not an electronic one. No hacking required."

Ha! I knew I was right about that. No way was that elevator delay a coincidence.

Mariah lets out a low whistle. "That's old school. I like it."

Oz's face takes on a light pink tinge at the mild compliment. "It's a short-range solution," he mumbles. "I have to be nearby to make it work."

"Thus ensuring you're on site for troubleshooting," Mariah says with a nod. "Good thinking."

The light pink turns dark. I turn my attention to Jordan, wondering if she's witnessing this new, blushing Oz, but she's busy taking notes.

"Jordan, I'm hoping you can work something out with Simon to get the key code from Pierre, the guy who runs the place," I say. "Simon was telling me about a case he worked where the thieves put some kind of chemical on the victim's fingerprints and used that to figure out what buttons he pushed to get into his warehouse. Is that a thing?"

"Absolutely," Jordan says. "And I can take you one step further with a degrading fluorescent chemical. It'll leave residue behind while also making sure each print is fainter than the last. That way you can see the numbers *and* sequence."

"Excellent. I'll also need you two to either duplicate his key card or find a way to lift it. Riker refuses to tell me what you had planned for that, but I assume you can start there."

With that, I turn to my final mismatched pair.

"Riker and Cheryl, you guys are in charge of the ATM camera outside the bank next door. Christopher is obviously camera-shy, so there's no way he's going to follow through if he thinks he'll get caught on video. That means we need to do more than just hack in and turn it off like you guys were thinking. He needs to *see* that steps have been put in place to secure an exit."

"Spray paint?" Cheryl asks.

Riker shakes his head. "Wouldn't work. The bank guards would pick up on it in seconds."

"Smash it with a rock?"

He shakes his head again. "Too obvious. See above."

For a moment, I think it was a mistake to hand poor Cheryl over to Riker, who obviously intends to sneer circles around her, but she turns to him with her most quelling look and asks, "How about *smoke and mirrors*?"

We all laugh again, but Riker perks up, looking at Cheryl with something akin to admiration.

"I'll also need everyone to come up with ideas for handling security that night," I say. "I have it on good authority that they've hired additional staff, and there isn't enough time for one of us to get hired on. We'll need to find another way to circumvent them."

I take a deep breath and survey the assembled crew with a heartfelt pang. For the longest time, I've seen these two parts of my life as diametric opposites—my good half and my bad half, irreconcilable in every way—and navigating between them has been exhausting. I'm no one without the good half; even less without the bad. This group of people is as close to a literal translation of my dilemma as you can get.

Yet here we are. Sitting together. Working together. There is no monkey in the middle here.

"I've ordered room service and requested that no one disturb you unless absolutely necessary," I continue. "I know it's asking a lot for you to sit here for the next forty-eight hours and plan the theft of a necklace we don't get to keep, but you're all I have. You're all Grant has. No matter what else happens, we can't let Christopher try to take him away from us."

I pause, waiting for my rallying cheer, but all I get is a lot of blinking and two enthusiastic thumbs up from Oz. Good ol' Oz. At least one of us has seen the same heist movies as me.

"Any questions before I head out?" I ask.

"I have one."

We turn as a group to face the door, where a woman appears to have slipped through, unseen by all except my father and his ever-watchful eye. Dressed to impress in a mint-green pencil skirt and a cropped white top that shows off the perfect curve of her stomach, Tara is—as usual—a sight to behold.

"Yes?" I ask, refusing to be intimidated by her presence.

"It's a good plan and all, but how can you be so sure Chris will fall for it?"

There's that *Chris* again—mocking me, taunting me—but I suspect I know what it is now. It's the last-ditch effort of a woman who wants to be relevant. It's her desperate need to play along.

"Easy," I say and smile. "Because it's my job to make him."

Although I'd like nothing more than to start working on my part of the plan, I have to return to the hospital to check on Grant and assure him that I'm still in one piece. Enough time has passed that he's probably climbing the walls, if he hasn't already torn them down one by one.

It's a testament to his mother's calming influence that he's in his bed sleeping peacefully when I arrive.

"Oh, there you are, dear," Myrna says as I tiptoe through the door. I doubt the soap opera she's watching is the same one as before, but her gaze is fixated on the screen, and it doesn't look like she's changed position at all. It feels as though I've been gone eight minutes instead of eight hours. "It's good that you're here."

"Why? Is everything okay?" My fears of waking

Grant disappear as I fly to his side, scanning the machines he's hooked up to as if I have a clue what any of them mean.

"Oh, he's fine. He almost ripped his IV out and went looking for you when it started to get dark outside, but I convinced him to keep it in."

"How?" I ask, genuinely curious. That seems like a trick I should know.

She turns her mild gaze my way. "I don't know, dear. How do *you* get him to do the things you want?"

You mean, other than breaking his heart by telling him I have no intention of changing my ways and that I plan to make decisions regardless of his wishes? "I don't," I admit. "He's impossible once he gets like this, so I usually ignore him and do my own thing."

"As do I." Her smile spreads, and a twinkle reaches her eyes, which aren't like Grant's at all. While he has those dark, almost inky irises, hers are bright green, full of warmth and light. "I told him to go ahead and act like a barbarian who doesn't have enough faith in his wife to let her five feet out of his sight. I intend to keep you in the divorce, so his actions have no bearing on *me*."

My chest tightens. Her words hit closer to home than she realizes.

"Do you need to take a break for a few hours?" I ask. "The guest room is all set up for you at the house, so if you want to settle in…"

"I'm comfortable right where I am. Don't worry about me." She does look comfortable, but then, she always does. She's not one to be put out by circumstance. "But there was a young man here looking for you."

"For me?" The only young men I know are Riker and Oz, and I've already seen both of them.

"Well, he wasn't here to see me, and he wouldn't even come past the door to see Grant. You'd think my son had bones sticking out of his skin for how green the poor boy turned at the sight of him."

Dread and anticipation flood through me. "Was he about six feet tall? Golden hair? A cleft chin that looks like it could crack stone?"

"It *was* a rather forceful chin, now that you mention it," she says, only partly paying attention. Someone on the television set ran out of a wedding in a white dress, so I don't take it personally. "Grant's father had something like it. I hated it. I can't tell you how happy I was when our baby came out nicely flat and square."

I murmur a vague excuse for ducking out of the room, but she waves me off with the opinion that Grant will sleep for at least twelve more hours, so I'm free to roam the hospital at large. Which is exactly what I intend to do, except I get all of three feet from the door when Christopher pounces.

Like a lion.

Like a would-be assassin.

Like a man I'm not letting anywhere near my husband.

"Christopher?" I say, doing my best to keep the hard edge of anger from my voice. He looks peaky, as Myrna mentioned, so I focus on that to garner enough sympathy to face him. This plan will only work if he believes my forgiveness is sincere. "I didn't expect to see you here. Did you come to visit Grant?"

For a moment, the green, uneasy look lifts from his face. "Is he asking for me?"

"No." I'm prepared to lie for the sake of what needs to happen, but only to a point. That point doesn't include putting this man and my husband in the same room anytime soon. "He's asleep."

"Oh. Of course."

"And he's not feeling up to having visitors, so even when he is awake…"

"You mean he's not feeling up to having *me* as a visitor."

I take Christopher's arm and pull him away from the door. Even in the quiet wing of a hospital, his voice is overloud and overeager, his whole body strung full of energy.

"You did shoot him," I point out.

"I didn't!" Then, when a nurse walks by and shushes him with a harsh glare, he amends his outburst. "Well, I did shoot him, but I didn't *mean* to. It was an accident."

I'm unable to keep my hostility at bay. "You accidentally pulled a gun and shot a fellow agent in the back?"

"I know how it looks."

No, he has no idea how it looks, or he wouldn't be standing here with me. If he had any idea what sort of revenge lay in wait for him, he'd be changing his name, his hair color, his goddamned *chin* in hopes that I never track him down.

"His mom has him under a careful watch, and she's strict about who she lets in, so I don't suggest you try." I lead him to the elevator and push the button. Up, down, to the moon—I don't care as long as it gets Christopher off this floor and out of Grant's vicinity. "Did you know she's the person who taught him how to shoot a gun? You wouldn't think to look at her, but she carries more heat than most of the FBI agents I know, Grant included."

It's a lie, bald-faced and brazen, but I don't care. Christopher is *not* going to creep in and finish the job.

As the elevator arrives with a cheerful chime, Christopher steps back to allow me on. Even now, slick with remorse and some unnamed motive, he's ever the gentleman. We get on, and I press the number for the cafeteria level. That seems as good a place as any to lay out the trap I have for him.

"What's she like?" Christopher asks suddenly.

"Grant's mom? I just told you. She has great aim."

He laughs uneasily and reaches up to adjust his tie in what I suspect is a nervous tic, considering he's not wearing one. He's in jeans and a nicely pressed shirt with a jacket over the top, almost as if he wanted to get dressed for work but forgot, halfway through, that he's suspended.

Well, it could be a nervous tic, or it could be phenomenal acting. If this man is trying to get me to lower my guard, this would be a great way to go about it.

Too bad I have no intention of falling for it.

"No, I mean, what's she like as a person?" he asks.

"She's nice," I say, answering with honesty. "Laid-back. It's hard to get her riled up about anything, but once you do, good luck trying to get her to back down again. As soon as she commits to something, she's immovable."

He smiles faintly. "That sounds familiar."

I can't help but agree, but I press my lips in a firm line. I didn't mean it as a compliment—it was supposed to be a warning.

I follow Christopher to the cafeteria, where he buys

me a cup of coffee and a slice of chocolate cake. I accept them only because they're put into my hands directly from the woman behind the counter.

"They took my gun and badge," he says as soon as we're seated, saving me the task of introducing the topic myself.

"Oh?" I can't say I'm sad to hear about that. I don't particularly like the idea of ending up in a hospital bed next to Grant's.

"Yeah. I might not get them back again."

I have a hard time mustering up the pity he's so obviously angling for. "You fired a gun in a public place without cause and shot a man under your command," I say. "People have a way of reacting badly to that sort of thing."

"But you aren't mad." It's more statement than question.

"I'm furious," I respond, surprised at how calm I'm able to make myself sound. "I hope the FBI bars you from employment and makes it impossible for you to use a handgun for the rest of your life."

He eyes me askance. "That's fair."

"He almost died, Christopher."

"I know." An expression of misery washes over him, and I don't know where to look. As an actor, this man has some serious chops. "For what it's worth, I'm sorry. More sorry than you know."

"Is that why you came here? To apologize?" *Or to finish the job you started?* It's not out of the realm of possibility—he has to know that Grant won't stop now, that one wiped video isn't a free pass for all his other crimes.

"I only wanted…" He takes a deep breath and cradles his head in his hands. "Just make sure he knows how sorry I am. Please? I know he has no reason to believe me, but it was never my intention to take things this far."

I stop in the middle of lifting a bite of cake to my mouth. "This far?"

"Yeah. I should have stopped a long time ago, walked away while I still had the chance. But I kept going despite my better judgment, and now look what's happened."

I'm not sure what I'm supposed to say or how I should react. Is he about to confess over dry cake and sour coffee?

He glances at me, sharp and earnest. "*You* understand, don't you? How hard it is to step away while you're in the thick of things? To give up when you're so close?"

Lord help me, but I nod. This man robbed my grandmother's friends and almost killed my husband, caused more problems in my marriage than any stranger should be allowed to, but still I nod.

Because I do get it. I do understand.

It's wrong to break the law, and it's wrong to take things that don't belong to you, but when it's the only thing you know—when it's the only thing you have—it's almost impossible to envision a life of anything else. It would be so easy to draw a line between me and Christopher, to point out that no matter how bad things get, I'd never hurt another human being. I'd never hurt *Grant*. But the reality is, I already have.

He wants the happy wife and the comfortable home and the neat picket fence protecting them both—but he'll never have that unless I'm willing to change my entire worldview or cut him loose. And I tried that first one. For six whole months, I tried. My worldview, it seems, is permanently fixed.

Cutting him loose might be the only other option I have.

"Would you like to come with me to the Black and White Ball?" I ask suddenly.

Christopher blinks, understandably startled by my request. "What?"

"My grandmother got me tickets to the Black and White Ball—the one they're holding at the Conrad Museum on Saturday. Grant was supposed to go with me, but that's obviously not going to happen now. From what I understand, a girl can't go to these things alone, so I'll need a date. Would you like to be mine?"

I thought it would be difficult to get the request out, but it's surprisingly easy. I guess that's what happens when you have as much in common with your husband's enemy as you do your actual husband.

"Really? You mean it?" The smile that spreads across Christopher's face would be heartbreaking if I didn't know the true motivation behind it. "I can't tell you how much I'd like that."

I know. He couldn't get easier access to the necklace if it was handed to him on a tray. Which, in a way, is exactly what I intend to do.

"It'll be fun," I say and dazzle him with my brightest smile. "I still need to get a dress, and you'll need a tuxedo, but I'm sure you won't have any problems with that."

"You don't think Grant will mind?"

Oh, Grant will mind. Grant will mind so much, he

might take it upon himself to get out of bed and stop us both.

So I laugh. "I don't know about you, but I, for one, don't intend to tell him."

THE HEIST
(REPRISE)

IT'S A SHAME GRANT ISN'T MY DATE TO THE BALL tonight, because I look freaking amazing.

I haven't been in the right frame of mind to apologize to Tara for believing her to be the Peep-Toe Prowler all these weeks, so I passed on her offer of a dress loan, opting instead to use Jane as my guide. She was happy to take me and happier still to foot the bill, which was nice but not at all necessary.

We walked into Barneys—my choice—where she moved straight to the most beautiful dress in the place and said we were done.

"But it's red," I pointed out, even as I admired the slinky material. I look great in slinky. "I thought everyone was going to be in black or white. That's what I'm supposed to wear."

"That's all the more reason not to, don't you think? If I could still pull it off, I'd do it. Just imagine the looks on their faces. It'll be fun."

Again, I agreed. Most of the time, my goal would be to blend in the night of a big heist, to slither around like a shadow, but I need to make sure everyone sees me there—or, rather, that they see the man escorting me. Christopher Leon might be able to wipe a video feed while the FBI's back is turned, but even he can't change the firsthand reports of several hundred witnesses.

"It *is* beautiful…" I said, trailing my fingers over the fabric.

Jane was all decision. "Then this is the one you want. You're a size four? Don't look so surprised—your mom was, too. I was always jealous of how easy she made it look. She wore a red dress just like this to prom."

Flustered by the reference to my mother, I accepted both the compliment and the dress.

I'm in it now as I wait for Christopher to arrive, my hair piled on top of my head and secured by about fifty bobby pins. Half of them stab my head any time I make a sudden movement, but it feels good knowing they're there. That's fifty lock-picking kits no one will question me having in my possession.

Plus, the coiled loops of my hair are strategically placed to hide the small transmitter behind my right ear. I'm hooked up and plugged in to an alarmingly high-tech federal communication system that Mariah and Cheryl stole from the office.

Those women had way more fun with this than national security allows.

I also have Cheryl's letter opener strapped to one thigh and my red peep-toe heels on, but those parts go without saying. The shiv is for my safety—Cheryl insisted on it—and the shoes, while not functional, were a gift from my husband, who's still lying in a hospital bed with his beautiful body torn open.

Forget functionality. I'm wearing the goddamned shoes.

Christopher arrives precisely on time, looking as handsome and nervous as if he's picking me up for a real date. I can tell as soon as I open the front door that his tuxedo is one he owns, tailored to his body and pulled out for many such occasions.

He's done this before. He does this all the time.

It's that realization, more than the image of Grant, that has me greeting him with a semblance of calm. This is the last time Christopher Leon puts on a tux and pretends to be something he's not.

"Oh, you look so nice!" I say in a tone that anyone who knows me would recognize as a clear and patent lie. "You FBI agents sure do clean up well."

A dark flash fills his eyes, and I'm reminded how important it is to tread lightly. "I'm not an FBI agent tonight."

Of course he's not. And if all goes well, he never will be again.

"You can take the badge away from the man, but you can't take the man away from the badge," I say breezily. It's true, too. I doubt even decades away from the job would force Grant to budge so much as an inch. "But let's not think about that tonight. I've been cooped up inside the hospital for days. I don't know about you, but I feel a need to stretch my wings."

Christopher pulls his muscle car up to valet parking right on time.

Almost everything about the Conrad Museum's exterior looks the same as it did before, save for the expensive cars spewing out well-dressed men and women and the two large, intimidating men at the door checking off the guest list. The bouncers are standard protocol at an event of this magnitude, and they're possible to circumnavigate only by begging your grandmother to add a few fake names to the list without asking questions about it.

Of course, if you zoom out a little, things take on a more interesting light. To the left, a few feet away from an ATM machine on the side of the bank, a masked magician and his middle-aged assistant are setting up. It's an odd time of night and an even stranger location for a street show, but people are already pausing to watch them work. Clad in crushed velvet and with a swatch of black hair—a lock of which keeps falling over his eye—the magician looks exactly like the dark, brooding sort to put on a good show.

How much magic Riker actually *knows* is anyone's guess, though I suspect his fast hands will lend themselves well to the task. Not that it matters. The tricks don't have to be good. They just have to include a few well-timed smoke bombs to guarantee obscured vision—including electronic vision—for a full thirty minutes.

Cheryl gave Riker his smoke after all.

"That's a strange place for a street magician," Christopher murmurs as we make our way past the pair. Riker's mask renders him unidentifiable, and Cheryl looks like a completely different person in sequins and a long blond wig, so I'm not too worried about him making the connection.

"Isn't it?" I ask blithely. "I wonder what made them set up there. They're going to be in everyone's way. People can't even get to the ATM machine."

I'd rather he not spend *too* much time questioning their presence—yet—so I wind my arm through his and steer him past the guards.

"Do you do this sort of thing often?" Christopher asks. "The high society functions, I mean?"

"I have been lately," I say. "They're more interesting than you think—you'd be surprised what you can get away with."

He turns his head in sudden interest, but I catch sight of my favorite mustachioed museum curator and beeline straight for him.

"Pierre!" I say with genuine pleasure. If he looked dapper before, he's downright quixotic now. He's in tails—actual tails—and the bright white of the vest underneath his tuxedo jacket looks like something out of a 1920s gangster movie. He also looks like he's *in* a gangster movie, but not as the guy with the tommy gun. He's definitely the guy on the other end, nervous and trying not to show it.

Poor man. I wish I could reassure him that he has seven talented people looking out for him tonight. You couldn't ask for a better personal security team.

"Ah, the beautiful Liliana Dupont returns," he replies with a shake of his head. "Though I suppose it's not fair to keep calling you that. You're quite lovely in your own right."

"Pierre knew my mother when they were younger," I explain to my date. "He thinks I look like her."

"Then she must have been very pretty," Christopher

replies with an easy promptness that robs the compliment of its value.

Pierre is wearing white gloves to match his outfit,
but that's a nonissue. A carefully disguised Oz came by
to look at the contents of the first floor of the museum
yesterday, and the chemical formula Jordan concocted
was transferred to Pierre's hand via handshake. After
that, all Oz had to do was reach in his pocket and toy
with the elevator's remote controls, which he did before
the chemical wore off. Pierre, alarmed at the malfunc-
tioning elevator, promptly went upstairs to check on his
beloved collection.

With any luck, the UV flashlight currently tucked
down the front of my bra will show us not only the
numbers on the keypad, but the order in which they
were used.

I only wish the crew had been half as inventive when
it came to getting their hands on his key card. No amount
of brainstorming provided a way to get that card, repli-
cate it, and return it within the small window of time we
had. And my friends' old plan had been discarded as
soon as Mariah pried it out of them.

It was Tara, of course. She would have been sent to
seduce it out of him.

Since no one except Cheryl offered to step in and take
her place, it's up to me to get my hands on it tonight
before I slip upstairs. I'm guessing, from the way Pierre
keeps nervously patting his chest, that it's tucked into
an interior pocket.

It's not great news. The curator is nice and all, but
we're not on such good terms that I can run my hands
up his torso without giving myself away.

Pierre catches sight of another guest and goes off to greet them, so Christopher offers me his arm and escorts me toward the food tables near the back. For reasons I'm sure only my grandmother understands, they used a circus theme for the appetizers as well as the charity. The shrimp are arranged in literal rings of fire.

"Your mom must have been rich if she grew up in all this," Christopher says as he passes over the flaming food in favor of a glass of champagne, which he gulps in one quick motion.

"Yeah, but she gave it up for love," I say. "You have to admire her for that."

He eyes me askance.

It's not difficult for me to interpret that look. "My dad has money *now*, but it wasn't always like that," I say defensively. "We had our share of lean times. Besides, when he married my mom, he always planned to give up his criminal ways. He never got the chance, that's all."

Christopher pauses. "It takes a lot of strength to walk away like that."

It doesn't take strength, I want to tell him. *It takes superhuman capabilities*. Superhuman capabilities that I, unfortunately, don't have. I feel more alive right now than I have in ages.

"Penelope, there you are!" My attention is pulled away by my grandmother, who hails me from the small crowd gathered around her. She's wearing her regular pantsuit—I swear that woman never wears anything else—but this one is white and dressed up with a sequined blouse and a gleaming string of pearls I would have advised her to leave safely locked up at home. "I must say I was worried about how you'd turn out, but you look almost presentable this evening. Flashy and obvious, but presentable."

"Jane helped pick my dress," I say modestly and nod at the woman in question. Unlike me, she's opted for black. Her dress has a full, puffed skirt that stops just above the knee, fifties-style. I wonder if it's an homage to the collection upstairs. "You look great, by the way."

"So does your date," Jane says pointedly. I remember, too late for manners, that Christopher is standing patiently by my side awaiting an introduction. To be honest, he's more of a burden than a date at this point. It would be so much easier if I could stash him in a closet until I'm ready to make my way upstairs to lure him into the trap.

Which, if the melting clock/artwork installation is to be believed, is soon. Crap. I need to get that card from Pierre.

As if to remind me of the ticking clock, I hear a tinny buzz and then the soft sound of Jordan's voice announcing that Riker's smoke bomb has just gone off. *T minus thirty minutes and counting*.

I make a round of hasty introductions, hoping the well-bred inanities required in this sort of situation will leave me enough time to scan the room for Oz and Simon. I know they're here, mingling among the guests under assumed names, but they're either hiding where I can't see them or putting the final touches into place.

Help. I need help.

It comes from an unlikely source.

"Who are you looking for?" Jane asks, watching me as my eyes roam the floor of the museum for the second time. "Your friend Olivia? I saw her earlier—she's in a frothy white gown that looks like a puff pastry. You can't miss her."

"No, I was hoping to talk to Pierre."

"Pierre?" Her eyes open wider. "Whatever for?"

"I, uh—" I hadn't thought that far ahead, actually.

She hands me yet another out. "You're going to see what else he can tell you about your mom, aren't you? You're so sweet. Remind me to introduce you to that woman standing by the champagne fountain later. She was another friend of ours, and she's eager to meet you."

I flash a grateful smile, feeling like a traitor. These people have nothing but fondness and affection for the memory my mother left behind—and by extension, have nothing but fondness and affection for *me*. Yet here I am, lying and sneaking around, gauging how I can best use them to break in upstairs.

"I've got just the thing to get you two together," Jane adds with a wink. "That man never lets a dance pass him by." She turns to my date. "Christopher, you said your name was?"

Christopher nods.

"Be a dear and tell the quartet behind the von Schuettenberg to strike up a waltz. I believe it's time the dancing portion of this ball got underway."

I can barely believe my good luck. No sooner does Christopher lean down to murmur something in the piano player's ear than Jane is leading Pierre straight to me. He still looks anxious, especially now that people are moving and rustling en masse, but true to her words, he perks up as the strains of a waltz begin.

"Your mother was a heavenly dancer," Pierre confesses as he takes me into his arms. In my peep-toes, I'm the same height as he is, so it's a strange sensation. I'm used to being dwarfed by Grant's massive frame.

"Was she?" I ask. "I bet Erica made her take all kinds of formal lessons as a kid. Unlike me. I can feel her judging me from the other side of the room."

His mustache twitches in laughter. "Nonsense. Your grandmother is proud of you—she wouldn't have brought you here otherwise. And your dancing is perfectly acceptable."

It *is* fine, since my time as a rec center ballet teacher taught me a thing or two about fancy footwork, but I pretend to falter anyway. My fumbling movements are the perfect cover for me to beg Pierre to teach me the steps. The faltering one-two-three, one-two-three is the perfect cover for slipping a hand inside his coat pocket and extracting the card, so I accept.

And it's a good thing, too. With no more than a sharp turn, a wobbling heel, and an intoxicated couple at our back, I have the key card in my grip.

While Pierre struggles to help the fallen couple back to their feet, I stick the card down the front of my dress alongside the UV flashlight. It's getting awfully crowded in there, especially since I don't have much in the way of cleavage to hide all that technology, but the music comes to a miraculous halt before Pierre notices.

"Thank you for the dance," I manage, breathless with the exertion of the waltz and the exhilaration of success.

"Any time," he says, more out of politeness than a desire to hold me in his arms again.

Not that I mind in the slightest. Now that I have the key card in hand, it's time to take this party upstairs.

Christopher performs the waltz to admiration with my grandmother, and he looks as though he has every intention of doing the same with me, but I draw him away from the dance floor before he can get an arm around my waist.

"It was nice of you to take my grandmother out for a whirl," I say, struggling to keep the obvious excitement from my voice. In less than ten minutes, Christopher Leon and I will have our hands on the Starbrite Necklace. In less than ten minutes, I'll know him for what he is.

And Simon will be waiting outside to arrest him.

"It was my pleasure. I tried to ask your friend Jane, but she was needed for a minor catering emergency. Something about stale canapés."

"She's one of the women in charge of the event," I explain, only giving him half an ear. I'm too distracted scouring the room for signs of Simon getting ready.

According to our original headcount, there are a dozen security guards on staff at the Conrad—all of whom are working on high alert tonight. The firm they hired for additional support supplied the two bouncers at the door as well as two men posted outside the elevator and two more at the back emergency exit. Eighteen all together, each of them on the lookout for anything out of the ordinary. We've never attempted a heist with so much on-site muscle before, and if we didn't have Simon on our side, I doubt we ever would.

But we do have Simon. And Simon has a badge.

I see him out of the corner of my eye, wearing a dark suit and tie, looking uncomfortable. He nods once, which is my cue to start moving. Whirling Christopher so he faces away from his coworker, I push my date toward the opposite side of the room. The last thing we need is for him to witness Simon flashing his credentials to the security guards and asking them for help with the belligerent magician outside whose smoke is conveniently obscuring the ATM camera.

"Have you been to this museum before?" I ask conversationally, leading Christopher in the general direction of the elevators. We're not close enough to those double metal doors to draw suspicion, but we are close enough to slip inside as soon as the guards are distracted. "I came last week and looked at the collection upstairs. It's breathtaking."

"Uh, no. This is my first time. I don't usually do this sort of thing, to be honest."

"This sort of thing as in…" Museums? Fancy parties? *Theft?*

"I don't know. Socializing, I guess? I don't get out much."

"Really?" I'm puzzled by the angle he's trying to play. Christopher is an attractive, single man with a job and a nice car. He's officious and loud, of course, but he's still charming for all that. And with all the jewels he's taken, he's got to be pretty wealthy by now. He must have friends in the hundreds. "But you've had such a successful career and everything. Grant says you've practically shot up the ranks at the FBI. *Someone* must like you."

His eyes—those dark, familiar eyes—settle on me with uncomfortable intensity. "That's not about me. That's about something else."

My heart picks up, and for the first time since everything started, I feel how dangerous a situation I've placed myself in. All of Grant's warnings and worries slam into me at once. Ten million dollars isn't something to take lightly. It's more money than most people see in a lifetime, more money than most people need to feel justified in resorting to extremes, as this man has already proven.

People kill for this kind of money. People die.

A waiter whizzes past us carrying a tray of hors d'oeuvres, his head ducked low, and I recognize him—just barely—as Oz. Simon stands talking to a pair of security guards on the other side of the room, gesturing outside at where Riker and Cheryl are putting on the show of a lifetime. Mariah is sitting in a dark room somewhere, furiously hacking into the laser system so it will be timed to go down as we walk in. Jordan is in my ear and ready to step in the moment I need her. And even my grandmother is helping, standing back and watching with something like admiration as I take control of this ballroom and all the people in it.

Unlike Christopher, I'm not alone.

"Look, Penelope, there's something I should tell you, something I should have told you from the start." Christopher runs his hand through his hair. "Can we go somewhere quiet to talk?"

Yes, actually. And I know just the place.

"Do you want to go see the necklace?" I ask and point upstairs.

He blinks. "You have access?"

Oh, I have access. Don't you worry your proud lion's head about that. "Of course," I say, trying on a breezy laugh. If it falls a little flat, Christopher doesn't seem to notice. "I'm Erica Dupont's granddaughter, after all."

As if by magic, the guards standing in front of the elevator doors shift their attention to the front doors of the museum, where Simon leads a few men out. They don't give up their posts, but a clumsy waiter crashes into them at that exact moment, sending a flaming ring of shrimp flying.

In their haste to prevent fire from catching on all the trailing gowns in the room, the guards don't notice when the waiter reaches into his pocket and fiddles with a control. They also don't notice when the elevator doors swish open and two people slip quietly inside.

It's showtime.

THE 31 GRAB

CHRISTOPHER SHOWS A SLIGHT CONCERN WHEN THE ELEVATOR takes us to the second floor without my pushing a single button. That concern hitches up a notch when I walk up to the alarm panel, slip a pair of gloves on my hands, and extract a key card from the front of my dress, swiping it through with a cool efficiency.

When I extract the UV flashlight and hold it up to the keypad, he even goes so far as to attempt to stop me. It's not a surprise; I assume he's being careful not to give too much of his interest away yet. Until he can actually *see* the necklace, it's smart to have an exit strategy.

"Uh, what are you doing?" he asks as I lean in to see what trace I can make. The oval road maps of Pierre's prints glow an eerie purple under my light thanks to the chemical, faint but visible. As expected, the two is the darkest, and an eight is so faint it's almost invisible. *First and last*, no problem.

Unfortunately, the middle three numbers *are* a problem. From the smudged prints, I can tell that both the one and the seven have been pressed—which would be fine, except we know the code is five digits long, so one of them had to be pressed twice.

It's figuring out which one that's slowing me down. With my light held close, I can see they're about equal in terms of visibility, which tells me nothing except that I'm stuck.

Gah. Repeated digits. Why didn't we think of this?

"Penelope? Are you sure we should be up here?"

"It's fine," I say. "Will you look at this and tell me what you think? Does it seem like the seven is fainter than the one, or is it the other way around?"

He leans in, his head next to mine. "The seven is fainter, but only because the one covers a wider area," he says after a slight pause. "Like, ah, the seven came first, maybe? And then the one was doubled up. But I'm not—"

A professional? I beg to differ. I'm running out of time, so I go with his gut. With only a minor wince of anticipation, I press the code 2-7-1-1-8 and hold my breath. Even though only a fraction of a second passes, it feels like an eternity before the familiar whir and click fills the air, and the door opens easily under my hand.

I release a breath. That was a close one.

Now that Christopher sees the collection for himself—even if it is in the dark—he's starting to lose the feigned innocence. Just as I planned, the excitement of the heist is getting the better of him. It's not long now until he reveals himself. He takes a large step forward, as if to plunge right in, but I fling up my arm to stop him.

He's heavy—all these tightly packed FBI agents are—and I grunt as I force him to remain in place.

"Not yet," I say as I put all my strength into preventing him from setting off every alarm in the place. "We have to make sure the lasers are off first."

Crouching low, I reach into my brassiere trove and pull out a compact of face powder, which I brought for this sole purpose. Time to touch up my makeup in the ladies' room wasn't put on the schedule. My gentle breath over the surface of the powder sends a cloud of particles into the room, where they catch the light of the network of lasers, all of which are still hot.

"Dammit," I say. "She was supposed to have them off by now."

"Who was supposed to have them off?" Christopher asks.

I wave him off and press the chip on the back of my ear. "Are you there?" I ask in a hushed voice, not wanting to crackle too loudly on Jordan's end of the line. "I'm ready for the lasers to go down."

The crackle of her response comes through. "*They are down.*"

"No, they're not. I'm looking at them right now."

"*Well, they were down. Mariah confirmed it. Hang on a sec.*"

Jordan's end of the line goes silent for a moment, and I use the opportunity to study Christopher, who's watching me with an unreadable look on his face. Ah, the unreadable look. So familiar to me, especially through those eyes. I imagine he's contemplating all the ways he can smuggle the necklace out of here while leaving me behind to take the blame. A bullet in the back, perhaps? Or a neat blow over the head?

"*She says they were down five minutes ago, as planned. They must be on an automatic cycle. Are you behind schedule?*"

"There were some complications with the password, but I'm in now," I say, unwilling to go into more detail while I'm still crouched and staring at lasers. "Can she shut them down again?"

Another pause, another long look from Christopher, even more sweat building up on my brow.

"*She says no, not without it triggering a fail-safe hardwired into the system.*"

"Well, shit." I rock back on my heels. "So that's it? The mission is over?"

"*Not yet—hang on—*"

I expect a lengthy pause as Mariah tries to come up with a backdoor plan, but it's only a few seconds before another voice takes over the conversation. "*Pen? Do you still have that compact? The one with the mirror?*"

I groan at the sound of Riker's ill-contained glee. "Yeah. I have it."

"*Excellent. It looks like we're going to have to do this my way, after all.*"

He pauses expectantly.

"We don't have time for you to gloat," I grumble, but I know him well enough to accept that gloating will need to be worked in. "Fine. You're a genius criminal mastermind, and I can't do this without you. Happy now?"

"*Getting there,*" he says with a cackle. "*Now. I need you to count how many detectors there are. They're*" *what the lasers are pointed at, the trigger that will go off if the flow of light is interrupted in any way. Can you do that?"*

I scan the room and grimace. It's big and dark, and without a steady influx of face powder, we can't see the lasers to trace their path. As much as I hate to admit it, some of Riker's smoke would come in handy right about now.

"No, I don't think I can," I admit. "What do they look like?"

"It depends on how sophisticated the system is. Most likely they're small black boxes along the base of the wall."

Small black shadows are everywhere. "I can't. It's too hard to tell in this light."

"What about the reflectors? Can you see those?"

"Yes. Maybe. No." This is starting to feel futile. I don't even know what a reflector is. "I'm not good at tech systems. You know that. You're the one who handles this sort of thing."

A gentle cough sounds from behind me. "May I?"

I turn to find Christopher standing over my shoulder, taking in the same scene with a much calmer, almost distinguished air. *Finally.* Gone is the bumbling pretense—no more do we have to pretend he's going to stop me from going through with this. The Peep-Toe Prowler is ready to act at last.

"Do you know a lot about disabling laser alarm systems?" I ask.

"I assume you have someone on the line to walk you through it?" He doesn't wait for me to reply before beckoning. "Give it to me."

Since there isn't much else I can do short of crawling

on my hands and knees and hoping I don't trigger the network, I comply. Pulling the earpiece—which I'm sure he recognizes as one of the FBI's own—from behind my ear, I step back and wait, curious to see what he'll do next.

"There's one detector," Christopher says in a clipped voice, his normal volubility controlled for once. There's a pause while I assume Riker adjusts to the change before Christopher speaks again. "No, not lasers specifically, but I'm a fast learner."

Another lengthy pause ensues before Christopher shifts position and tries again. "From what I can tell, there's just the one near the back of the room. Eight reflectors—three on the left, five on the right. We can't see the pattern of the lasers, but I can make a good guess based on the angles. You think it's as easy as redirection?"

Redirection doesn't sound easy to me, not by a long shot, but Christopher is already playing with the mirror in his hand, flexing it on its hinge until it separates from the powder half. Regret at wasting this man's talents by sending him to prison twinges in my stomach until I remind myself what he's done. *He might play well, but he doesn't play fair*.

"I see what you're saying, but I'd need a second reflective surface to make that work," Christopher says over the earpiece. He turns to me. "I don't suppose you have another mirror down the front of your dress, do you?"

Alas, even my bag of tricks comes to an end. I shake my head.

"I could try breaking it in half," he says doubtfully. Shattered shards of glass seem like an unstable resource—not to mention a safety hazard—so I shake my head again, this time with meaning. Hitting a dead end this far along is the worst. It's a door slammed in the face, a knife stabbed in the gut—

"Oh, wait!" I cry, louder than I intend. More moderately, I add, "I do have this," and reach for the bottom hem of my dress. I feel another pang that it's Christopher here with me instead of my husband, because I have never felt sexier or more badass than when I expose the length of my thigh and unstrap Cheryl's shiny letter opener from my leg. God bless that woman's foresight. "Here. Will this do?"

Christopher smiles in full dimple mode. "Oh, yeah. That'll do fine."

My role after that is to occasionally blow a puff of compact powder into the air when Christopher requests it, watching as the particles dance and shimmer in the light of the laser beam. It's pretty in a dangerous, this-could-be-the-thing-that-sends-me-to-jail-forever sort of way.

"Okay, I think I have it calculated." He hands me the mirror. "On my mark, you're going to place this on top of that display case at this exact angle. We're going to redirect the laser to this knife, which will then bypass the laser beam straight to the detector. But we have to time it perfectly, or it won't work. There can't be a delay."

"That sounds hard."

"It *is* hard, but no more so than any of the other tasks you've pulled off this evening. I assume you have a plan for getting the necklace out of here undetected?"

I can't help but grin. "Did you see the magician outside the bank getting ready for his show? He's got all cameras blocked. We're clear."

His glance is sharp but admiring. "You set that up?"

He pauses as I assume Riker corrects him as to the true power behind that piece of work. Another one of those deep, dimpled smiles greets my eyes, and Christopher holds up his fingers.

"On my count of three. Ready?"

I nod.

"Okay, here goes nothing. One. Two. Thr—"

We place the mirrors, our movements swift and sure, our hands steady in a way that belongs solely to surgeons and jewel thieves. There's no way to see the lasers being redirected, so all we can do is stand and wait for the inevitable alarm. When it doesn't come, I pull out the compact and give the powder one final blow.

The lasers sparkle and shimmer…a good five feet away from the center of the room.

"It worked," Christopher says in a stunned voice.

"Of course it worked." I lead the way to the Starbrite Necklace with a confident step, borne mostly of the fact that I'm just as stunned by our success as he is. "Isn't it beautiful?"

Knowing firsthand what an ugly piece of craftsmanship the necklace is, I offer the compliment to encourage Christopher to make the first move at smashing through the glass.

Which is why it comes as such a surprise when I finally look down to see it.

"Wait—where's the necklace? Why is the case empty?" I look to my new partner in alarm. He'd been within eyesight all evening, so there's no way he could have already snuck up here and stolen it.

An accomplice? An earlier heist? *A setup?*

My heart thuds heavily. *No*. It can't be.

"Are you sure it's supposed to be in here?"

"Yes, I'm sure!" I look around the rest of the room, eyes narrowed as I try to pick out the glint of jewels in the dark. The rest of it appears to be there—the jade and the emeralds, the chunky metalwork I remember so clearly from my last visit—but when I whirl back to the Starbrite case, it's still very much empty. "Did they move it? It has to be there! I need it to—"

I glance at Christopher, hoping to find some sign of guilt on his face. But if he feels any, it's well hidden. "Yes, Penelope?" he prods. "You need it to what?"

To put in his pocket so I can send him out the door and into Simon's waiting arms. To end this thing once and for all.

As if on cue, the overhead fluorescent lights turn on in a bright flash of white. The laser system, so neatly bypassed by Christopher's adept ministrations, goes off in a whirlwind of sirens and warning lights. I don't have to look to know that Pierre is standing in the doorway, flushed and frantic at having found himself relieved of his key card, flanked by heavily armed guards on both sides.

"You!" he cries, striding forward as if he'd like to waltz me into oblivion. "Little Lily Dupont! How could you do this?"

I moan, wishing I had an answer other than stupid pride and even stupider folly. Grant warned me that this would happen, that Christopher Leon only wanted a fall guy and would go to any lengths to secure one, but I, in my stubbornness, refused to believe that such a disaster could befall me.

But here I am. The necklace is gone. I'm standing in the room where it went missing, where it's only my word against a federal agent and the museum curator that I didn't do it.

And in this damnable red dress, about a hundred people saw me come up here.

"I didn't…" I begin feebly, but no one is listening to me.

What happens next is a blur, emotion and panic combining to overwhelm me, but there are two things I know to be true. The first is that Christopher Leon, the man who shot my husband and set me up as the Peep-Toe Prowler, inexplicably inserts himself between me and the security guards. The second is that with the sudden illumination, I can now see a panel cut into the wall opposite the pedestal—the faint outline of an opening carved into the drywall, into the insulation, into the metal siding, layer after layer painstakingly cut away to provide an alternate access route. That must have been how Christopher's accomplice got in.

I'm screwed.

Or so I think until Christopher speaks up. "Stop right there," he says. "I'm FBI." And then, harsher, "Penelope, go."

I spin, confused by the sound of that command. It's Grant but not Grant, his voice of authority and concern in a place he can't possibly be.

He lifts his hands as the guards move forward, shifting to keep his bulk between me and them. "You need to go," Christopher says, shattering all my expectations. Saving me. "*Now*."

I don't hesitate the second time around. With no more

thought than my own selfish, cowardly survival, I fly to the panel someone else cut into the wall and pull it aside.

And then I do what Penelope Blue has always done best.

I squeeze myself into the smallest shape possible and crawl.

THE 32 ESCAPE

THE TUNNEL LEADS, AS MOST TUNNELS DO, NOWHERE GOOD.

As soon as I pop my head out the end of it, I realize there's nothing preventing me from falling twenty feet to the ground outside the Conrad Museum except a rope that dangles from the rooftop. Since I'm unable to fly, and heading back inside doesn't sound appealing, I kick off my shoes and climb that sucker so fast, I'll bear the rope burns on my upper arms for weeks to come.

Only to find myself climbing over the roof's edge to stare at none other than Tara Lewis.

For the first time since I've had the misfortune to know Tara Lewis, I'm dressed better than she is. My ball gown is a stark contrast to the black shirt, black leggings, black beanie, and—hey, are those *my* boots?— she's wearing. If it weren't for the perfect makeup and wisp of platinum blond hair trailing out of the bottom of her hat, I probably wouldn't have recognized her.

Especially since she's pointing a gun at me.

"Oh, my God." I don't try to move off the outer ledge where I'm perched, opting instead to remain perfectly still so as to avoid being shot and sent hurtling to the pavement below. I wish I could say that the only thing I feel right now is fear for my life, but I'm aware of another sensation creeping through my veins.

Disappointment. And for Tara Lewis, of all people.

"It really *was* you?" I ask. "This whole time?"

"Penelope?" Her gun comes down a fraction. "What are you doing up here?"

"Fleeing for my life, obviously."

Even though I'm not fleeing—I'm not moving at all, to be honest—she doesn't balk at my confession. "Where's Christopher?"

"Why do you care?" I ask. But then I pause, aware of one very good reason why she might care, and my confusion mounts. I'm having a hard time following the thread of my own suspicions, as Christopher and Tara and potential unnamed accomplices take shape around me. "Does this mean he's your partner after all? You guys planned this together?"

This time, she does balk, her brow lowered as she tries to puzzle out my meaning. "I don't understand. Where's Jane?"

"Jane Bartlett?" I don't wait for an answer. Since Tara doesn't seem to be on the verge of pumping me full of lead, I climb down from the ledge to the rooftop below. Having that small barrier between me and the swirling vertigo of death goes a long way in lowering my heart rate, but my pulse is hot and frantic at the base of my throat.

"I think she's still at the party," I say as soon as I'm

on solid ground. "Unless they've started evacuating people by now."

I take my eyes off Tara long enough to spare a glance to the sidewalk below. It doesn't look as though the guests are streaming out in panic and fear, but that doesn't mean the police won't arrive soon to clear the building. Oh, how I wish I'd thought to get the earpiece back from Christopher. I could use my friends right about now.

"Then we need to move fast," Tara says. "Here."

In the five seconds my attention was distracted, Tara silently closed the distance between us and reached for my hand. The gun is now tucked securely in her waist-band—I think that's my utility belt, too, the thief—but her grip is so strong, she manages to drag me halfway across the roof before my bare feet find enough purchase on the rooftop tiles to stop her.

"I'm not going anywhere with you," I say, digging my heels in. "Where is it? Did you shove it down the front of your shirt? Or did you pass it off to someone else before I got up here?"

"For God's sake, Pen, I don't have it—and neither will you, if you don't hurry. She'll get away with it. She'll get away with it all."

The action of the past few hours is taking its toll on me, because I still don't understand. "*Who* will get away with it all?"

"Jane. Your new best friend. I thought I got up here in time to catch her, but apparently, I didn't. Come on. She can't have gone far—and the only way off this rooftop is through the museum."

The last place I want to go is back inside the building

I just fled on hands and knees, but I follow Tara down the rooftop access stairwell as fast as my bare feet will allow. There's still so much I don't understand, but certain truths are starting to poke through.

Namely, that I don't have the necklace, and Christopher doesn't have the necklace, and unless Tara shoved it somewhere no woman should place diamond spikes of that magnitude, I don't think she has it either.

But *Jane*?

I expect there to be chaos and mass hysteria when we arrive back on the main floor, but the party appears to be in full swing. The lights are low, the champagne is flowing, and every other woman is dressed in black, making it difficult to pick anyone out of the crowd.

"Wait, Tara, *wait*." I force her to a halt. "What makes you so sure it's her?"

It's clear from Tara's furtive movements and tense grip that she doesn't care to answer me, but she does anyway. "I'm not. It's a hunch."

"A hunch? We're lingering at the scene of a crime for a *hunch*?"

A figure in black lace flashes by, and Tara's eyes widen. "I think I see her. Come on."

We start moving again, this time skirting the edge of the room to avoid making a scene. We're just two people trying to dash furtively along the walls of a party. I probably look like a woman who's had too much to drink, but Tara is as out of place as they come. People are starting to notice.

We make it outside the front doors—now abandoned by the guards—and to an alley on the side of the building before we catch up with her. The light sound of traffic indicates that we're not alone, but this area is remote enough that we feel isolated.

"Jane!" I call, mostly as a test.

Sure enough, she turns around. My mom's best friend, a woman Tara would have me believe is somehow both the owner of a world-renowned cosmetics company and a jewel thief, turns with a serene smile. She looks as cool as always, no sign of diamond spikes anywhere near *her* lady parts either.

"Penelope, there you are," she says. "I was looking everywhere for you. I thought maybe you'd gone outside for some air."

"Um. Well. No." Her air of perfect calm is the opposite of Tara's panicked plunge through the crowd, which has left me embarrassingly out of breath. "I was in the restroom."

"Oh, dear. I hope you're not feeling sick again," she says and raises her hand to my forehead for another maternal test of my health.

Tara huffs in disapproval, drawing Jane's attention.

"And who's this?" she asks. "I don't believe we've met before. I'm Jane. Jane Bartlett. I was a friend of Penelope's mother."

Not one to be outdone, Tara straightens her posture and glares the older woman down. "Oh, yeah? Well, I'm Tara. Tara Lewis. And I *am* Penelope's mother."

Jane laughs in clear disbelief, but I find myself looking at the evil stepmother I've hated for so long through bewildered eyes.

"Penelope?" Jane asks. "What's going on? Who is this woman?"

"She's my…" I struggle to find the right word to

explain Tara. It's not easy, especially considering the past few weeks we've had.

"I told you," Tara says. "I'm her mother."

"Nonsense. Her mother was Liliana Dupont. You're much too young to have known her."

I halt at the sound of my real mother's name, unsteady on my feet.

"I never met the woman, but believe me, I know her." Tara's normally breathy voice is hard. "I know her better than I know myself. How many people loved her, how much her family would have preferred having her around instead of me. You could say we're old friends that way."

Jane laughs lightly. "Don't take it personally. No one could compete with Liliana. It was foolish of you to try. Tell her, Penelope."

I recoil from the command. Even though I agree with her—that I'll never be as good as my mother—hearing the words aloud feels wrong. These past few weeks, I've heard so many conflicting stories of my mom's personality. According to one side, she was impetuous and uncontrollable and defied a lifetime of careful upbringing for the sake of love. She caused mischief for no reason other than the joy of it and got away with it most of the time, too. According to the other side, she was kind and warm and the best person in the world. In fact, she was worth giving up a life of crime for.

In other words, she was human. She was a complicated mix of good and bad, right and wrong.

She was just like me.

Noises from inside the building prevent me from telling Jane any of this. Raised voices and panicked shouts indicate that the standoff upstairs has come to an end. I don't know who's won, but I don't intend to stick around long enough to find out. Jane and Tara hear it, too, and both women look to me to choose a side. The woman my mother called friend and the one I call enemy, both of them wearing similar expressions of expectation.

I can't do it.

The sounds of mass evacuation hit us at once. An alarm from inside the museum starts driving people out the door and all over the place, robbing me of the time I need to make a decision. Jane and Tara tense and prepare to run with the crowd. One moves off to the right, the other to the left, splitting as neatly as if they'd planned it—splitting me along with them.

One is telling the truth; the other is lying to suit her own ends.

One is going to get away; the other is going to stay and face the music.

And it's up to me to decide which.

Without waiting another second, I grab the gun from out of Tara's waistband and point. "Don't even think about it," I warn. "You're staying right where you are."

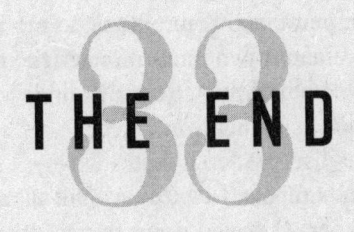

THE END

"ARE YOU CRAZY? SHE'S GETTING AWAY!"

I don't turn my head to follow the path of Jane's gaze, which is trained on Tara as she blends in with the dispersing crowd. I'm too intent on holding the gun steady.

"Penelope, you won't really shoot me," she tries again, her tone more pleading this time. "I was your mother's friend. Her *best* friend. No one knew her like I did."

"Then tell me about her," I say. The gun wavers in my grip, but I manage to keep it upright. Even though I'm a lousy shot, I'm standing close enough to Jane that any quick movement on her part would be a painful mistake. "Tell me a story about her, and I'll let you go."

Jane licks her lips nervously. With a strange sense of detachment, I note that the deep red color stays in place. Owning a cosmetics company must come with its perks.

"What kind of story?" she asks. "What do you want to hear?"

"Tell me what you loved about her."

At my request, Jane makes a jerky movement to her right, but I hold firm. Most of the people have left the museum now, and the confusion is dying down. I figure I have about two more minutes before someone in a position of authority—Simon or one of the security guards—finds us hiding over here.

I intend to use my two minutes wisely.

"Tell me," I repeat.

"Everything—I loved everything," she says, her voice almost wild. "She was smart and beautiful and fun. She had money and friends and a family that loved her so much, they couldn't bear her loss. She could do no wrong in the eyes of the world."

"No," I hear myself saying, as if from afar. "That's not true."

"It *is* true, and you know it," Jane insists. "Ask anyone about her, and they'll tell you the same thing."

I know they will—which is why I find myself holding the gun steady now. "She might have been all those things, but you didn't love her for it, did you? You hated her."

Jane starts, but she doesn't take a step.

"You hate her just as much as Tara does. Except she's willing to admit it."

"I never hated her!" Jane cries, but there's a feral look in her eyes—that of a trapped animal. *A jaguar.* "And I don't hate you, either. All you have to do is let me go, and I'll help clean this up for you. No one has to know you were involved."

"But I am involved," I say, seeing things clearly for the first time. "I did this. I pulled a team of mismatched people together, I orchestrated a heist in one of the most-watched museums in New York, and I broke dozens of laws to do it. And I'd do it all again in an instant. Not because it's the right thing to do, but because it's who I am."

And there it is, the reality of it all. I'm a woman who makes mistakes. I'm a woman who strives to do her best every day—sometimes with good results, sometimes with catastrophic ones. I'm a woman who's deeply, irreversibly flawed, and who deserves to be loved in spite of it.

Who deserves to be loved *because* of it.

"I'm not perfect," I say and lower my gun a fraction. "And it's ridiculous to assume that anyone is. Even you, Jane. Even my mom."

"Are you letting me go?" Jane asks, seeing only the gun going down.

"Yes, but I doubt you'll get very far." I nod my head behind her, where my reinforcements have finally arrived. "I think it's time I handed this over to the real professionals."

* * *

I've never been present at an arrest before.

Well, that's not true—I've been at *lots* of arrests, including that of my father and a few of my own when I was a teenager. It would be more accurate to say I've never stood on the side of the good guys, watching as someone I helped catch is carted away.

I can't say it feels very good. Especially since, when it comes down to it, the only thing separating me from Jane Bartlett is timing.

"You have the right to remain silent," Simon says in a voice of proud authority as he slaps a pair of handcuffs on Jane. He walks her toward the car that's pulled up to escort her back to the FBI building, in his element as he continues reciting her rights.

She's going to need them. They found the diamond necklace smuggled under her fifties-style dress. The pouf was perfect for hiding the telltale bulge of those diamond spikes.

"He loves this part, doesn't he?" I ask Christopher, who's standing beside me.

He arrived only a few seconds after Simon did, the pair of them working together to create as much of a scene as possible. I thought, at first, that they were playing up the theatrics because they couldn't help themselves, but it turns out they were trying to give the rest of the team—Riker and Jordan and Cheryl and Mariah and Oz—enough time to clear away evidence of our involvement.

As far as the authorities are going to be concerned, this was a takedown orchestrated and pulled off entirely by Simon, with a little help from Christopher and me. No need for *everyone* to get put on another watch list.

"Every agent loves this part," Christopher says ruefully. "Some of us don't get as many opportunities to do it, that's all. He's lucky."

"Maybe you should stop shooting innocent men, and then you'll get a turn."

He winces, frowning heavily.

I wince, too. He just spent the past half hour trying to explain my innocence to a group of very angry, very incredulous security guards. He did a good job, too, stalling them long enough for me to get away and catch the real culprit. I *could* be more generous with him.

"Sorry," I say. "Too soon?"

He holds up his fingers in the approximation of an inch.

"What will happen to her?" I ask.

"My guess?" He shrugs. "She'll use her connections and position to try and cut a deal. The high profile ones always do."

"Will that work?"

He levels me with a careful stare. "That depends. Do you *want* it to work?"

I'm startled by the question, as I seem like the least relevant part of the judicial process. I *was* instrumental in laying an underhanded plot to catch her, obviously, but that doesn't make me qualified to don a robe and carry a gavel. I think.

"It doesn't have anything to do with me, does it?" I ask.

"She's your friend. I might not have my badge right now, but I'm not without connections. And neither, might I add, is your husband."

As I watch Jane being led away, her head held proud, I wonder if letting her go would be the worst thing in the world.

"I thought you were going to be different, Penelope," she says when she sees me watching her. "But you're just as bad she was."

For a moment, I think she's talking about Tara, but she continues. "She acted the same way when I took that dress from Bergdorf's. I was only borrowing it, like I said. I was going to give it back."

It takes me a moment to place her confession, but then I remember. *A fight about something stupid, a dress I borrowed and didn't return, and that was the last I ever saw of her.*

"For a lousy thief, you sure are uptight when other people steal things," she says. "I take back what I said before—I did hate her—and you."

Only half of her spiteful words have any impact on me. "I am *not* a lousy thief," I declare hotly. "I'm a very good one."

Next to me, Christopher chokes on a laugh.

I turn to him with a shake of my head. "She's not my friend. Don't intervene on my behalf."

"I won't." He hesitates before putting an awkward hand on my shoulder. "Um, and for what it's worth, I think she's wrong. That was a hell of a heist you pulled off tonight."

I can't help but laugh. "Thank you for helping me in the museum," I say. "And for protecting me when the guards came in. You didn't have to do that—especially since I'm pretty sure you've had me fingered as the Peep-Toe Prowler for a while now."

A blossom of red covers his face. "Yes, well. Maybe a little."

"Was it Millie Ralph's that convinced you?" I ask.

"You *were* leaving the scene on foot."

"And you were fleeing by car! What were you doing on the Upper East Side anyway?"

He shrugs again. "An old friend of my mom's lives around there. He helps me out from time to time."

"Oh." I want to ask more, but it seems like a touchy subject, so I don't. "One thing I'm confused about, though—if you thought I was the Peep-Toe Prowler, why were you helping me steal the necklace?"

He shrugs. "I knew you were going after it with or without me. Shooting Grant in the back was an accident—I swear it on my life—and I know it will be hard for him to overlook that. But if he found out I let you come to any harm while he's in recovery? I doubt he could see his way past that one."

That is so sweet and so misguided, I almost tear up. "You would have helped me get away with the theft of a ten-million-dollar necklace just to get on Grant's good side?"

"Yeah, basically."

"Wow. I don't know what that man has done to earn such undying loyalty from you, but I'm glad." I turn to him with my hand outstretched. "Thank you, Christopher. I mean it. For being my date tonight, for helping me almost steal a necklace, and for being so nice to me now. I don't think I'll ever be able to repay you, but—"

"Convince Grant to see me."

The request comes so rapidly, it takes me a moment to process it. I drop my hand. "I'm sorry?"

"One meeting, a few minutes at most. That's all I need." He rubs the back of his neck. "Remember when I said I had something I wanted to say, that I haven't been up-front with you?"

"Ye-es. And then I made you break into the second floor of the museum and play with lasers, so we didn't get to it."

He's too distracted by his own confession to smile, which is saying a lot. That was pretty funny.

"I told you that after my mother died, I didn't have anyone. Well, that's not strictly true. I have a father out there somewhere, but more importantly than that, I have the son he bore from a previous marriage. I have a half brother." He takes a deep breath and points those oh-so-familiar eyes right at me. "I have Grant."

GRANT

THERE IS NOTHING MORE AGONIZING THAN BEING STUCK IN a bed while your wife risks life and limb.

I don't care about the Peep-Toe Prowler. I don't even care about my career. I'd trade both if she would enter this hospital room and tease me about being a surly beast of a man who doesn't deserve the bed linen he's lying on.

"She said she'll be here in an hour," my mother says in the maddening voice she's been using the whole time she's had watch over my room. No jailer has ever been more dedicated to her task. "It's been thirty-eight minutes. Calm down."

"I *am* calm," I say calmly. My heart monitor spikes with a loud beep, which only serves to irritate me further.

Please. I'm not going to die. As long as I remain married to Penelope Blue, I don't have that luxury.

"Knock, knock," a singsong voice at the door calls.

I turn at the sound of that voice and try to rise out of

bed before my body reminds me that sitting up is not a smart move. The ever-present dull ache turns into a slice of metal gutting me from the inside out.

"It's about goddamned time," I say, the pain turning my voice hoarse. "Where have you been?"

As soon as I catch sight of her, I realize what a stupid question that is.

I've seen my wife dressed up before, of course. We've been married twice, and she gave herself up to the demands of fashion both times—but those were demure, appropriate gowns. Whatever concoction she's got on now is a tantalizing mixture of skin and fabric, her waist and back exposed, one leg visible all the way up to the thigh.

She looks as if she's been to war and back, too, which has always been a good look on her. Her hair must have been up at one point, but wisps of it frame her face in what can only be termed a rat's nest. She's exhausted, her eye makeup is smeared, and her bare feet are almost black on the bottom.

She's fucking gorgeous, and I've never been so happy to see her in my life.

"Penelope," I manage.

"Get back in that bed," she commands, entering the room with a sweep of her long red dress. "You look like hell."

"I look like hell because that's where I am. *You* spend two days wondering where your wife is and what she's doing while your warden of a mom keeps watch, and—"

"Hey, I'm sitting right here."

"I know. You haven't let me forget it once."

My mom rises to her feet, picking up the stack of

gossip magazines she's taken to reading aloud to me as torture, and sighs. "That's gratitude for you. Honestly, Penelope, I don't know how you put up with him. You're an angel for taking on the task, I'll give you that much." She smiles in her maddeningly knowing way. "I'll give you some privacy. You two look like you could use it."

She makes it as far as the door before she stops. "You're back, too, huh? Good luck."

Craning my neck, I look around my wife and mother to see who she's talking to. At first, he's nothing more than a shadow, and I think it's yet another doctor coming to check on me. But the man in the tattered tuxedo is no doctor.

"Get him out of here," I snap.

"Grant, before you go crazy—"

I cut Penelope off. "Out. I want him out. I don't want to see his face, I don't want to hear his voice, I don't..." I'm suddenly hit with the sight of them standing side by side. *Both in formal wear*.

"What's going on?" I ask.

"Grant, Christopher has a few things he wants to say to you, and I promised him you'd listen."

"Penelope..."

"I *promised*." She sits on the edge of my bed, and simply having her near me—smelling her, feeling her reassuring weight, knowing she isn't dead or gone or giving me up as a lost cause—is enough to make me offer her the world. "He saved me tonight, in case you were wondering. He's not what we thought him to be. Be nice, okay?"

She leans down and presses a kiss on my forehead. It's not the most sensual kiss we've shared, not by a long shot, but I don't know when I've ever felt more moved by her presence—by soft lips, firm pressure, the potential for so much more.

Please let there be more.

"I'll be nice," I say gruffly.

"*Really* nice," she bargains. Always, she bargains.

"I'll be really nice," I promise. Always, I promise.

"Okay. I'll come and see you when he's done."

I want to hold on to her hand and beg her to stay, but I can't—not while that traitorous bastard is present—so once again, I have to watch her go. Understandably, this doesn't leave me in the greatest of moods.

"This had better be good," I say with a snarl. Maybe too fierce of a snarl, if Christopher's expression is anything to go by. But he doesn't run, and he doesn't cower, and maybe my esteem goes up the slightest bit because of it.

"It's not. At least, I doubt you'll think so." Christopher lifts his lips in an attempt at a smile, but when I don't return the gesture, he stops. "The good news is that thanks to your wife, we caught the Peep-Toe Prowler tonight."

I'm on my feet before I know what I'm doing. "*What?*"

A hot blade runs through me. I make it farther out of that bed than I have in days, but at the small cost of my dignity. Doubled over, sure I ripped open every last stitch, it takes Christopher damn near lifting me off the ground and hauling me back into the bed to get me settled. Even then, I have to take the glass of water he offers me, forcing sips down my throat to even my breathing, before I'm able to remember where I am or how I got here.

"Sorry," he says. "I didn't mean for it to come out like that."

"Of all the shit you've pulled, *that's* what you're sorry for?"

He takes a seat on the chair recently vacated by my mom, his body falling to the vinyl with a heavy *whump*.

"I'm sorry for everything," he says, eyeing me to make sure I'm not going to make another attempt to get out of bed and throttle him. "But it'll probably be better for us both if you wait until the end to get mad."

"I'll do my best," I say dryly. "And only because my wife asked me to."

"Thank you," he says without irony and proceeds to tell me of the evening's activities.

It's difficult for me to know which part of his tale enrages me the most—my wife putting herself in the worst possible position for exposure and danger, or my friends for aiding and abetting her. I knew bringing Mariah into the mix came with risks, but Cheryl? *Simon?* We're going to have some serious talks later.

"And you managed to keep her out of the whole thing, you and Sterling?" I ask when he's done, sounding more anxious than I care to admit. "There's no reason for the FBI to assume it was anything but careful work between the two of you?"

"We can't guarantee that Jane Bartlett won't try and bring her into it, but Simon is taking steps to ensure her cooperation. As far as everyone else knows, we're the sole heroes of the day. There's even a chance I might get reinstated."

"How nice for you."

"I know you have no reason to believe me, but the

shot *was* an accident. I saw Penelope fleeing the crime scene earlier that day. I covered her tracks the way I've been doing this whole time, but when you said there was a video feed—"

I shake my head as if to clear it. "Wait, what?"

"Covering her tracks. Making sure the evidence was blurred before you got to it. I realize now that I should've taken your word for it that Penelope wasn't involved, but—"

"That's why you kept messing up my crime scenes?"

His gaze doesn't meet mine. "All signs pointed to her, Emerson—for this and several other crimes. Lots of people at the Bureau still believe her to be active."

"*I* don't believe it," I say coldly.

"I know. I was trying to protect you from the truth."

Protect me. A strange thing to hear coming from this man's lips—and not a fully welcome one, either. I'm beginning to see why Penelope bristles at the sound of it.

"That didn't give you the right to shoot me in the back," I say.

"It wasn't on purpose, I swear! When you said there was a video camera, I panicked. I knew it would contain footage of me deliberately tampering with the crime scene. I had to get to it before you did, but you wouldn't listen. I was just going to scare you a little, get you to back down long enough for me to erase it before you saw."

"That's one hell of a scare tactic."

"My finger slipped on the trigger." Christopher drops his head into his hands with a groan. "I'm a terrible marksman. Guns make me nervous—they always have. It's why I was so quick to take that deal during our first training exercise together. I wanted so badly to make a good impression on you, to show you I was up to your weight. I didn't think about how mad you'd get at me for shooting you out of the game before you were ready."

"How the hell did you manage to get promoted so often if you can't handle a gun?"

He has the decency to look chagrined. "The associate deputy director dated my mom when I was younger. I know it sounds bad—it *is* bad—but he knew about my interest in the FBI and offered to give me a leg up. Paid for my education, covered up a stupid mistake I made as a teenager, called in a few favors to get me placed, the whole thing. And when my mom died, he felt so guilty for not being there, he got me a promotion to go along with it."

It's difficult to tell a man what you think of him when he talks about his dead mom, so I clamp my mouth shut. It's a lesson to me, because with silence comes introspection, and with introspection comes my wife's voice telling me to see what's right in front of my stubborn, unseeing eyes.

His Ivy League education. His case files wiped of any mention of armed robbery.

"Your ten-month leave," I say. "*Fuck*."

He shrugs. "Yeah. There wasn't anyone else to take care of her, so I took some time off. Breast cancer."

"Jesus. I'm sorry, Christopher."

His shrug this time is less pronounced. "Thank you. It was better, toward the end, for her to go. But it was hard. My dad left when I was young, so she was all I had growing up. She's all I've ever had."

"I'm sure that's not true," I begin, but Christopher stops me short.

"It is true, and we both know it." He draws a deep breath. "The other guys at the Bureau don't like me. I may be a joke, but I'm not stupid. I can see how little they respect me when I walk into a room. I notice how they turn their backs and change the topic of conversation. It's fine. I'm used to it. For as long as I can remember, I've been the poor kid, the weird kid, the kid who tries too hard."

"You *do* try too hard. You could scale it back a little."

He offers me a self-deprecating smile. "I could, but how else was I supposed to get you to notice me?"

There's an odd flattery to that statement, but it's an uncomfortable flattery. I've never asked for that kind of admiration from anyone except my wife, and she's the one person who refuses to give it to me. "Why do you care so much what I think?"

"You haven't discovered it by now? I thought for sure you would."

Despite my reservations, I ask the question he wants to hear. "Discovered what?"

"That your dad who left and my dad who left were one and the same." He rises from his chair and approaches me with his hand outstretched, and I'm too stunned to stop him. "It's nice to finally meet you, Grant Emerson. Bet you didn't know you had a little brother, did you?"

If anyone had told me that I would spend a full hour talking to Christopher Leon while my beautiful, exhausted wife waited in a dingy hospital hallway, I would have laughed them out of the room. In terms of life priorities, she rests unquestionably at the top. My mom takes up her share, and I'd give my life for my teammates and partners, but other than that, I lead a fairly straightforward existence. Food, work, wife. My needs are few.

But by the time Christopher convinces me of the truth and we sort out the details of our painfully similar childhoods, a large chunk of time has passed. I also wouldn't admit to a grudging respect for the man I once considered my nemesis, but that's there, too.

Christopher Leon might be a terrible agent and a shitty shot, but he's persistent—I'll give him that much. It takes a strong man to keep pushing after all the crap I've loaded on him—and from the sound of it, I have him to thank for keeping Penelope out of a bigger mess than even I could extricate her from.

Which is why, when she finally walks into the room, I'm so relieved to see her intact that my first words are gruff.

"You perfect idiot," I say as soon as I catch sight of her. "Do you have any idea what could have happened tonight?"

She's changed out of the dress and into a pair of hospital scrubs on loan from some nurse she cajoled into doing her bidding. She's trouble, that wife of mine. She could charm gold ore out of an iron mine.

"Oh, lots of things," she says. "Don't worry. We accounted for them."

"Really? Christopher made it sound like he's the only thing that stood between you and a lifetime behind bars."

"Christopher was trying to sweet-talk you into not hating him. He can't be trusted." Her hesitant smile and hitched breath give her away. "You used his first name. Does this mean you're not mad at him anymore?"

I hold my hand out to her. "Of all the things we have to talk about, the thing worrying you the most is how I feel about *him*?"

"He's your half brother." She takes my hand but doesn't draw any nearer. If ever there was a case for the travesties of being bedridden, the inability to whisk your wife into your arms is it. "I know what it's like to feel alone in this world, to believe no one understands or cares. After all this time, he deserves some family."

I clasp her fingers even tighter. "Is that what you think? That you're alone? That no one understands you?"

She turns her head, showing me the neat line of her profile. Even from the side, she's achingly beautiful, the image of her seared into my soul so deeply, she's become part of it. "Yes. No. Sometimes. These past few months have been hard for me."

"Penelope." I wait for her to turn to me, but she doesn't, so I sit up—or try to, anyway. *That* gets her attention, but it's officious and maternal, the care of my physical body instead of my heart. So I say it again. "Penelope Blue. Look at me."

She does, and I can see the shimmer of tears in her gaze.

"I tried to make you proud of me," she says, her voice so small, it cuts through me. "I tried to make it work. I played housewife and pretended gardening was some-thing I cared about. I gave up my old habits and made new, more socially acceptable ones."

Her lips wobble.

"I hate it." A tear falls down her cheek, catching on the edge of her lips. "I don't want to hurt you, but I can't lie anymore. Not to you, and not to myself."

This time, I accept the price of knives in my back for pulling my wife into my arms. She comes softly and readily, curled up next to me on this sterile, antiseptic hospital bed I've hated since the moment I woke up in it.

All of a sudden, it feels like home.

"I'm sorry. I'm so sorry," she says, her body rocking against mine. "I wanted it to be enough. I wanted *you* to be enough. But I need there to be more."

I tighten my hold on her and still her rocking movements, forcing the dual beat of our hearts to compensate for it.

"Is this about our deal?" I ask as soon as I'm able to find my voice. "About my demand that you find something safe and ordinary to do? Because I'll take that off the table right now. It was a stupid idea to begin with."

She sniffles against my chest. "It's not about the deal. I kind of like making deals with you. It's fun."

Her words, which would have set my heart soaring a few days ago, only make me grow cold. "Is it because I'm always trying to protect you? I can do better, give you more space. I didn't realize how condescending it sounds until Christopher said something similar to me."

"It's not that, either. I mean, it *is* annoying, but I'm used to it by now."

"Then is it me? Is being married to me the problem?" I can barely get the words out, but I force them anyway. "Penelope, you're everything that matters to me in this world. I mean to stay true to our vows until the day I die, but if your freedom is what you need to be happy, then I give it to you, without question and under any terms you request. I don't like it—I'm not so selfless I can pretend otherwise—but I'll do it. For you."

She doesn't reply, and my heart cracks a little. She feels so small, so vulnerable, so *sad*.

"And if that's not what you want, if what you'd rather have is for me to quit the FBI and start breaking into jewelry stores with you, then we'll do that instead. Starting tomorrow. Right now, if you want."

Her soft laughter moves the bed—and me with it.

It's a promising start, and I bury my face in her neck, breathing the sweet scent of her skin.

"I'm not kidding. I would rob a bank tonight, in this condition, if that's what it takes to make you happy."

She shifts to face me, her movements gentle as she navigates around my IV and bandages. "Of course I wouldn't make you do that. You'd be terrible at it."

"I beg your pardon. I'd make an excellent bank robber. I know more about security than anyone on your team."

She buries her head in my chest, pressing her cheek against the beat of my heart. "Yes, but it would eat you up inside. To be bad, to break rules—it would kill you. What kind of a monster would I be if I tried to change you?"

The very worst kind. The kind I was in danger of becoming in my overzealous need to keep this woman safe. But if there's one thing I've realized over the past few days, it's that holding my wife back is the worst thing I can do to her. You don't cage a woman like Penelope Blue. She's at her best when she's wild and free.

"I care much less for the laws of mankind than I do for your happiness," I say. "And you know how much I enjoy rules, so that's saying something."

"But we're so fundamentally different, Grant. I *want* to see our future the way you do, but it's hard. What happens if I can't stay out of trouble for very long? What if I keep stealing things? What if this is all I am? I had a revelation, you know. I'm pretty sure this is as good as I get. If you want me in your life—the *real* me—then that's something you're going to have to get used to."

My intentions to stay calm and in control snap.

"I wouldn't have it any other way," I say, so vehemently, I startle her. "Penelope, I know I've been overbearing these past few months, and I wish I could go back and change things, but I can't. Please believe that I look at you and feel nothing but admiration. I always have. You're brilliant and sneaky and fearless. You can bend the hardest people to your will using nothing more than a smile and a laugh. Every morning, I wake up next to you and feel that my life is infinitely brighter because you're in it."

She releases a soft huff of disbelief, her breath warm.

"Oh, you're still a pain in my ass, no question about that," I say. "I have no doubt you'll cause me any number of problems at work, and keeping you and your friends out from behind bars will be a full-time job for the rest of my life."

That noncompliment is naturally the only one to make it through, so I follow it quickly with, "But all of that is just details. What really matters is that you have more heart than anyone I've ever met, and you never hesitate to share it with others. You're everything to me—good, bad, and all the stuff that exists in between."

Her breath catches. "You really think that?"

"I *know* it." I put a finger under her chin and tilt her

head so her clear, glittering gaze meets mine. "I love you, Penelope Blue."

She pauses to digest this, her thoughts marching neatly across her face. She doesn't want to believe me, but even she can't deny a truth that's so patent, it's literally holding her in its arms.

"You know, there might be a way we could make this work," she says slowly. "But I'll need something from you first."

"Name it, and it's yours." Anything, everything—all she has to do is ask.

A smile begins to form on the edges of her mouth. "I wouldn't get too excited. A few weeks ago, you told me Christopher wanted to bring me into the office, and I freaked out about it. Do you remember?"

Do I remember? With her warm, pliant body against mine and my heart so near to breaking? Yeah, I remember. I was wearing only a towel at the time, and the way her eyes devoured me, like I was a piece of cake for her delectation, made me feel stronger and more powerful than I'd ever felt before. I wanted to tell her that everything I possess—everything I am— exists for her alone.

"You said he wanted me to come in on a consult. Obviously, we thought it was a trap at the time, but since it turns out he's not an evil master criminal, he must have been sincere." She takes a deep breath. "Is that a thing? Consulting for the FBI? Is that something I could do?"

My heart stops. When it picks back up again, I feel more alive than I have in months.

A solution. Another chance. This woman has no

idea how much she gives me every day she remains in my life.

"Yes, it's a thing. We sometimes work with independent contractors who lend us their, uh, expertise in exchange for an inordinate amount of money."

All the breath leaves her body. "And would you let me do something like that?"

Two weeks ago, I know what my answer to that question would have been. *No*. Consulting for the FBI means putting her close to the very people who can harm her most, and the last thing I want is to expose her to them.

But—"You don't need my permission, Penelope. It's your life. I trust you to do what feels right with it."

"Okay. Then that's what I want to do." She wraps her arms so tight around my torso, it hurts like the pain of death all over again. I don't care. Some things are worth dying for. "But you have to promise to give me all the dangerous, scary cases."

Oh, fuck. What did I just do?

"No."

"Murders especially. I think I'd be good at murders."

"Nope."

"Oooh, or serial killers. Do you get many of those?"

"Absolutely not."

She squeezes me tighter, and even though I want her to hold me that way forever, the pain eventually gets the better of me. I grunt.

"Oh, God! You poor thing. I squished you."

She flies to her feet and starts making a fuss over me, performing useless tasks like smoothing already smooth blankets and forcing me to eat ice chips. I'm so happy to see her moving again, back to her usual, bouncy self, I let her continue for as long as she wants.

With any luck, she'll want to keep doing it forever.

"I'll have to get business cards made, of course," she says as she scrapes a chair along the floor to sit at my bedside. She grabs a pen and pad of paper from the nurse's table to start jotting notes. "Riker and Jordan won't be happy to find me switching teams, but I'm sure I can get them to come around. And of course, I'll want top security clearance."

"I beg your pardon?" I ask as I struggle to sit up. At this rate, I'm going to need new stitches by morning.

"Well, you can't expect me to do my job well if I don't have all the facts, can you? Just look at what a disaster this last one was."

"You'll get exactly as much information as you need," I growl.

She makes a gentle tsking sound and reapplies herself to the pad of paper. "We'll see about that. Maybe I can even head up my own department someday. You can come work for me, if you want."

I can't help but laugh. Penelope is in charge and on the case, and there's nothing I can do but play along.

I don't care. As long as she's here with me, I'm just happy to have a seat at the table. No matter how this hand unfolds, the FBI couldn't ask for a better consultant.

And I, lucky bastard that I am, couldn't ask for a better wife.

EPILOGUE

"HELLO, MOTHER."

At the sound of my voice, Tara looks up in alarm from the Lombardy bar—a turn of events I'm quite pleased to have orchestrated on my own. It's no fun being startled all the time by someone sneaking around in the background. Let's see how much she likes it.

"What are you doing?" she snaps. "Don't call me that."

I ignore her and gesture to the bartender, who's pretending not to watch us. "I'd like a club soda, please, and get my mother here another of whatever she's having."

"For God's sake, Pen. Keep your voice down." To the bartender, she purrs, "I'm not her mother. She's delusional."

"My mother likes to crack jokes, but she's quite loving once you get to know her."

"I'll call security and have you escorted out," she warns. "One look at the two of us sitting here, and I promise they'll think you're the crazy one."

She's not wrong. In her skintight orange minidress, Tara has never looked less like anyone's mother, let alone mine.

I roll the suitcase I've been dragging behind me up to the bar and take a seat, pressing the handle down with a click. "I brought your clothes back. I don't think I'll be needing them anymore."

"Oh?" She swivels her stool back to face the bar, feigning disinterest. "Did your grandmother decide it's too risky to have you accompany her to future events? Have you been banned from polite society?"

"Actually, no." I swivel my own stool so we match— two ladies out on the town, sitting side by side and having drinks. "She's quite proud of me for uncovering the truth about Jane. Apparently, we Duponts are the only ones capable of seeing through deception to a person's true motives. It's one of our many talents."

Tara has to clap a hand over her mouth to keep her drink from spewing back out. "Like hell you are. *I'm* the one who saw through her deception."

"Yes, but you fled the scene before you could take any credit for it. So I took it all." I press a cocktail napkin against my lips in a gesture of genteel tranquility. "Grandmother is so pleased, she's going to take me on a shopping spree to outfit me properly. Apparently, she's tired of me dressing like a harlot—*her* words, so you can put that knife down. I'm afraid I'm going to end up with a closet full of pantsuits."

Tara laughs. "Serves you right."

It does serve me right, but then, so would a lot of things—including Tara marching out of here without a word of explanation. She doesn't, though. I turn to her with a question on my lips, grateful for this opportunity to voice it.

"How did you know it was Jane?" I ask.

She allows herself a moment of careful consideration before turning the question back on me. "How did *you*?"

"I didn't—that's the point," I say. "The whole time, I suspected you and Riker and Jordan and Christopher… not once did I think Jane was the culprit. I didn't have the smallest clue it was her."

"But you did," she insists. "When you stood outside the museum facing the pair of us, both equally likely suspects, you turned the gun on her instead of me. Why?"

It's an easy question, but it doesn't have an easy answer—and I should know, because I've been trying to figure it out for days. Grant says it was my inherent brilliance, but that's because he's trying to get me to sign him out of the hospital a week early.

"I have no idea," I say with perfect honesty. "It was mostly a feeling I had. From all the stuff she said about my mom, it was obvious she admired her, but… I don't know. She made her seem so perfect, so untouchable. That's not what love is."

I don't think Tara's going to like this next part, but I say it anyway.

"Love isn't putting a person on a diamond pedestal, or even carrying a picture of them in your wallet years after they're gone." I know that now. It's recognizing their flaws and imperfections, loving them in spite—and because—of them. It's finding a common ground between a life of crime and the FBI. It's this crazy thing Grant and I have somehow managed to make for ourselves. "Jane only said those things about my mom to try and get me on her side. You've never sugarcoated how you feel about either of us."

Tara pauses so long, I'm afraid I pushed the subject too far, but she eventually takes a drink from her martini glass and turns to me. "You know what your problem is, Pen?"

"I only have one?"

She ignores the insouciance of my reply. "You don't trust your gut enough. I've always thought that."

"Really?"

"Don't be too flattered—most of my observations spring from professional jealousy, not personal interest. What would you say was your first impression when you met Christopher Leon?"

I need only a moment to gather my thoughts. "Oh, the poor guy. I felt like he was way too nice and uneasy to be any good as a federal agent. That ended up being painfully accurate, didn't it?"

"What about Jane?"

That one requires even less time. "I thought she was a jaguar, all sleek and muscled. Predatory. But then she claimed to know my mom, and—"

"And you mistrusted your initial reaction." She stops. "What about me?"

No time at all. "You were the devil incarnate, come to earth to ruin my life."

Her smile isn't quite as pronounced this time. "Also painfully accurate. That was exactly what I did."

"Tara, I—" I begin, but this next part doesn't come so easy. I bite my lip as I think best how to capture my thoughts—about Tara's role in my painful youth, about the overtures of friendship she's been extending lately, even the way she hinted at Jane's true motivations the day she gave me my mom's picture. There are so many different things I feel about this woman, all of them swirling until I don't know if they can be untangled anymore.

In the end, I decide it doesn't matter. "I'm glad it wasn't you," I say.

She doesn't reply—at least not right away—and when she does finally speak, it's to provide more of that semi-maternal advice. "Trust your intuition, Pen, and you'll be fine. You have an unerring talent for handling people."

"I do?"

"Of course." She waves an airy hand, but the gesture feels forced. "Just look at your life, at everyone who came out of the woodwork the moment you needed help. I never thought I'd live to see the day three federal agents would willingly team up with four jewel thieves to work toward a common goal, but you pulled it off."

I flush. "They didn't do that for me. They did it for Grant."

"They did it for *you*," she says firmly. "Just like you asked them to. Just like you knew they would. I don't know how, but you've managed to surround yourself with a group of people who love you without question. Grant, Jordan, Oz, Riker, Warren, Simon, Cheryl, Mariah, your grandmother…"

She holds her breath and looks at me askance. I hold my breath and wait.

"…and me," she finishes, unsteady. "You have to know that there isn't anything we wouldn't do for you."

I open my mouth to speak, but no words come out.

"I'm not nearly as good as you at seeking out loyal allies, obviously, but I do tend to get an accurate read on people. Christopher Leon is a perfect example. I never knew the guy, of course, but I did hear that he was working with Grant—and that there was friction between them. From there, it was easy to rile you up."

"That wasn't very nice of you."

"No, it wasn't—which was part of the reason I took such a keen interest in Jane. I wanted to prove to you that I'm not all bad. And she seemed too good to be true, dropping in like she did, full of promising stories about your mother when she never bothered to look you up before." She shrugs. "I dug into her background a little, saw that her cosmetics company wasn't enjoying robust stocks lately, and put the pieces together. It made sense. I once told you you'd be surprised what you can get away with by acting like you belong somewhere. That's exactly what Jane did. She walked upstairs when everyone else was busy and took what she wanted."

Jane confessed as much to the FBI a few days ago. She also admitted to knowing that my mom married a jewel thief and that I was the product of that union. She never intended to copy my methods, but when I showed up and paved the way for the theft of the Starbrite Necklace, she jumped at the chance.

"I'm sorry I didn't believe you when you tried to warn me about her."

She laughs softly. "That's okay. I didn't expect you to. What reason did you have to listen to me? Besides—I wasn't one hundred percent sure myself. I didn't want to accuse your newfound mother figure without proof. Not after you were already so mad at me for keeping that picture all those years."

It seems a strange thing to be mad about now. I love

that picture of my mother, love even more that I'm in there with her, but having it in my possession doesn't mean anything. It's as futile as putting her on a pedestal. She's still gone, and I'm still me. Those are things I'll never be able to change, no matter what happens.

What I can change, however...

Without waiting for Tara to sense—and counter-act—my intentions, I throw my arms around her and bury my nose in her neck.

"Oh, God." She lifts her arms to try and force me back. "What are you doing? Stop that. Stop that right now."

"You can't make me," I say and hold on tighter. "*Mom*."

Keep reading for a sneak peek at the next
book in the Penelope Blue series

SEEKING
MR. WRONG

COMING MARCH 2018!

THE HEIST

"I'M TELLING YOU, SIMON, IT'S THE ONLY WAY WE'RE getting in." I stab at the blueprints spread out on the table in front of us. "You can set up as many detonation devices as you want, but that steel is impenetrable. All you'll do is make a lot of noise and announce yourself to every single person within a two-block radius. Is that what you want?"

Federal Agent Simon Sterling—a man most noted for his ability to freeze the happiness out of every human heart—crumples the blueprints in a fit of pique.

"Fine," he says. "You want to spend ten hours crouched inside a ceiling panel on the off chance the security guard will take an extra undocumented break that day? Be my guest. I'm not going to stop you."

"Thank you," I say and grab the wadded-up papers from the floor. I make as much noise as possible as I lay them flat again, which serves to infuriate my husband's partner even more. He doesn't like that I'm right—hates even more that of the two of us, I'm the one behaving most like a professional.

Penelope Blue: former expert jewel thief turned FBI consultant by day, loving and totally underappreciated FBI wife by night. My talents know no bounds.

"And it's not as if the guard's going to *randomly* take an extra break," I explain in as level a voice as possible. One thing I've learned working with Simon over the past few months—he's a lot easier to go up against if you make yourself sound as much like a robot as possible. "We'll make sure he's indisposed beforehand."

His interest gets the better of him. Although I wouldn't go so far as to say his icy exterior *cracks*, it does thaw a little. "How will you do that?"

"Oh, there are lots of ways. I'm sure Jordan can think of something." I wave my hand. "Eye drops in the coffee will do in a pinch, but that approach lacks a certain *savoir faire*, don't you think?"

I take his annoyed exhalation of breath as a yes.

"Okay, so he's out of the way and you can slip down and grab the amulet from above," Simon says. "What then? The guard's going to notice that it's missing the second he returns. How do I extract you before he sounds the alarm?"

"Aha! That's where things start to get interesting." I lean closer to the page, but I don't get a chance to outline the details of my plan. Before I so much as point out the drainage duct my team and I uncovered during a routine walk-through, a *real* alarm starts to sound.

I look up, startled, as an intermittent flash of red and the screaming whir of a fire alarm fill the conference room Simon and I share. To the best of my knowledge,

I haven't done anything to warrant an office-wide panic. In fact, the heist I'm outlining isn't even real. It's part of an exercise Simon and I are devising to help beef up the Major Thefts training program.

"What did you do?" Simon asks, his own thoughts taking a similar turn. Like me, he doesn't bolt at the sudden alarm, even though we can hear several people in the hallway starting to evacuate. "What are you trying to steal from the FBI this time?"

"Nothing!" I protest. "And I resent the implication that I'm involved in *every* alarm that goes off around here."

For one, I haven't stolen anything in almost three months. Ever since I became a consultant for the New York field office of the Federal Bureau of Investigations, I've been a model citizen in every sense of the word. I don't steal, I don't lie, and I even pay my own taxes now—real IRS taxes. Did you know the government takes almost twenty percent of everything you earn? And people think *I'm* a thief.

For another, I would never do something so clumsy as set off an alarm like this. Full-scale fire alarms are great if you want to bring every police and fire official in the city running—but that's something that rarely works in a thief's favor. The idea is not just to get the goods, but to get *away* with them. The less involved the authorities are, the better.

In fact, the only reason I can think of to set off an alarm would be because someone wants to create a distraction. If, for example, there was an event taking place inside this building that I wanted to interrupt...

My head snaps up. "Oh, no. It can't be. He wouldn't dare."

Simon's questioning gaze meets mine.

"Simon, what time is Grant's physical?"

"Four thirty," he says without hesitation. He has a computerlike memory for schedules and lists. It's infallible most of the time, but don't bother asking him to remember a girl's birthday or where she prefers to order lunch, even when you know the answer will never be the sushi place around the corner.

"And what time is it right now?" I ask.

He doesn't have to look at his watch, either. Clocks are programmed into his android brain. "Four thirty. Why? You don't think—"

No, I don't think. I *know*.

"That sneaky, lying bastard," I say as I bolt out of my chair and head for the door. Normally, making sudden movements around Simon isn't a good idea, as he enjoys pulling out his handcuffs on any pretext he can find. For once, however, I have nothing to worry about. My husband's partner and I are in perfect unity. "I thought it was weird when he scheduled the meeting for so late on a Friday," I mutter. "I should have known he was up to something."

I dash out of the conference room with Simon on my heels. With a quick glance up and down the hallway, I scan for evidence that we're all going to die in a fiery blaze. I don't see or smell smoke coming from either direction, nor is anyone evacuating at a pace other than an annoyed walk.

Just as I thought—a false alarm.

"What's the standard protocol for an alarm like this?" I ask, mentally calculating the time it will take for the building to go on lockdown and open back up again. I don't like my odds.

Simon hesitates, which goes to show how little he trusts me even after all this time. We spend almost twenty hours a week together now, planning fake heists and advising foreign nationals on the safest way to transport their jewels, but he'd still happily consign me to the trunk of his car, should the opportunity arise. Fortunately, he's the one person who knows Grant better than I do, and he eventually reaches the same conclusion as me: *We've been duped*.

"They'll evacuate the civilians, close off the floors at each end, and post a team at every exit," he says, his tone clipped. "As soon as the all clear comes through, they'll open it back up again."

"And how long will that take?"

"Long enough for him to get what he wants." He sighs. "I don't know, Blue. He's awfully determined. Maybe we should just let him—"

"No way." I take off for the emergency exit. The medical offices are located five floors down, and they're five floors I intend to take at a flying pace. Forget the teams at the exits and metal fire doors coming to a close—I'm light on my feet and nimble enough to squeeze through any open space. And I will, too.

My husband might be able to send the entire FBI building scattering, and he might be able to push even Simon beyond the limits of his patience, but there's one person he can't order around—no matter how hard he tries.

The answer, as he well knows, is *me*.

As expected, I find my husband flashing his most disarming, crinkly-eyed smile at the doctor trying to exit the medical office in accordance with standard evacuation protocols.

"But Dr. Lee, I need a quick signature here at the bottom, and I'm good to go." He hands her a slip of paper. "I'm afraid I won't see you again today with all this going on. Would you mind skipping the exam just this once?"

Dr. Lee, who's both far too young and far too unmarried to withstand a smile like Grant's, takes the piece of paper. "I don't know, Agent Emerson. This is highly unethical."

"You know as well as I do that this is only a formality. I passed the physical test last week and have never felt better. Please? For me?"

"Don't do it," I warn from the doorway. It's difficult to hear me over the sound of the fire alarm still clanging in the distance, but I can make myself heard when I set my mind to it. And my mind, to put it mildly, is set. "He's lying through his teeth. He passed the physical test, yes, and re-injured himself to the point where he can't even stand up straight."

I can't hear Grant's low, muttered curse, but I can imagine it just fine—I've heard it plenty enough times in my life for that.

"Look at him," I add. "He's not fit for anything but another round of therapy."

He turns to me with a scowl. He also stands up incredibly straight, though I don't miss the grimace of pain that crosses his face as he does it. That one is going to cost him.

"The building is under evacuation, Penelope," he says. His voice is easy even if his stance isn't. "Civilians are supposed to be outside by now."

Yes, which would explain why he pulled the alarm in the first place. Step one, get rid of the wife. Step two, flirt with the doctor to get his way. Step three, return to work against the advice of countless medical professionals and the screaming pain of his own body telling him to slow down.

I love my husband, I really do, but as a master planner, he sucks big time. Those are the worst three steps I've ever heard.

"I'm not going anywhere until you give me that release form." I fold my arms and firm my stance. Grant narrows his eyes in a look of cunning, so I hastily amend my command. "That *unsigned* release form. Believe me—I'm not a woman you want to cross right now."

Dr. Lee looks at the form in alarm.

"Don't listen to her," Grant wheedles as he hands the doctor a pen. "She'll do or say anything to get what she wants."

Ha. Talk about a man willing to go to any means to achieve his ends. I don't know how illegal it is to fake a fire at an FBI building just to harass a doctor into signing a medical release, but I can't imagine it's looked upon with favor. Not that he cares about any of that. I've never met a man so dishonorably honorable as my husband. Sure, he fights crime and locks up bad guys for a living, but you wouldn't believe the kind of rules he breaks to do it—and without so much as a twinge of conscience.

Behold, our marriage in a nutshell.

"And he's trying to trick you into clearing him for a job that he's in no way, shape, or form ready for," I reply. "Give it to me, or I'll have to report you both."

Grant turns on his heel to face me. "Penelope, so help me—"

I turn on my heel to face him. "Grant, so help *me*—"

"Maybe I should give you two a minute," Dr. Lee says with a nervous laugh. "I get the feeling this isn't really about a health release form."

I ignore her. A health release form is *exactly* what this is about—nothing more, nothing less. See, three months ago, my husband was shot in the line of duty. A bullet entered his back and emerged through his abdomen, narrowly missing his spine and all major internal organs. He's lucky to be walking—luckier still to be alive—but to hear him tell the tale, his injury is nothing more than a scratch that needs a kiss and a bandage.

The thing is, I *have* kissed him and I *have* changed his bandages—and still I've watched him struggle for the past ninety days to reconcile the body he once had and the one he's stuck with now. He's not healing the way he's supposed to. He pushes too hard and tries to do too much. The summation of all his life goals is to get cleared to return to field duty, and he's worked single-mindedly toward that goal since the day he was discharged from the hospital, common sense be damned.

But he's not ready. I know it and Simon knows it and, yes, even Grant knows it. Getting him to admit that out loud, however, is an exercise in head-against-the-wall futility.

"Poke him," I suggest with a gesture at Grant's stomach. "Go ahead. Stick a finger out and jab him right in the scar. See what happens."

Grant's scowl lightens to a half-smile, his lips turned up at the corners. "Is that a challenge, my love?"

Despite the fact that I would like to poke this man into full-on obedience, I can't resist that smile or the playful way his coffee-black eyes twinkle in the flashing red alarm. There's nothing he loves more than turning our arguments into a game. He thinks he has a better chance of winning that way.

"Sure, if you want to call it that," I concede. "Let's make it a challenge. If Dr. Lee pokes you as hard as she can and you don't flinch, I'll let you keep your stupid form, signed or not."

"And if I do flinch?"

"You don't return here until *I* decide you're ready." I hold his gaze. "You're not the only one who can be stubborn, you know."

He extends a hand at me, holding it steady until I slip my palm against his. The rough texture of his skin is warm and familiar, as is the way he lingers over the perfunctory handshake a second too long.

"Then it's a deal." He turns to Dr. Lee. "You heard my wife. If you poke me and I don't move a muscle, you can go ahead and sign the form. We'll be on our way and won't bother you again."

Dr. Lee blinks at him, her green eyes owlish behind their frames. "That's, um, not how any of this works. You guys know that, right?"

"And if he does move a muscle, you need to prescribe him at least four more weeks of physical therapy," I counter, ignoring her. "You might also want to throw in psychological counseling, because the man clearly needs it."

Grant takes a step my direction. "I beg your pardon," he says, his low voice grumbling. "There's not a damn thing wrong with my brain, and there never has been. Except for maybe the day I married you."

I match my step to his, drawing so close we're practically chest to chest. "If that's not clear proof you're out of your mind, then I don't know what is. A *fire* alarm, Grant? Really? Have I taught you nothing?"

As if on cue, the siren turns off, plunging the three of us into a ringing silence. I pause a moment before I move, allowing myself time to adjust to the sudden alteration in my surroundings.

"Huh," Grant says. He casts a glance at the clock on the wall and frowns. "That didn't take nearly as long as I wanted it to."

"Probably because I sent Simon to go call in the false alarm," I say and turn to the doctor. "Does this mean you'll have time to do a full exam now? I wasn't kidding before—he's good at hiding it, but he's in a lot of pain."

"No way." She holds up her hands. "I'm not doing anything except maybe sending you *both* down to psych."

"Hey, now!" I protest. "There's no call for drastic measures."

"Yeah," Grant agrees with a laugh. "I'm probably okay, but you can't send my wife down there. She'd never make it out again."

Grant and I turn toward the doctor as one, aligning together to defend ourselves against her. The way we conduct our marriage may be unorthodox, but there's no denying I have Grant's best interests at heart.

One of has to.

Unfortunately, there's no time for me to convince the doctor to perform her test after all, because Simon appears at the door, breathless and red-faced.

"Oh, good. You're both still here." He nods in Grant's direction. "I was up in the section chief's office calling off the alarm, and you'll never guess what just got the all clear."

"No way," Grant says, his eyes lighting from within. "They actually approved it?"

"I've got the paperwork signed, sealed, and delivered." Simon rubs his hands together. "Complete that release form, doc, and let my man get back to the field. We've got work to do."

"Simon!" I cry. I thought he was supposed to be on my side.

"Sorry, Blue," he says, sounding like the least apologetic man of all time. "But you're going to want to get in on this one. Leon called an emergency meeting up in his office. If all goes according to plan, you two ship out Monday."

"Tamara Morgan keeps readers turning the pages of this fun and feisty contemporary romance."
—*Night Owl Book Reviews* for *Love is a Battlefield*